PENGUIN CLASSICS

CHILDHOOD, BOYHOOD, YOUTH

COUNT LEO NIKOLAYEVICH TOLSTOY was born in 1828 at Yasnaya Polyana in the Tula province, and educated privately. He studied Oriental languages and law at the University of Kazan, then led a life of pleasure until 1851 when he joined an artillery regiment in the Caucasus. He took part in the Crimean war and after the defence of Sevastopol he wrote *The Sevastopol Stories*, which established his reputation. After a period in St Petersburg and abroad, where he studied educational methods for use in his school for peasant children in Yasnaya, he married Sophie Andreyevna Behrs in 1862. The next fifteen years was a period of great happiness; they had thirteen children, and Tolstoy managed his vast estates in the Volga Steppes, continued his educational projects, cared for his peasants and wrote *War and Peace* (1865–68) and *Anna Karenin* (1874–76). *A Confession* (1879–82) marked an outward change in his life and works; he became an extreme rationalist, and in a series of pamphlets after 1880 he expressed theories such as rejection of the state and church, indictment of the demands of the flesh, and denunciation of private property. His teaching earned him numerous followers in Russia and abroad, but also much opposition, and in 1901 he was excommunicated by the Russian holy synod. He died in 1910 in the course of a dramatic flight from home, at the small railway station of Astapovo.

ROSEMARY EDMONDS was born in London and studied English, Russian, French, Italian and Old Church Slavonic at universities in England, France and Italy. During the war she was translator to General de Gaulle at Fighting France Headquarters in London and, after the liberation, in Paris. She went on to study Russian Orthodox Spirituality, and translated Archimandrite Sophrony's *The Undistorted Image* (since published in two volumes as *The Monk of Mount Athos* and *The Wisdom from Mount Athos*), *His Life Is Mine*, *We Shall See Him As He Is*, *Saint Silovan the Athonite* and other works. She also researched and translated Old Church Slavonic texts. Among the many translations she made for Penguin Classics are Tolstoy's *War and Peace*, *Anna Karenin*, *Resurrection*, *The Death of Ivan Ilyich/The Cossacks/Happ*

Boyhood, Youth; Pushkin's *The Queen of Spades and Other Stories*; and Turgenev's *Fathers and Sons*. She also translated works by Gogol and Leskov.

Rosemary Edmonds died in 1998, aged 92.

L. N. TOLSTOY

CHILDHOOD
BOYHOOD
YOUTH

TRANSLATED AND
WITH AN INTRODUCTION BY
ROSEMARY EDMONDS

PENGUIN BOOKS

PENGUIN BOOKS

Published by the Penguin Group
Penguin Books Ltd, 80 Strand, London WC2R 0RL, England
Penguin Putnam Inc., 375 Hudson Street, New York, New York 10014, USA
Penguin Books Australia Ltd, Ringwood, Victoria, Australia
Penguin Books Canada Ltd, 10 Alcorn Avenue, Toronto, Ontario, Canada M4V 3B2
Penguin Books India (P) Ltd, 11 Community Centre, Panchsheel Park, New Delhi – 110 017, India
Penguin Books (NZ) Ltd, Cnr Rosedale and Airborne Roads, Albany, Auckland, New Zealand
Penguin Books (South Africa) (Pty) Ltd, 24 Sturdee Avenue, Rosebank 2196 South Africa

Penguin Books Ltd, Registered Offices: 80 Strand, London WC2R 0RL, England

www.penguin.com

This translation first published 1964

28

Translation and Introduction copyright © Rosemary Edmonds, 1964

Printed in Great Britain by Antony Rowe Ltd, Chippenham, Wiltshire
Set in Monotype Bembo

ISBN: 978-0-140-44139-0

CONTENTS

1/8   7-71

INTRODUCTION

LEV NIKOLAYEVICH TOLSTOY was twenty-three and convalescing in Tiflis after mercury treatment for 'the venereal sickness' when he completed the first part of *Childhood*, which appeared in a Petersburg monthly in September 1852, above the initials L.N. It created an immediate sensation, one reviewer writing: 'If this is the first production of L.N. Russian literature must be congratulated on the appearance of a new and remarkable talent.' It was Tolstoy's first published work and first attempt at fiction. The original plan comprised a great novel (with the general title of *Four Epochs of Growth*) founded – but only founded – on the reminiscences and traditions of his family, so that Tolstoy was displeased when the magazine altered his *Childhood* to *The History of My Childhood*. 'The alteration is especially disagreeable,' he complained to the editor, 'because, as I wrote to you, I meant *Childhood* to form the first part of a novel.'

Childhood is fiction but fiction rooted in reality (for Tolstoy '*l'art égale la vie*') and in autobiography – Tolstoy produced no work which did not contain a portrait of himself. When still only a boy of nineteen he confided to his Diary that he wanted to know himself through and through, and from then until his death at the age of eighty-two he observed and described the morphology of his own soul. He is little interested in invention: his concern is with the experienced and the perceived; and half a century later, when he was planning a 'perfectly truthful account' of his life and, anxious not to repeat himself, re-read *Childhood, Boyhood, Youth*, he regretted the book 'so ill and (in a literary sense) insincerely is it written. But it could not have been otherwise, in the first place because my intention was to relate not my own story but that of my childhood friends, and this resulted in an incoherent jumble of events from their childhood and my own, and secondly because at the time of writing it I was far from being independent in my forms of expression but was strongly under the influence of two writers: Sterne (his *Sentimental Journey*) and Töpffer (*La Bibliothèque de mon oncle*).'

Incidentally, Tolstoy disliked the last two parts, *Boyhood* and *Youth*, even more, not only because they contained fewer autobiographical elements and seemed to him an 'awkward mixture of fact and fiction' – but for their insincerity: their 'desire to put forward as good and important what I did not then consider good and important, namely, my democratic turn of mind'.

But the child is father of the man, and the prototype is here. It does not take overmuch hindsight to discern in this semi-autobiographical story the man and the writer Tolstoy was to become. We have Tolstoy the moralist who regarded life from beginning to end as a 'serious matter' to be lived accordingly; Tolstoy the fanatical seeker after God and justice among men, though an early period of scepticism had brought him to 'the verge of insanity'. The boy with his RULES OF LIFE foreshadows the man whose search for the meaning of life – how to live in relation to God, to one's fellows and to oneself – was eventually to preoccupy him to the total exclusion of his literary work. Unrestrained by any Anglo-Saxon *mauvaise honte*, Tolstoy constantly reveals his spiritual condition and gives us 'the whole diapason of joy and sorrow' – and shame. With the sixteen-year-old who retires to the box-room to scourge his bare back in order to harden himself to physical pain, and then – suddenly remembering that death may come for us mortals at any moment – casts his lesson-books aside and for three days lies on his bed, enjoying a novel and eating honey-cakes bought with the last of his pocket-money, we live the conflict in Tolstoy between Puritan and Epicurean. At a very early age he recognized that his 'tendency to philosophize' was to do him 'a great deal of harm', the weary mental struggle yielding nothing save an artful elasticity of mind which weakened his will-power, and a habit of perpetually dissecting and analysing, which destroyed spontaneity of feeling and clarity of reason. It was not intellectual curiosity, nor hunger after wisdom through knowledge, that drove Tolstoy to spend his life from first to last in observing and recording: it was despair and the fear of death, of nothingness. 'Wherefore live, seeing that life is so horrible?' he asks with Ecclesiastes. He had no dreams of another world to comfort and inspire him: his act, as Carl Nötzel said, was an architecture of the depths, not of the heights.

The dramatis personae of *Childhood, Boyhood, Youth* are a mélange of real people and imagined characters of whom perhaps the most deeply felt portrait is that of the old housekeeper, who 'accomplished the best and greatest thing in life – she died without regret or fear'. (The older he grew the more Tolstoy was to turn to the common people for sincerity and wisdom – and to the end of his life he himself retained much that was Orthodox.)

The searchlight of Tolstoy's eye falls with like penetration on the world of nature, which for him is equally divine (in the Homeric sense) with human beings. We are caught up in the violence of the storm, we *feel* the 'sublime moment of silence' before the thunder-clap; we smell the damp smell of rotting leaf-mould in the orchard, hear the anxious twittering of the sparrows disturbed in the bush overhead and peer up and see the round green apples, 'lustrous as bone', hanging high on the old apple-tree, close to the burning sun.

Tolstoy was always an ardent admirer of Rousseau and *Childhood* reveals their kinship – but Tolstoy is a more profound, more radical thinker than Rousseau. He has the Russian consciousness of guilt, absent in Rousseau, and a dual nature to contend with: a vegetarian without the vegetarian temperament, a man full of earthly passions and lust for life, proud and given to black rages, yet with a persistent hunger after asceticism. 'The arbiter of what is good and evil is not what people say and do, nor is it progress, but it is my heart and I,' and even in childhood his heart gave him no peace.

In 1857, when the third part of this trilogy was published, Druzhinin, the critic and translator of Shakespeare, wrote to Tolstoy:

> You have an inclination to super-refinement of analysis. Each of your defects has its share of strength and beauty, and almost every one of your qualities bears with it the seed of a defect.
>
> Your style quite accords with that conclusion: you are most un-grammatical, sometimes with the lack of grammar of a reformer and powerful poet reshaping a language his own way and for ever, but sometimes with the lack of grammar of an officer sitting in a casemate and writing to his chum. One can say with assurance that all the pages you have written with love are admirable – but as soon as you grow cold your words get entangled and diabolical forms of speech appear ... Above all avoid long sentences. Cut them up into two or three; do not be sparing of full-stops ... Do not stand on ceremony with the particles, and strike out by dozens the words *which, who,* and *that.*

There are very few passages in *Childhood, Boyhood, Youth* where Tolstoy might be suspected of having grown cold; and certainly no later self-portrait is quite so expressive as this first one, which he wrote in order to learn to know himself, not to instruct or convert. Tolstoy possessed the rare quality of empathy: he stirred the very foundations of the human conscience and his characters belong to any and every age. Reading him, our own life-experience is widened and intensified.

London, 1961   ROSEMARY EDMONDS

Except in one instance (on page 28) the footnotes have been added by the translator.

CHILDHOOD

I · OUR TUTOR, KARL IVANYCH

On the 12th of August 18–, exactly three days after my tenth birthday, for which I had received such wonderful presents, Karl Ivanych woke me at seven in the morning by hitting at a fly just over my head with a flap made of sugar-bag paper fastened to a stick. His action was so clumsy that he caught the little ikon of my patron-saint, which hung on the headboard of my oak bedstead, and the dead fly fell right on my head. I put my nose out from under the bedclothes, steadied with my hand the ikon which was still wobbling, flicked the dead fly on to the floor, and looked at Karl Ivanych with wrathful if sleepy eyes. He, however, in his bright-coloured quilted dressing-gown, with a belt of the same material round the waist, a red knitted skull-cap with a tassel on his head and soft goat-skin boots on his feet, continued to walk round the room, taking aim and smacking at the flies on the walls.

'Of course I am only a small boy,' I thought, 'but still he ought not to disturb me. Why doesn't he go killing flies round Volodya's bed? There are heaps of them there. But no, Volodya is older than me: I am the youngest of all – that is why I am tormented. All he thinks of every day of his life is how to be nasty to me,' I muttered. 'He is perfectly well aware that he woke me up and startled me, but he pretends not to notice it . . . disgusting man! And his dressing-gown and the skull-cap and the tassel too – they're all disgusting!'

While I was thus mentally expressing my vexation with Karl Ivanych he went up to his own bed, looked at his watch which was suspended above it in a little shoe embroidered with glass beads, hung the fly-swat on a nail and turned to us, obviously in the best of moods.

'*Auf, Kinder, auf!* . . . *'s ist Zeit. Die Mutter ist schon im Saal!*'[1] he cried in his kindly German voice. Then he came over to me, sat down at the foot of my bed and took his snuff-box from his pocket. I pretended to be asleep. Karl Ivanych first took a pinch of snuff, wiped his nose, snapped his fingers, and only then began on me. With a chuckle he started tickling my heels. '*Nun, nun, Faulenzer!*'[2]

1. Get up, children, get up! . . . It's time! Your Mother is already in the dining-room!
2. Now then, lazy-bones!

Much as I dreaded being tickled, I did not jump out of bed or answer him but merely hid my head deeper under the pillow and kicked out with all my might, doing my utmost to keep from laughing.

'How nice he is, and how fond of us!' I said to myself. 'How could I have had such horrid thoughts about him just now?'

I was annoyed with myself and with Karl Ivanych; I wanted to laugh and cry at the same time. I was all upset.

'*Ach, lassen Sie*,[1] Karl Ivanych!' I cried with tears in my eyes, thrusting my head from under the pillows.

Karl Ivanych was taken aback. He stopped tickling my feet and began to ask anxiously what was the matter with me? Had I had a bad dream? His kind German face and the solicitude with which he tried to discover the cause of my tears made them flow all the faster. I felt ashamed and could not understand how only a moment before I had hated Karl Ivanych and thought his dressing-gown, skull-cap and the tassel repulsive. Now, on the contrary, I liked them all very much indeed and even the tassel seemed to be a clear testimony to his goodness. I told him I was crying because of a bad dream: I had dreamt that mamma was dead and they were taking her away to bury her. I invented all this, for I really could not remember what I had been dreaming that night; but when Karl Ivanych, affected by my story, tried to comfort and soothe me it seemed to me that I actually had dreamt that awful dream and I now shed tears for a different reason.

When Karl Ivanych left me and sitting up in bed I began pulling my stockings on my little legs my tears ceased somewhat but the melancholy thoughts occasioned by the dream I had invented still haunted me. Presently Nikolai, who looked after us children, came in, a neat little man, always grave, conscientious and respectful, and a great friend of Karl Ivanych. He brought our clothes and foot-wear: boots for Volodya, but I still wore those detestable shoes with bows. I would have been ashamed to let him see me cry; besides, the morning sun was shining cheerfully in at the windows and Volodya was mimicking Marya Ivanovna (our sister's governess) and laughing so gaily and loudly as he stood at the wash-stand that even the sober-minded Nikolai, a towel over his shoulder, soap in one hand and a basin in the other, smiled and said:

'That's enough, Vladimir Petrovich. Please wash now.'

1. Oh leave me alone.

I quite cheered up.

'*Sind Sie bald fertig?*'[1] Karl Ivanych called from the schoolroom.

His voice sounded stern: the kindly tone which had moved me to tears had vanished. In the schoolroom Karl Ivanych was an entirely different person: there he was the tutor. I dressed myself quickly, washed and with the brush still in my hand smoothing down my wet hair appeared at his call.

Karl Ivanych, spectacles on nose and book in hand, was sitting in his usual place between the door and the window. To the left of the door were two shelves: one of them belonged to us children – the other was Karl Ivanych's *own* shelf. On ours were all sorts of books – lesson-books and story-books, some standing, others lying flat. Only two big volumes of *Histoire des Voyages* in red bindings rested decorously against the wall, and then came tall books and thick books, big books and little, bindings without books and books without bindings, since everything got pushed and crammed in anyhow when playtime arrived and we were told to tidy up the 'library', as Karl Ivanych pompously labelled this shelf. The collection of books on his *own* shelf, if not so large as ours, was even more miscellaneous. I remember three of them: a German pamphlet on the manuring of cabbages in kitchen-gardens (minus a cover), one volume of a *History of the Seven Years' War*, bound in parchment with a burn at one corner, and a complete course of hydrostatics. Karl Ivanych spent most of his time reading and had even injured his eyesight by doing so; but except for these books and the *Northern Bee* he never read anything else.

Among the things that lay on Karl Ivanych's shelf was one which recalls him to me more than all the rest. It was a round piece of cardboard attached to a wooden stand which could be moved up and down by means of small pegs. A caricature of a lady and a wig-maker was pasted on to the cardboard. Karl Ivanych, who was very clever at that sort of thing, had thought of and made this contrivance himself to protect his weak eyes from any very strong light.

I can see before me now his tall figure in the quilted dressing-gown and his thin grey hair visible beneath the red skull-cap. I see him sitting beside a little table on which stands the cardboard circle with the picture of the wig-maker; it casts its shadow on his face; he holds his book in one hand, the other rests on the arm of his chair; near him lie his watch with the figure of a huntsman painted on the dial, a chequered

1. Are you nearly ready?

pocket-handkerchief, a round black snuff-box, his green spectacle-case and a pair of snuffers on their tray. Everything is arranged so precisely and carefully in its proper place that this orderliness alone is enough to suggest that Karl Ivanych's conscience is clear and his soul at peace.

If we got tired of running about the *salon* downstairs and crept upstairs on tiptoe to the schoolroom – there was Karl Ivanych sitting by himself in his arm-chair and reading one or other of his beloved books, with a calm, stately expression on his face. Sometimes I caught him when he was not reading: his spectacles had dropped down on his big aquiline nose, his half-closed blue eyes had a peculiar look in them, and a sad smile played on his lips. All would be quiet in the room: his even breathing and the ticking of the watch with the huntsman on the dial were the only sounds.

Sometimes he did not notice me and I used to stand at the door and think: 'Poor, poor old man! There are a lot of us, we can play and enjoy ourselves; but he is all alone with no one to make a fuss of him. It is true what he says when he talks about being an orphan. And the story of his life is such a dreadful one! I remember him telling Nikolai about it – how awful to be in his position!' And I would feel so sorry for him that sometimes I would go up and take his hand and say, '*Lieber* Karl Ivanych!' He liked to have me say that, and would always pet me and show that he was touched.

On the other wall hung maps, nearly all of them torn but skilfully mended by Karl Ivanych. On the third wall, in the middle of which was the door leading to the stairs, on one side hung two rulers – the first all hacked and scored, that was ours, and the other, a new one, his *own* private ruler, used by him more for urging us on than for ruling lines; on the other side was a blackboard on which our more serious misdeeds were marked with noughts and our little ones with crosses. To the left of the board was the corner where we were made to kneel when we were naughty.

How well I remember that corner! I remember the shutter on the stove, the ventilator in the shutter and the noise it made when it was reversed. Sometimes you had to kneel and kneel in that corner until your knees and back ached and you would think: 'Karl Ivanych has forgotten me. No doubt he is sitting comfortably in his soft arm-chair reading his hydrostatics – but what about me?' And to remind him of oneself one would begin gently opening and shutting the damper, or picking bits of plaster off the walls; but if an extra large bit of plaster fell noisily on the floor the fright of it was worse than any punishment. One would peep round at Karl Ivanych, and there he sat, book in hand, apparently not noticing a thing.

In the middle of the room stood a table covered with torn black oil-cloth under which in many places it was possible to see the edges of the table all cut with penknives. Round the table there were several wooden stools, unpainted but polished by long use. The last wall was taken up by three windows. This was the view from them: directly in front, the road, every pot-hole, every stone, every rut of which had long been familiar and dear to me; beyond the road an avenue of close-clipped lime-trees, with here and there a wattle-fence visible behind it; across the avenue lay the meadow, on one side of which was a thresh-ing-floor, and opposite to this a wood. Deep in the wood one could see the watchman's hut. From the window on the right part of the veran-dah was visible, where the grown-ups generally sat before dinner. Sometimes while Karl Ivanych was correcting a page of dictation it was possible to steal a glance that way and see mamma's dark head and somebody's back, and hear faint sounds of conversation and laughter coming from that direction. And one would feel cross because one could not be there, and would think: 'When *shall* I be a big boy and stop learning lessons, and sit with people I love instead of poring over *Dialogues*?' Vexation would turn to sadness and one would fall into such a reverie, heaven knows why and what about, that one did not even hear Karl Ivanych raging over mistakes.

Karl Ivanych took off his dressing-gown, put on his blue swallow-tail coat with the padding and gathers on the shoulders, adjusted his cravat before the looking-glass, and led us downstairs to say good morning to our mother.

2 · MAMMA

Mamma was sitting in the parlour pouring out tea. In one hand she held the teapot and with the other the tap of the samovar, from which the water poured over the top of the teapot on to the tray. But though she was staring intently at it she did not realize either this, or that we had come in.

So many memories of the past arise when one tries to recall the features of somebody we love that one sees those features dimly through the memories, as though through tears. They are the tears of imagination. When I try to recall my mother as she was at that time I can only picture her brown eyes which always held the same expression of goodness and love, the mole on her neck just below the place where the short hairs grow, her embroidered white collar, and the delicate dry hand which so often caressed me and which I so often kissed; but the complete image escapes me.

To the left of the sofa stood an old English grand piano at which sat my rather sallow-skinned sister, Lyuba, her rosy fingers just washed in cold water playing Clementi's studies with evident effort. Lyuba was eleven. She wore a short gingham frock and white lace-trimmed drawers, and could only manage an octave as an arpeggio. Beside and half turned towards her sat Marya Ivanovna, wearing a cap with pink ribbons and a short blue jacket; her face was red and cross, and assumed a still more forbidding expression as soon as Karl Ivanych came in. She looked severely at him and without returning his bow went on tapping the floor with her foot and counting '*Un, deux, trois; un, deux, trois*' more loudly and imperatively even than before.

Karl Ivanych, paying no attention whatsoever to this, after his usual fashion went straight to kiss my mother's hand. She roused herself, shook her head as if to drive away sad thoughts, gave Karl Ivanych her hand and kissed him on his wrinkled temple while he kissed her hand.

'*Ich danke, lieber*[1] Karl Ivanych,' and continuing in German she asked: 'Did the children sleep well?'

Karl Ivanych was deaf in one ear and now, thanks to the noise from the piano, he heard nothing at all. He stooped nearer to the sofa, rested one hand on the table and, standing on one foot, with a smile which seemed to me then the pinnacle of refinement he raised his skull-cap above his head and said:

'You will excuse me, Natalya Nikolayevna?'

Karl Ivanych, for fear of catching cold in his bald head, always wore his red cap but every time he entered the parlour he begged permission to keep it on.

'Put it on, Karl Ivanych . . . I was asking you if the children slept well?' said mamma, moving towards him and speaking fairly loudly.

But again he heard nothing, covered his bald head with the red skull-cap and smiled more amiably than ever.

1. Thank you, dear Karl Ivanych.

'Stop a moment, Mimi,' said mamma to Marya Ivanovna with a smile. 'We can't hear anything.'

When mamma smiled, beautiful as her face was, it became incomparably lovelier and everything around seemed to grow brighter. If in the more painful moments of my life I could have had but a glimpse of that smile I should not have known what sorrow is. It seems to me that what we call beauty in a face lies in the smile: if the smile heightens the charm of the face, the face is a beautiful one; if it does not alter it, the face is ordinary, and if it is spoilt by a smile, it is ugly.

When she had said good morning to me mamma took my head in both her hands and tilted it back, then looked fixedly at me and said:

'Have you been crying this morning?'

I did not answer. She kissed my eyes and asked in German:

'What were you crying about?'

When talking to us with particular intimacy she always used that language, which she knew to perfection.

'I cried in my sleep, mamma,' I said, remembering my invented dream in all its details and involuntarily shuddering at the recollection.

Karl Ivanych corroborated my words but kept silent about the dream itself. After speaking of the weather – a conversation in which Mimi also took part – mamma put six lumps of sugar on a tray for certain specially esteemed servants, got up and went over to her embroidery-frame which stood in the window.

'Now, children, run along to papa, and tell him to be sure and come to me before he goes to the threshing-floor.'

The music, the counting and the black looks began again, and we went off to papa. Passing through the room which still retained from grandpapa's time the name of 'the pantry', we entered the study.

3 · PAPA

He was standing by his writing-table and pointing to some envelopes, papers, and piles of money spoke with anger – heatedly explaining something to his steward, Yakov Mihailov, who stood in his usual place between the door and the barometer with his hands behind his back, rapidly twisting and turning his fingers in all directions.

The angrier papa grew the more rapidly the fingers twitched, and in the same way, when father paused the fingers came to rest too; but as soon as ever Yakov himself started to speak the fingers betrayed extreme agitation and flew desperately here, there and everywhere. It seemed to me one could guess Yakov's secret thoughts by the movements of his fingers, but his face was invariably placid – expressing consciousness of his own dignity and at the same time deference, saying as it were, 'I am right but nevertheless have your own way!'

When papa saw us he merely said:

'Wait a moment,' and by a nod of his head directed one of us to shut the door.

'Oh, gracious heavens! What is the matter with you today, Yakov?' he continued to the steward, jerking one shoulder (which was a habit of his). 'This envelope with 800 roubles in it . . .'

Yakov moved his abacus a little, marked off eight hundred and fixed his gaze on some indefinite spot while he waited for what would come next.

'. . . is for general expenses during my absence. Do you understand? For the mill you ought to get a thousand roubles . . . is that right or not? From the Treasury mortgage you should get back eight thousand; for the hay, of which by your own reckoning there should be 7,000 poods[1] for sale, at, say, forty-five kopecks a pood, you will get three thousand roubles; so altogether you will have . . . how much? twelve thousand . . . is that so or not?'

'Just so, sir,' said Yakov.

But by the rapidity with which his fingers moved I saw that he had an objection to make; papa interrupted him.

'Well, out of this money you will send ten thousand to the Council for the Petrovskoe estate. Now as to the money which is in the office,' continued papa (Yakov pushed back the twelve thousand he had shown on the abacus and cast on twenty-one thousand) – 'you will bring it to me and enter it as paid out today.' (Yakov shook up his abacus again and turned it over, no doubt to intimate that the twenty-one thousand would disappear in like fashion.) 'And this envelope with the money in it you will deliver for me to the person to whom it is addressed.'

I was standing near the table and glanced at the address. It was to 'Karl Ivanych Mauer'.

Papa must have noticed that I had read something I had no business to know for he put his hand on my shoulder and with a slight pressure

1. 1 pood = 40 Russian pounds = about 36 English pounds.

indicated that I was to move away from the table. I did not understand whether this was a caress or a rebuke but at all events I kissed the large muscular hand that lay on my shoulder.

'Yes, sir,' said Yakov. 'And what are your orders with regard to the Khabarovka money?'

Khabarovka was mamma's estate.

'Keep it in the office and on no account make use of it without my instructions.'

For several seconds Yakov was silent; then suddenly his fingers began to twitch with increased rapidity, and altering the look of servile stupidity with which he had listened to his master's orders to his natural expression of sly intelligence he drew the abacus towards him and began to speak:

'Permit me to report to you, Piotr Alexandrych, it's just as you please, but we cannot pay the Council on time. You were pleased to say,' he went on with deliberation, 'that monies are due to come in from the deposits, from the mill and from the hay . . .' (As he mentioned each item he cast on to the abacus) 'but I am afraid we may be wrong in our reckoning,' he added after a pause and with a thoughtful look at papa.

'How so?'

'Be pleased to consider: take the mill now – the miller has twice been to see me begging for a deferment and swearing by Christ the Lord that he has no money . . . Why, he is even here now: perhaps you would like to speak to him yourself?'

'What does he say?' asked papa, shaking his head to show that he had no wish to speak to the miller.

'The same old story. He says there was no grinding to do; that what little money there was all went on the dam. And suppose we turn him out, sir, what good would it do us? As to the deposits you were pleased to mention, I think I have already reported that our money is locked up there and cannot be got hold of at a moment's notice. I sent a load of flour to town the other day for Ivan Afanassich and with it a note about this business, and the answer is again the same: "I should be glad to do anything I could for Piotr Alexandrych but the matter does not depend on me," and it looks as if it will be at least another couple of months before you receive settlement. You were pleased to mention the hay – let us suppose it does sell for three thousand . . .'

He cast three thousand on the abacus and was silent for about a minute, looking now at the abacus, now into papa's eyes, as much as to say:

'You can see for yourself that it is too little! And again, the hay will have to be sold first: if we sell now, you know yourself...'

It was plain that he still had a large fund of arguments ready, and probably for that reason papa interrupted him.

'I am not going to change my orders,' he said, 'but if there should really be a delay in receiving these sums it can't be helped, you will take what is necessary from the Khabarovka money.'

'Yes, sir.'

The expression of Yakov's face, and his fingers, showed that this last order afforded him great satisfaction.

Yakov was a serf, and a very zealous and devoted man. Like all good stewards he was extremely close-fisted on his master's account, and had the queerest notions as to what was advantageous for him. He was for ever endeavouring to increase his master's property at the expense of his mistress's, and to prove that it was absolutely necessary to use the income from her estate for Petrovskoe – the estate where we lived. He was triumphant at the present moment because on this point he had been successful.

Having wished us good morning, papa said that we had kicked our heels in the country long enough, that we were no longer little boys and it was time for us to do lessons in earnest.

'I think you know that I am going to Moscow tonight, and I am taking you with me,' he said. 'You will live at grandmamma's, and mamma will remain here with the girls. And be sure that her one consolation will be to hear that you are doing well in your studies.'

The preparations which had been in progress for some days past had made us expect something unusual but this news was a terrible shock. Volodya turned red and in a trembling voice repeated mamma's message.

'So that is what my dream foreboded?' I thought. 'God grant there may be nothing worse to follow.'

I felt very very sorry to leave mamma, and at the same time pleased at the idea that we were now really big boys.

'If we are going away today I don't suppose there will be any lessons. That's fine!' I thought. 'But I am sorry about Karl Ivanych. He is certainly going to be sent away, otherwise they would not have prepared that envelope for him ... It would be better to go on having lessons for ever, and not go away and leave mamma and hurt poor Karl Ivanych. He is so very unhappy as it is!'

These reflections flashed through my mind. I stood still and stared hard at the black bows on my shoes.

After a few words to Karl Ivanych about a fall in the barometer, and telling Yakov not to feed the dogs so that he might go out after dinner and make a farewell trial of the young hounds, papa, contrary to my expectations, sent us to the schoolroom, comforting us, however, with a promise to take us out hunting with him.

On my way upstairs I ran out on to the verandah. At the door my father's favourite borzoi, Milka, lay in the sun with her eyes shut.

'Good dog, Milka,' I said, patting and kissing her on the muzzle. 'We are going away today. Good-bye! We shall never see each other again.'

My feelings overcame me and I burst out crying.

4 · LESSONS

Karl Ivanych was in a very bad humour. This was evident from his frowning brows and the way he flung his frock-coat into a drawer and angrily tied the girdle of his dressing-gown, and the deep mark which he made with his nail across the book of *Dialogues* to indicate how far we were to learn by heart. Volodya set to work diligently; but I was so upset that I could do positively nothing. I gazed long and stupidly at the *Dialogues* but could not read for the tears which gathered in my eyes at the thought of the parting before us. When the time came to recite to Karl Ivanych, who was listening to me with half-closed eyes (that was a bad sign), just at the place where someone asks, '*Wo kommen Sie her?*'[1] and the answer is '*Ich komme vom Kaffeehaus*'[2] I could no longer keep back my tears, and sobs prevented my uttering '*Haben Sie die Zeitung nicht gelesen?*'[3] When it came to writing, the tears that fell on the paper made such blots that it looked as if I had been writing with water on brown paper.

Karl Ivanych got angry, ordered me on my knees and kept saying that it was obstinacy and all humbug (a favourite expression of his),

1. Where do you come from?
2. I come from the coffee-house.
3. Have you not read the newspaper?

threatened me with the ruler and demanded that I should say I was sorry, though I could not get a word out for my crying. At last he must have felt that he was being unjust for he went off into Nikolai's room and slammed the door.

In the schoolroom we could hear the conversation in the other room.

'I suppose you have heard, Nikolai, that the children are going to Moscow?' said Karl Ivanych as he went in.

'Indeed, sir, I have.'

Probably Nikolai started to his feet for Karl Ivanych said: 'Sit down, Nikolai,' and then shut the door. I left the corner and went to the door to listen.

'However much you do for people, however devoted you may be, gratitude is not to be expected, apparently, Nikolai,' said Karl Ivanych with feeling.

Nikolai, who was sitting by the window mending a boot, nodded affirmatively.

'Twelve years have I lived in this house, Nikolai,' went on Karl Ivanych, lifting his eyes and his snuff-box towards the ceiling, 'and I can say before God that I have loved them and taken more interest in them than if they had been my own children. You remember, Nikolai, when Volodya had fever, you remember how for nine days I sat beside his bed without closing my eyes. Yes, then I was "dear kind Karl Ivanych", then I was wanted; but now,' he added with an ironical smile, 'now *the children are growing up, they must study in earnest. Just as if they were not doing any learning here, Nikolai!* Eh?'

'I can't see how they could learn more,' said Nikolai, laying his awl down and pulling the waxed thread through with both hands.

'Yes, I am no longer needed now, I must be sent away; but where are their promises? Where is their gratitude? Natalya Nikolayevna I revere and love, Nikolai,' he said, placing his hand on his heart, 'but what can *she* do here? Her wishes are of no more account in this house than that,' and he flung a strip of leather on the floor with an expressive gesture. 'I know whose doing this is, and why I am no longer needed: it is because I do not flatter and fawn, like *some people*. I am accustomed to speak the truth at all times and to all persons,' he continued proudly. 'Oh well! They won't grow any the richer by my not being here, and I – God is merciful – I shall find a crust of bread for myself . . . isn't that so, Nikolai?'

Nikolai raised his head and looked at Karl Ivanych as though desirous of assuring himself that he would indeed be able to find a crust of bread; but he said nothing.

Karl Ivanych went on at great length in this strain. In particular he said how much better his services had been appreciated at a certain general's where he had once lived (I was awfully upset to hear that). He spoke about Saxony, about his parents, about his friend the tailor, Schönheit, and so on and so forth.

I sympathized with his distress and it grieved me that my father and Karl Ivanych, whom I loved almost equally, had not seen eye to eye. I betook myself back to my corner, where I squatted on my heels and pondered how understanding might be restored between them.

When Karl Ivanych returned to the schoolroom he told me to get up and prepare my exercise-book for dictation. When everything was ready he lowered himself majestically into his arm-chair and in a voice which seemed to issue from a great depth began to dictate as follows:

'*Von al-len Lei-den-schaf-ten die grau-samste ist* . . . *haben Sie ge-schrieben?*'[1] Here he paused, slowly took a pinch of snuff, and continued with renewed energy – '*die grausamste ist die Un-dank-bar-keit* . . . *ein grosses U.*'[2] I looked at him after I had written the last word, expecting the next sentence.

'*Punctum,*'[3] he said with a scarcely perceptible smile and made a sign for us to hand him our copy-books.

He read this dictum, which gave utterance to his innermost thought, several times over with varying intonations and with an expression of the greatest satisfaction. Then he set us a history lesson and seated himself at the window. His face was not so morose as it had been: it was now eloquent of the gratification a man feels who has worthily avenged an insult.

It was a quarter to one. But Karl Ivanych apparently had no intention of letting us go: he kept setting us new tasks. Lassitude and hunger increased in equal proportion. I noted with great impatience all the signs which betokened the near approach of dinner. There was the woman with her dishcloth to wash the plates; now I could hear the rattling of china in the pantry, and the dining-room table being pulled out and chairs put in place. Then Mimi came in from the garden with Lyuba and Katya (Katya was Mimi's twelve-year-old

1. Of all passions the most re-volting is . . . have you got that down?
2. The most re-volting is In-gra-ti-tude . . . with a capital I.
3. Full stop.

daughter); but nothing was to be seen of Foka – Foka was the major-domo who always appeared to announce that dinner was ready. Only then could we throw aside our books and race downstairs, regardless of Karl Ivanych.

Footsteps now on the stairs; but it was not Foka! I knew his step by heart and could always recognize the sound of his boots. The door opened and there stood a figure totally unknown to me.

5 · 'GOD'S FOOL'

Into the room walked a man of about fifty with a long pale pock-marked face, long grey hair and a scanty reddish beard. He was so tall that to get through the door he was obliged not only to incline his head but to bend his whole body. He wore a tattered garment, something between a peasant tunic and a cassock; in his hand he carried a huge staff. As he entered the room he used the staff to strike the floor with all his might and then, wrinkling his brows and opening his mouth extremely wide, he burst into a terrible and unnatural laugh. He was blind in one eye, and the white iris of that eye darted about incessantly and imparted to his face, already ill-favoured, a still more repellent expression.

'Aha, caught!' he shouted, running up to Volodya with short steps, and seizing him by the head he began a careful examination of its crown. Then with a perfectly serious face he left Volodya, came up to the table and started blowing under the oil-cloth and making the sign of the cross over it. 'O-oh, what a pity! . . . O-oh, sad! . . . The dears . . . will fly away,' he said in a voice trembling with tears, gazing feelingly at Volodya and wiping away the tears, which were actually falling, with his sleeve.

His voice was rough and hoarse, his movements hasty and jerky, his speech devoid of sense and incoherent (he never used any pronouns), but his intonations were so touching and his grotesque yellow face at times assumed such a frankly sorrowful expression that as one listened to him it was impossible to repress a mingled feeling of compassion, fear and sadness.

He was the saintly fool and pilgrim, Grisha.

Where had he come from? Who were his parents? What had in-duced him to adopt the wandering life he led? No one knew. All I know is that from the age of fifteen he had been one of 'God's fools', who went barefoot winter and summer, visited monasteries, gave little ikons to those he took a fancy to, and uttered enigmatic sayings which some people accepted as prophecies; that nobody had ever known him otherwise, that occasionally he would visit my grandmother's house and that some said he was the unfortunate son of wealthy parents, a pure soul, while others held that he was simply a lazy peasant.

At last the long-wished-for and punctual Foka appeared and we went downstairs. Grisha, sobbing and continuing to talk all sorts of nonsense, followed us, thumping every step on the stairs with his staff. Papa and mamma were walking up and down the drawing-room arm in arm, discussing something in low tones. Marya Ivanovna sat stiffly in one of the arm-chairs that were symmetrically arranged at right angles near the sofa, and in a stern but subdued voice exhorted the girls who sat beside her. As soon as Karl Ivanych entered the room she glanced at him and immediately turned away, her face assuming an expression which might have been interpreted to mean: 'You are beneath my notice, Karl Ivanych.' It was plain from the girls' eyes that they had some very important news to communicate to us at the first possible opportunity; but to jump up and come over to us would have been a breach of Mimi's rules. We had first to approach her and say, 'Bonjour, Mimi,' with a bow and a scrape, and only after that were we allowed to speak.

What an intolerable creature that Mimi was! One could hardly talk about anything in her presence: she considered everything unseemly. In addition, she was continually nagging us, 'Parlez donc français!'[1] and that, of course, just when we wanted to chatter in Russian. Or at dinner just when you were beginning to enjoy something specially nice and wanted to be left in peace she would be sure to come out with her 'Mangez donc avec du pain'[2] or 'Comment est-ce que vous tenez votre fourchette?'[3] – 'What business are we of hers?' we would think. 'Let her see to the girls, we have Karl Ivanych to look after us.' I fully shared his dislike for some people.

'Ask mamma to make them take us hunting too,' Katya said to me in a whisper, catching hold of me by the jacket when the grown-ups had preceded us into the dining-room.

1. Speak French now!
2. Eat bread with that.
3. Look how you are holding your fork!

'All right, we'll try to.'

Grisha ate in the dining-room but at a separate table; he did not lift his eyes from his plate, and every now and then sighed and made terrible faces, and kept saying, as if to himself: 'A pity! flown away . . . the dove will fly to heaven . . . Oh, there is a stone on the grave! . . .' and so on.

Mamma had been upset ever since the morning; Grisha's presence, his words and his behaviour seemed to make her more so.

'Oh yes, there is something I almost forgot to ask you,' she said, handing my father a plate of soup.

'What is it?'

'Please have your dreadful dogs shut up: they nearly bit poor Grisha as he crossed the courtyard. They might attack the children too.'

Hearing himself mentioned, Grisha turned towards our table and began to exhibit the torn tails of his clothes and, continuing to chew, he muttered:

'Wanted to bite to death . . . God would not allow. Sin to set dogs on a person! A great sin! Don't beat, elder,[1] why beat? God will forgive . . . Times are different now.'

'What is he saying?' asked papa, scrutinizing him sharply and severely. 'I don't understand a word.'

'I do,' answered mamma. 'He was telling me how one of the huntsmen set the dogs on him, on purpose, so he says, "Wanted them to bite him to death but God would not allow it," and he asks you not to punish the man for it.'

'Oh, so that's it!' said papa. 'How does he know I intended to punish the man? You know I'm not over-fond of fellows like this,' he continued in French, 'but this one I particularly dislike, and no doubt . . .'

'Oh, don't say that, my dear,' mamma interrupted, as if she were frightened at something. 'What do you know about them?'

'I should think I have had opportunity and to spare to study the species – enough of them come to you, and they are all after the same pattern. It's everlastingly the same story . . .'

I could see that mamma held an entirely different opinion but did not want to argue the point.

'Pass me a patty, please,' she said. 'Are they good today?'

'No, it makes me angry,' went on papa, picking up a patty but hold-

1. He called one and all *elder*. [*The author.*]

ing it at such a distance that mamma could not reach it. 'No, it makes me angry when I see sensible, educated people letting themselves be deceived!'

And he struck the table with his fork.

'I asked you to give me a patty,' she repeated, holding out her hand.

'The police are quite right,' continued papa, drawing his hand back, 'to put such people under arrest. All they are good for is to upset certain individuals whose nerves are not strong as it is,' he added with a smile, seeing that mamma did not like the conversation at all, and he handed her the patty.

'I have only one remark to make to you on the subject: it is difficult to believe that a man who in spite of his sixty years goes barefoot winter and summer and under his clothes wears chains weighing over seventy pounds, which he never takes off, and who has more than once declined a comfortable life with everything found – it is difficult to believe that such a man does all this out of laziness.

'As to their predictions,' she added with a sigh, after a few moments' silence, *'je suis payée pour y croire:*[1] I think I have told you how Kiryushka prophesied my father's death to him to the very day and hour.'

'Oh, what *have* you gone and done to me!' said papa, smiling and putting his hand up to his mouth on the side where Mimi was sitting. (When he did this I always listened with all my ears, expecting something funny.) 'Why did you remind me of his feet? I looked at them and now I shan't be able to eat a thing.'

Dinner was nearly over. Lyuba and Katya kept winking at us, fidgeting in their chairs and generally evincing extreme restlessness. The winking signified, 'Why don't you ask them to take us out hunting?' I nudged Volodya with my elbow. Volodya nudged me and finally, summoning up his courage, explained, first in a timid voice, then firmly and loudly, that as we were going away that day we should like the girls to come to the hunt with us, in the wagonette. After a short consultation among the grown-ups the question was decided in our favour and, what was better still, mamma said that she would accompany us herself.

1. I have good cause to believe in them.

6 · PREPARATIONS FOR THE HUNT

During dessert Yakov was sent for and orders were given about the carriage, the dogs and the saddle-horses – all in great detail, each horse being mentioned by name. Volodya's horse was lame; papa said one of the hunters was to be saddled for him. The word 'hunter' sounded strange in mamma's ears: she imagined that a hunter must be some sort of ferocious beast that would certainly bolt and kill Volodya. Despite the assurances of papa and Volodya, who declared with wonderful bravado that it was nothing, and that he liked a horse to run away, poor mamma continued to protest that she would be in torment the whole outing.

After dinner the grown-ups went to the study to drink coffee, while we scampered out into the garden to scrape our feet along the paths, which were covered with fallen yellow leaves, and to talk. We began about Volodya riding a hunter, and said what a shame it was that Lyuba did not run as fast as Katya, and what fun it would be if we could see Grisha's chains, and so forth; but we said nothing about our having to part. Our conversation was interrupted by the clatter of the approaching carriage, with a serf-boy perched on each of the springs. Behind the trap rode the hunt-servants with the dogs, and behind them the coachman, Ignat, on the horse intended for Volodya, and leading my ancient Kleper by the bridle. We rushed to the fence where we could see all these interesting things, and then, shrieking and stamping, we flew upstairs to dress, and to dress so as to look as much like huntsmen as possible. One of the best ways to do this was to tuck one's trousers inside one's boots. We set to work without losing a moment, making haste to complete the operation and run out on to the steps, there to feast our eyes on the hounds and the horses and to have a chat with the hunt-servants.

The day was hot. White, fantastic clouds had been hovering all the morning on the horizon; then a light breeze drove them closer and closer together until at times they obscured the sun. But it was evident that for all their menacing blackness they were not destined to gather into a storm and spoil our last day's pleasure. Towards evening they began to disperse again: some grew paler, lengthened out and fled to the horizon; others, just overhead, changed into transparent white scales; only one large black cloud lingered in the east. Karl Ivanych always knew where any cloud would go: he declared that this cloud would go to Maslovka, that there would be no rain, and that the weather would be lovely.

Foka, in spite of his advanced years, ran down the steps most nimbly and quickly, and called out: 'Drive up!' and, planting his feet far apart, took his stand in the middle of the entrance between the lowest step and the place where the coachman was to halt, his posture that of a man who had no need to be reminded of his duties. The ladies came out and after a brief discussion as to who should sit on which side, and who should hold on to whom (though I didn't think there was any need to hold on), they took their seats, opened their parasols and drove off. As the wagonette moved off mamma pointed to the hunter and asked the coachman with a voice that trembled:

'Is that the horse for Vladimir Petrovich?'[1]

When the coachman said it was she waved her hand and turned away. I was frantic with impatience: I clambered on to my horse's back (I was just tall enough to see out between his ears) and proceeded to perform various evolutions in the courtyard.

'Mind you don't ride over the hounds, sir,' said one of the huntsmen.

'Never fear, I am not out for the first time,' I replied haughtily.

Volodya mounted the 'hunter', not without some quaking in spite of his unflinching character, and asked several times as he patted the animal:

'Is he gentle?'

He looked very well on horseback – like a grown-up man. His thighs in their tight trousers sat so well on the saddle that I felt envious – especially as, so far as I could judge by my shadow, I was far from presenting so fine an appearance.

And now we heard papa's footsteps on the stairs; the kennel-man rounded up the hounds; the huntsmen with the borzoi dogs called them in and mounted their horses. The groom led a horse up to the steps; papa's leash of dogs who had been lying about in various picturesque attitudes rushed to him. And Milka in her bead collar, the metal disc at the end jingling, bounded out joyfully from behind his heels. When she came out she always greeted the kennel-dogs, sporting with some, sniffing or growling at others, while on some she would bite for fleas.

Papa mounted his horse and we set off.

1. The formal way of addressing or referring to Volodya.

7 · THE HUNT

The whipper-in, whose name was Turka, rode ahead on a hook-nosed pale-grey. On his head he wore a shaggy cap and had a huge horn slung across his shoulders and a knife in his belt. He looked so black and fierce that he might have been riding to mortal combat instead of on a hunting expedition. Round about the hind legs of his horse ran the harriers, all excited and jostled together like a speckled ball. It was pitiful to see the fate that befell any unfortunate dog that took it into its head to lag behind. Only with the greatest effort could it hold back its companion, and when it had succeeded in this one of the kennel-men riding behind would be sure to slash at it with his whip, shouting 'Back to the pack, there!' When we emerged from the gate papa told the huntsmen and us to keep to the road while he himself turned into the rye-field.

Harvesting was in full swing. The brilliant yellow field was bounded on one side only by the tall bluish forest, which seemed to me then a very distant and mysterious place beyond which either the world came to an end or some uninhabited regions began. The whole field swarmed with sheaves and peasants. Here and there among the tall thick rye where the sickle had passed could be seen the bent back of a woman reaping, the swing of the ears as she grasped the stalks between her fingers, a woman in the shade bending over a cradle, and scattered sheaves upon the stubble which was dotted all over with cornflowers. In another quarter were peasants clad only in their shirts, without their tunics, standing on carts loading the sheaves and raising the dust in the dry scorched field. The village elder, in boots and with a coat thrown over his shoulders and tally-sticks in his hand, seeing papa in the distance, took off his felt hat made of lamb's wool, wiped his ginger hair and beard with a towel, and bawled at the women. The little chestnut horse papa rode trotted along with a light prancing gait, from time to time bending his head to his chest, pulling at the reins and swishing his thick tail to and fro to brush away the gadflies and ordinary flies that clung ravenously to him. Two borzois with their tails curved tautly in the shape of a sickle, and lifting their feet high, leaped gracefully over the tall stubble, behind the horse's heels. Milka was always in front, with her head down seeking for the scent. The chatter of the peasants, the tramp of the horses and the creaking of the carts, the merry whistle of quail, the hum of insects hovering in the air in motionless swarms, the smell of wormwood, straw and horses' sweat, the thousand different lights and shadows with which the burning sun flooded the light yellow stubble, the dark blue of the distant forest and the pale lilac of the clouds, the white gossamer threads which floated in the air or lay stretched across the stubble – all these things I saw, heard and felt.

When we reached the Kalina woods we found the carriage already there and, surpassing all our expectations, a one-horse cart in the middle of which sat the butler. We could see, packed in straw, a samovar, a tub with an ice-cream mould and various other attractive-looking packets and boxes. There could be no mistake: it meant tea out of doors, with ice-cream and fruit! At the sight of the cart we gave vent to uproarious joy, for to drink tea in the woods on the grass, and where no one had ever drunk tea before, was the greatest of treats.

Turka rode up to the little clearing, stopped, listened carefully to papa's detailed instructions as to where to line up and where to come out (though he never conformed to such instructions but did as he chose), unleashed the dogs, slowly and deliberately strapped the leashes to his saddle, remounted his horse and disappeared, whistling, behind the young birch-trees. The first thing the hounds did on being released was to express their happiness by wagging their tails, shaking themselves and taking stock generally; then sniffing and still wagging their tails, they moved off at a slow trot in different directions.

'Have you a handkerchief?' asked papa.

I pulled one out of my pocket and showed it to him.

'Well, tie that great dog to it.'

'Zhiran?' I said, with the air of an expert.

'Yes, and now run along the road. When you come to the glade, stop. And mind you don't return to me without a hare!'

I tied my handkerchief round Zhiran's shaggy neck and rushed headlong for the spot indicated to me. Papa laughed and called out:

'Hurry up, hurry up, or you'll be too late!'

Zhiran kept stopping, pricking his ears and listening to the hallooing of the huntsmen. I was not strong enough to drag him on and I began to shout 'Tally-ho! Halloo!' Then he would pull so hard that I could scarce hold him and I fell over more than once before we reached my post. Selecting a shady level place at the foot of a tall oak, I lay down in the grass, made Zhiran sit beside me, and waited. My imagination as usual on such occasions far outstripped reality. I fancied that I was pursuing at least my third hare when, as a matter of fact, the first hound was only just giving tongue in the woods. Turka's voice reverberated ever louder and with more animation through the forest; the hound gave cry and its baying came more and more frequently. Then another joined in with a deep base note, and then a third, and a fourth . . . Now they fell silent, now interrupted each other. The sounds gradually grew louder and more continuous until at last they united into one ringing clamorous din. *The island-glade had found a tongue and the hounds bayed in chorus.*

When I heard this I stiffened at my post. With my eyes fixed on the edge of the forest I smiled inanely while the perspiration poured from me, and though the drops tickled me as they ran down my chin I did not wipe them off.

It seemed to me that there could be nothing more critical than this moment. The tension was too unnatural to last long. The harriers now bayed close to the outskirts of the wood, then they retreated; there was no hare. I began looking around me. It was the same with Zhiran: at first he tugged and yelped, then lay down at my side, put his nose on my lap and was quiet.

Around the bare roots of the oak under which I sat the grey parched earth, the withered oak-leaves, the acorns, the dry moss-grown twigs, the yellowy-green moss and the thin green blades of grass which pushed their way through here and there teemed with swarms of ants. They hurried one after another along the smooth tracks they had made for themselves, some carrying burdens, others unladen. I picked up a twig and barred their way. It was a sight to see how some of them, despising the danger, crawled underneath and others climbed over it; while some, especially those who had loads to carry, quite lost their heads: they stopped, not knowing what to do, looked for a way round, or turned back, or came up the twig to my hand with the idea, I think, of crawling up the sleeve of my jacket. My attention was diverted from these interesting observations by a butterfly with yellow wings fluttering most alluringly before me. No sooner had it attracted my notice than it flew a little way off and, circling a few times about a nearly dead wild white clover-flower, alighted on it. I do not know whether it was warming itself in the sun or sucking nectar from the flower, at all events it seemed very happy. Every now and then it fluttered its wings and pressed closer to the flower; at last it became perfectly still. I propped my head on both hands and gazed at the butterfly with delight.

All at once Zhiran began to whine, and tugged with such force that I nearly rolled over. I looked round. Along the edge of the wood skipped a hare with one ear drooping, the other erect. The blood rushed to my head and forgetting everything for a moment I shouted in a frantic voice, loosed the dog and rushed after it. But hardly had I done so than I began to regret it – the hare squatted for a second, gave a bound, and I saw no more of him.

But what was my mortification when, following the hounds who came out into the open in full cry, Turka appeared! He had seen my mistake (which had consisted in my not biding my time) and now threw me a contemptuous look as he merely said: 'Oh, master!' But you should have heard the tone in which he said it! I would rather he had hung me to his saddle like a hare.

For a long time I stood where I was in deep despair, without attempting to recall the dog and only repeating as I slapped my thighs:

'Heavens, what have I done!'

I could hear the hounds coursing on in the distance, hear the hallooing on the other side as they caught a hare, and then Turka with his huge horn summoning the dogs back – but still I did not budge.

8 · WE PLAY GAMES

The hunt was over. A rug was spread in the shade of some young birch-trees and the whole company disposed themselves in a circle on the rug. Gavrilo, the butler, having stamped down the lush green grass around him, was wiping plates and taking out of the box plums and peaches wrapped in leaves. The sun shone through the green branches of the young birches and cast round quivering medallions of light on the pattern of the rug, on my legs and even on Gavrilo's perspiring bald head. A light breeze fluttering through the foliage of the trees on to my hair and burning face refreshed me beyond measure.

When we had had our share of ice-cream and fruit it was no use sitting on the rug any longer so in spite of the scorching heat of the oblique rays of the sun we got up and proceeded to play games.

'Well, what shall it be?' said Lyuba, screwing her eyes up in the sun and hopping about on the grass. 'Let's play Robinson!'

'No . . . that's too dull,' said Volodya, sprawling on the grass and chewing some leaves. 'It's always Robinson! If you must do something, we'd better build a summer-house.'

Volodya was obviously putting on airs: probably he was proud of having ridden the hunter and was pretending to be very tired. Or perhaps even at that age he was too matter-of-fact and had too little imagination really to enjoy playing at Robinson, which consisted in performing scenes from *The Swiss Family Robinson* which we had read not long before.

'Please do . . . why won't you do what we want?' the girls insisted. 'You can be Charles, or Ernest, or the father, whichever you like,' said Katya, trying to pull him up from the ground by the sleeve of his jacket.

'I really don't want to – it's a silly game!' said Volodya, stretching himself and at the same time smiling smugly.

'It would have been better to stay at home if no one wants to play,' declared Lyuba in tears.

She was an awful cry-baby.

'All right, come along then; only please don't cry. I can't stand it!'

Volodya's condescension afforded us very little satisfaction: on the contrary his lazy bored look destroyed all the fun of the game. When we sat on the ground and pretending we were going fishing began to row with all our might Volodya sat with folded arms in an attitude which had nothing in common with the attitude of a fisherman. I told him so but he retorted that by waving our arms about more vigorously or less we should not gain or lose anything, and should not travel any the further. I could not help agreeing with him. When I pretended to go hunting and set off into the woods with a stick over my shoulder Volodya lay down on his back with his hands behind his head and told me he would pretend to be coming too. Such talk and behaviour had a damping effect on the game and were extremely distasteful, the more so because in one's secret heart one had to admit that Volodya was right.

I knew myself that not only could I not kill a bird with a stick but that I could not even make it fire. It was just a game. Once you begin arguing like that it becomes equally impossible to ride out for a drive on chairs; and, I thought, Volodya must remember how in the long winter evenings we covered an arm-chair with a shawl to turn it into a carriage. One of us sat in front as the coachman, someone else was a

footman, and the girls sat in the middle. Three chairs were the horses –
and we were off. And what adventures we used to meet on the way, and
how gaily and swiftly those winter evenings passed! . . . If you only go
by what's real there won't be any games. And if there are no games,
what is left?

9 · SOMETHING IN THE NATURE OF FIRST LOVE

Pretending that she was picking some kind of American fruit off a tree,
Lyuba plucked a leaf with a huge caterpillar on it, flung it to the ground
in horror, raised her hands and sprang back as though afraid something
might rush out of it. Our game stopped and we all dropped down on
the ground with our heads together to examine this rare specimen.

I looked over Katya's shoulder: she was trying to pick up the caterpillar on a leaf she placed in its path.

I had noticed that many girls had a way of twitching their shoulders
to bring a low-necked frock that had slipped back into its proper place.
And I remembered that this always made Mimi cross. '*C'est un geste de
femme de chambre,*'[1] she would say. Bending over the caterpillar, Katya
did just this, and at the same time the wind lifted the kerchief from her
little white neck. Her shoulder was within two inches of my lips. I was
no longer looking at the caterpillar: I looked and looked at Katya's
shoulder and kissed it as hard as I could. She did not turn round but I
saw that she blushed to her very ears. Volodya, without raising his head,
said scornfully:

'Spoony!'

But my eyes were full of tears.

I never took my eyes off Katya. I had long been used to her fresh
fair little face and had always liked it; but now I began to look at it
more attentively and I liked it still better.

When we returned to the grown-ups papa to our great delight
announced that at mamma's request our departure had been put off to
the following morning.

We rode back beside the wagonette. Volodya and I, trying to outdo
one another in horsemanship and daring, caracolled round about. My
shadow was longer than before and, judging by it, I fancied I must
present the appearance of a rather fine rider; but my self-satisfaction

1. Like a chambermaid.

was speedily upset by the following incident. Hoping finally to captivate every one in the carriage, I dropped a little behind; then using my
whip and my heels I urged my horse on and at the same time assumed an
easy graceful attitude, with the intention of dashing past the side of the
carriage where Katya sat. My only doubt was whether to gallop past in
silence or to halloo as I did so. But my insufferable pony in spite of all
my urging stopped so abruptly when we were level with the carriage
horses that I was pitched out of the saddle on to its neck and nearly
tumbled off.

10 · WHAT KIND OF MAN WAS MY FATHER?

He was a man of the last century and possessed that indefinable chivalry
of character and spirit of enterprise, the self-confidence, amiability and
sensuality which were common to the youth of that period. He regarded the young people of our day with a contempt arising partly
from an innate pride and partly from a secret feeling of vexation that
he could not in our time enjoy either the influence or the success he had
had in his own. The two chief passions of his life were cards and
women: he had won several million roubles in the course of his life and
had had affairs with innumerable women of all classes.

A tall imposing figure, a strange tripping gait, a habit of jerking one
shoulder, small perpetually twinkling eyes, a large aquiline nose,
slightly crooked lips that set in a rather odd but pleasing way, a speech
defect – a kind of lisp – and an entirely bald head: such was my father's
exterior as far back as I can remember him. It was an exterior which
not only won him the reputation of being a man à bonnes fortunes[1] but
made him liked by every one without exception – by people of all sorts
and conditions, and especially by those he desired to please.

He could impose his will on all those he came in contact with.
Although never a member of the *very highest society* he had always
mixed with these circles and in a way that made him generally esteemed. He understood the exact degree of pride and self-confidence
which without causing offence raised a man in the eyes of the world.
He was eccentric but not always so; sometimes he made his eccentricity serve instead of good breeding or wealth. Nothing on earth
could surprise him: however exalted the circumstances in which he

1. A lady-killer.

might find himself he always seemed born to them. He was so good at hiding from others and putting away from himself the dark side of life with its fill of the petty vexations and disappointments familiar to every one of us that it was impossible not to envy him. He was a connoisseur in all things conducing to comfort and enjoyment, and knew how to avail himself of them. He was particularly proud of his distinguished connexions, which he possessed partly through my mother's family and partly through the companions of his youth, with whom in his secret heart he was angry because they had all risen high in rank while he remained a retired lieutenant of the Guards. Like all retired military men he had no talent for choosing fashionable dress; but he made up for it by dressing with originality and elegance. He always wore light loose-fitting clothes and beautiful linen with large turn-down cuffs and collars . . . Indeed, everything suited his tall figure and powerful build, the bald head and quiet assured movements. He was emotional and even easily moved to tears. Often when reading aloud and he came to a pathetic passage his voice would falter, tears would appear in his eyes and he would put down the book in vexation. He loved music and accompanying himself on the piano sang the love-songs of his friend A— or the gipsy ballads or arias from operas; but he found no pleasure in classical music and regardless of accepted opinion frankly said that Beethoven's sonatas sent him to sleep and bored him, and that he knew nothing finer than *Do not wake me, a young girl* as sung by Semionova and *Not alone* when the gipsy girl Tanyusha sang it. He had a nature that required his good deeds to be noted. And he only approved what was approved by the public. Heaven only knows whether he had any moral convictions. His life was so full of all kinds of amusements that he had no time to form convictions, and besides, he was so fortunate in life that he saw no necessity to do so.

As he grew older his opinions set and his rules of conduct became immutable – but solely on practical grounds. Those actions and the manner of life which afforded him happiness or pleasure he considered right, and held that everybody else should behave likewise. He talked very persuasively and this faculty, it seemed to me, increased the elasticity of his principles: he could describe one and the same action as the most delightful piece of mischief or as the most abject villainy.

II · IN THE STUDY AND THE DRAWING-ROOM

It was getting dark by the time we reached home. Mamma sat down at the piano and we children fetched paper, pencils and paints, and settled ourselves at the round table to draw. I only had blue paint; but for all that I took it into my head to draw a picture of the hunt. After representing in very lively style a blue boy on a blue horse, and some blue dogs, I stopped, uncertain whether one could paint a blue hare, and ran into papa's study to consult him. Papa was reading something and in answer to my question 'Are there blue hares?' replied without lifting his head, 'Yes, my dear, there are.' Returning to the round table, I painted a blue hare but then found it necessary to turn it into a bush. I did not like the bush either and made it into a tree, then the tree into a hayrick, and the hayrick into a cloud, until finally I had so smeared my whole sheet of paper with blue paint that I tore it up in vexation and went off to meditate in the high-backed arm-chair.

Mamma was playing the second concerto of Field, her music-master. I sat day-dreaming, and airy luminous transparent recollections appeared in my imagination. She started playing Beethoven's *Sonate pathétique* and my memories became sad, oppressive and gloomy. Mamma often played those two pieces and so I well remember the feelings they aroused in me. They resembled memories – but memories of what? It almost seemed as if I were remembering something that had never been.

Opposite me was the door into the study and I saw Yakov and some other men, bearded and in peasant coats, go in. The door immediately closed behind them. 'Well,' I thought, 'they have begun business now!' It seemed to me that nothing in the world could be more important than the business which was being transacted in the study. This idea of mine was confirmed by the fact that generally everybody who approached the study door spoke in whispers and walked on tiptoe; while from the study came the sound of papa's loud voice and the scent of his cigar – which always attracted me very much, I don't know why. Half asleep, I suddenly heard a familiar squeak of boots in the butler's pantry. Karl Ivanych with some papers in his hand crept up to the door on tiptoe but with a gloomy and determined look, and knocked lightly. He was admitted and the door shut fast again.

'If only something dreadful does not happen,' I thought. 'Karl Ivanych is angry: he might do anything . . .'

Again I dozed off.

But no disaster occurred: about an hour later the same creaking of boots woke me. Karl Ivanych emerged from the study, with his handkerchief wiping away the tears which I could see on his cheeks and muttering to himself as he went upstairs. Papa followed him out and came into the drawing-room.

'Do you know what I have just decided?' he said in a cheerful voice, laying his hand on mamma's shoulder.

'What, my dear?'

'I am taking Karl Ivanych with the children. There is room for him in the trap. They are used to him and apparently he is really attached to them; and seven hundred roubles a year won't make any difference to us, *et puis au fond c'est un très bon diable.*'[1]

I could not understand why papa called Karl Ivanych a devil.

'I am very glad both for the children's sakes and for his,' said mamma. 'He is a worthy old man.'

'You should have seen how affected he was when I told him he could keep the five hundred roubles as a present . . . but the most amusing thing of all is this account he brought me. It's worth looking at,' he added with a smile, handing her a note in Karl Ivanych's writing. 'Quite delightful!'

This is what the note contained:[2]

	roubles	kopecks
2 fishing-rods for the children	0	70
Coloured paper, gold border, glue and a dummy for making boxes for presents	6	55
Book and a bow, presents to the children	8	16
Trousers for Nikolai	4	00
Promised by Piotr Alexandrych from Moscow in the year 18– –, a gold watch	140	00
Total due to Karl Ivanych Mauer over and above his salary	159 r.	41 k.

1. And at heart he's not at all a bad old devil.
2. Karl Ivanych's bill is written in atrocious Russian, full of spelling and grammar mistakes.

Reading this note, in which Karl Ivanych demanded payment of all the money he had spent on presents, and even the price of a present promised to himself, anyone would conclude that Karl Ivanych was nothing but an unfeeling mercenary egoist – and every one would be mistaken.

When he entered the study with this account of his in his hand and a speech ready prepared in his head he intended to set forth eloquently before papa all the injustices he had endured in our house; but when he began to speak in that touching voice and with the feeling intonations he used when dictating to us his eloquence reacted chiefly on himself, so that when he reached the place where he said: 'Sad as it will be for me to part with the children' – he quite lost his thread, his voice trembled and he was obliged to pull his chequered handkerchief out of his pocket. 'Yes, Piotr Alexandrych,' he said through his tears (this passage did not occur in his prepared speech) 'I am so used to the children that I don't know what I shall do without them. It would be better for me to serve you without salary than not at all,' he added, wiping his eyes with one hand while with the other he presented his bill.

That Karl Ivanych was speaking in all sincerity at that moment I can affirm for I know what a kind heart he had; but how he reconciled the bill with his words remains a mystery to me.

'If you are grieved, the idea of parting from you would grieve me even more,' said papa, patting him on the shoulder. 'I have now changed my mind.'

Just before supper Grisha entered the room. From the moment he had come to our house he had never left off sighing and weeping, which in the opinion of those who believed in his powers of prediction portended some calamity to our family. He began to take leave of us for tomorrow (he said) he was moving on. I winked at Volodya and went out of the room.

'What is it?'

'If you want to see Grisha's chains let's go upstairs to the menservants' quarters. Grisha sleeps in the second room – so we can wait splendidly in the attic and see everything.'

'Fine! Stay here and I'll call the girls.'

The girls ran out and we betook ourselves upstairs. Having decided, not without some arguing, who should be the first to have to enter the dark attic, we settled down and waited.

12 · GRISHA

We were all scared in the dark garret: we huddled close together and did not say a word. Almost immediately Grisha arrived with his soft tread. In one hand he had his staff, in the other a tallow candle in a brass candlestick. We held our breaths.

'Lord Jesus Christ! Most Holy Mother of God! To the Father, the Son and the Holy Ghost . . .' he kept saying, drawing the air into his lungs and speaking with the different intonations and abbreviations peculiar to those who often repeat these words.

With a prayer he placed his staff in a corner of the room and inspected his bed; after which he began to undress. Unfastening his old black girdle, he slowly divested himself of his tattered nankeen coat, folded it carefully and hung it over the back of a chair. His face no longer wore its usual precipitant obtuse look: on the contrary, he was composed, pensive and even majestic. His movements were deliberate and thoughtful.

Clad only in his shirt and undergarment he gently lowered himself on the bed, made the sign of the cross all round it, and with an effort (for he frowned) adjusted the chains beneath his shirt. After sitting there for a while and anxiously examining several tears in his linen he got up and, lifting the candle with a prayer to the level of the glass case where there were some ikons, he crossed himself before them and turned the candle upside down. It spluttered and went out.

An almost full moon shone in through the windows which looked towards the forest. The long white figure of the fool was lit up on one side by its pale silvery rays; from the other its dark shadow, in company with the shadow from the window-frames, fell on the floor, on the walls and up to the ceiling. Outside in the courtyard the watchman was striking on his iron panel.

Folding his huge hands on his breast, Grisha stood in silence with bowed head before the ikons, breathing heavily all the while. Then with difficulty he sank to his knees and began to pray.

At first he softly recited familiar prayers, only emphasizing certain words; then he repeated them, but louder and with much animation. Then he began to pray in his own words, making an evident effort to express himself in Church Slavonic. Though incoherent, his words were touching. He prayed for all his benefactors (as he called those who received him hospitably), among them for our mother and us; he prayed for himself, asking God to forgive him his grievous sins, and he kept repeating: 'Oh God, forgive my enemies!' He rose to his feet with a groan and repeating the same words again and again, fell to the floor and again got up despite the weight of his chains, which knocked against the floor every time with a dry harsh sound.

Volodya gave me a very painful pinch on the leg but I did not even turn round: I only rubbed the place with my hand and continued to follow all Grisha's movements and words with childish wonder, pity and awe.

Instead of the amusement and laughter I had expected when we entered the garret I was trembling and my heart beat.

For a long time Grisha continued in this state of religious ecstasy, improvising prayers. Now he would repeat several times in succession *Lord, have mercy* but each time with renewed force and expression. Then he prayed *Forgive me, O Lord, teach me how to live . . . teach me how to live, O Lord* so feelingly that he might be expecting an immediate answer to his petition. Then piteous sobs were all that we could hear . . . He rose to his knees, folded his hands on his breast and was silent.

I poked my head softly round the door and held my breath. Grisha was not moving; heavy sighs escaped his chest; a tear . . . . stood in the dim pupil of his blind eye which was lit up by the moon.

'Thy will be done!' he exclaimed suddenly in an inimitable tone, sank with his forehead on the floor and sobbed like a child.

Much water has flowed under the bridges since then, many memories of the past have lost their meaning for me and become dim recollections; even the pilgrim Grisha has long ago completed his last journey; but the impression he made on me and the feeling he evoked will never fade from my memory.

O truly Christian Grisha! Your faith was so strong that you felt the nearness of God; your love was so great that the words poured from your lips of themselves – you did not measure them with your reason . . . And what lofty praise you brought to glorify His majesty when, finding no words, you fell weeping to the floor! . . .

The emotion with which I listened to Grisha could not last long; in the first place because my curiosity was satisfied, and, secondly, because I had pins and needles in my legs from sitting in one position for so long, and I wanted to join in the general whispering and commotion I heard behind me in the dark garret. Someone caught my hand and

asked in a whisper: 'Whose hand is it?' It was quite dark in the attic
but I knew at once by the touch and by the voice whispering just above
my ear that it was Katya.

Quite without premeditation I took hold of her bare elbow and
pressed my lips on her arm. Katya must have been surprised and she
drew away her arm: in doing so she pushed against a broken chair
which stood in the garret. Grisha raised his head, looked slowly round
and murmuring a prayer made the sign of the cross towards each of the
four corners of the room. Talking in whispers, we scampered from the
garret.

13 · NATALYA SAVISHNA

In the middle of the last century a plump red-cheeked girl called
Natasha, wearing a coarse linen frock, used to run barefoot but gay
about the homesteads of the village of Khabarovka. In return for the
faithful services of her father, the clarinet-player Savva, and at his
request my grandfather took her 'upstairs' – that is to say, made her
one of my grandmother's female servants. As a maid Natasha distinguished herself by her gentleness and zeal. When mamma was
born and a nursemaid was required this duty was entrusted to Natasha.
In her new post the girl earned both praises and rewards for her loyalty
and devotion to her young mistress. However, the powdered head, the
stockings and the buckled shoes of the smart young footman Foka,
whose work brought him in constant contact with Natasha, captivated
her unsophisticated but loving heart. She even ventured to go herself
and ask my grandfather's permission to marry Foka. Grandpapa regarded this wish of hers as a sign of ingratitude towards himself, flew
into a passion and to punish her banished poor Natasha to a cattle-farm
on a property of his in the steppes. Six months later though, as no one
had been found to fill her place, Natasha was brought back to the
estate and reinstated in her former position. Returning in her coarse
linen dress from her exile, she went to grandpapa, fell at his feet and
begged him to restore her to favour and affection and to forget the
folly that had possessed her and which, she swore, would never occur
again. And she was true to her word.

From that day Natasha became Natalya Savishna and wore a cap
like a married woman. All the store of love in her heart she transferred
to her young lady.

When it was time for mammà to have a governess instead of a nursemaid Natalya Savishna was given the keys of the store-room and all the household linen and provisions were placed in her charge. These new duties she fulfilled with the same zeal and love. She put her whole life into care for her master's property, trying her utmost to remedy the waste, damage and pilfering which she saw everywhere.

On the day mamma married, wishing in some way to show her gratitude to Natalya Savishna for twenty years' service and devotion, she sent for her and expressing in the most flattering terms her affection and appreciation presented her with a certificate which bore a government stamp and declared that Natalya Savishna was a free woman.[1] My mother added that whether Natalya Savishna continued to serve in our house or not she should always have a pension of 300 roubles a year. Natalya Savishna heard all this in silence, then took the document, looked at it angrily, muttered something between her teeth and ran out of the room, slamming the door behind her. Not understanding the reason for such strange behaviour, mamma presently followed her to her room. She was sitting on her trunk with tear-stained eyes, twisting her handkerchief in her fingers and staring at the torn fragments of her deed of emancipation scattered on the floor in front of her.

'Dearest Natalya Savishna, what is the matter?' asked mamma, taking her hand.

'Nothing, ma'am,' Natalya Savishna replied. 'I must have displeased you somehow, that you are turning me out of the house ... Well, I am going.'

She pulled her hand away and hardly able to restrain her tears rose to go. Mamma stopped her, embraced her and they both began to cry.

Ever since I can remember anything I remember Natalya Savishna and her love and tenderness; but only now have I learnt to appreciate their worth – it never occurred to me at the time to think what a rare and wonderful creature that old woman was. Not only did she never speak but it seems that she never even thought of herself: her whole life was compounded of love and self-sacrifice. I was so used to her disinterested tender affection for us that I could not imagine things otherwise. I was not in the least grateful to her and never asked myself whether she were happy and content.

1. It was not until 1861 that serfdom generally was abolished by the Peasant Reform under Alexander II.

Sometimes on the imperative plea of necessity I would escape from lessons to her room, to sit and dream aloud, not in the least embarrassed by her presence. She was always busy, either knitting a stocking or rummaging in the chests which filled her room, or making a list of the linen, while she listened to all the nonsense I uttered – about how when I became a general I would marry a great beauty and buy a chestnut horse, build myself a crystal house and send for Karl Ivanych's relations from Saxony; and so on. She would keep saying, ' Yes, my dear, yes.' Usually when I got up to go she would open a blue chest, inside the lid of which – I can see them now – were pasted a coloured sketch of a hussar, a picture off a pomade-box and one of Volodya's drawings, and take out an aromatic pastille, which she would light and wave about, observing:

'This, my dear, is still one of the Ochakov pastilles. When your sainted grandfather – may the Kingdom of Heaven be his! – went against the Turks he brought it back. This is the last bit,' she would add with a sigh.

The trunks which crowded her room contained absolutely everything. Whatever was wanted, the cry was always: 'Ask Natalya Savishna for it,' and sure enough after a certain amount of searching she would produce the required article, saying, 'It's lucky I put it away.' In these trunks were thousands of objects about which nobody in the house but herself either knew or cared.

Once I lost my temper with her. This is how it happened. One day at dinner when I was pouring myself out some *kvass*[1] I dropped the decanter and stained the tablecloth.

'Call Natalya Savishna to come and admire what her darling has done!' said mamma.

Natalya Savishna came in, saw the mess I had made and shook her head. Then mamma whispered something in her ear and she went out, shaking her finger at me.

After dinner I was on my way to the ball-room and skipping about in the highest of spirits when all at once Natalya Savishna sprang out from behind the door with the tablecloth in her hand, caught hold of me and despite desperate resistance on my part began rubbing my face with the wet cloth, repeating: 'Don't thee go dirtying tablecloths, don't thee go dirtying tablecloths!' I was so offended that I howled with rage.

1. A non-intoxicating drink made of rye malt.

'What!' I said to myself, pacing up and down the room and choking with tears, 'To think that Natalya Savishna – no, plain *Natalya* says *thee* to *me*, and hits me in the face with a wet tablecloth as if I were a serf-boy. It's abominable!'

When Natalya Savishna saw that I was gasping with fury she immediately ran off, while I continued to walk to and fro considering how I could pay out the impudent *Natalya* for the way she had insulted me.

A few minutes later Natalya Savishna returned, came up to me timidly and started trying to pacify me.

'Hush now, dearie, don't cry . . . Forgive an old fool . . . it was all my fault . . . Pray forgive me, my pet . . . Here's something for you.'

From under her shawl she took a screw of red paper in which there were two caramels and a grape, and offered it to me with a trembling hand. I could not look the kind old woman in the face; with averted eyes I accepted her present, my tears flowing faster than ever, but from love and shame now, and no longer from anger.

14 · PARTING

Towards noon on the day following the events I have described the barouche and the chaise stood at the front door. Nikolai was dressed for travelling – that is to say, his trousers were tucked into his boots and the belt round his old coat was tied as tightly as possible. He stood in the trap packing greatcoats and cushions under the seat. When the pile seemed to him too high he sat on the cushions, bounced up and down and flattened them.

'For mercy's sake, Nikolai Dmitrich, can't you get the master's dressing-box in with your things?' pleaded papa's valet, panting and thrusting his head out of the carriage. 'It isn't big . . .'

'You should have spoken before, Mihei Ivanych,' Nikolai snapped back, angrily hurling a parcel with all his might to the floor of the trap. 'By heaven, my head's in a whirl as it is, and you come along with your dressing-boxes,' and he lifted his cap to wipe away the large drops of perspiration from his sunburned forehead.

Men-servants bare-headed, in peasant-coats, tunics or shirt-sleeves, women in coarse linen dresses with striped kerchiefs on their heads and babies in their arms, and bare-footed children stood around the steps looking at the vehicles and chatting among themselves. One of our coachmen, a bent old man wearing a winter cap and cloth coat, held the pole of the carriage and feeling it here and there thoughtfully examined the way it moved. The other, a good-looking young fellow in a white blouse with gussets of red calico under the arms, and a conical black lamb's-wool cap which he tilted first over one ear and then over the other as he scratched his curly fair hair, laid his coat on the box, slung the reins over it and cracked his little plaited whip as he looked now at his boots now at the coachmen who were greasing the trap. One of them was straining to hold the brake; the other, bent over the wheel, was carefully greasing the axle and hub, and, in order not to waste the remainder of the grease with which he was lubricating, smearing it on the rim below. Weary unmatched post-horses stood by the fence, brushing the flies away with their tails. Some of them planted their shaggy swollen legs far apart, blinked their eyes and dozed; others in sheer boredom rubbed against one another or nibbled the fronds and stalks of the coarse dark-green ferns that grew beside the porch. A number of borzoi dogs lay panting in the sun, while others were walking about in the shade under the carriage and the trap, licking the grease round the axles. The air was full of a sort of dusty mist and the horizon was purplish-grey, but there was not a single cloud in the sky. A strong wind from the west raised columns of dust from the roads and the fields, bent the tops of the tall lime- and birth-trees in the garden, and bore far away their falling yellow leaves. I sat by the window waiting impatiently for all these preparations to come to an end.

When we were all assembled by the round table in the drawing-room, to spend the last few minutes together, it never entered my head what a painful moment awaited us. The most trivial thoughts flitted through my mind. Which driver would drive the carriage and which the trap, I wondered. Who would travel with papa and who with Karl Ivanych? And why did I have to be muffled up in a scarf and wadded coat?

'Am I so delicate? No fear of my freezing. I wish all this were over quickly and we could take our seats and be off!'

'Who shall I give the list of the children's underclothes to?' asked Natalya Savishna, coming in with her eyes swollen with tears and a list in her hand, addressing mamma.

'Give it to Nikolai and then come and say good-bye to the children.'

The old woman tried to speak but suddenly stopped, covered her face with her handkerchief and with a gesture of her hand left the room.

Something seemed to stab at my heart when I saw that gesture of hers but impatience to be off was stronger than my feeling and I continued to listen quite indifferently to my father's conversation with mamma. They were talking about things which obviously did not interest either of them: what should be bought for the house, what to say to Princess Sophie and to Madame Julie, and whether the roads would be good!

Foka entered, stopped at the door and in exactly the same tone with which he announced 'Dinner is served' said 'The horses are ready'. I noticed that mamma started and turned pale at this announcement, as though she had not expected it.

Foka was told to close the doors of the room.[1] This amused me highly – 'as if we were all hiding from somebody!'

When we were all seated Foka too sat down on the edge of a chair but hardly had he done so before the door creaked and every one looked round. Natalya Savishna hurried in and without raising her eyes took refuge near the door on the same chair as Foka. To this day I can see Foka's bald head and wrinkled set face and the bent figure of the kindly old woman with the grey hair showing beneath her cap. They sat squeezed together on the one chair, and both of them felt awkward.

I continued to feel unconcerned and impatient. The ten seconds we sat with the doors shut seemed like a whole hour. At last everybody got up, crossed themselves and began to say good-bye. Papa embraced mamma and kissed her several times.

'Don't, my dear,' said papa. 'We are not parting for ever.'

'All the same it is painful!' said mamma, her voice choking with tears.

When I heard that voice and saw her quivering lips and tear-filled eyes I forgot everything else: I felt so sad and miserable and terrible that I wanted to run away rather than say good-bye to her. At that moment I realized that when she embraced papa she was taking leave of us all.

She started kissing Volodya and making the sign of the cross over him so many times that I pushed forward, thinking she would now turn to me; but she kept on blessing him and hugging him to her breast.

1. It was the custom in Russia for those who were setting out on a journey to sit together in silence for a few moments before their departure. (Orthodox Russians still do this.)

At last I put my arms round her and clinging to her I wept and wept, thinking of nothing in the world but my grief.

When we were ready to take our seats in the vehicles the tiresome domestics waylaid us in the hall. Their 'Let me kiss your hand, please, sir', the resounding kisses they imprinted on our shoulders[1] and the smell of tallow from their heads excited in me something like the annoyance irritable people feel. Under the influence of this feeling I kissed Natalya Savishna very coldly on the cap when bathed in tears she came up to bid me farewell.

It is strange that I can see the faces of all those servants as if it were today, and could draw them in the minutest detail; but mamma's face as she looked at that moment escapes me entirely: perhaps because while all this was happening I could not once summon up enough courage to give her a glance. It seemed to me that if I did so her misery and mine would burst all bounds.

I flung myself into the carriage before anyone else and sat down on the back seat. As the hood was raised I could see nothing, but some instinct told me that mamma was still there.

'Shall I look at her again or not? . . . Well, for the last time then!' I said to myself, and leaned out of the carriage on the porch side. At that instant mamma, with the same thought, came to the opposite side of the carriage and called me by name. Hearing her voice behind me, I turned to her so quickly that our heads bumped together. She gave a mournful smile and kissed me convulsively for the last time.

When we had gone a few yards I made up my mind to look at her again. The wind was lifting the small blue kerchief which was tied round her head; with her head down and her face buried in her hands she was slowly climbing the steps of the porch. Foka was supporting her.

Papa sat beside me without speaking. I was choking with tears and there was a sensation in my throat that made me afraid I should stifle . . . As we drove out on to the highway we saw a white handkerchief someone was waving from the balcony. I started to wave mine and the action of doing so calmed me a little. I continued to cry and the thought that my tears were a proof of my sensitiveness pleased and consoled me.

After we had gone about three-quarters of a mile I settled down more comfortably and began gazing steadily at the nearest object which presented itself to my eyes – the flanks of the trace-horse trotting on my

1. The fashion in which inferiors saluted their superiors in Russia.

side. I watched how the piebald trace-horse flicked his tail, how he struck one hoof against the other, how the driver's plaited whip reached him and his hooves began to leap together. I looked at the harness shaking on his neck, and the rings on the harness jerking too. And I stared and stared until the harness near the piebald's tail became covered with lather. I began to look about me at the waving fields of ripe rye, at the dark fallow where I could see a plough, a peasant and a mare with a foal. I looked at the mile-posts, I even glanced at the coachman's box to find out who was driving us; and before the tears had dried on my face my mind was already far from my mother, from whom I had parted perhaps for ever. But my every recollection led to thoughts of her. I remembered the mushroom I had found in the birch avenue the day before, and how Lyuba and Katya had squabbled as to who should pick it, and I remembered how they had cried when saying good-bye to us.

'I am sorry to have left them! And sorry to have left Natalya Savishna, and the birch avenue, and Foka. Even that nasty Mimi – I am sorry to have left her. I am sorry about everything, everything! And poor mamma, what about her?' And the tears rushed to my eyes again; but it was not for long.

15 · CHILDHOOD

Oh the happy, happy, never-to-be-recalled days of childhood! How could one fail to love and cherish memories of such a time? Those memories refresh and elevate the soul and are a source of my best enjoyment.

Having run about to your heart's content you sit in your high chair at the tea-table. It is late, you have long ago finished your cup of milk with sugar in. So sleepy that you cannot keep your eyes open, still you do not stir from your place but sit and listen. And how can you help listening? Mamma is talking to someone and the sound of her voice is so sweet, so warm. Just the sound of it goes to my heart! With eyes drowsy with slumber I gaze at her face, and all at once she becomes quite quite little, her face no bigger than a button; but I see it just as plainly still: I can see her look at me and smile. I like seeing her so tiny. I screw my eyes tighter still, and now she is no bigger than a little boy reflected in the pupil of an eye, but I move and the spell is broken. I half close my eyes, change my position, trying in every way to revive the spell, but all in vain.

I get down and settle myself comfortably in an arm-chair, with my feet tucked up under me.

'You will fall asleep again, my little Nikolai,' mamma says to me. 'Why don't you go upstairs?'

'I don't want to go to bed, mamma,' I answer. And vague sweet visions fill your mind, the healthy sleep of childhood weighs your eyelids down, and in a moment you are fast asleep, till someone comes to rouse you. In your dreams you feel a gentle hand touching you: you recognize it by the touch alone and still asleep you instinctively seize hold of it and press it hard to your lips.

The others have all gone; one candle only burns in the drawing-room; mamma had said that she would wake me herself. It is she who has seated herself on the chair in which I am sleeping, and strokes my hair with her wonderful tender hand, and I hear the dear familiar voice say in my ear:

'Up you get, my darling: it is time to go to bed.'

There are no careless onlookers to restrain her and she is not afraid to pour out all her tenderness and love on me. I do not move but kiss and kiss her hand.

'Get up now, my angel.'

She puts her other hand round the back of my head and her slender fingers run over my neck, tickling me. It is quiet and half dark in the room; I feel all quivery with being tickled and roused from sleep; mamma is sitting close beside me; she touches me; I am aware of her scent and her voice. All this makes me jump up, throw my arms around her neck, press my head to her bosom and whisper breathlessly:

'Oh dear dear mamma, I do love you so!'

She smiles her sad bewitching smile, takes my head in both her hands, kisses me on the forehead and pulls my head on to her lap.

'So you love me very much?' She is silent for a moment and then says: 'Mind you always love me and never forget me. If mamma was no longer here, you would not forget her? You would not forget her, little Nikolai?'

She kisses me still more tenderly.

'No! Oh don't even talk like that, darling mamma, my own darling mamma!' I exclaim, kissing her knees while the tears stream from my eyes – tears of love and rapture.

After that perhaps I go upstairs and in my little quilted dressing-gown stand before the ikons, and what a wonderful feeling I have as I say: 'O Lord, bless papa and mamma.' Repeating the prayers which my baby lips had first lisped after my beloved mother, the love of her and the love of God in some strange fashion mingled into one feeling.

After saying my prayers I would tuck myself up in the bedclothes, and my heart would feel all light, buoyant and happy. Dreams would follow one another in quick succession – but what were they about? Elusive and intangible they were but full of pure love and hope of radiant joy. Maybe I would think of Karl Ivanych and his bitter lot (he was the only unfortunate person I knew) and I would feel so sorry for him and so fond of him that tears trickled from my eyes and I said to myself: 'God grant him happiness, let me help him and lighten his sorrow: I am ready to make any sacrifice for his sake.' Then I would make a place at the corner of the down pillow for a favourite toy – a china hare or a dog – and rejoice to see it lying there so snug and warm. Another prayer to God to make everybody happy and content and for the weather to be fine tomorrow for our outing, and I turn over on the other side, thoughts and dreams slide together until at last I fall gently and peacefully asleep, my face still wet with tears.

Will that carefree freshness, that craving for love, that force of love that one possesses in childhood ever return? What better time in our life can there be than when the two finest virtues – innocent gaiety and a boundless yearning for affection – are the only mainsprings of one's life?

Where are those ardent prayers? Where that finest gift of all – the pure tears of emotion? A guardian angel flew down from heaven with a smile to wipe away those tears and waft dreams into the uncorrupted imagination of infancy.

Has life left such heavy traces in my heart that those tears and that ecstasy have deserted me for ever? Can it be that only the memories of them abide?

16 · WRITING POETRY

Nearly a month after we moved to Moscow I was sitting upstairs in my grandmother's house at a large table, writing. Opposite me sat our drawing-master, putting some finishing touches to the head of a Turk in a turban, executed in black crayon. Volodya, craning his neck, was standing behind the drawing-master and looking over his shoulder. This head was Volodya's first effort in crayon and was to be presented to grandmamma that very day, her name-day.

'What about some more shadow here?' said Volodya, rising on tiptoe and pointing to the Turk's neck.

'No, it is not necessary,' said the master, putting away the crayon and holder into a box with a sliding lid. 'It is all right now: don't touch it any more. Well, Nikolai,' he added, standing up and continuing to examine the Turk out of the corner of his eye, 'won't you tell us your great secret at last – what are you going to give your grandmother? I really think it would have been better if you too had drawn a head. Well, good-bye young gentlemen,' he said, taking his hat and his ticket[1] and departing.

At that moment I was thinking myself that a head would have been better than what I was working at. When we had been told that it would soon be our grandmother's name-day and that we ought to prepare presents to give her the idea occurred to me of writing some verses for the occasion, and I immediately made up two verses with rhymes, hoping to do the rest just as easily. I really do not know how the idea – such a peculiar one for a child – entered my head but I do remember that I was very pleased with it and that to all questions on the subject I replied that I would certainly have a present for grandmamma but was not going to say what it was.

Contrary to my expectations I found that after composing two verses in the first heat of enthusiasm, try as I would I could not produce any more. I began to read the different poems in our books; but neither Dmitriev nor Derzhavin helped me at all – far from it, they convinced me still more of my own inability. Knowing that Karl Ivanych was fond of transcribing verses, I began surreptitiously burrowing among his papers, and among some German poems I found one in Russian which he must have written himself.

To Madame L— Petrovsk, 3 June 1825
Remember me near,
Remember me far,
O remember me
Henceforth and for ever.

1. A master was given a ticket at the end of each lesson which he saved and later presented for payment.

> Remember to my grave
> How truly I can love.

This poem, penned in a beautiful round hand on a sheet of fine letter-paper, attracted me by the touching feeling with which it was imbued. I immediately learned it by heart and decided to take it as a model. The matter then went much more easily. By the name-day twelve lines of good wishes were ready, and sitting at the schoolroom table I was copying them out on vellum.

Two sheets were already spoilt . . . not because I had found it necessary to make any alterations (my verses seemed to me perfect) but because after the third line the tail-end of each successive one would go curving up and up so that even from a distance they looked crooked and no good at all.

The third sheet came out as sloping as the others but I decided not to do it again. In my poem I wished grandmamma many happy returns of the day, and concluded thus:

> To comfort thee we shall endeavour,
> And love thee like our own dear mother.

This ought to have sounded really quite fine yet in a strange way the last line offended my ear.

'And to lo-ve thee li-ike our own dear mo-ther,' I kept repeating to myself. 'What other rhyme could I use instead of *mother*? . . . Oh, it will do! It's better than Karl Ivanych's anyhow.'

Accordingly I added the last line to the rest. Then in our bedroom I read the whole composition aloud with expression and gestures. There were some lines that did not scan at all but I did not dwell on them: the last line, however, struck me even more forcibly and disagreeably than before. I sat on my bed and pondered:

'Why did I write *like our own dear mother*? She is not here so there was no need ever to bring her in; it is true, I do love and respect grandmamma, still she is not the same as . . . Why did I put that? Why did I write a lie? Of course it's only poetry but I needn't have done *that*.'

At this point the tailor entered with our new suits. 'Well, it can't be helped!' I thought irritably, stuffing my verses under the pillow in my vexation, and ran to try on my Moscow clothes.

They were splendid: the cinnamon-brown jackets with their bronze buttons fitted tightly – not as they made them in the country to allow for growing. The black trousers, also close-fitting, showed up our muscles and came down over our boots.

'At last I've got real trousers with straps!' I reflected, beside myself with delight as I examined my legs from every side. Although the new garments felt very tight and uncomfortable I concealed the fact from everybody and declared that, on the contrary, they fitted comfortably and if there was any fault about them it was that they were, if anything, a shade loose. After that I stood for a long time before the looking-glass, brushing my generously pomaded hair; but strive as I would I could not smooth down the tufts of hair on the crown of my head: so soon as, to test their obedience, I stopped pressing them with the brush they rose and stuck out in all directions, imparting to my face a most ridiculous look.

Karl Ivanych was dressing in another room, and his blue frock-coat and some white things were carried in to him through the schoolroom. The voice of one of grandmamma's maids was heard at the door which led downstairs and I went out to see what she wanted. She was holding in her hand a stiffly starched shirt-front which she told me she had brought for Karl Ivanych, and that she had been up all night to get it washed in time. I undertook to deliver the shirt-front and asked whether grandmamma was up yet.

'I should say so! She's had her coffee and now the priest is here. What a fine fellow you look!' she added with a smile, surveying my new clothes.

This remark made me blush. I whirled round on one leg, snapped my fingers and gave a little skip, to let her feel that she still did not thoroughly appreciate what a very fine fellow I was.

When I took Karl Ivanych his shirt-front he no longer needed it: he had put on another and, stooping before a small looking-glass that stood on a table, was holding the magnificent knot of his cravat in both hands and trying whether his smoothly shaved chin could move easily in and out. After pulling our clothes straight all round and asking Nikolai to do the same for him he took us down to grandmamma. I laugh when I remember how strongly all three of us smelt of pomatum as we descended the stairs.

Karl Ivanych was carrying a little box he had made himself, Volodya had his drawing and I my verses; and each of us had on the tip of his tongue the greeting with which he intended to offer his present. When Karl Ivanych opened the drawing-room door the priest was putting on his vestments and we heard the first sounds of the *Te Deum*.

Grandmamma was already in the drawing-room: with her head bowed and resting her hands on the back of a chair she was standing by the wall, praying devoutly; papa stood beside her. He turned towards us and smiled as he saw us hastily hide our presents behind our backs and stop just inside the door in an effort to escape notice. The whole effect of a surprise, on which we had counted, was lost.

When the time came to go up and kiss the cross I suddenly felt myself suffering from an insurmountable paralysing fit of shyness, and feeling that I should never have the courage to give my present I hid behind the back of Karl Ivanych who, having expressed his good wishes in the choicest of phrases, transferred his little box from his right hand to his left, presented it to grandmamma and stepped a few paces to one side to make way for Volodya. Grandmamma seemed delighted with the box, which had gilt strips pasted round the borders, and expressed her gratitude with the sweetest of smiles. It was evident, however, that she did not know where to put the box, and probably for this reason she asked papa to look at it and see how wonderfully skilfully it was made.

After satisfying his curiosity papa handed it to the priest, who apparently admired the little article very much indeed: he nodded his head, gazing with interest first at the box, then at the craftsman who could make such a beautiful object. Volodya presented his Turk, and he too received the most flattering praise from all sides. I was the next and grandmamma turned towards me with an encouraging smile.

Those who have experienced what it is to be shy know that the sensation increases in direct proportion to its duration, and that one's resolution diminishes in the same ratio: in other words, the longer the condition lasts the more invincible it becomes and the less resolution remains.

The last remnants of courage and resolution forsook me while Karl Ivanych and Volodya were offering their presents, and my shyness reached its climax: I felt the blood continually rushing from my heart to my head, my face kept changing colour and great drops of perspiration stood out on my forehead and my nose. My ears were burning, I felt my whole body trembling and cold with perspiration, and I shifted from one foot to the other but did not budge from the spot.

'Well, Nikolai, show us what you have got – is it a box or a drawing?' papa said to me. There was no help for it: with a shaking hand I held out the crumpled fatal roll; but my voice utterly refused to serve me and I stood before grandmamma in silence. I could not get away from the dreadful idea that instead of the expected drawing my good-for-nothing verses would be read out in front of everybody, and the words *like our own dear mother* would clearly prove that I had never loved her and had forgotten her.

How can I describe my sufferings when grandmamma began to read my poem aloud, and when, unable to make it out, she paused in the middle of a line to glance at papa with what seemed to me then a mocking smile, or when she failed to give a word the expression I had intended, and when, on account of her weak eyesight, she handed the sheet to papa before she had finished, and asked him to read it all over again from the beginning. I thought she did so because she had had enough of reading such stupid crookedly-written verses, and so that papa might read for himself that last line which was such plain proof of want of feeling. I expected him to give me a rap on the nose with the verses and say, 'You horrid boy, you are not to forget your mother ... take that!' But nothing of the kind happened: on the contrary, when it had been read to the end grandmamma said *'Charmant!'*[1] and kissed me on the forehead.

The little box, the drawing and the poem were laid out in a row beside two cambric handkerchiefs and a snuff-box with a portrait of mamma on the lid on the adjustable flap of the arm-chair in which grandmamma always sat.

'The Princess Varvara Ilinichna!' announced one of the two huge footmen who stood behind grandmamma's carriage when she drove out.

But grandmamma was gazing thoughtfully at the portrait set in the tortoise-shell snuff-box, and made no reply.

'Shall I show her in, your ladyship?' repeated the footman.

17 · PRINCESS KORNAKOVA

'Yes, show her in,' said grandmamma, settling deeper into her chair.

The princess was a woman of about forty-five, small, frail, lean and bilious-looking, with disagreeable greeny-grey eyes whose expression entirely contradicted the unnaturally suave curves of her small mouth. Beneath her velvet bonnet with its ostrich feather some fair carroty hair

1. Delightful!

was visible; her eyebrows and eyelashes appeared paler and more carroty still against the unhealthy colour of her face. But in spite of all this, owing to the ease of her movements, her tiny hands and the peculiar aridity of all her features, there was something aristocratic and forceful about her general appearance.

The princess was a great talker and in the way she spoke belonged to the category of people who give the impression that they are being contradicted though no one has uttered a word: she would alternately raise her voice and let it die away gradually, then suddenly begin to speak with fresh animation and gaze round at those who were present but taking no part in the conversation, as though she hoped to gain support by so looking.

In spite of the fact that the princess had kissed grandmamma's hand and continually called her *ma bonne tante*[1] I noticed that grandmamma was displeased with her: she raised her eyebrows in an odd kind of way as she listened to explanations as to why Prince Mihailo could not come in person to give grandmamma his good wishes 'as he would so very much like to have done'; and, answering in Russian to the princess's French, said in a singular drawl:

'I am very much obliged to you, my dear, for your thoughtfulness; and as for Prince Mihailo's not having come, pray do not mention it ... He always has such a mass of things on hand; and besides, what pleasure could he find in seeing an old woman like me?'

And not giving the princess time to protest she went on –

'And how are your children, my dear?'

'Quite well, I am thankful to say, *ma tante*: they grow, do their lessons and get into mischief, especially Etienne, the eldest, who is becoming such a scapegrace that we can't do anything with him; but then he's very intelligent – *un garçon qui promet.*[2] Just fancy, *mon cousin*,' she continued, addressing herself exclusively to papa since grandmamma, not in the least interested in the princess's children but wanting to brag about her own grandchildren, was carefully taking my verses from under the little box and beginning to unfold them: 'Just fancy, *mon cousin*, what he did the other day ...'

And the princess, leaning over to papa, began to tell him something with great animation. When she had finished her tale, which I did not hear, she burst into a laugh and looking inquiringly into papa's face said:

1. My kind aunt.   2. A promising boy.

'What a boy, eh *mon cousin*? He deserved a whipping but the prank was so clever and amusing that I forgave him, *mon cousin*.'

And fixing her eyes on grandmamma the princess continued to smile without saying anything more.

'Do you really *beat* your children, my dear?' asked grandmamma, raising her eyebrows significantly and laying particular emphasis on the word *beat*.

'Ah, *ma bonne tante*,' the princess replied in a sweet voice after a swift glance at papa, 'I know your opinion on that subject; but you must allow me to disagree with you in this one particular. I have thought and read a great deal, and taken much advice about this matter, but experience has all the same convinced me that children must be governed through fear. To make anything of a child, fear is indispensable . . . is it not so, *mon cousin*? And what, *je vous demande un peu*,[1] do children fear more than the birch?'

Saying this, she threw an inquiring look in our direction, and I confess at that moment I felt rather uncomfortable.

'Say what you like but a boy up to the age of twelve, or even fourteen, is still a child. Now with a girl it is different.'

'How lucky,' I thought to myself, 'that I am not her son.'

'Yes, that is all very fine, my dear,' said grandmamma, folding up my verses and putting them away under the box as though after that she did not consider the princess worthy of hearing such a work. 'That is all very well, only tell me, please, what delicacy of feeling can you expect in your children after that?'

And considering this unanswerable grandmamma added, in order to put an end to the conversation:

'However, every one has a right to his own opinion on that subject.'

The princess made no reply but merely smiled condescendingly, to show that she forgave these strange prejudices in one whom she respected so much.

'Oh, but do introduce me to your young people,' she said, looking at us and smiling affably.

We stood up and fixed our eyes on the princess's face but we did not in the least know what we ought to do to show that we had become acquainted.

'Well, kiss the princess's hand,' said papa.

'I hope that you will love your old aunt,' she said, kissing Volodya

1. I ask you now.

on the hair. 'Though I *am* a distant relation I value friendship more than I do degrees of relationship,' she added, directing her remark chiefly to grandmamma; but grandmamma was still displeased with her and answered:

'Oh, my dear, just as if kinship of that kind counted nowadays!'

'This is going to be my young man of the world,' said papa, pointing to Volodya, 'and this is the poet,' he added, just as I was kissing the princess's dry little hand, at the same time very distinctly picturing to myself a birch in that hand, and a bench beneath the birch, and so on and so on.

'Which one?' asked the princess, detaining me by the hand.

'This little fellow with the tufts of hair sticking up,' answered papa with a merry smile.

'What have my tufts done to him? Is there nothing else to talk about?' I thought, and retreated into a corner.

I had the strangest possible conceptions of beauty – I even thought Karl Ivanych one of the handsomest men in the world, but I knew very well that I was not good-looking, and in this I was in no wise mistaken, so that any allusion to my personal appearance offended me deeply.

I can remember quite well how one day during dinner – I was six years old at the time – they were discussing my looks and mamma, trying to discover something nice about my face, said that I had intelligent eyes and a pleasant smile, and then, yielding to papa's arguments and to the obvious, had been forced to admit that I was plain; and afterwards, when I was thanking her for the dinner[1] she patted my cheek and said:

'Remember, my little Nikolai, that no one will love you for your face so you must try to be a sensible good boy.'

These words not only convinced me that I was no beauty but made me determined by all the means in my power to be a good and clever boy.

But in spite of this I often had moments of despair, fancying that there could be no earthly happiness for a person with such a broad nose, such thick lips and such small grey eyes as I had; and I prayed for a miracle that would transform me into a handsome man, and I would have given all I possessed and everything I might have in the future in exchange for a handsome face.

1. After a meal Russians always thank whoever has provided it.

18 · PRINCE IVAN IVANYCH

After the princess had heard the verses and showered praises upon their author grandmamma relented. She began talking to her in French and stopped calling her 'you, my dear'[1] and invited her to return that evening with all her children. The princess accepted the invitation and after staying a little longer took her leave.

So many visitors called with their good wishes that day that throughout the morning there were always several carriages by the entrance in the courtyard.

'Bonjour, chère cousine!' said one of the callers as he entered the room and kissed grandmamma's hand.

He was a tall man of about seventy, in military uniform with large epaulets and a large white cross showing beneath his collar, and having a calm frank expression of countenance. I was struck by the freedom and simplicity of his movements. Though only a thin semicircle of hair was left on the back of his head, and the set of his upper lip clearly betrayed a scarcity of teeth, his face was still notably handsome.

While he was still very young at the end of the last century Prince Ivan Ivanych had made himself a brilliant career, thanks to his honourable character, good looks, remarkable courage, distinguished and powerful connexions and, above all, good fortune. He continued in the Service and very soon his ambition was so thoroughly satisfied that there was nothing more for him to wish for in that respect. From his earliest youth he had behaved as if he were preparing himself to occupy that exalted position in the world in which fate eventually placed him. Consequently, though in the course of his brilliant and somewhat vainglorious life he encountered reverses, disappointments and afflictions like any other man, his invariably calm disposition, his elevated cast of mind, his profound moral and religious principles never once failed him, and he had won universal respect not so much for his brilliant position as for his perseverance and integrity. He was not a man of great intellect but due to the eminence of his station which allowed him to look down on all the vain turmoil of life his views were lofty. He was kindly and sympathetic but cold and rather arrogant in his dealings with others – since, occupying a position in which he could

1. Instead of the more friendlier, intimate *thou*.

be useful to many people, he endeavoured by his cold manner to protect himself from the continual requests and cajolery of those who only wanted to avail themselves of his influence. Even so this coldness was mitigated by the indulgent courtesy of a man of the highest society. He was well educated and well read; but his education had stopped at what he had acquired in his youth, that is, at the end of the last century. He had read everything of note that had been written in France in the field of philosophy and rhetoric during the eighteenth century; he was thoroughly acquainted with all the best works of French literature, so that he was able to quote and liked quoting passages from Racine, Corneille, Boileau, Molière, Montaigne and Fénelon; he was splendidly versed in mythology, and in French translations had studied with profit the ancient monuments of epic poetry; he had acquired a sufficient knowledge of history from Ségur but he knew nothing at all of mathematics beyond arithmetic, nor of physics, nor of contemporary literature; in conversation he knew how to be silent, or to utter a few commonplaces about Goethe, Schiller and Byron but he had never read them. Notwithstanding this classical French education, of which so few examples still exist nowadays, his conversation was always simple and this very simplicity both concealed his ignorance of certain things and showed his good breeding and tolerant disposition. He hated every kind of eccentricity, declaring that eccentricity was an expedient of vulgar people. Society life was a necessity to him wherever he might be: whether in Moscow or abroad he always lived in the same open fashion and on certain days entertained the whole town at his home. His standing was such that a note of invitation from him would serve as a passport to any drawing-room, and many young and pretty women willingly offered him their rosy cheeks, which he kissed as it were paternally; and others, to all appearances very important and superior persons, were delighted beyond words when they were asked to one of the prince's receptions.

There were very few people left to the prince now, who, like our grandmamma, were of the same circle as himself, had been brought up in the same way, had the same outlook on things and were of the same age; so he set particular store on his long-established friendship with her and always showed her the greatest esteem.

I could not take my eyes off the prince: the respect he evoked from all sides, his huge epaulets, the way grandmamma was always so glad to see him, and the fact that he was the only person she did not seem to inspire with fear – indeed, he was quite at his ease with her, even daring to address her as *ma cousine* – filled me with a regard which equalled, if it did not excel, that which I felt for grandmamma. When my verses were shown to him he called me to his side and said:

'Who knows, *ma cousine*, but this may turn out to be a second Derzhavin?'

Thereupon he pinched my cheek so painfully that if I did not cry out it was only because I guessed it must be meant as a caress.

The visitors had departed, my father and Volodya had gone out of the room: only the prince, grandmamma and I were left in the drawing-room.

'How is it our dear Natalya Nikolayevna did not come?' asked Prince Ivan Ivanych suddenly, after a momentary silence.

'Ah, *mon cher*,' answered grandmamma, lowering her voice and laying a hand on the sleeve of his uniform, 'she would certainly have come were she at liberty to do what she wants to. She wrote that Pierre had offered to bring her but that she had declined because, according to her, they are getting no income at all this year; and she adds: "Besides, there is no real reason why the whole family need come to Moscow this year. Lyuba is still too young, and as to the boys – they will live at your house and I shall feel even more secure about them than if they were with me." All very nice!' continued grandmamma in a tone which plainly showed that she did not consider it nice at all. 'It was high time to send the boys here that they might learn something and become accustomed to society, for what sort of an education could they have got in the country? . . . Why, the eldest will soon be thirteen and the other eleven . . . You have noticed, *mon cousin*, that they are just like savages here . . . they do not even know how to enter a room.'

'Still I cannot understand these perpetual complaints of straitened circumstances,' replied the prince. '*He* has a very handsome fortune, and I know Natalya's Khabarovka estate (where once upon a time you and I used to play in theatricals together) like the back of my hand – it is a marvellous property and must bring in a splendid income.'

'I will tell you as a true friend,' grandmamma interrupted him with a sad expression on her face, 'that it seems to me these are only excuses for *him* to live here alone, to gad about from club to club, go to dinner-parties and do heaven knows what, and she does not suspect a thing. You know what an angel of goodness she is – she trusts *him* in everything. He assured her that the children had to be taken to Moscow and that she ought to remain in the country with the stupid governess – and she believed it. If he were to tell her the children should be whipped as Princess Kornakova whips her children I think she would agree even to that,' said grandmamma, turning in her arm-chair with an expression of great contempt. 'No, my dear friend,' she continued after a brief pause, and taking one of her two handkerchiefs to wipe away a tear which had showed itself, 'I often think that *he* is incapable either of appreciating or understanding her, and that, for all her goodness, her affection for him and her endeavour to conceal her grief (which I know very well exists) – she cannot be happy with him; and mark my words, if he does not . . .'

Grandmamma covered her face with her handkerchief.

'Come, *ma bonne amie*,' said the prince reproachfully, 'I see you haven't grown one scrap more sensible – you are always distressing yourself and weeping over imaginary sorrows. Fie, for shame! I have known *him* for a long time and I am sure he is an attentive, kindly and excellent husband, as well as (which is the chief thing of all) a most honourable man, *un parfait honnête homme*.'[1]

Having involuntarily overheard a conversation I was not meant to hear, I tiptoed out of the room in a fine state of excitement.

19 · THE IVINS

'Volodya, Volodya! The Ivins are here!' I cried, seeing through the window three boys in blue overcoats with beaver collars crossing to our house from the opposite pavement behind their smart young tutor.

The Ivins were relations of ours and almost the same age as we were, and soon after our arrival in Moscow we had made their acquaintance and become friends.

The second Ivin, Seriozha, had dark curly hair, a firm turned-up little nose, very fresh red lips which seldom entirely closed over his rather prominent upper white teeth, fine dark blue eyes and an uncommonly lively face. He never smiled but either looked perfectly serious or laughed outright a ringing clear and extraordinarily captivating laugh. His unusual beauty struck me at first sight. I felt irresistibly attracted to him. To see him was sufficient to make me happy, and at the time my whole soul was concentrated on that one desire. Should

1. A thorough gentleman.

three or four days go by without my seeing him I began to fret and was miserable enough to shed tears. All my dreams, waking or sleeping, were of him: when I went to bed I willed myself to dream of him; shutting my eyes I saw him before me and hugged the vision to me as my choicest delight. To no one in the world could I have brought myself to confess this feeling, so precious was it to me. Perhaps because he was sick of having my anxious eyes constantly fixed upon him, or simply because he felt no liking for me, he evidently preferred to play and talk with Volodya rather than with me; but for all that I was quite content, wished for nothing, demanded nothing and was ready to make any sacrifice for him. Besides the passionate fascination he exercised upon me his presence inspired another feeling in a no less powerful degree – a dread of upsetting, offending or displeasing him in any way. Was it because his face wore such a haughty expression or because, despising my own looks, I valued beauty too highly in others, or, most probably of all, because awe is an infallible sign of affection, that I feared him as much as I loved him? The first time Seriozha spoke to me I was so taken aback by such unexpected happiness that I turned pale, then blushed, and could not answer him. He had a bad habit of fixing his eyes on one spot when he was pondering something, and continually blinking while twitching his nose and eyebrows. Everybody thought that this habit greatly spoiled his looks but I found it so attractive that I involuntarily began to do the same thing until a few days after we had got to know him grandmamma asked me whether my eyes were hurting me, since I was blinking like an owl. No word of affection ever passed between us; but he sensed his power over me and in our childish dealings with one another used it unconsciously but tyrannically; as for me, much as I longed to bare my soul to him, I was too afraid of him to venture to be frank: I tried to appear indifferent, and submitted to his will without a murmur. At times his influence seemed to me oppressive and intolerable but I could not cast it off.

It makes me sad to remember that fresh beautiful feeling of disinterested boundless affection which died away without ever finding vent or being reciprocated.

How strange it is that when I was a child I tried to be like a grownup, yet as soon as I ceased to be a child I often longed to be like one. Again and again in my relations with Seriozha this desire – not to behave like a child – stopped me from pouring out my feelings and forced me to dissimulate. Not only did I never dare kiss him as I often longed to, or take his hand and tell him how glad I was to see him, but I never even dared to call him by his pet name, Seriozha, but always kept to Sergei, as everyone else did in our house. Any expression of sentiment was regarded as proof of babyishness, and any one who permitted himself anything of the sort was still a *little boy*. Ignorant still of the bitter experiences which cause grown-up people to be cautious and cold in their relations with one another, we deprived ourselves of the pure joys of a tender attachment between children merely from a strange desire to resemble *grown-ups*.

I met the Ivins in the hall, exchanged greetings with them and rushed headlong to grandmamma and in a tone suggesting that the news must make her completely happy announced that the Ivins had come. Then without taking my eyes off Seriozha I followed him into the drawing-room, watching his every movement. When grandmamma said that he had grown a great deal, and fixed her penetrating gaze on him, I experienced the same sensation of fear and hope which an artist must feel when waiting for a revered critic's opinion of his work.

The Ivins' young tutor, Herr Frost, with grandmamma's permission went out into the garden with us, seated himself on a green bench, gracefully crossed his legs, placed his bronze-headed cane between them and lit a cigar with the air of one highly satisfied with what he is doing.

Herr Frost was a German but a German of quite a different type from our good Karl Ivanych. In the first place he spoke Russian correctly and French with a bad accent, and generally enjoyed, especially among the ladies, the reputation of being a very learned man. Secondly, he had red moustaches, wore a large ruby pin in his black satin cravat, the ends of which were tucked under his braces, and trousers of light blue shot material, with straps. Thirdly, he was young, had a handsome self-satisfied appearance and unusually fine muscular legs. It was evident that he particularly prized this last superiority and considered its effect irresistible to every female, and no doubt for this reason he always tried to place his legs in the most conspicuous position and whether standing or sitting always twitched his calves. He was a typical young Russo-German who aspires to be a gay fellow and a lady-killer.

We had great fun in the garden. Our game of 'robbers' never went better; but an incident occurred that nearly put a stop to it completely. Seriozha was the robber and while pursuing the travellers at full tilt he

stumbled and struck his knee so violently against a tree that I thought
he must have shivered it to splinters. Though I was the gendarme and
it was my duty to catch him I went up to him and began to ask with
concern if he were hurt. Seriozha flared up at me: he clenched his
fists, stamped his foot and in a voice which plainly betrayed that he had
hurt himself badly shouted:

'What's the matter with you? How can we play the game properly?
Well, why don't you catch me? Why don't you catch me?' he repeated several times, with a side glance at Volodya and the eldest
Ivin who were the travellers and so were running and jumping along
the path; then with a sudden wild yell he hurled himself after them,
laughing loudly.

I cannot express how impressed and enthralled I was by this heroic
behaviour: in spite of terrible pain he not only did not cry – he did not
even show that he was hurt, or for a moment forget the game.

Soon after that, when Ilinka Grap joined us and we went upstairs
before dinner, Seriozha had occasion still further to captivate and
impress me by his astonishing courage and strength of mind.

Ilinka Grap was the son of a poor foreigner who had once lived at
my grandfather's and was under some obligation to him, and now
considered it his imperative duty to send his son to us as often as possible. If he supposed his son would derive any honour or pleasure from
acquaintance with us he was quite mistaken, for not only were we not
friendly with Ilinka but we only took any notice of him when we
wanted to make fun of him. Ilinka Grap was a boy of about thirteen,
thin, tall and pale, with a bird-like face and a good-natured submissive
expression. He was very poorly dressed but his hair was so abundantly
pomaded that we declared that on sunny days the pomatum melted on
his head and trickled down under his jacket. As I recall him now I see
that he was a very obliging quiet kind-hearted boy; but at the time he
seemed such a contemptible creature that he was not worth pitying or
even thinking about.

When we had finished playing at robbers we went upstairs and began to romp about and show off gymnastic feats to one another. Ilinka
watched us with a timid smile of admiration and when we invited him
to do the same he made excuses, saying that he was not strong enough.
Seriozha looked marvellously nice: he had taken his jacket off, his face
and eyes shone, he laughed and continually devised new tricks; he
jumped over three chairs placed in a row, turned somersaults right down

the room, stood on his head on Tatishchev's dictionaries which he piled in the middle of the room for a pedestal, and at the same time did such funny things with his feet that it was impossible to help laughing. After this last trick he thought for a bit, blinking his eyes, and with a perfectly serious air suddenly went up to Ilinka and said: 'You try that: it really isn't difficult.' Grap, seeing everybody's attention fixed on him, blushed and in a scarcely audible voice said that he could not possibly do it.

'Now, really, why won't he do some trick for us too? He's not a girl . . . He has just *got* to stand on his head.'

And Seriozha grabbed him by the hand.

'Yes, yes, he must stand on his head!' we all shouted, surrounding Ilinka, who at that moment obviously took fright and went pale, and we seized him by the arm and dragged him towards the dictionaries.

'Let me go, I'll do it by myself! You'll tear my jacket!' cried the unfortunate victim. But his cries of despair only encouraged us the more. We were doubled up with laughter: his green jacket was bursting at all its seams.

Volodya and the eldest Ivin pushed his head down and placed it on the dictionaries. Seriozha and I seized the poor boy by his thin legs, which he was kicking in all directions, rolled his trousers up to the knee and with a shout of laughter jerked his legs up in the air, while the youngest Ivin tried to preserve the balance of the whole body.

Suddenly after our boisterous laughter we all fell quite silent and it was so quiet in the room that the only sound heard was the heavy breathing of the unhappy Grap. At that moment I did not feel entirely convinced that all this was funny and amusing.

'Now you're a good chap,' said Seriozha, giving him a slap.

Ilinka was silent and, endeavouring to free himself, kicked out right and left. In one of these desperate thrusts he caught Seriozha in the eye so forcibly with his heel that Seriozha immediately let go of the legs, put one hand to his eye which was shedding involuntary tears, and pushed Ilinka with all his might. No longer supported by us, Ilinka crashed heavily to the floor and could only mutter through his tears:

'Why do you bully me?'

We were struck by the pitiful figure of poor Ilinka with his tear-stained face, dishevelled hair and the rolled up trousers showing the unblacked tops of his boots. No one said anything and we tried to force a smile.

Seriozha was the first to recover.

'There's an old woman for you! Cry-baby!' he said, lightly touching Ilinka with his foot. 'It's no good trying to have a joke with him. Well, that's enough now, get up.'

'I told them all you were a nasty boy,' said Ilinka angrily, and turning away he burst into loud sobs.

'Oh, oh, kicks out with its heels and then starts calling names!' cried Seriozha, seizing one of the dictionaries and flourishing it over the unfortunate youth, who made no pretence of defending himself but merely covered his head with his arms.

'That's what I think of you!... Let's leave him alone if he can't take a joke... Come on downstairs,' said Seriozha, laughing unnaturally.

I glanced with compassion at the poor lad who lay on the floor and hiding his face among the dictionaries wept so bitterly that it seemed a little more and he would have died of the convulsions which shook his whole body.

'Oh Sergei!' I said. 'Why did you do that?'

'That's good!... I didn't cry, I hope, when I cut my leg nearly to the bone today.'

'Yes, that's true,' I thought. 'That Ilinka's nothing but a cry-baby, but Sergei now – he's a fine fellow... What a fine fellow he is!...'

It never occurred to me that poor Ilinka was probably crying not so much from physical pain as at the thought that five boys whom he may have liked had for no reason at all conspired to detest and persecute him.

I am quite unable to explain to myself my cruel behaviour. How was it I did not go up to him, did not protect or console him? Where was my tender heart which often caused me to sob wildly at the sight of a young jackdaw pushed out of its nest, or a puppy being thrown over a fence, or a chicken the cook was going to make soup of?

Can it be that all those good instincts were stifled in me by my affection for Seriozha and my desire to appear in his eyes as fine a fellow as he was himself? Contemptible then were both the affection and my wish to be a fine fellow, for they left the only dark spots on the pages of my childhood's recollections!

20 · VISITORS ARRIVE

To judge by the unusual activity in the butler's pantry, by the brilliant lighting which lent a novel and festive appearance to all the things so long familiar to me in the drawing-room and ball-room, and especially by the fact that Prince Ivan Ivanych would not have sent his orchestra without some reason, it seemed that we were to have a large party that evening.

Every time a carriage rattled past I ran to the window, put the palms of my hands to my temples and leaned against the window-pane, peering into the street with impatient curiosity. Out of the darkness, which at first hid everything outside the window, there gradually emerged – opposite, the familiar little shop with its lantern, diagonally across the road, the large house with two lighted windows on the ground floor and in the middle of the street an open cab with a couple of passengers or an empty carriage returning at a foot pace; but at last a carriage drove up to our door and feeling sure that it was the Ivins who had promised to come early I ran to meet them in the hall. Instead of the Ivins two feminine figures appeared behind the liveried arm which opened the door: one of them tall, in a blue coat with a sable collar, the other much shorter and wrapped in a green shawl from beneath which only her little feet in fur boots were visible. Without paying any attention to my presence in the hall – although I had thought it my duty to make them a bow when they came in – the little one stepped up to the taller lady and silently stood in front of her. The latter unwound the shawl that completely covered the little one's head, unbuttoned her mantle and when the liveried footman had received these articles into his charge and had pulled off her fur boots the muffled-up individual turned out to be a wonderful little girl of about twelve in a short low-necked muslin frock, white pantalettes and tiny black slippers. She had a black velvet ribbon round her snow-white neck; her little head was a mass of dark chestnut curls which suited her pretty face and bare shoulders so well that I would not have believed it even if Karl Ivanych himself had told me that her hair curled like that because it had been twisted up ever since the morning in bits of the *Moscow News*, and been crisped with hot curling tongs. She looked as if she had been born with that head of curls.

The most striking feature of her face was the extraordinary size of her prominent half-veiled eyes which formed an odd but pleasing contrast to her very small mouth. Her lips were closed and her eyes so grave that the general expression of her face suggested no promise of a smile, and therefore the smile when it did come was all the more bewitching.

Trying not to be noticed, I slipped through the door into the ball-room, and deemed it necessary to walk up and down in thought and quite unaware that guests had arrived. When they were half-way through the room I as it were came to myself, bowed and brought my feet together, and informed them that grandmamma was in the drawing-room. Madame Valakhina, whose face I liked very much, more especially as I discerned in it a strong resemblance to that of her daughter, Sonya, nodded to me graciously.

Grandmamma apparently was very pleased to see Sonya. She made her come up closer, set to rights a curl which fell over her forehead, and looking earnestly into her face said: '*Quelle charmante enfant!*'[1] Sonya smiled, blushed, and looked so charming that I blushed too as I watched her.

'I hope you will not find it dull here, my dear,' said grandmamma, raising Sonya's face by the chin. 'Pray enjoy yourself and dance as much as ever you can. See, we have one lady and two *beaux* already,' she added, turning to Madame Valakhina and stretching out her hand to me.

This coupling of Sonya and myself pleased me so much that I blushed again.

Feeling that my shyness was increasing and hearing another carriage drive up, I thought it best to beat a retreat. In the hall I met Princess Kornakova with her son and an incredible number of daughters, who all looked alike – they resembled the princess and were all plain so not one of them attracted attention. As they took off their mantles and boas they all talked together in thin voices, and bustled about and laughed at something – probably at there being so many of them. Étienne was a tall fleshy boy of about fifteen, with a bloodless face, sunken eyes that had dark shadows under them, and hands and feet which were enormous for his age. He was clumsy and had a disagreeable rough voice but seemed very well satisfied with himself, and according to my idea was precisely the sort that a boy who was beaten with a switch would be.

1. What a charming child!

We stood for some time confronting and scrutinizing one another without uttering a word. Then we moved closer, meaning, I think, to kiss, but after looking once more into each other's eyes for some reason we changed our minds. When the dresses of all his sisters had rustled past us, in order to start a conversation I asked him whether they had not been very crowded in the carriage.

'I don't know,' he answered indifferently. 'You see I never ride inside the carriage because as soon as I get in I feel sick, and mamma knows that. When we go anywhere in the evening I always sit on the box – it is much more fun, you can see everything. Filip gives me the reins, and sometimes the whip too. So that now and then the passers-by get a taste of it' – he added with a significant gesture. 'It's fine!'

'Your excellency,' said a footman coming into the hall, 'Filip wants to know where you have put the whip.'

'Put the whip? Why, I gave it back to him.'

'He says you didn't.'

'Well then, I hung it on the carriage-lamp.'

'Filip says it is not on the lamp either, and you had better say you took it and lost it, or Filip will have to pay out of his own money for your mischief,' continued the angry footman, getting more and more worked up.

The footman, who looked a glum honest man, seemed to be very warmly on Filip's side and determined to get to the bottom of the affair. Prompted by an instinctive feeling of tactfulness I stepped aside as if I had not noticed anything, but the other footmen who were there behaved quite differently: they drew nearer and stared approvingly at the old servant.

'Well if I lost it, I lost it,' said Étienne, avoiding further explanations. 'What the whip cost I'll pay. Did you ever hear anything so absurd?' he added, coming up to me and impelling me towards the drawing-room.

'No, allow me, sir, how will you pay? I know the way you pay: for more than seven months now you have been going to pay Marya Vassilyevna her twenty kopecks, and I have been waiting for over a year, and there's Petrushka . . .'

'Hold your tongue, will you!' shouted the young prince, turning pale with rage. 'See if I don't tell everything.'

'Tell everything, tell everything!' repeated the footman. 'It is not good, your excellency,' he added with particular stress on the title as we entered the ball-room and he departed to the chest with the cloaks.

'Quite right, quite right!' remarked someone approvingly from the hall behind us.

Grandmamma had a peculiar faculty for expressing her opinion of people by addressing them in a special tone of voice and in certain circumstances now in the second person plural, now in the singular. Though she used the pronouns 'you' and 'thou' quite contrary to the usual way of doing so, these distinctions assumed a very different significance on her lips. When the young prince went up to her she said a few words to him, calling him 'you' and looking at him with such disdain that had I been in his shoes I should have been utterly abashed; but Étienne was evidently not a boy of that stamp: he not only did not take any notice of grandmamma's reception of him but even took none of her, and bowed to the whole company, if not gracefully at least with perfect ease.

Sonya claimed my whole attention: I remember that when Volodya, Étienne and I were chatting in a part of the ball-room where I could see Sonya and she could see and hear us, I enjoyed talking; and when I happened to say anything that seemed to me smart or amusing I raised my voice and glanced towards the drawing-room door; but when we moved to another part of the room from which we could not be heard or seen from the drawing-room I was silent and took no further pleasure in the conversation.

The drawing-room and ball-room gradually filled with guests; among their number, as is always the case at children's parties, were some older girls and boys who did not want to miss a chance of enjoying themselves and dancing, though they pretended to do so only to please the hostess.

When the Ivins arrived, instead of the pleasure it generally gave me to be with Seriozha I was conscious of a certain strange vexation with him that he would see Sonya and she would see him.

21 · BEFORE THE MAZURKA

'Ah, you are having some dancing, I see,' said Seriozha, coming from the drawing-room and pulling a new pair of kid gloves from his pocket. 'I must put my gloves on.'

'Goodness, what shall I do? We have no gloves,' I thought. 'I must go upstairs and try and find some.'

But although I rummaged through every chest of drawers all I found was, in one, our green travelling mittens, and in another a single kid glove which could be of no use to me – in the first place because it was exceedingly old and dirty, secondly because it was too large, and above all because the middle finger was missing, having most likely been cut off long ago by Karl Ivanych for a sore finger. However, I put on this remnant of a glove and contemplated that part of my middle finger which was always ink-stained.

'Now if Natalya Savishna were here she would surely have found me some gloves. I can't go down like this because if they ask me why I don't dance, what can I say? But I can't stay here either for they are certain to miss me. What am I to do?' I said to myself, swinging my arms backwards and forwards.

'What are you doing here?' asked Volodya, running into the room. 'Go down quick and invite a lady to dance . . . they are just beginning.'

'Volodya,' I said, displaying my hand with two fingers sticking out of the dirty glove, and speaking in a voice bordering on despair, 'Volodya, you never thought of this!'

'Of what?' he asked impatiently. 'Oh, you mean gloves,' he added with indifference when he caught sight of my hand. 'No, I didn't. We must ask grandmamma what she thinks,' and without further ado he ran downstairs.

The composure with which he met a situation that had seemed to me so grave relieved my mind and I hurried to the drawing-room, quite forgetting the horrid glove on my left hand.

Cautiously approaching grandmamma's arm-chair and lightly touching her sleeve, I whispered:

'Grandmamma, what are we to do? We have no gloves!'

'What, my dear?'

'We have no gloves,' I repeated, coming closer and closer and putting both my hands on the arm of her chair.

'And what is this?' she said, suddenly seizing my left hand. '*Voyez, ma chère,*' she went on, turning to Madame Valakhina, '*voyez comme ce jeune homme s'est fait élégant pour danser avec votre fille!*'[1]

Grandmamma held my hand firmly and gazed seriously and with a

1. Look, my dear – look how elegant this young man has made himself to dance with your daughter.

look of inquiry at the company present until all had satisfied their curiosity and the laughter had become general.

I should have been much chagrined had Seriozha seen me vainly endeavouring to pull my hand away, scowling with embarrassment, but I did not feel at all ashamed in front of Sonya, who laughed so much that the tears came into her eyes and her ringlets danced about her flushed little face. I realized that her laughter was too full and too natural to be sarcastic; on the contrary, the fact that we were laughing together and were looking at one another seemed to draw us together. The episode with the glove, though it might have ended badly, turned out to be to my advantage, for it put me at my ease with the circle which had always seemed the most dreadful of all – the drawing-room circle. After that I no longer felt at all shy in the ball-room.

The sufferings of shy people spring from their doubts as to the opinion others have formed of them. So soon as that opinion is clearly expressed – be it what it may – the suffering ceases.

How charming Sonya Valakhina was as she danced the French quadrille opposite me with the awkward young prince! How sweetly she smiled when she gave me her hand in the *chaîne*! How prettily the brown curls on her head swung in time to the music, how naïvely she made the *jeté-assemblé* with her tiny feet! In the fifth figure, when my partner left me to run to the other side and I, waiting for the beat, was preparing for my solo, Sonya compressed her lips gravely and looked the other way. But she need not have been nervous for me. I did my *chassé en avant, chassé en arrière* and *glissade* with aplomb, and as I approached her laughingly showed her the glove with the two fingers sticking out. She burst into a helpless laugh and tripped still more enchantingly over the parquet floor. I remember, too, how when we all joined hands to form a ring she bent her head and without letting go of my hand rubbed her little nose with her glove. I can see it all now and can still hear the music of the quadrille from *The Maid of the Danube* to the strains of which all this took place.

Then came the second quadrille, which I danced with Sonya. When we were sitting out together I felt overcome with shyness and positively did not know what to say to her. Finally, after my silence had lasted so long that I began to be afraid she would take me for an idiot, I decided at all hazards to rescue her from any such mistaken notion on my account. '*Vous êtes une habitante de Moscou?*' I asked, and on receiving a reply in the affirmative continued: '*Et moi, je n'ai encore jamais fréquenté la capitale,'*[1] relying particularly on the effect of the word *fréquenté*. I was conscious however that, though this was a very brilliant beginning and fully proved my profound knowledge of the French tongue, I was incapable of continuing the conversation in the same style. It would be some time before it was our turn to dance, and silence fell again. I looked anxiously at her in the hope of discerning what impression I had made and waiting for her to help me. 'Where did you find such a funny glove?' she asked all of a sudden, and the question afforded me immense satisfaction and relief. I explained that the glove belonged to Karl Ivanych, and then went on to speak, rather ironically even, of Karl Ivanych himself – how comical he looked when he took off his red cap, and how once in his green overcoat he had fallen off his horse right into a puddle, and so on. The quadrille passed unnoticed. This was all very well – but why did I ridicule Karl Ivanych? Should I really have forfeited Sonya's good opinion had I described him to her with the affection and esteem I undoubtedly felt for him?

When the quadrille was over Sonya said *merci* to me in such a pretty manner, as if I had really earned her gratitude. I was in the seventh heaven – beside myself with delight – and could hardly recognize myself: where had I obtained such courage, assurance, even daring? 'Nothing in the world can abash me now!' I thought, light-heartedly strolling about the ball-room. 'I am ready for anything!'

Seriozha asked me to be his *vis-à-vis*. 'All right,' I said. 'I have not got a partner yet but I will find one.' Glancing round the room with a confident eye, I saw that all the ladies were engaged except one of the big girls who was standing by the drawing-room door. A tall young man was just approaching her with the intention, so I concluded, of inviting her to dance: he was within a couple of paces from her, while I was at the opposite end of the ball-room. In a twinkling I flew across the space that separated us, doing a graceful *glissade* over the polished floor, and clicking my heels together asked her in a firm voice for the next quadrille. The grown-up young lady, smiling condescendingly, gave me her hand and the young man was left without a partner.

I was so conscious of my power that I did not even take any notice of the young man's annoyance; but I heard afterwards that he had asked who the tousled boy was who had darted past him and snatched his partner from under his nose.

    1. Are you an inhabitant of Moscow? . . . For my part I have never before frequented the capital.

22 · THE MAZURKA

The young man whom I had robbed of his lady was leading, in the first pair of the mazurka. He sprang from his place and holding his partner by the hand, instead of doing the *pas de Basque* which Mimi had taught us, simply ran forwards and on reaching the corner stopped, spread his legs, struck the floor with his heel, turned and with a spring did another run.

As I had no partner for the mazurka I sat behind grandmamma's high-backed chair and looked on.

'Whatever is he doing?' I wondered to myself. 'That's not a bit what Mimi taught us: she always said everybody danced the mazurka on their toes, moving their feet in a semicircle; but now I find it's not danced that way at all. And there are the Ivins and Etienne and the others all dancing without any *pas de Basque*; and our Volodya, too, has adopted the new style. It's not bad either!... And what a darling Sonya is! There she goes...' I felt extraordinarily happy.

The mazurka was nearing an end. Several of the older ladies and gentlemen came up to take leave of grandmamma and departed. Footmen, avoiding the dancers, were carefully carrying supper things into the back room. Grandmamma was obviously tired and spoke slowly, as if she had to make an effort. The band began lazily playing the same tune for the thirtieth time. The grown-up girl with whom I had danced caught sight of me as she was doing a figure, and with a disingenuous smile – she probably hoped to please grandmamma – led Sonya and one of the innumerable princesses up to me. '*Rose ou ortie?*'[1] she asked.

'Oh there you are!' said grandmamma, turning round in her chair. 'Go, my dear, go.'

Although at that moment I felt more like hiding my head under grandmamma's chair than coming out from behind it, how could I refuse? I got up, said '*Rose*' and glanced timidly at Sonya. Before I could recover myself someone's white-gloved hand lay in mine and the princess started forward with the pleasantest of smiles, not suspecting in the least that I had no idea what to do with my feet.

I knew that the *pas de Basque* would be out of place, unsuitable, and

1. Rose or nettle?

might even put me to shame; but the familiar sounds of the mazurka acting upon my ears communicated a certain movement to my acoustic nerves which in turn passed it on to my feet; and these, quite involuntarily and to the surprise of all spectators, began to evolve the fatal circular gliding *pas* on the toes. So long as we proceeded straight ahead we got on after a fashion but at the turn I perceived that unless I took care I should certainly get in front of my partner. To avoid such a catastrophe I stopped short, intending to make the same kind of figure the young man in the first couple had executed so beautifully. But just at the moment when I separated my feet and was preparing to spring the princess, circling quickly round me, looked at my legs with an expression of blank inquiry and amazement. This look undid me. I got so confused that instead of dancing I stamped my feet up and down on one spot in the strangest manner, neither in time to the music nor in relation to anything else, and at last came to a dead standstill. Everybody was staring at me: some in surprise, some with curiosity, some derisively, others with sympathy: only grandmamma looked on with complete indifference.

'*Il ne fallait pas danser, si vous ne savez pas!*'[1] said papa's angry voice just above my ear, and gently pushing me aside he took my partner's hand in his, danced a turn with her in the old-fashioned style and to the loud applause of the onlookers led her back to her seat. The mazurka was at an end.

'O Lord, why dost Thou punish me so dreadfully?'

. . . .

'Every one despises me, and it will always be so . . . Every road is closed to me – the road to friendship, to love, to honour . . . all is lost! Why did Volodya make signs to me which everybody could see and which were no help to me? Why had that disgusting princess looked at my feet like that? Why did Sonya . . . she is a darling but why had she smiled at that moment? Why had papa gone red and seized me by the arm? Can even he have been ashamed of me? Oh, this is frightful! Now if mamma were here she would never have blushed for her little Nikolai . . .' And my imagination carried me far away in pursuit of that beloved figure. I recalled the meadow in front of the house, the tall lime-trees in the garden, the clear pond over which the swallows swooped and swirled, the blue sky dappled with motionless transparent

1. You should not dance if you do not know how.

white clouds, the fragrant stacks of new-mown hay; and many another peaceful happy memory flitted through my troubled mind.

23 · AFTER THE MAZURKA

At supper the young man who had danced in the first couple seated himself at the children's table and treated me with an amount of attention which would have flattered my self-esteem had I been in a state to feel anything after the catastrophe that had befallen me. But the young man seemed determined to cheer me up at any cost: he joked with me, called me a fine fellow, and whenever none of the grown-ups was looking helped me to wine, first from one bottle and then from another, and made me drink it up. Towards the end of supper, when the butler had only filled my glass a quarter full from the champagne bottle wrapped in a table-napkin and the young man had insisted on his filling it right up and got me to empty it at a draught, I felt a grateful warmth diffusing itself through my whole body and an especial goodwill towards my lively patron, and for some reason I burst into loud laughter.

Suddenly the sounds of the *Grossvater*[1] reached our ears from the ball-room and everybody rose from the table. My friendship with the young man came to an abrupt end: he joined the grown-ups while I, not daring to follow him, approached Madame Valakhina, curious to hear what she and her daughter were saying.

'Just another half hour,' Sonya was imploring her.

'We really mustn't, my love.'

'To please me – just this *once*?' Sonya coaxed.

'Will it make you happy if I am ill tomorrow?' said Madame Valakhina, and was incautious enough to smile.

'There, you agree! We can stay?' cried Sonya, jumping for joy.

'What is to be done with you? Well, go along and dance . . . See, here is a partner for you,' said her mother, pointing to me.

Sonya gave me her hand and we ran into the ball-room.

The wine I had drunk and Sonya's presence and high spirits made me forget all about the unfortunate incident of the mazurka. I executed the most amusing tricks with my feet: I trotted like a horse, proudly lifting my feet, or I stood stamping on one spot like a ram angry with a dog, and all the time I laughed for all I was worth, regardless of the

1. Generally the last dance at a ball, and very popular in Russia.

impression I might produce on the spectators. Sonya too did not stop laughing: she laughed at our holding each other's hands and circling round, she laughed when she saw an elderly gentleman laboriously lift his feet to step over a handkerchief, pretending that this was a very difficult operation, and she nearly died of laughing when I leaped almost to the ceiling in proof of my agility.

Passing through grandmamma's boudoir I glanced at myself in the glass: my face was bathed in perspiration, my hair was untidy, all the tufts sticking up more than ever, but my general expression was so happy, good-tempered and healthy that I liked the look of myself.

'If I were always like this,' I thought, 'people might find me nice-looking.'

But when I turned again to my partner's lovely face and I saw there, besides the gaiety, health and light-heartedness that had pleased me in my own, so much exquisite gentle beauty I felt dissatisfied with myself and realized how foolish it was of me to hope to attract the attention of so wonderful a being.

I could not hope that my feelings might be reciprocated – indeed, I could not even think of it: my soul was overflowing with joy without that. I could not imagine that the love which filled my heart with delight could call for still greater happiness or desire anything more than that this feeling might last for ever. I felt perfectly content as it was. My heart fluttered like a dove, the blood rushed to it continually, and I wanted to cry.

When we were going through the passage past the dark lumber-room under the stairs I glanced at it and thought what bliss it would be to live for all time with her in that dark lumber-room, nobody knowing we were there.

'It's been very jolly tonight, hasn't it?' I said in a low trembling voice and quickened my steps, scared not so much at what I had said as at what I had in mind to say.

'Yes . . . very!' she replied, turning her pretty head towards me with such an unmistakably friendly expression that I ceased to be afraid.

'Especially since supper . . . But if you only knew how sorry –' (I wanted to say how 'miserable' but did not dare to) – 'I am that you are soon going away and we shall not see one another again.'

'But why shouldn't we see one another?' she said, gazing intently at the toes of her slippers and running a finger along the trellis screen by which we were passing. 'On Tuesdays and Thursdays mamma and I always drive on the Tverskoy Boulevard. Don't you ever go out for a walk?'

'We will certainly ask to go out next Tuesday, and if they won't let me I will run off by myself – without my hat. I know the way.'

'Do you know what?' Sonya said suddenly. 'I call some of the boys who come to our house *thou*. Shall we say *thou* to each other too? Wouldst thou like to?' she added, throwing back her little head and looking me straight in the eyes.

Just then we were entering the ball-room, and the other lively part of the *Grossvater* was beginning.

'Yes with . . . you,' I said when the music and the noise were loud enough to drown my exact words.

'With *thee*, not with *you*,' Sonya corrected me with a laugh.

The *Grossvater* was over before I had succeeded in saying a single sentence with *thou* in it, even though I had been trying all the time to think of some in which the pronoun might be repeated more than once. My courage failed me. I kept hearing 'Wouldst thou like to?' and 'With thee' and they produced a kind of intoxication in me: I saw nothing and nobody but Sonya. I watched her mother lift her ringlets and push them back behind her ears, exposing parts of her forehead and temples I had not seen before; I saw them wrap her up so completely in the green shawl until only the tip of her nose was left visible; I observed that if she had not made a little opening for her mouth with her rosy fingers she would surely have suffocated, and I saw her turn round quickly and nod to us as she followed her mother down the stairs and vanished through the door.

Volodya, the Ivins, the young prince and I had all fallen in love with Sonya and standing on the staircase we followed her with our eyes. To whom in particular she nodded I do not know but at that moment I was firmly convinced that it was done for me.

When the Ivins said good-bye to us I spoke in a free and easy, even rather cool manner to Seriozha, and shook hands with him. If he realized that from that day he had lost my affection and his power over me I suppose he regretted it although he did his best to appear quite indifferent.

For the first time in my life I had been faithless in love, and for the first time experienced the sweetness of that sensation. I was glad to exchange the worn-out feeling of habitual devotion for the first flush of a love full of mystery and the unknown. Besides, to fall out of love and in love at the same time is to love twice as deeply as one did before.

24 · IN BED

'How could I have been so passionately devoted to Seriozha and for so long?' I wondered as I lay in bed. 'No, he never understood, or appreciated or deserved my love ... But Sonya ... what a darling she is! "Wouldst thou?" – "It is thy turn to begin" ...'

I jumped up on my hands and knees in bed, vividly picturing her face to myself, covered my head with the bed-clothes, tucked them round me on all sides and when there was no opening left anywhere I lay down and feeling cosy and warm immersed myself in sweet visions and memories. Staring fixedly at the lining of my quilt, I saw her as clearly as I had an hour before; I talked to her in my mind, and though there was no sense in the conversation at all it gave me indescribable pleasure because the words *thou, to thee, with thee* and *thine* continually occurred in it.

My imaginings were so vivid that the sweet excitement of them kept me awake and I longed to share my over-abundant happiness with someone.

'Dearest Sonya!' I said almost aloud, suddenly turning over on the other side. 'Volodya, are you asleep?'

'No,' he answered in a sleepy voice. 'What do you want?'

'I am in love, Volodya! Head over heels in love with Sonya.'

'Well, what of it?' he replied, stretching himself.

'Oh Volodya, you can't imagine what is going on inside me ... Here I have been lying tucked up in the quilt and I could see her so plainly – so plainly – and I talked to her: it was simply marvellous! And do you know what – when I lie and think of her, goodness knows why but I feel sad and awfully want to cry.'

Volodya stirred.

'I only wish for one thing,' I continued, 'and that is to be with her always, to see her always. Just that. Are you in love? Confess the truth, Volodya.'

It was strange but I wanted every one to be in love with Sonya and every one to say so.

'What has that to do with you?' said Volodya, turning his face towards me. 'Perhaps.'

'You don't want to sleep, you were only pretending!' I exclaimed, perceiving by his shining eyes that he had no thought of sleep, and I threw off the quilt. 'Let's talk about her. Isn't she a darling? . . . Such a darling that if she said, "Nikolai, jump out of the window," or "Throw yourself in the fire," I swear I would do it at once and gladly. Oh, how lovely she is!' I added, vividly imagining her before me, and in order to enjoy the picture to the full I jerked myself over on the other side and thrust my head under the pillow. 'I terribly want to cry, Volodya.'

'What a little idiot!' he said smiling, and then after a short pause: 'I am not a bit like you: I think, if it were possible, I should like first of all to sit beside her and talk . . .'

'Ah, so you are in love too?' I interrupted him.

'Then,' continued Volodya, smiling tenderly, 'then I would kiss her little fingers, her eyes, her lips, her little nose, her feet – I would kiss all of her.'

'How stupid!' I cried out from under the pillow.

'You don't understand a thing,' said Volodya scornfully.

'I *do* understand, it's you who don't understand and talk nonsense,' I said through my tears.

'Anyhow, there's nothing whatever to cry about. You're a regular girl!'

25 · THE LETTER

On the 16th of April, nearly six months after the day I have just described, father came upstairs while we were having lessons and told us that we were going to the country with him that night. My heart contracted at this news and my thoughts at once turned to mamma.

The cause of such an unexpected departure was the following letter:

Petrovskoe, 12th April

I have only just this moment, at ten o'clock in the evening, received your kind letter of April 3rd and as usual I answer it at once. Fiodr brought it from town yesterday but as it was late he only gave it to Mimi this morning. And Mimi, on the pretext that I was not well and upset, kept it from me all day. It is a fact that I have been a little feverish and to confess the whole truth this is the fourth day I have not been well and have stayed in bed.

Pray do not be alarmed, my dearest: I am feeling pretty well now and if Ivan Vassilyevich will let me I hope to get up to-morrow.

Last Friday I took the girls for a drive but just at the turning which goes to the high road, near that little bridge which always terrifies me, the horses stuck in the mud. It was a lovely day and I thought I would walk as far as the high road while the carriage was being extricated. On reaching the chapel I felt very tired and sat down to rest but as it was half an hour or so before people could be got to pull the carriage out I began to feel cold, especially my feet for I only had thin boots on and they were wet through. After dinner I felt shivery and had a temperature but carried on as usual and after tea sat down to play duets with Lyuba. (You would hardly know her, she has made such progress!) But fancy my sur-prise when I found that I could not count the beats. Several times I began to count but was quite muddled in my head and there were strange noises in my ears. I would begin 'One – two – three' and then suddenly go on '– eight – fifteen –' and, worst of all, I was conscious that I was talking nonsense, and yet could not help it. At last Mimi came to my aid and practically put me to bed by force. There, my dear one, you have the detailed account of how I fell ill and how it was all my own fault. Next day I had quite a high tem-perature and our kind old Ivan Vassilyevich came and is still stay-ing here but promises soon to let me out into God's fresh air. What a wonderful old man Ivan Vassilyevich is! When I was feverish and delirious he sat up all night by my bedside, not closing his eyes; and now, knowing that I am writing this letter, he is in the sitting-room with the children and from my bedroom I can hear him telling them German fairy tales, and them doubled up with laughter as they listen.

'La belle Flamande', as you call her, has been staying with us since last week because her mother has gone away somewhere on a visit, and by her care of me shows her sincere attachment. She confides all her secrets to me. If she were in good hands she might become in all respects a fine young woman, with her lovely face, her kind heart and her youth; but the society in which she moves, according to her own account, will be the ruin of her. It has occurred to me more than once that if I had not so many children of my own it would be doing a good deed to take her into our family.

Lyuba wanted to write to you herself but has torn up three sheets of paper already. 'I know what a tease papa is,' she says. 'If you make one single little mistake he shows it to everybody.' Katya is as sweet as ever, and Mimi as kind as she is tiresome.

Now let us speak of more serious matters: you write that your affairs are not going well this winter and that you will have to break into the Khabarovka revenues. It seems strange to me that you should think it necessary to ask my consent even. Surely what belongs to me belongs equally to you?

You are so kind-hearted, my dear one, that for fear of worrying me you conceal the real state of your affairs; but I can guess: no doubt you have lost a great deal at cards and I assure you, I am not at all troubled about it. So if matters can be arranged all right, pray do not think overmuch about it, and don't worry yourself needlessly. I am accustomed not to count on your winnings for the children, nor, forgive me, even on any of your property. Your gains give me as little pleasure as your losses cause me anxiety. The only thing that grieves me is your unfortunate passion for gambling which robs me of a portion of your tender affection and obliges me to tell you such bitter truths as (heaven knows with what pain) I am doing now. I never cease to pray God for one thing – that He will preserve us, not from poverty (what does poverty matter?) but from any terrible situation in which the children's interests, which I should have to defend, conflicted with our own. Till now the Lord has heard my prayer – you have never yet overstepped the limit beyond which we should be forced either to sacrifice the property, which no longer belongs to us but to our children, or . . . but it is too dreadful to think of even, this horrible misfortune which continually hangs over our heads. Yes, it is a heavy cross that the Lord has laid on us both!

You also write about the children and return to the old point of difference between us: you ask me to let them be sent away to school. You know my objection to that kind of upbringing . . .

I do not know, my dear one, if you will agree, but in any case I implore you by your love for me to give me your promise that, so long as I live, and after my death if it be God's will to part us, you will never do this.

You write that you have got to go to Petersburg in connexion with our affairs. May Christ be with you, my dearest; go, and come back soon. We all miss you so much. Spring here is incredibly lovely: the double door of the balcony has already been taken down, while the path to the hot-house has been quite dry for the past four days and the peach-trees are in full blossom. The snow lingers in a few places only, the swallows have returned, and to-day Lyuba brought me the first spring flowers. The doctor says that in two or three days' time I shall be all right again and able to breathe the fresh air and bask a little in the April sun. *Au revoir*, my dear one, do not worry either about my illness or your losses. Finish your business as speedily as possible and come back with the children to spend the whole summer with us. I am making wonderful plans for it, and it only wants your presence to realize them.

The next part of the letter was written in French, in a close and uneven hand on another scrap of paper. I translate it word for word:

Do not believe what I have written to you about my illness: no one suspects how serious it is. I only know that I shall never leave my bed again. Do not lose a moment but come at once and bring the children. Perhaps I shall be able to embrace them once again, and give them my blessing; that is my one last wish. I know what a terrible blow I am inflicting on you with this news but sooner or later, from me or from others, you would have had to hear it; so let us try to bear this calamity with fortitude and trust in God's mercy. Let us submit to His will.

Do not think that what I am writing is some delusion of my sick imagination: on the contrary, my thoughts are remarkably clear at this moment and I am perfectly composed. Nor must you comfort yourself with the vain hope that these are the unreal, confused forebodings of a timid spirit. No, I feel, I know – and I know because it has pleased God to reveal it to me – that I have but a very short time to live.

Will my love for you and the children cease with this life? I have come to realize that this is impossible. As I write I feel too deeply to be able to believe that this ability to feel, without which I cannot conceive of existence, could ever be extinguished. My soul cannot exist without its love for you, and I know that it will live for ever if only for the reason that such a feeling as my love could never have come into being if it were not destined to be eternal.

I shall no longer be with you but I am firmly convinced that my love will never leave you, and the thought is so comforting to my heart that I await the approach of death calmly and without fear.

I am at peace, and God knows that I have always regarded and still regard death as the passage to a better life. Yet why do the tears choke me? Why must the children be deprived of a beloved mother? Why must such a heavy and unexpected blow fall upon you? Why must I die, when your love has made my life so boundlessly happy?

His holy will be done.

I cannot write more for tears. Maybe I shall not see you again. Thank you, my precious love, for all the happiness with which you have surrounded me in this life. There in the next life I shall pray God to reward you. Farewell, dearest friend: remember that, though I am no more, my love will never leave you wherever you may be. Farewell, Volodya, farewell my angel. Farewell, my Benjamin – my little Nikolai.

Is it possible that the day will come when they forget me?

With this letter was enclosed a note in French from Mimi, the contents of which were as follows:

The sad presentiments of which she speaks are only too well confirmed by what the doctor says. Last night she ordered this letter to be taken to the post at once. Thinking she was delirious, I waited till this morning and then decided to open it. No sooner had I broken the seal than Natalya Nikolayevna asked me what I had done with the letter and told me to burn it if it had not been posted. She keeps talking about it, and says that you will never get over it. Do not postpone your departure if you wish to see the angel before she leaves us. Excuse this scrawl. I have not slept for three nights. You know how I love her!

Natalya Savishna, who had spent the whole night of April the 11th in our mother's bedroom, told me that when she had written the first part of the letter mamma laid it on the little table beside her and dozed off.

'I confess,' continued Natalya Savishna, 'that I dozed off too in my arm-chair, and the stocking I was knitting slipped from my hands. Then (it was some time after midnight) in my sleep I heard a sound as if she were talking. I opened my eyes and looked: and there was my darling sitting up in bed with her hands folded like this, and the tears pouring from her eyes in three streams. "So it is all over?" was all she said, and she covered her face with her hands.

'I jumped up and asked her what was the matter.

'"Oh, Natalya Savishna, if you only knew whom I have just seen!"

'But in spite of all my questioning she would say no more. She only told me to move the little table nearer, added something to her letter, ordered me to seal it in her presence and send it off at once. After that everything went worse and worse.'

26 · WHAT AWAITED US IN THE COUNTRY

On the 18th of April we climbed out of the carriage at the porch of our Petrovsk house. Papa had been very thoughtful and preoccupied when we left Moscow, and when Volodya asked him whether *maman* was ill papa looked at him sadly and nodded his head without speaking. During the journey he grew noticeably more composed but as we drew nearer home his face became more and more mournful, and when he asked Foka, who came running up out of breath as we were getting out of the carriage, 'Where is Natalya Nikolayevna?' his voice was unsteady and there were tears in his eyes. The good old Foka glanced stealthily at us, lowered his gaze and opening the front door answered with his face turned away:

'This is the sixth day she has not left her bedroom.'

Milka, who, I was afterwards told, had whined piteously since the day mamma fell ill, sprang joyfully to meet papa, jumped up on him and licked his hands with an occasional yelp; but he pushed her aside and passed on to the drawing-room and from there to the sitting-room, the door from which led straight into the bedroom. The nearer he approached the bedroom the more did every movement of his body betray his agitation; on entering the sitting-room he walked on tiptoe, hardly daring to breathe, and made the sign of the cross before he could bring himself to turn the handle of the door. At that moment Mimi, dishevelled and tearstained, rushed in from the passage. 'Ah, Piotr

Alexandrych!' she whispered with an expression of unfeigned despair, and then, seeing that papa was turning the door handle, she added almost inaudibly: 'You can't go in that way – you must go in through the maids' room.'

Oh how sadly all this affected my childish imagination, which was stirred by a dreadful foreboding and expecting anguish!

We went to the maids' room. In the passage we encountered the idiot boy Akin, who always amused us by his grimaces; but at this moment he not only did not seem funny to me but nothing struck me so painfully as his vacant indifferent face. In the maids' room two maids sitting at their sewing rose to greet me with such sad faces that I felt frightened. Passing next through Mimi's room, papa opened the bedroom door and we entered. To the right of the door were two windows curtained over by shawls; at one of these windows sat Natalya Savishna with her spectacles on her nose, knitting a stocking. She did not kiss us as she usually did but only rose, looked at us through her spectacles, and the tears rolled down her cheeks. I did not at all like the way everybody began to cry immediately they set eyes on us, although they had been quite calm and composed until then.

To the left of the door stood a screen, and behind the screen the bed, a little table, a small medicine-chest and a big arm-chair in which the doctor was dozing. Beside the bed stood a very fair, remarkably beautiful young girl in a morning gown: she had pushed up her sleeves a little and was applying ice to mamma's head, but mamma herself I could not see at that moment.

The girl was *la belle Flamande* of whom mamma had written and who afterwards played such an important part in the life of our whole family. As soon as we entered she withdrew one hand from mamma's head and arranged the folds of her gown over her bosom, and then said in a whisper: 'She is unconscious.'

I was in great distress at that moment, yet I automatically noticed every little detail. It was almost dark in the room, and very hot; there was a mingled smell of mint, eau-de-cologne, camomile and Hoffmann's drops. The smell struck me so forcibly that, not only when I happen to smell it but when I even recall it, my imagination instantly carries me back to that dark stifling room and reproduces every minute detail of that terrible moment.

Mamma's eyes were wide open but she saw nothing . . . Oh, never shall I forget that dreadful look! It expressed so much suffering.

We were led away.

When I asked Natalya Savishna afterwards about mamma's last moments this is what she told me:

'After you were taken away my poor birdie tossed about for a long time as though she was being suffocated just here; then her head slipped off the pillows and she fell into a doze, all quiet and peaceful like an angel from heaven. I went out for a moment to see why they had not brought her her drink – and when I returned my sweetheart was throwing the bedclothes all about her and beckoning your papa to come to her. He bent over her but 'twas plain she hadn't the strength to say what she wanted to: she could only open her lips and moan: "O God, O Lord . . . the children, the children!" I was just going to run and fetch you but Ivan Vassilyevich stopped me and said: "It will only upset her more, better not." After that she would just raise her hand and drop it again. What she meant by it, the good God only knows. I think she was blessing you in your absence; aye, it seems God would not let her see her children before the end. Then she sat up, did my little dove, moved her hands like this, and suddenly spoke, in a voice I cannot bear to remember: "Mother of God, do not forsake them . . ." And then the pain reached her heart; you could see by her eyes that the poor dear was suffering terribly. She fell back on the pillows and seized the sheet with her teeth, while the tears fairly streamed down her cheeks.'

'Yes, and what then?' I asked.

Natalya Savishna could say no more: she turned away and wept bitterly.

Mamma died in dreadful agony.

27 · GRIEF

Late the following evening I thought I would like to look at her once more. Overcoming an involuntary feeling of terror, I softly opened the door and slipped on tiptoe into the music-room.

On a table in the middle of the room lay the coffin. Around it were candles that had burnt low in their tall silver candlesticks. In the far corner sat the chanter reading the Psalter in a low steady tone.

I stopped at the door and looked but my eyes were so swollen with weeping and my nerves so unstrung that I could distinguish nothing. The light, the gold brocade, the velvet, the tall candlesticks, the pink

lace-trimmed pillow, the frontlet,[1] the cap with ribbons, and something else of a transparent wax-like colour – all ran together in a
strange blur. I climbed on to a chair to look at her face but there in its
place I again saw the same pale-yellow translucent object. I could not
believe that this was her face. I began to stare hard at it and gradually
began to recognize the dear familiar features. I shuddered with horror
when I realized that this was she. But why were the closed eyes so sunken? Why that dreadful pallor, and the blackish spot under the transparent skin on one cheek? Why was the expression of the whole face
so stern and cold? Why were the lips so pale and their shape so beautiful, so majestic and expressive of such unearthly calm that a cold shiver
ran over my spine and hair as I looked at them?

I gazed and felt that some incomprehensible, irresistible power
attracted my eyes to that lifeless face. I did not take my eyes from it,
yet my imagination sketched for me one picture after another of puls-
ing life and happiness. I kept forgetting that the dead body which lay
before me and which I gazed at so absently, as on some object that had
nothing to do with my memories, was *she*. I imagined her now in one,
now in another situation: alive, gay and smiling; then suddenly some
feature in the pale face before my eyes arrested my attention and I
remembered the dreadful reality, and shuddered but continued to
look. Then again visions replaced the reality, to be shattered by the
consciousness of the reality. At last my imagination grew weary, it
ceased to deceive me. The consciousness of the reality vanished too
and I became oblivious of everything. I do not know how long I
remained in this state, nor what it was: I only know that for a time I
ceased to be aware of my existence and experienced a kind of exalted,
ineffably sweet, sad happiness.

It may be that as she flew towards a better world her lovely spirit
looked pityingly at the one in which she was leaving us; she had seen
my grief and in pity for it with a heavenly smile of compassion had
descended to earth on the pinions of love, to comfort and bless me.

The door creaked and another chanter entered the room to relieve
the first one. The noise roused me and the first thought that came to
my mind was that as I was not crying but stood on a chair in an attitude
which had nothing pathetic about it the chanter might take me for a

1. A ribbon of satin or paper with pictures showing the Saviour, the Mother
of God and St John which is laid upon the brow of the corpse in the Orthodox
rite.

heartless boy who had climbed on the chair out of commiseration or curiosity; and I made the sign of the cross, bowed and began to cry.

As I recall my impressions now it seems to me that only that momentary forgetfulness of self was genuine grief. Before and after the funeral I never ceased to cry and be miserable, but it makes me ashamed when I think back on that sadness of mine, seeing that always in it was an element of self-love – now a desire to show that I prayed more than any one else, now concern about the impression I was producing on others, now an aimless curiosity which caused me to observe Mimi's cap or the faces of those around me. I despised myself for not experiencing sorrow to the exclusion of everything else, and I tried to conceal all other feelings: this made my grief insincere and unnatural. Moreover, I felt a kind of enjoyment in knowing that I was unhappy and I tried to stimulate my sense of unhappiness, and this interest in myself did more than anything else to stifle real sorrow in me.

Having slept soundly and peacefully all that night, as is always the case after great distress, I awoke with my eyes dry and my nerves soothed. At ten o'clock we were called to the service which was celebrated before the body was borne away. The room was filled with weeping servants and peasants who had come in to take leave of their mistress. During the service I wept as befitted the occasion, crossed myself and bowed to the ground, but I did not pray in spirit and was more or less unmoved: I was more concerned with the fact that the new jacket they had dressed me in was too tight under the arms; I thought about how not to dirty the knees of my trousers when I knelt down, and kept stealthily observing all the people who were present. My father stood at the head of the coffin. He was as white as a sheet and obviously had difficulty in restraining his tears. His tall figure in a black frock-coat, his pale expressive face and his movements, graceful and assured as ever when he crossed himself, bowed, touching the floor with his fingers, took a candle from the priest's hand or approached the coffin were extremely effective; but, I don't know why, I did not like him being able to show himself off so effectively at that moment. Mimi was leaning against the wall and seemed hardly able to stand on her feet; her dress was crumpled and had bits of down sticking to it, her cap was awry, her swollen eyes were red, her head shook and she sobbed incessantly in a heart-rending manner and kept covering her face with her handkerchief and her hands. I fancied she did so in order to hide her face from the spectators and rest a moment from forced sobbing. I remembered how the day before she had told papa that mamma's death was such a terrible blow for her that she could never hope to recover from it; that it had deprived her of everything; that that angel (as she called mamma) had not forgotten her at the last and had expressed her wish to secure her future and Katya's. She had shed bitter tears while relating this, and perhaps her grief was genuine but was not entirely pure and disinterested. Lyuba in a black frock trimmed with weepers, her face all wet with tears, stood with bent head. From time to time she glanced at the coffin and her face expressed nothing but childish terror. Katya stood beside her mother and in spite of the long face she put on was as rosy as ever. Volodya's frank open disposition was open and frank in his grief too: he stood pensive, staring straight before him at something. Then suddenly his lips would begin to quiver and he would hastily cross himself and bow his head again. All the outsiders who were present at the service I found intolerable. The expressions of sympathy they addressed to my father – that she would be better off there, that she was not for this world – aroused a kind of anger in me.

What right had they to talk about her and mourn for her? Some of them in referring to us called us *orphans*. As if we did not know without their assistance that children who have lost their mother are known as orphans! Probably (I thought) they enjoyed being the first to give us that name, just as people generally are in a hurry to call a newly-married girl *Madame* for the first time.

In the far corner of the room, almost hidden by the open door of the butler's pantry, knelt a bent grey-haired old woman. With clasped hands and eyes raised to heaven she was not weeping but was praying. Her soul went out to God, and she besought Him to let her join the one she had loved more than anything on earth, and earnestly hoped that it would be soon.

'There is one who loved her truly,' I thought, and I felt ashamed of myself.

The service was over; the face of the deceased was uncovered, and all present, excepting ourselves, went up to the coffin, one after another, to kiss her.

One of the last to approach and take leave of her was a peasant woman carrying a pretty five-year-old girl whom she had brought with her, heaven knows why. At that moment I dropped my wet handkerchief by mistake and was just stooping to pick it up when I was startled by an awful piercing cry of such horror that I shall never forget it if I live to be a hundred: whenever I think of it a cold shudder runs down my body. I raised my head – the peasant woman was standing on a stool by the coffin and struggling to hold the little girl in her arms. The child was pushing with her little fists, throwing back her frightened little face and staring with dilated eyes at the dead woman as she uttered a succession of dreadful frenzied shrieks. I too uttered a cry that, I think, must have been even more terrible than the one which had startled me, and ran from the room.

Only now did I understand whence came the strong and oppressive smell which, mingling with the incense, filled the whole room; and the thought that the face that but a few days ago had been so full of beauty and tenderness, the face of the person I loved most in the world, could inspire horror, as it were for the first time revealed the bitter truth to me and overwhelmed my soul with despair.

28 · LAST SAD MEMORIES

Mamma was no more but our life continued on the old lines: we went to bed and got up at the same time as before and in the same rooms; morning and evening tea, dinner, supper – all took place at the usual hours; tables and chairs stood in the same places; nothing had changed in the house or in our way of life: only she was not there.

It seemed to me that after adversity of such magnitude everything ought to be different; our ordinary course of life seemed to me an affront to her memory, and too acutely reminded me of her absence.

On the day before the funeral, after dinner, I felt sleepy and went to Natalya Savishna's room, meaning to install myself on her soft feather-bed under her warm quilt. When I entered I found Natalya Savishna herself lying on the bed, apparently asleep. Hearing the sound of my footsteps, she sat up, threw off the woollen shawl with which she had protected her head from the flies, straightened her cap and seated herself on the side of the bed.

Since in the old days it had frequently happened that I came for an after-dinner nap in her room she immediately guessed why I was there and getting up said:

'Well, I dare say you have come to have a rest, eh dearie? Lie down.'

'What an idea, Natalya Savishna!' said I, holding her back by her arm. 'I did not come for that at all . . . I just came . . . and you are tired yourself: you'd better lie down.'

'No, my dear, I am quite rested,' she said (I knew she had not slept for three days). 'Besides, I don't feel like sleep now,' she added with a deep sigh.

I wanted to talk to Natalya Savishna about our trouble: I knew how honest and loving she was, and so it would have been a comfort to me to have a good cry with her.

'Natalya Savishna,' I said after a pause and sitting down on the bed, 'did you expect it?'

The old woman gave me a puzzled surprised look, probably not understanding why I asked her that.

'Who could have expected it?' I repeated.

'Ah, my dearie,' she replied, casting me a look of tenderest sympathy, 'not only did I not expect it but I can't believe it even now. I'm an old woman now, and my old bones ought to have been laid to rest long ago – and yet I have lived to see my old master, your grandpapa, Prince Nikolai Mihailovich, into his grave (God rest his soul), two of my brothers, my sister Anna – I have buried them all, and them all younger than me, my dearie; and now, for my sins no doubt – I must outlive her too. His holy will be done! He went and took her because she was worthy to go and He needs good souls in heaven.'

This simple thought impressed me as comforting and I moved closer to Natalya Savishna. She folded her hands on her bosom and looked upwards; her hollow rheumy eyes expressed deep but tranquil sorrow. She firmly trusted that God had not parted her for long from the one on whom all the power of her love had been centred for so many years.

'Yes, my dear, it does not seem long since I dandled her and swaddled her, and she called me "Nasha". She used to come running up to me, put her tiny arms round me and kiss me, saying, "My Nasha, my darling, my ducky!" and I'd answer in fun: "No, miss, you don't love me. Just you wait: when you grow up into a big girl, you'll get married and forget your old Nasha." She would look thoughtful, and "No," she'd say. "I'd rather not marry if I can't take Nasha with me. I'm not going to leave Nasha ever." And now she's gone and left me and didn't wait for me. And how she did love me, my little dead lamb! And was there anyone in the world she did not love? No, my dearie, you mustn't forget your mamma: she was not a creature of this earth, she was an angel from heaven. When her soul reaches the heavenly kingdom she will still love you and be proud of you even there.'

'Why did you say, "When she reaches the heavenly kingdom," Natasha Savishna?' I asked. 'I should think she is there now.'

'No, dearie,' said Natasha Savishna, lowering her voice and settling closer to me on the bed. 'Her soul is here now.'

And she pointed upwards. She spoke almost in a whisper and with such feeling and conviction that I involuntarily raised my eyes and looked up at the ceiling as if I expected to see something there.

'Before the souls of the righteous enter paradise they have to pass through forty trials, my dear, for forty days, and during that time they may hover around their earthly home . . .'

She continued for a long time in this strain, speaking with the same simplicity and conviction as though she were relating quite ordinary things which she had seen herself and concerning which it could never enter any one's head to doubt. I listened to her, holding my breath, and though I did not understand all she said I believed every word.

'Yes, my dear, she is here now looking at us and perhaps hearing what we are saying,' concluded Natalya Savishna.

And lowering her head she fell silent. Wanting a handkerchief to dry the falling tears, she got up, looked fixedly at me and in a voice trembling with emotion said:

'The Lord has brought me many degrees nearer to Him through this. What is there left for me here? Whom have I to live for? Who have I to love?'

'Don't you love us then?' I said reproachfully and hardly restraining my tears.

'The good God knows I love you, my duckies, but I never did and never can love any one as I loved her.'

She could say no more but turned her head away and sobbed aloud.

I no longer thought of sleep and we sat silently opposite one another and wept.

Foka came into the room. Seeing us like that and probably not wishing to disturb us, he stopped short at the door, looking at us timidly and not saying anything.

'What is it you want, Foka?' asked Natalya Savishna, wiping away her tears.

'A pound and a half of raisins, four pounds of sugar and three pounds of rice for the *kutya*, please.'[1]

'Here you are,' said Natalya Savishna, hurriedly taking a pinch of snuff and trotting briskly to the provision chest. The last traces of the grief aroused by our conversation vanished when she set about her duties, which she looked upon as of prime importance.

'Why four pounds?' she grumbled, getting out the sugar and weighing it on the balance. 'Three and a half will do,' and she took a few lumps from the scales.

'And what do they mean, asking for more rice when I gave out eight pounds only yesterday? You may do what you like, Foka Demidych, but I am not letting them have any more rice. That Vanya is pleased the house is upside down: he thinks things won't be noticed. But I am not shutting my eyes to any extravagance with my master's goods. Who ever heard of such a thing – eight pounds?'

'What's to be done? He says it's all gone.'

'Oh well, here it is, take it. Let him have it.'

I was struck by the change from the touching emotion with which she had been speaking to me to this captiousness and concern over petty trifles. Thinking back on it afterwards, I realized that whatever she might be feeling she was still able to give her mind to her duties, and the force of habit impelled her to busy herself with her usual occupations. Grief had taken such a hold of her that she did not find it necessary to conceal that she was nevertheless able to attend to everyday matters; she would not even have understood how such an idea could occur to any one.

Self-conceit is a sentiment entirely incompatible with genuine sorrow, and yet it is so firmly engrafted on human nature that even the most profound sorrow can seldom expel it altogether. Vanity in sorrow expresses itself by a desire to appear either stricken with grief or unhappy or brave: and this ignoble desire which we do not acknowledge but which hardly ever leaves us even in the deepest trouble robs our grief of its strength, dignity and sincerity. But Natalya Savishna was so utterly stricken by her unhappiness that not a single desire lingered in her soul and she went on living only from habit.

When she had let Foka have the provisions he had come for, and reminded him about the pasty that must be made to set before the

1. Rice boiled with raisins and sugar, and partaken of by the mourners at an Eastern Orthodox funeral.

clergy, she let him go and, taking up her knitting, seated herself by my side again.

We began to talk about the same thing as before, and again we mourned and once more dried our tears.

These talks with Natalya Savishna were repeated day after day: her gentle tears and calm devout words eased me and brought me comfort.

Soon, however, we were parted: three days after the funeral we moved with all our belongings to Moscow and I was destined never to see her again.

Grandmamma learned the terrible news only on our arrival and her grief was extreme. We were not allowed in her room because for a whole week she was beside herself and the doctors feared for her life, for she not only refused to take any medicines but would not utter a word to any one and did not sleep or have any food. Sometimes as she sat alone in her room in her easy chair she suddenly began to laugh or burst into dry sobs; she was seized with convulsions and in a frenzied voice shouted meaningless or frightful words. It was the first great sorrow she had known and it brought her to despair. She had to blame some one for her unhappiness and she would say dreadful things, with extraordinary energy threaten some one, jump up from the chair and stride rapidly up and down the room and end by falling unconscious to the floor.

Once I went into her room: she was sitting as usual in her arm-chair and seemed quiet and composed but I was struck by her expression. Though her eyes were wide open her gaze was vacant and dull: she was looking straight at me but did not appear to see me. Her lips stretched slowly into a smile and she began to speak in a pathetic tender tone. 'Come here, my love; come, my angel.' I thought she was speaking to me and moved closer but she was not looking at me. 'Oh, if you knew, my treasure, how I have suffered and how glad I am now that you have come . . .' I realized that she imagined she saw mamma, and I stood still. 'And they told me you were no more,' she continued, frowning. 'What nonsense! As if you could die before me!' And she burst into terrible hysterical laughter.

Only people capable of loving deeply can experience profound grief; but the very necessity they feel to love serves as an antidote to grief and heals them. This is why the human spirit is more tenacious of life than the body. Grief never kills.

A week later grandmamma was able to weep and she began to recover. Her first thought when she came to herself was of us, and her love for us increased. We stayed near her chair and she cried quietly, talked of mamma and caressed us tenderly.

It would never have occurred to any one who saw her grief that she was exaggerating it, and the expressions of that grief were heartfelt and moving; yet for some reason or another I felt more in sympathy with Natalya Savishna and to this day I am convinced that no one loved and mourned mamma so truly and sincerely as that simple-hearted and affectionate creature.

With my mother's death the happy period of childhood ended for me and a new epoch began – the epoch of boyhood; but since my memories of Natalya Savishna, whom I never saw again and who had such a powerful and beneficent influence on the bent of my mind and the development of my sensibility, belong to that first period I will add a few more words about her and her death.

I heard later from servants who were left on the estate that after our departure she found time hang very heavy on her hands. Although all the clothes-presses were still in her charge and she never ceased to turn over their contents, re-arranging, airing and unfolding, she missed the noise and bustle of a country house inhabited by the family, to which she had been accustomed from her childhood. Grief, the changed manner of life and the absence of household responsibilities soon combined to develop in her a senile ailment to which she had a tendency. Exactly a year after my mother's death she became affected with dropsy and took to her bed.

It must have been hard for Natalya Savishna to go on living and still more to die – alone in that great empty house at Petrovskoe, without relations or friends around her. Every one in the house esteemed and was fond of Natalya Savishna but she was not intimate with any of them and prided herself on the fact. She considered that in her position of housekeeper enjoying her master's confidence and having charge of so many chests full of all sorts of goods a friendship with any one would inevitably lead to partiality and wrongful connivance; for this reason, or perhaps because she had nothing in common with the other servants, she kept them all at a distance and used to say that she had no cronies to gossip with in the house and that she would not shut her eyes where her master's property was concerned.

She sought and found consolation in fervent prayer to God; but sometimes, in those moments of weakness to which we are all subject, when man finds his best comfort in the tears and sympathy of a living being, she would take her little pug-dog on to her bed (it would lick her hands and fix its yellow eyes on her) and talk to it, crying quietly as she fondled it. When the dog began to whimper plaintively she would try to soothe it, and say, 'There, that will do: I know without your telling me that my time is soon.'

A month before her death she took some white calico, white muslin and pink ribbon out of her trunk, and with the help of the girl who looked after her made a white gown and a cap for herself, and arranged everything for her funeral down to the last detail. She also sorted out the chests belonging to her master and handed them over to the steward's wife together with an inventory which she had compiled with scrupulous accuracy. Next she got out two silk gowns and an ancient shawl that my grandmother had given her at some time or other, and my grandfather's gold-laced military uniform which had also been presented to her to dispose of as she liked. Thanks to the care she had taken of them the embroidery and the gold lace on the uniform looked as good as new and the cloth had not been touched by moths.

Before her death she expressed a wish that one of these gowns (the pink one) should be given to Volodya for a dressing-gown or a *beshmet*,[1] and the other, the brown checked one, to me for the same purpose, and the shawl to Lyuba. She bequeathed the uniform to whichever of us should first become an officer. All the rest of her property and money (except forty roubles which she set aside for her funeral and for prayers for her soul) she left to her brother. Her brother, who had long before been enfranchised, was living a most dissolute life in some distant province; so she had had no intercourse with him during her lifetime.

When this brother arrived to claim his legacy and found that its sum-total only amounted to twenty-five paper roubles[2] he would not believe it and said it was quite impossible that an old woman who had lived with a wealthy family for sixty years and been in charge of everything, who had led a miserly life and grudged even a duster, should have left nothing. Yet it was a fact.

Natalya Savishna was ill for two months and bore her sufferings

1. Quilted jacket.
2. Paper roubles were the depreciated currency in use after the Napoleonic wars. Later they were converted at the rate of $3\frac{1}{2}$ to one silver rouble, whose value was about 38 pence.

with truly Christian patience: she did not grumble or complain but only kept calling on God, as was her wont. An hour before her death she made her confession with quiet joy and received the sacrament and was anointed with holy oil.

She begged forgiveness of everyone in the household for any wrong she might have done them, asked her confessor, Father Vassily, to tell us all that she did not know how to thank us for our kindness to her and that she asked us to forgive her if through stupidity she had offended anyone – 'but I have never been light-fingered and I can say that I never filched so much as a thread of cotton that belonged to my master'. That was the one virtue she prided herself on.

Having put on the gown and cap she had prepared, and propping an elbow on the pillow, she conversed with the priest up to the very last. Remembering that she had not left anything for the poor, she got out ten roubles and asked him to distribute them in the parish. Then she crossed herself, lay back and breathed her last, with a peaceful smile and the name of God on her lips.

She quitted this life without a pang: she did not fear death but welcomed it as a blessing. This is often said but how seldom is it really true! Natalya Savishna could face death without fear because she died steadfast in her faith and having fulfilled the Gospel commandments. Her whole life had been one of pure unselfish love and self-sacrifice.

What if her beliefs might have been more lofty and her life directed to higher aims – was that pure soul any the less deserving of love and admiration?

She accomplished the best and greatest thing in life – she died without regret or fear.

They buried her where she wished to rest, not far from the chapel that stands over our mother's grave. The little mound overgrown with nettles and burdock beneath which she lies is surrounded by a black railing, and I never forget after visiting the chapel to go to this railing and bow down before her grave.

Sometimes I pause in silence between the chapel and that black railing. Painful memories suddenly flood my soul. The thought comes to me: Can Providence really have united me with those two beings only in order that I should for ever mourn their loss?

[1852]

BOYHOOD

Once more two vehicles are drawn up at the porch of the Petrovsk house – one a closed carriage in which Mimi, Katya, Lyuba and a maid-servant take their seats, with the steward, Yakov, on the box; the other, a chaise, for Volodya, myself and the footman, Vassily (a serf lately taken into our service).

Papa, who is to follow us to Moscow in a few days' time, stands bare-headed in the porch and makes the sign of the cross before the carriage window and the chaise.

'Well, God bless you! Off you go!' Yakov and the coachmen (we are travelling with our own horses) take off their caps and cross themselves. 'Gee up! God be with us!' The carriage and the chaise begin to jolt along the uneven road, and the birch-trees of the great avenue fly past us one by one. I do not feel in the least depressed: my thoughts are turned not to what I am leaving but to what awaits us. The farther the objects connected with the painful memories which up to now have filled my mind retreat into the distance, the more do these memories fade and give way to a buoyant consciousness of life full of vigour, freshness and hope.

I have seldom spent days – I won't say so gaily, for I still felt some-how guilty at the idea of yielding to gaiety – but so pleasantly as those four days of our journey. My eyes were confronted neither by the closed doors of mamma's room, which I could not pass without a shudder, nor the piano with its lid down, which we not only avoided approaching but looked at with a sort of pang, nor our mourning garments (we were all wearing ordinary travelling clothes), nor any of the things which by acutely reminding me of my irreparable loss made me avoid any appearance of animation for fear of offending against *her* memory in some way. Here on the contrary a continual succession of new and picturesque scenes and objects attract and divert my attention, and nature in its spring garb imbues my soul with a cheerful sense of satisfaction in the present and bright hopes for the future.

Very very early in the morning the merciless Vassily (over zealous as people always are with new duties) pulls off my blanket and announces that it is time to start and everything is ready. Snuggle down and rage and contrive as you will to prolong even for another quarter of an hour your sweet morning slumber, you see by Vassily's determined face that he is inexorable and prepared to pull off the blanket another twenty times; so you jump up and run out into the courtyard to have a wash.

In the passage the samovar into which Mitka, the postilion, flushed red as a lobster, is blowing is already on the boil. Out of doors it is damp and misty, as though steam were rising from an odorous dung-heap. In the eastern part of the sky the sun diffuses a bright cheerful radiance and makes the dew sparkle on the thatched roofs of the spacious penthouses around the courtyard. In these lean-to outhouses we can see our horses tethered to their mangers, and hear their chewing. A shaggy mongrel which had settled down for a nap before daybreak on a dry heap of manure now lazily stretches itself and wagging its tail trots slowly off to the opposite side of the yard. A bustling peasant-woman opens some creaking gates and drives her dreamy cows into the street, where we already hear the stamping, lowing and bleating of the herd, and exchanges a word with her sleepy neighbour. Filip, his shirt-sleeves rolled above the elbow, winds up a bucket from the deep well, and splashing the clear water pours it into an oak trough beside which some wide-awake ducks are already paddling about in a puddle, and it gives me pleasure to watch Filip's dignified face with its thick broad beard and see the well-developed sinews and muscles stand out so sharply on his strong bare arms with every exertion.

Behind the partition-wall where Mimi and the girls had slept and through which we had talked the evening before there is a sound of movement. Masha, the maid, keeps running past concealing various articles from our inquisitive eyes by covering them with her apron. At last the door opens and we are called in to tea.

Vassily, in a superfluous fit of zeal, repeatedly runs into the room, first for one thing, then for another, winking at us and imploring Marya Ivanovna in every way he can think of to make an early start. The horses are harnessed and show their impatience by every now and then jingling their bells. Portmanteaux, trunks, boxes large and small are packed in again, and we take our places. But each time we find a mountain inside the chaise instead of a seat, so that we cannot make out how all the things got packed in the day before, and how we are to sit down now. One walnut tea-caddy with a three-cornered lid which is put into our chaise underneath my seat in particular arouses me to strong indignation. But Vassily says things will soon right themselves, and I have no choice but to believe him.

The sun has only just risen above the dense white cloud which had covered it, and all the country round about is bathed in quietly radiant light. Everything around me looks so beautiful and my heart feels so light and peaceful. The road winds before us like a wild broad ribbon between fields of dry stubble and meadows sparkling with dew. Here and there we come upon a gloomy willow or a young birch-tree with small sticky leaves, casting a long motionless shadow on the dry clayey ruts and the short green grass of the highway ... The monotonous rumble of our wheels and the tinkling of the bells do not drown the singing of the larks which whirl round close to the road. The smell of moth-eaten cloth, dust and something sour which is peculiar to our chaise is overpowered by the fragrance of the morning, and I feel a pleasant restlessness, a longing for action – the true sign of enjoyment.

I had not time to say my prayers at the inn but as I have noticed more than once that some misfortune happens to me when for one reason or another I forget to perform that duty I try to make good the omission: I take off my cap, turn my face to the corner of the chaise, say my prayers and cross myself under my jacket so that nobody shall see. But a thousand different objects distract my attention and I absent-mindedly repeat the same prayer words several times over.

There on the footpath which winds beside the road some slowly moving figures appear in sight: they are women pilgrims. Their heads are enveloped in dirty shawls, on their backs they carry knapsacks of birch-bark, their legs are swathed in dirty ragged leg-bands and they wear heavy bast shoes. Swinging their staffs in regular rhythm and scarcely throwing us a glance, they move along one after the other with slow heavy steps. 'Where are they going?' I wonder to myself. 'And what for? Will their journey be a long one, and how soon will the tall shadows they cast on the road join the shadow of the willow which they must pass?' Here is a calash with four post-horses rushing quickly towards us. Another two seconds and the faces looking at us with friendly curiosity from a couple of yards away have flashed past, and it seems strange that these people have nothing in common with me and it may be I shall never see them again.

Here come two shaggy sweating horses galloping along the side of the road in their halters, with the traces tucked under their harness, and behind them, his long legs in enormous boots dangling astride a

horse on whose neck hangs a shaft-bow[1] with a bell that gives an
occasional tinkle rides a post-boy, his felt cap cocked over one ear,
singing a long-drawn-out song. His face and attitude express so much
indolent careless ease that it seems to me it must be the height of
happiness to be a post-boy and to ride the horses home, singing sad
songs. Over there, far beyond the ravine, a village church with a green
roof shows up against the light-blue sky; that way is the village, and
the red roof of the manor house with its green garden. Who lives in
that house? I wonder if there are any children in it, with their father,
their mother, a tutor? Why should we not drive up to that house and
make the acquaintance of its owners? Here comes a long train of enormous hooded carts, each drawn by three well-fed stout-legged horses,
to pass which we must get to the side of the road. 'What have you got
there?' Vassily asks the first carter who, dangling his huge legs over the
splash-board and flourishing his little whip, regards us for some time
with a stolid vacant stare and only answers when we are too far off to
catch what he says. 'What goods are you carrying?' Vassily asks the
driver of the next cartload, who is lying on the front bar covered with
new matting. A light brown head with a red face and a small russet
beard thrusts itself from under the matting, casts an indifferent contemptuous glance at our chaise and disappears again – whereupon I
conclude that these carters probably do not know who we are, where
we come from and where we are going.

For about an hour and a half after this I am absorbed in various
observations and pay no heed to the slanting figures on the mile-posts.
But now the sun starts to scorch my head and back more fiercely, the
road becomes increasingly dusty, the triangular lid of the tea-caddy
begins to cause me acute discomfort and I change my position several
times: I begin to feel hot, cramped and bored. My whole attention is
on the mile-posts and the figures marked on them, and I make various
calculations as to when we can reach the next station. 'Twelve versts
are one-third of thirty-six, and there are forty-one versts to Liptsi, so
we have done one-third plus how much?' and so on.

'Vassily,' I say, when I see he is beginning to nod on the box, 'let
me sit on the box, there's a dear.' Vassily agrees. We change places: he
immediately begins to snore and stretches himself out so that there is
no room left for anybody else in the chaise; but from the height
I occupy the most delightful picture presents itself – our four

1. Part of the Russian harness to which the shafts are fixed.

horses, Neruchinskaya, Sexton, Left-Shaft and Apothecary, whom I know down to the minutest details and shades of the peculiarities of each.

'Why is it Sexton is on the off-side instead of the near-side today, Filip?' I inquire somewhat timidly.

'Sexton?'

'And Neruchinskaya is not pulling at all,' say I.

'Sexton can't be harnessed on the near-side,' says Filip, disregarding my last remark. 'He is not that kind of horse to be harnessed on the near-side. The near-side needs a horse that is a horse, so to speak, and he is not that sort of horse.'

And with these words Filip leans over to his right and, jerking the rein with all his might, begins to lash poor Sexton over the tail and legs in a peculiar manner from below, and though Sexton tries for all he is worth and pulls the whole chaise to one side Filip only abandons this proceeding when he feels it necessary to take a rest and push his hat, for some unknown reason, askew, though till then it had sat very firmly and well on his head. I seize this favourable opportunity to ask Filip to let me drive. Filip gives me one rein first, then another, and at last all six reins and the whip are transferred to me and I am utterly happy. I try to imitate Filip in every way and ask him whether I am doing well but it generally ends by his not being satisfied with me, saying that one horse pulls too hard while another does not pull at all, and finally he thrusts his elbow against my chest and takes the reins away from me. It gets hotter and hotter; fleecy clouds float up and up like soap-bubbles, run together and turn dark grey. A hand holding a bottle and a small package is thrust out of the carriage window and Vassily with surprising agility jumps down from the chaise while it is moving and brings us a bottle of kvass and some cheese-cakes.

At a steep descent we all get out of the vehicles and perhaps have a race to the bridge while Vassily and Yakov, after putting a drag on the wheels, support the carriage on both sides with their hands, as though they could hold it should it upset. Then, with Mimi's permission, either I or Volodya get into the carriage and Lyuba or Katya climbs into the chaise. This change vastly pleases the girls because, as they rightly say, it is much more fun in the chaise. Sometimes when the heat is at its most intense and we are passing through a grove we linger behind the carriage, tear off some green branches and make a sort of arbour over the chaise. The moving arbour races full speed after the carriage and

Lyuba gives the most piercing shrieks, a thing she never fails to do on every occasion which affords her great pleasure.

But here is the village where we are to dine and rest. We have already caught the smell of a village – smoke, tar, cracknels – and heard the sound of voices, steps and wheels; and our harness bells already sound differently from what they did in the open fields; and on both sides we catch glimpses of thatched huts with their small carved wooden porches and red or green shutters to their little windows, where here and there an inquisitive old woman thrusts her head out. Here are little peasant boys and girls with nothing on but their smocks: with wide-open eyes and arms outstretched to us they stand stock-still, or run barefoot through the dust after our carriages with quick little steps and regardless of Filip's threatening gestures try to climb on the portmanteaux which are strapped on behind. Now two red-haired inn-keepers come running, one each side of our vehicles, and with inviting words and signs vie with each other to attract the travellers. 'Whoa!' The gates creak, the cross-bars to which the traces of the side-horses are attached scrape the gate-posts, and we drive into the yard of an inn. Four hours of rest and freedom!

2 · THE STORM

The sun was sinking to the west and its slanting rays burned my neck and cheeks beyond endurance: it was impossible to touch the scorching sides of the chaise; dense clouds of dust rose from the road and filled the air. There was not a breath of wind to carry it away. Keeping a regular distance in front of us rolled the tall dusty body of the carriage with our luggage on top, and beyond this every now and then we caught glimpses of the whip the coachman was flourishing, his hat and Yakov's cap. I did not know what to do with myself: neither Volodya's face black with dust as he dozed by my side, nor the movements of Filip's back, nor the long shadow of our trap which followed us at an oblique angle afforded me any diversion. My whole attention was concentrated on the mile-posts which I could see from a distance, and on the clouds which had been scattered over the horizon but had now assumed a menacing blackness and were gathered into one great dark storm-cloud. From time to time there was a distant rumble of thunder. This last circumstance more than anything else increased my impatience to reach the inn. Thunderstorms always gave me an indescribable feeling of depression and dread.

The nearest village was still about seven miles off and the large dark-purple cloud (heaven knows where it had come from) was advancing swiftly towards us though there was no wind. The sun, not yet obscured by the clouds, casts a vivid light on the sombre mass and the grey streaks which run from it right to the horizon. At intervals lightning flashes in the distance, followed by low rumbles steadily increasing in volume and drawing nearer and nearer until they swell into broken peals which embrace the entire firmament. Vassily half stands and raises the hood of the chaise; the coachmen put on their greatcoats and at each clap of thunder take off their caps and cross themselves; the horses prick up their ears and puff out their nostrils as though to smell in the cool air wafted from the approaching storm-cloud; and the chaise speeds along the dusty road. I am frightened and feel the blood coursing faster through my veins. But now the nearest clouds begin to veil the sun, which peeps out for the last time, lights up the terribly sombre part of the horizon and disappears. The landscape all around suddenly changes and takes on a leaden aspect. The aspens in the wood quiver; the leaves turn a kind of dull whitish colour and stand out sharply against the purple background of the cloud; they rustle agitatedly. The tops of the tall birch-trees begin to sway, and tufts of dry grass fly across the road. Martins and white-breasted swallows, as though minded to stop us, whirl round the chaise and sweep close to the very breasts of the horses; jackdaws with ruffled wings fly sideways to the wind; the flaps of the leather apron we have buttoned over ourselves begin to lift, admitting gusts of damp wind and blowing and beating against the sides of the trap. The lightning seems to flash right into the trap, blinding us and cleaving the obscurity for a second to reveal the grey cloth and braid of the inside and Volodya's figure crouching in the corner. At the same instant a majestic peal of thunder resounds directly overhead. It seems to rise higher and higher and spread wider and wider in a huge spiral, gradually swelling louder and ending in a deafening crash, which made us tremble and involuntarily hold our breaths.

The wrath of God! What poetry there is in that popular conception!

The wheels revolve faster and faster; by the backs of Vassily and Filip, who is furiously shaking the reins, I notice that they are alarmed too. The chaise bowls swiftly downhill and rattles on to a wooden bridge. I am afraid to move, and expect every moment that we shall all perish.

'Whoa!' A cross-bar has come off and in spite of the unceasing deafening peals of thunder we are obliged to stop on the bridge.

Leaning my head against the side of the chaise, with bated breath and sinking heart I watch in despair the movements of Filip's thick black fingers as he slowly ties a loop and adjusts the traces, pushing the side-horse now with the palm of his hand, now with the whip handle.

My worried sensation of uneasiness and dread increased with the violence of the storm, but when the sublime moment of silence came which usually precedes the thunder-clap my nervousness reached such a pitch that had this state of things lasted another quarter of an hour I am sure I should have died of alarm. At that very moment from under the bridge a human being suddenly appears clad in a dirty tattered shirt, with a bloated vacant face, a shaking close-cropped totally bare head, crooked bandy legs, and in place of a hand a red shiny stump which he thrusts into the chaise.

'Ma-a-shter! Something for a cripple, for Christ's sake!' groans a feeble voice, and at each word the beggar crosses himself and bows from his waist.

I cannot describe the chill horror which seized my soul at that moment. A shiver ran through my hair and my eyes were riveted in blank terror on the mendicant.

Vassily, whose business it is to distribute the alms on our journey, is busy giving Filip directions about putting the cross-bar right and only when everything is ready and Filip, gathering up the reins, is climbing back on to the box does he start getting something out of his side pocket. But just as the chaise is moving off a blinding flash of lightning fills the whole hollow with fiery light, causes the horses to stop short and is accompanied simultaneously by such an ear-splitting clap of thunder that it seems as if the whole vault of heaven were crashing about us. The wind blows harder than ever: the horses' manes and their tails, Vassily's cloak and the flaps of the leather apron are swept in one direction and flutter desperately in the raging gusty wind. A great fat rain drop falls heavily on the leather hood of the chaise . . . another, a third, a fourth, and suddenly as though some one were beating a drum over our heads the whole countryside resounded with the steady patter of falling rain. I notice by the jerking of Vassily's elbow that he is untying his purse; the beggar, still crossing himself and bowing, keeps so close to our wheels that at any moment we expect to see him run over. 'Give in Christ's Name.' At last a copper coin flies past us and the poor wretch in his coarse rags that are wet through and cling to his thin limbs stops bewildered in the middle of the road, swaying in the wind, and is lost to my sight.

The slanting rain driven by the violent wind pours down as from a bucket; the water streams down the back of Vassily's frieze coat into the muddy pools that have collected on the apron. The dust, which at first had been beaten into little pellets, was transformed into liquid mud which stuck to the wheels; the jolts became fewer and streams of turbid water flowed along the clayey ruts. The lightning grew paler and more diffuse and the rolling of the thunder sounded less awful when heard through the monotonous downpour.

But now the rain abates, the thunder-cloud begins to divide itself into fleecy cloudlets and grow lighter where the sun should be, and a patch of clear blue is visible through the light-grey edges of the cloud. A minute later a shy sunbeam glistens in the puddles along the road, on the long lines of rain now falling thin and straight as from a sieve, and on the shining newly-washed grass by the roadside. A great cloud still lours black and threatening as ever on the far horizon but I am not afraid of it now. I experience an inexpressibly joyous feeling of optimism which rapidly replaces my oppressive sensation of dread. My soul smiles, like Nature refreshed and rejoicing. Vassily turns down the collar of his cloak, takes off his cap and shakes it. Volodya throws back the apron. I lean out of the chaise and eagerly drink in the fresh and fragrant air. The shining well-washed body of the carriage with its boxes and portmanteaux sways along in front of us; the horses' backs, the harness, the reins, the tyres on the wheels are all wet and glitter in the sun as if they had just been varnished. On one side of the road a vast field of winter grain, intersected here and there by shallow channels, its wet earth and vegetation shining bright, stretches away like a shadowy carpet to the very horizon; on the other side an aspen grove with an undergrowth of nut-bushes and wild cherry stands as if in an excess of happiness, without a rustle, while sparkling drops of rain slowly drip from its clean-washed branches on to last year's dry leaves. Crested skylarks circle all about us with glad songs and downward swooping. Small birds flutter and bustle in the dripping bushes, and from the heart of the wood the clear note of the cuckoo reaches our ears. So bewitching is the wonderful fragrance of the wood after that early spring storm – the fragrance of birch-trees, violets, rotting leaves, mushrooms and the wild cherry – that I cannot stay in the chaise. So I jump from the step and run towards the bushes, and though raindrops shower over me I break off wet branches of the flowering wild cherry, stroke my face with them and revel in their glorious scent. Heedless even of the fact that great lumps of earth are sticking to my boots and my stockings are wet through long ago, I run splashing through the mud to the carriage window.

'Lyuba! Katya!' I cry, handing in some branches of wild cherry. 'Look how lovely!'

The girls squeal and exclaim; Mimi shouts to me to go away or I shall certainly be run over.

'But you just smell how delicious it is!' I cry.

3 · A NEW POINT OF VIEW

Katya sat beside me in the chaise and with her pretty head bent was gazing thoughtfully at the dusty road which ran back under our wheels. I watched her in silence and wondered at the sad expression, so unnatural in a child, which I noticed for the first time on her rosy little face.

'We shall soon be in Moscow now,' I said. 'What do you think it will be like?'

'I don't know,' she replied reluctantly.

'Well, but what do you think? Is it bigger than Serpuhov or not?'

'What?'

'Oh nothing.'

But the instinctive feeling which enables one person to guess the thoughts of another and which serves as a guiding thread in conversation made Katya realize that I was hurt by her indifference: she lifted her head and turned to me.

'Did papa tell you we are to live at grandmamma's?'

'Yes, he did: grandmamma wants us to live with her for good.'

'All of us?'

'Of course. We shall live upstairs on one side, you on the other and papa in the wing; but we shall all have our dinner together downstairs with grandmamma.'

'*Maman* says your grandmother is such a grand lady – is she bad-tempered?'

'No–o. She only seems so at first. She is grand but not a bit bad-tempered. On the contrary, she is very kind-hearted and jolly. You should have seen the ball there on her name-day!'

'All the same, I am scared of her; besides, heaven alone knows whether we shall . . .'

Katya suddenly stopped and once again became thoughtful.

'Wha-at?' I asked anxiously.

'Nothing particular.'

'Yes, but you said: "Heaven knows . . ."'

'And you were saying about the ball at your grandmother's.'

'Yes, it's a pity you weren't there. There were heaps of guests – about a thousand – and music, and generals, and I danced . . . Katya!' I said suddenly stopping in the middle of my description, 'you are not listening?'

'Yes, I am. You were saying you danced.'

'Why are you so miserable?'

'One can't always be gay.'

'But you have changed a lot since we came back from Moscow. Tell me truly,' I went on, turning towards her with a determined look, 'what makes you so sort of strange?'

'Strange?' replied Katya with an animation which showed that my remark had aroused her interest. 'I am not a bit strange.'

'Well you are not the same as you used to be,' I persisted. 'Once upon a time every one could see that you were just like us, that you looked on us as relations and were as fond of us as we are of you, but now you have become so serious and you avoid us . . .'

'I don't at all.'

'No, let me finish,' I interrupted, already beginning to feel a slight tickling in my nose which preceded the tears that always rose to my eyes whenever I tried to give utterance to any long-pent-up and deeply-felt idea. 'You avoid us and talk to no one but Mimi, as if you did not wish to have anything to do with us.'

'But one can't always remain the same: one must change some time,' answered Katya, who had a habit when she did not know what to say of putting everything down to some kind of fatalistic necessity.

I remember how once in a quarrel with Lyuba who had called her a stupid little girl she had retorted: 'Every one can't be clever: there must be stupid people too.' But I was not satisfied with her argument that one must change some time and I went on with my interrogation.

'Why must one?'

'Well, you see, we shan't always be living together,' replied Katya, flushing slightly and staring hard at Filip's back. '*Maman* was able to be with your dead mother because she was her friend but who knows if she will get on with the countess, who, they say, is so irritable? Besides, some time or other we shall have to part anyhow: you are rich – you have Petrovskoe, but we are poor, my mamma hasn't anything.'

'You are rich, we are poor . . .' These words and the ideas connected with them seemed very curious to me. According to my conceptions at that time only beggars and peasants could be poor, and my imagination could not at all associate the notion of poverty with the graceful pretty Katya. I had thought that Mimi and Katya would go on living with us just as they always had, and we would share everything equally. It could not be otherwise. But now thousands of new confused thoughts regarding their lonely state swarmed in my head, and I felt so ashamed that we were rich and they poor that I coloured up and had not the courage to look at Katya.

'What does it matter that we are rich and they poor?' I thought. 'And why does that make it necessary for us to part? Why should we not divide what we have between us?' But I realized that it would not do to say so to Katya, and some practical instinct in defiance of all logical reasoning was already telling me that she was right and it would be out of place to explain my ideas to her.

'Are you actually going to leave us?' I said. 'How can we live apart?'

'What else can we do? I am sorry too. Only if it does happen I know what I shall do . . .'

'Become an actress? . . . What nonsense!' I broke in, knowing that to be an actress had always been a favourite dream of hers.

'No, I used to say that when I was little . . .'

'What will you do then?'

'Go into a convent and live there and wear a black dress and a velvet cap.'

Katya began to cry.

Has it ever happened to you, dear reader, at any point in your life to become aware all at once that your outlook on things has completely changed, as though all the objects that had hitherto been before your eyes had suddenly presented to you another, unfamiliar side?

Such a volte-face occurred to me for the first time during that journey of ours, from which I date the beginning of my boyhood.

For the first time I envisaged the idea that we – that is, our family – were not the only people in the world, that not every conceivable interest was centred in ourselves but that there existed another life – that of people who had nothing in common with us, cared nothing for us, had no idea of our existence even. I must have known all this before but I had not known it as I did now – I had not realized it; I had not felt it.

An idea changes to a conviction in a way of its own, often a quite unexpected one and different from that by which other minds arrive at the same conclusion. This conversation with Katya, which affected me deeply and caused me to reflect upon her future position, was the way in my case. As I looked at the villages and towns through which we passed, in every house of which lived at least one family like our own, at the women and children who stared with momentary curiosity at our chaise and then disappeared from our sight for ever, at the shop-keepers and peasants who not only did not bow as I was accustomed to see them do in Petrovskoe but did not even bestow a glance on us, I asked myself for the first time: What could they have to think about if they aren't thinking about us? And this question gave rise to others: How and on what do they live? How do they bring up their children? Do they give them lessons? Do they let them play? How do they punish them? And so on and so on.

4 · IN MOSCOW

With our arrival in Moscow the change in my outlook on things and people, and my own relation to them, became still more evident to me.

When I first saw grandmamma again, and noticed her thin wrinkled face and dim eyes, the mingled respect and fear I used to have for her gave place to compassion; and when with her cheek pressed against Lyuba's head she began to sob as if the body of her beloved daughter lay before her eyes my compassion turned to affection. I did not like to see her so afflicted by grief when she saw us; I realized that we ourselves meant nothing to her, that she cherished us only because we reminded her of mother. I felt that every kiss she showered on my cheeks expressed but one thought: 'She is no more, she is dead, I shall never see her again.'

Papa, who hardly paid any attention to us in Moscow and who only appeared at dinner, perpetually looking worried and wearing a black frock-coat or dress-suit, had – together with his wide open-necked shirt-collars, his dressing-gown, his village-elders, stewards, expeditions to the threshing-floor and his hunting – lost much of his prestige in my eyes. Karl Ivanych, whom grandmamma called the 'school-usher' and who – heaven knows why – had suddenly taken it into his head to exchange his venerable long-familiar baldness for a red wig with a canvas parting almost in the middle, looked so strange and ridiculous to me that I was surprised he had never struck me so before.

Between the girls and ourselves, too, there arose a sort of invisible barrier: they had their own secrets as we had ours; they seemed to like showing off to us their ever-lengthening skirts, just as we gave ourselves airs with our trousers with straps. As for Mimi, she came down to dinner the first Sunday in such a fine gown and with so many ribbons in her cap that it was at once apparent that we were no longer in the country and that everything was to be different now.

5 · MY ELDER BROTHER

I was only a year and some months younger than Volodya; we grew up, studied and played together. No distinction of elder and younger was made between us; but just about the time I am speaking of I began to realize that I was no companion for him, either in age, in interests or in ability. It even seemed to me that Volodya himself was aware of his superiority and was proud of it. This idea (it may have been a wrong one) was inspired by my vanity – which suffered every time I came in contact with him. He was better than I in everything: at games, at lessons, in arguments and in manners, and all this estranged me from him and occasioned me moral anguish which I could not understand. If I had said frankly when Volodya was given tucked linen shirts for the first time that I was vexed at not having shirts like that, I am sure I should have felt happier and not thought every time he arranged his collar that it was only done to annoy me.

What tormented me most was that it sometimes seemed to me

Volodya understood what was going on inside me but tried to hide this.

Who has not noticed those mysterious unspoken relations which manifest themselves in a barely perceptible smile, a gesture or a look between people who live together – brothers, friends, husband and wife, master and servant – especially when they do not cultivate mutual frankness in all things? How many unuttered desires, thoughts and fears of being understood are expressed in one casual glance, when eyes meet shyly and hesitantly!

But perhaps my inordinate sensitiveness and tendency to analyse deceived me in this case. It may be Volodya did not feel at all as I did. He was impulsive, candid and fickle in his enthusiasms. Carried away by the most diverse interests, he flung himself into them heart and soul.

He would suddenly conceive a passion for pictures, himself take up painting, spend all his money buying them and beg them of his drawing-master, of papa and of grandmamma. Then it would be a rage for curios with which to adorn his table, collecting them from every room in the house; or a mania for novels, which he obtained on the sly and read all day and all night ... I could not help being enticed by his hobbies but I was too proud to imitate him and too young and not independent enough to choose a line for myself. But there was nothing I envied so much as Volodya's happy big-hearted disposition, which showed itself most strikingly when we quarrelled. I always felt that he was behaving well but I could not do likewise.

Once when his passion for ornaments was at its height I went up to his table and there accidentally broke an empty brightly-coloured little scent-bottle.

'Who asked you to touch my things?' demanded Volodya, coming into the room and seeing how I had upset the symmetry of the different treasures on his table. 'And where is the scent-bottle? You must have ...'

'I knocked it over by accident and it broke. What does it matter?'

'Do me the favour – never *dare* touch my things again,' he said, putting the pieces of the broken flask together and looking at them sorrowfully.

'And you please don't issue orders,' I retorted, 'that's all. What's there to talk about in that?'

And I smiled, though I did not feel in the least like smiling.

'Yes, it's nothing to you but it does matter to me,' pursued Volodya, jerking his shoulder, a gesture he had inherited from papa. 'He goes and breaks it, and then laughs, the nasty little *brat*!'

'I'm a little brat; and you're big but you're stupid.'

'I am not going to quarrel with you,' said Volodya, giving me a slight push. 'Go away.'

'Don't push!'

'Get away!'

'Don't push, I tell you!'

Volodya took my arm and tried to drag me away from the table; but I was beside myself now: I got hold of the leg of the table and tipped it over. 'There now!' And all his china and glass ornaments crashed to the floor.

'You disgusting little boy!' cried Volodya, trying to save some of his falling treasures.

'Well, now it is all over between us,' I thought as I left the room. 'We have quarrelled for good.'

We did not speak to each other till evening. I felt myself in the wrong and was afraid to look at him, and could not settle to do anything all day. Volodya, on the contrary, did his lessons well, and after dinner talked and laughed with the girls as usual.

As soon as afternoon lessons were over I left the room. I was too scared and uncomfortable and ashamed to be alone with my brother. After our history lesson in the evening I took my exercise books and started towards the door. As I passed Volodya, though I wanted to go up to him and make friends, I scowled and put on an angry expression. At that moment Volodya raised his head and with a faintly perceptible good-naturedly derisive smile looked me full in the face. Our eyes met and I knew that he understood me, and knew that I knew that he understood me; but some irresistible feeling made me turn away.

'Nicky!' he said in a most natural voice without a scrap of pathos. 'Don't be cross any more. Forgive me if I offended you.'

And he held out his hand.

Something that welled higher and higher seemed to be pressing my chest and hindering my breathing; but this only lasted a second; tears came to my eyes, and I felt better.

'Forgive ... m-me, Vol-dya,' I stammered, squeezing his hand. Volodya looked at me as if he could not make out at all why there should be tears in my eyes.

6 · MASHA

But none of the changes which took place in my outlook on things was
so startling to myself as that which made me cease to regard one of our
housemaids as a female servant and begin to see in her a *woman* on
whom to a certain extent my peace and happiness might depend.

As far back as I can recollect I remember Masha being in our house
with me; and never till the occasion that entirely altered my idea of
her, and which I will relate presently, had she received the slightest
attention from me. Masha was about twenty-five when I was fourteen. She was very pretty but I am afraid to describe her lest my
imagination should again present to me the bewitching and delusive
image which filled my mind at the time of my infatuation. To avoid
any mistake of the kind I will only say that she had an uncommonly
fair skin, a voluptuous figure, and she was a woman – while I was
fourteen.

In one of those moods when lesson-book in hand you pace up and
down the room trying to keep strictly to one particular chink between
the floor-boards, or hum some absurd tune, or daub the edge of the
table with ink, or mechanically repeat some phrase over and over again
– in short, in one of those moods when your mind refuses to work and
your imagination takes the upper hand and seeks new impressions one
day I slipped out of the schoolroom and idly wandered down to the
landing.

Some one in slippers was coming up the lower flight of the
staircase. Of course I wanted to know who it was, but all of a
sudden the footsteps ceased and I heard Masha's voice, 'Now then,
what are you up to? If Marya Ivanovna comes there will be a fine
to-do!'

'She won't come,' Volodya's voice whispered, and directly after
that there was a noise as if he were trying to detain her.

'Now now what are you doing with your hands? For shame!'
And Masha ran past me with her kerchief all awry and exposing her
plump white neck.

I cannot describe my amazement at this discovery; but astonishment
soon gave place to a kind of fellow-feeling with Volodya: I found
that the action itself did not surprise me but I wondered how he had

managed to find out that it was pleasant to behave so, and I could not help yearning to follow suit.

I would spend hours on end on that landing with not a thought in my head, straining to catch the slightest movement upstairs; but I never had the courage to copy Volodya, though I longed to more than anything in the world. Sometimes, hidden behind a door, I listened with a painful mixture of envy and jealousy to the romping going on in the maids' room, until the thought would occur to my mind, 'How if I were to go upstairs now and, like Volodya, try to kiss Masha? What should I say when she asked me, with my broad nose and my tufts of hair sticking up on my head, what I wanted?' Several times I heard Masha say to Volodya: 'What a nuisance you are! Why do you come pestering me? Go away, you naughty boy! ... Nikolai Petrovich never comes here and behaves silly . . .' She did not know that Nikolai Petrovich was at that very minute sitting at the foot of the stairs, and would have given all he possessed to be in the naughty Volodya's shoes.

I was bashful by nature but my bashfulness was still further increased by the conviction that I was ugly. I am quite sure that nothing has so much influence on a man's development as his outward appearance, and not his appearance itself so much as his opinion concerning its attractiveness or otherwise.

I was too conceited for resignation: I would seek comfort in persuading myself like the fox that the grapes were sour – that is, I tried to despise all the pleasure which I thought Volodya got as a result of his good looks and which I envied him with all my soul, and I exerted every ounce of brain and imagination to find enjoyment in haughty isolation.

7 · SMALL SHOT

'Heaven's above, gunpowder!' screamed Mimi in a voice choking with agitation. 'What are you doing? You will set the house on fire and be the death of us all . . .'

And with an indescribable expression of fortitude Mimi ordered everyone to stand back, and with long determined strides went up to some small shot that was scattered about the floor, and began to stamp it out, regardless of the danger from any sudden explosion. When in her opinion the peril was past she called Mihay in and commanded him to throw all this 'gunpowder' as far away as possible or, better still, into some water, and proudly tossing her cap she betook herself to the drawing-room. 'Well looked after, they are, I must say!' she muttered to herself.

When papa issued from the wing where he lived and we went with him to grandmamma's room Mimi was already there, sitting near the window and looking towards the door with a kind of enigmatic ministerial expression. In her hand she held something wrapped in several layers of paper. I guessed that this was some of the shot and that grandmamma already knew all about it.

Besides Mimi in the room was Gasha, one of the maids, who, as we could tell by her angry flushed face, was very much upset, and Dr Blumenthal, a short pock-marked man vainly endeavouring to calm Gasha by making mysterious pacifying signs to her with his head and eyes.

Grandmamma herself was sitting slightly sideways playing 'Traveller', a game of patience which always indicated an exceedingly inauspicious frame of mind.

'How are you feeling today, mamma? Had a good night?' said papa, kissing her hand respectfully.

'Excellent, my dear. I believe you know that I am always perfectly well,' replied grandmamma in a tone implying that papa's inquiries were out of place and insulting. 'Well, are you going to give me a clean handkerchief?' she continued, turning to Gasha.

'I *have* given you one,' answered Gasha, pointing to a snow-white cambric handkerchief that lay on the arm of grandmamma's chair.

'Take that dirty rag away and give me a clean one, my dear.'

Gasha went to the chiffonier, pulled out a drawer and slammed it so violently that all the windows in the room rattled. Grandmamma glanced round with a threatening look at all of us and continued to watch the maid's movements intently. When the girl handed her what appeared to me to be the very same handkerchief grandmamma said:

'And when will you rub my snuff for me, my dear?'

'When I have time.'

'What do you say?'

'I'll do it today.'

'If you do not wish to serve me, my dear, you should have said so; I would have let you go long ago.'

'It won't break my heart if you do,' muttered the maid under her breath.

Here the doctor was on the point of winking at her again but she looked at him so angrily and determinedly that he immediately dropped his eyes and busied himself with his watch-key.

'You see, my dear, how I am spoken to in my own house?' said grandmamma, addressing herself to papa after Gasha, still muttering, had left the room.

'Allow me to rub the snuff for you myself, *maman*,' said papa, evidently much embarrassed by this unexpected appeal.

'No, thank you. You see, she is impudent because she knows that no one else can rub my snuff the way I like it. Do you know, my dear,' grandmamma continued after a brief pause, 'that your children very nearly burned the house down today?'

Papa gazed respectfully and inquiringly at grandmamma.

'Yes, that is what they play with. Show him,' she said, turning to Mimi.

Papa took the shot in his hand and could not suppress a smile.

'Why, this is shot, *maman*,' he said, 'it is not at all dangerous.'

'I am very much obliged to you, my dear, for your instruction, but I am too old now . . .'

'Nerves, nerves!' whispered the doctor.

And papa immediately turned to us:

'Where did you get this? And how dare you play with such things?'

'Don't ask them, it's that useless *school-usher* of theirs you must ask,' said grandmamma, with particularly scornful emphasis on the term *school-usher*. 'What else is he for?'

'Voldemar says that Karl Ivanych himself gave him the *gunpowder*,' put in Mimi.

'There, you see how much good he is,' pursued grandmamma, 'and where is he, that *school-usher* – what's his name? Send him here.'

'I let him go out to visit some friends,' said papa.

'There's no sense in that; he should always be here. They are not my children but yours and I have no right to advise you because you know better than I do,' continued grandmamma, 'but I think it is high time to engage a regular tutor for them instead of this German peasant – who is a stupid peasant into the bargain, who can't teach them anything but bad manners and Tyrolean songs. Is it very necessary, I ask you, for the children to be able to sing Tyrolean songs? However, there is no one *now* to care about that, and you may do as you like.'

The word *'now'* meant 'now that they have no mother' and aroused sad memories in grandmamma's heart – she lowered her eyes to the snuff-box with the portrait on it, and was lost in thought.

'I have been thinking of that for some time,' papa hastened to say, 'and I wanted to consult you, *maman*: what about inviting St-Jérome here – he now gives them lessons by the hour?'

'You could not do better, my friend,' said grandmamma, no longer in the dissatisfied tone in which she had been speaking before. 'St-Jérome would at any rate be a proper tutor who knows how *enfants de bonne famille*[1] should be brought up, and not just a companion usher only fit to take them out for walks.'

'I will speak to him tomorrow,' said papa.

And indeed, two days after this conversation, Karl Ivanych was replaced by the young French dandy.

8 · KARL IVANYCH'S LIFE-STORY

Late in the evening before Karl Ivanych was to leave us for good he was standing beside his bed in quilted dressing-gown and red cap, bending over his portmanteau and carefully packing his things.

Karl Ivanych's manner to us had been peculiarly stiff of late: he seemed to want to avoid all contact with us. And so now when I entered the room, apart from a glance from under his brows in my direction, he continued with what he was doing. I lay down on my bed but Karl Ivanych, who before had always forbidden us to do this, said nothing, and the thought that he would never scold or stop us any more, that we were now no concern of his, brought the impending separation sharply home to me. I felt sorry that he had ceased to be fond of us, and wanted to express this to him.

'Let me help you, Karl Ivanych,' I said, going up to him.

Karl Ivanych glanced at me and again turned away, but in the fleeting look which he cast at me I read, not the indifference to which I had attributed his coldness, but genuine pent-up grief.

'God sees and knows everything and His holy will be done in all

1. Children of good family.

things,' he said, straightening up to his full height and giving a deep sigh. 'Yes, my Nikolai,' he continued, seeing the real sympathy in my face, 'it is my fate to be on'appy, from cradle to grave. I haf always been repaid by evil for the good I haf done peoples, and my reward is not here but there,' he said, pointing upwards. 'If you knew the story of my life and all that I haf endured! . . . I haf been a shoe-maker, I haf been a soldier, and a *desertair*, I haf vorked in a factory, I haf been a teacher, and now I am nothing, and like the Son of God haf nowhere to lay my head,' he concluded, closing his eyes and sinking into his arm-chair.

Seeing that Karl Ivanych was in that emotional state of mind in which he uttered his innermost thoughts, regardless of his hearers, I sat down quietly on the bed, not taking my eyes off his kind face.

'You are not a child, you can onderstand. I vill tell you the story of my life and all I haf had to go through. Some day you may remember and t'ink of the old friend who vass so fond of you children . . .'

Karl Ivanych leaned his elbow on the small table at his side, took a pinch of snuff and looking to heaven and showing the whites of his eyes began his tale, speaking in the peculiar monotonous guttural voice in which he generally read dictation to us.

'I vass on'appy already in my mudder's vomb. *Das Unglück verfolgte mich schon im Schosse meiner Mutter*!' he repeated in German with even more feeling.

As Karl Ivanych was afterwards to tell me his story more than once, using the same sequences and the same phrases and never departing from the same unvarying intonations, I think I can reproduce it almost word for word, except of course for the mistakes in language, of which the reader can judge by the first sentence. Whether it really was the history of his life or whether it was the product of his imagination evolved during the lonely time he spent in our house, and which he had from endless repetition come to believe in himself, or whether he merely embellished the actual events of his life with fantastic additions, I have never been able to decide. On the one hand there was too much lively feeling and orderly consistency – paramount tokens of veracity – in its recital for it not to be credible. On the other hand there was too much poetic beauty about his account, so that its very beauty tended to raise doubts.

'In my veins flows the noble blodd of the Counts of Sommerblat! *Im meiner Adern fliesst das edle Blut des Grafen von Sommerblat*! I vass born six veeks after the vedding. My mudder's husband (I called him papa) vass a tenant of Count Sommerblat. He could not forget my mudder's disgrace and did not like me. I had a little brudder, Johann, and two sisters; but I vass a stranger in my own family! *Ich war ein Fremder in meiner eigenen Familie!* Ven Johann vass naughty papa used to say: "I shall never have a moment's peace mit that child Karl," and I vass scolded and punished. Venever my sisters quarrelled papa said: "Karl vill never be a good obedient boy," and I vass scolded and punished. Only my kind mamma loved and petted me. Often she vould say to me: "Karl, come here into my room," and there with no one looking she kissed me. "Poor poor Karl!" she said. "No one loves you, but I vould not exchange you for anybody. One thing your mamma asks of you," she would say to me, "be diligent with your studies, and always be an honest man, and the gut Gott vill not forsake you! *Trachte nur ein ehrlicher Deutscher zu werden – sagte sie – und der liebe Gott wird dich nicht verlassen!*" And I tried. Ven I vass fourteen and could go to communion mamma said to my papa: "Karl iss a big boy now, Gustav. What shall we do mit him?" And papa said, "I don't know." Then mamma said: "Let us send him to town, to Herr Schultz: let him be a shoemaker!" And papa said: "Gut." *Und mein Vater sagte "gut".* For six years and seven months I lived in the town at the shoemaker's, und my master vass fond of me. "Karl iss a gut vorker," he said, "and soon he vill be my *Gesellel*"[1] But ... man proposes and God disposes ... In the year 1796 there vass conscription, and all able-bodied men between eighteen and twenty-one had to present themselves in the town.

'Papa and brudder Johann came to town and ve all vent together to draw lots who should be a soldier and who should not be a soldier. Johann drew a bad number – he vould haf to be a soldier. I drew a gut number – I did not haf to become a soldier. Und papa said: "I had an only son, and I must part mit him! *Ich hatte einen einzigen Sohn und von diesem muss ich mich trennen!*"

'I took his hand und said: "Vhy did you say that, papa? Come mit me und I vill tell you something." Und papa came. Papa came and ve seated ourselves at a little table in an inn. "Bring us two tankards of beer," I said, and they brought them. Ve had a glass each, and brudder Johann drank too.

'"Papa," I said, "don't speak like that – that you had an only son and you must part mit him. My heart is leaping out ven I hear sis.

1. Assistant.

Brudder Johann shall not serve – I vill be the soldier! . . . No one here vants Karl and Karl vill be soldier!"

'"You are a goot fellow, Karl Ivanych!" said papa to me, and kissed me. *"Du bist ein braver Bursche!" – sagte mir mein Vater und küsste mich!*

'Und I became a soldier!'

9 · CONTINUATION OF THE FOREGOING

'That vass a dreadful time, Nikolai,' continued Karl Ivanych, 'the time of Napoleon. He vanted to conquer Germany and ve vere defending our Vaterland to the last drop of our blodd! *und wir verteidigten unser Vaterland bis auf den letzten Tropfen Blut!*

'I vass at Ulm, I vass at Austerlitz, I vass at Wagram! *Ich war bei Wagram!'*

'Did you really fight too?' I asked, looking at him with astonishment. 'Did you really kill people too?'

Karl Ivanych immediately set my mind at ease on that point.

'Once a French grenadier lagged behind his comrades und fell down in the road. I sprang forward mit my musket to run him through, *aber der Franzose warf sein Gewehr und rief "Pardon"*[1] und I let him go.

'At Wagram Napoleon drove us on to an island and surrounded us so that there vass no escape anyvere. For three days ve had no provisions and stood up to our knees in vater. That miscreant Napoleon vould neither take us nor let us go! *und der Bösewicht Napoleon wollte uns nicht gefangen nehmen und auch nicht freilassen!*

'On the fourth day, thank Gott, they took us prisoner and led us off to a fortress. I vore blue trousers and a fine cloth uniform, I had fifteen thalers in money and a silver vatch – a present from my papa. A French soldier took it all from me. Luckily I had three gold pieces that mamma had sewn into my vest. No one found them!

'I did not vant to stop long in the fortress and I decide to run away. One day, ven it vass a big holiday I said to the sergeant who guarded us: "Mr Sergeant, today iss a big holiday, I should like to keep it. Please bring me two bottles of madeira und ve vill drink together." Und the sergeant said: "Very vell." Ven the sergeant brought the madeira and ve had each drunk a glass I took his hand and said: "Mr Sergeant,

---

1. But the Frenchman threw away his weapon and cried 'Pardon!'.

perhaps you haf a vater und mudder?" He said: "I haf, Mr Mauer" –
"My vater und mudder," I said, "haf not seen me for eight years und
they don't know if I am alife or if my bones haf long been lying in the
damp earth. Oh, Mr Sergeant – I haf two gold pieces that vere under
my vest: take them and let me go. Be my benefactor and my mamma
will pray to Almighty Gott for you all the days of her life."

'The sergeant emptied his glass of madeira und said: "Mr Mauer,
very much I like you and I am sorry for you but you are a prisoner und
I am a soldier!' I pressed his hand und said: "Mr Sergeant!" *Ich drückte
ihm die Hand und sagte: "Herr Sergeant!"*

'Und the sergeant said: "You are a poor man and I von't take your
money but I vill 'elp you. Ven I go to bed buy a bucket of brandy for
the soldiers and they vill sleep. I von't vatch you."

'He vass a gut man. I bought a pail of brandy and ven the *Soldaten*
vere all tipsy I put on my boots and my old greatcoat and crept out.
I vent on to the rampart and vass going to jump but there vass vater
below and I did not vant to spoil my last remaining clothes so I vent to
the gates.

'A sentry mit a mustket vass marching *auf und ab*[1] and looked at me.
"*Qui vive?*" *sagte er auf einmal,*[2] and I vass silent. "*Qui vive?*" *sagte er
zum zweiten Mal,*[3] and I vass silent. "*Qui vive?*" – *sagte er zum dritten
Mal,*[4] and I am running away. I spring in der vater, climb op on der oser
side and I go. *Ich sprang ins Wasser, kletterte auf die andere Seite und machte
mich aus dem Staube.*

'All night I run along the road but ven it grows light I am afraid of
being recognized, und I 'ide in some tall rye. There I knelt down, folded
my hands, thanked our Heavenly Vater for my safety und fell peacefully asleep. *Ich dankte dem allmächtigen Gott für Seine Barmherzigkeit
und mit beruhigtem Gefühl schlief ich ein.*

'I voke up in the evening und vent on. All at once a large German
vagon mit two black horses overtook me. In the vagon sat a vell-
dressed man smoking a pipe und looking at me. I valked slowly to let
the vagon pass me but I valked slowly and the vagon vent slowly and
the man vass looking at me. I valked faster und the vagon vent faster
und the man still looked at me. I sat down by the roadside; the man

1. Up and down.
2. 'Who goes there?' said he suddenly.
3. 'Who goes there?' said he a second time.
4. 'Who goes there?' said he a third time.

stopped his horses und looked at me. "Young man," he said, "Vere are you going so late at night?" I said: "I am going to Frankfurt." – "Get into my vagon, there iss room enough and I vill take you there ... Vy haf you got nothing mit you, vy iss your beard not shaven and vy are your clothes muddy?" he said to me ven I sat down beside him. "I am a poor man," I said, "I vant to find vork in a manufactory and my clothes are muddy because I fell down on the road." – "You are telling a lie, young man," he said, "the roads are dry now."

'And I kept silent.

' "Tell me the whole truth," the kind man said to me. "Who are you and vere do you come from? I like your face und if you are an honest man I vill 'elp you."

'And I tell him everyt'ing. He said: "Very vell, young man, come to my rope-factory. I vill gif you vork, clothes und money, und you shall live mit me."

'Und I said: "All right."

'Ve came to the rope factory und the kind man said to his wife: "Here iss a young man who has fought for his Vaterland und escaped from captivity. He hass no 'ome, no clothes, no food. He shall live in our 'ouse. Gif him clean linen und feed him."

'I lived a year und a half at the rope-factory and my gut master grew so fond of me that he did not vant to let me go. Und I vass 'appy. I vass a 'andsome man then. I vass young, tall, I had blue eyes and a Roman nose ... und Madame L. (I cannot mention her name), my master's wife vass a young und pretty lady. Und she fell in love mit me.

'Ven she saw me she said: "Mr Mauer, vat does your mamma call you?" I said: "Karlchen."

'Und she said: "Karlchen, sit here beside me."

'I sat down beside her und she said: "Karlchen, kiss me!"

'I kissed her und she said: "Karlchen, I love you so much that I cannot bear it any longer," und she began to tremble all over.'

Here Karl Ivanych made a long pause and turning his kindly blue eyes to the ceiling and slightly shaking his head began to smile as people do at a pleasant memory.

'Yes,' he began again, settling himself more comfortably in the armchair and wrapping his dressing-gown round him, 'I haf experienced much gut und much bad in my life; but here is my witness,' he said, pointing to a little ikon of the Saviour embroidered in wool which hung over his bed – 'nobody can say that Karl Ivanych vass dishonourable! I did not vish to repay Mr L's kindness to me mit black ingratitude und I decided to run avay. In the evening ven everybody vent to bed I wrote a letter to my master und put it on the table in my room. I took my clothes, three thalers of money und crept out into the street. No one saw me und I valked avay along the road.

10 · CONTINUATION

'I had not seen my little mudder for nine years and did not know vether she vass alive or vether her bones vere already lying in the damp earth. I vent to my Vaterland. Ven I came to the town I asked vere Gustav Mauer lived, who had rented land of Count Sommerblat. Und I vass told: "Count Sommerblat iss dead und Gustav Mauer now lives in the High Street und keeps a liquor shop." I put on my new waist-coat und a gut coat that my former master, the owner of the rope-factory, had given me, brushed my hair vell and vent to my papa's liquor shop. My sister Mariechen vass sitting in the shop und asked vot I vanted. I said: "May I haf a glass of liquor?" Und she said: "Vater! A young man iss asking for a glass of liquor." Und papa said: "Serve the young man mit a glass of liquor." I sat down at a small table, drank my glass of liquor, smoked a pipe und looked at papa, at Mariechen und at Johann, who had also come into the shop. Vile ve ver talking papa said to me: "You maybe know, young man, vere stands now our army?" I said: "I myself am coming from der army, and it iss near Vienna." – "Our son," said papa, "vass a soldier, and now he hassn't written to us for nine years, and ve do not know if he be alive or dead. My wife does nothing but veep about him . . ." I vent on smoking my pipe und said: "Vat vass your son's name, and vat regiment vass he in? Perhaps I know him . . ." – "His name iss Karl Mauer, und he vass serving mit the Austrian Jägers," said my papa. "He iss a tall und 'andsome man like yourself," said sister Mariechen. I said: "I know your Karl!" – "Amalia!" *sagte auf einmal mein Vater.*[1] "Komm here! Here iss a young man who knows our Karl." Und my dear Mudder she komm from der backroom. I did know her at once. "You know der Karl," she say, lookit at me und pale like pale trrremblt! "Yes, I haf seen him," I said und dared not lift my eyes to her; my heart visht to leap. "My Karl iss alive!" said mamma. "Thanks be to Gott! Vere iss

1. Said my father suddenly.

he, vere iss my dear Karl? I should die in peace if I could see him, see my beloved son once more; but it iss not Gott's vill." Und she begin to cry ... I could not ho–olt out .. ͵ "Mamma!" I said. "I am your Karl!" Und in my arms she fell ...'

Karl Ivanych closed his eyes and his lips quivered.

'"*Mutter!*" *sagte ich*, "*ich bin Ihr Sohn, ich bin Ihr Karl*" *und sie stürzte mir in die Arme,*'[1] he repeated, recovering a little and wiping the large teardrops that rolled down his cheeks.

'But it vass not Gott's pleasure that I should end my days in my native land. I vass doomed to misfortune! *das Unglück verfolgte mich überall!*[2] ... I lived in my own town only three months. One Sunday I vass at the coffee house, I bought a mug of beer, smoked my pipe und vass talking politics mit my acquaintances, about the Emperor Franz, about Napoleon, about the war, und each one vass speaking his opinion. Near us sat a stranger in a grey overcoat who drank his coffee, smoked his pipe und said nothing to us. *Er rauchte sein Pfeifchen und schwieg still.* Ven the night-watchman called ten o'clock I took my 'at, paid my money und vent 'ome. In the middle of the night some one knocked at the door. I woke up und said: "Who's there?"– "*Macht auf!*"[3] I called out: "Say who you are und I vill open." *Ich sagte: "Sagt, wer ihr seid, und ich werde aufmachen.*" – "*Macht auf im Namen des Gesetzes!*"[4] came from behind the door. Und I opened. Two Soldaten mit musket stood at the door und into the room komm the stranger in the grey overcoat who had been sitting near us in the coffee-house. He vass a spy! *Es war ein Spion!* ... "You must komm mit me!" said the spy. "Very vell," I said ... I put on my boots und trousers, buckled on my suspenders und paced up und down the room. My blodd vass up: I said to myself: "He iss a scoundrel!" Ven I came to the wall vere my sword vass 'anging I grabbed it und said: "You are a spy: defend yourself!" *Du bist ein Spion, verteidige dich!*" *Ich gab einen Hieb*[5] to the right, *einen Hieb* to the left, und vun on der 'ead. The spy fall. I snatched up my portmanteau und my money und jumped out of the window. *Ich nahm Mantelsack und Beutel und sprang zum Fenster hinaus. Ich kam nach Ems.*[6] There I made the acquaintance of General' – he pronounced it

1. 'Mamma!' said I, 'I am your son, I am your Karl!' and she threw herself into my arms.
2. Misfortune pursued me everywhere.
3. Open!   4. Open in the name of the law!
5. I give a blow.   6. I came to Ems.

Yeneral – 'Sazin. He took a fancy to me, got a passport for me from the ambassador und took me mit him to Russia to teach his children. Ven Yeneral Sazin died your mamma called me to her. She said: "Karl Ivanych! I gif you my children, lof them, und I vill never forsake you, I vill provide for you in your old age." Now she is no more und all iss forgotten. For my twenty years' service I must now in my old age go out into the streets to look for a crust of dry bread . . . Gott sees it und knows it und His holy vill be don. Only it griefs me to part from you kinder,' Karl Ivanych concluded, drawing me to him by my arm and kissing me on the head.

11 · THE BAD MARK

The year of mourning over, grandmamma recovered a little from the grief that had stricken her and began occasionally to receive visitors, especially children, boys and girls of our own age.

On Lyuba's birthday, the 13th of December, Princess Kornakova with her daughters, Madame Valakhina and Sonya, Ilinka Grap and the two youngest Ivins arrived before dinner.

The sounds of voices, laughter and running to and fro reached us from downstairs where all the company was assembled but we could not join them till we had finished morning lessons. The time-table hanging in the schoolroom mentioned: 'Lundi, de 2 à 3, maître d'Histoire et de Géographie',[1] and it was this maître d'Histoire whom we had to wait for, listen to and see out before we should be free. It was already twenty minutes past two but the history master so far was neither to be heard nor seen, not even in the street he had to come by and down which I looked with a great longing that I might never set eyes on him again.

'Lebedev doesn't seem to be coming today,' said Volodya, breaking away for a moment from Smaragdov's text-book which he was studying for his lesson.

'I hope not, please the Lord! . . . I don't know a single word . . . But there he is, I think,' I added in a dejected voice.

Volodya got up and went to the window.

'No, that's not him, that's a gentleman,' said he. 'Let us wait till half past two,' he added, stretching himself and at the same time

1. Monday, from 2 to 3, History and Geography master.

scratching the crown of his head as he usually did in moments of respite from his studies. 'If he doesn't come by half past we can tell St-Jérome and put away our exercise-books.'

'And what does he want to co-o-me for!' I said, also stretching myself and shaking Kaydanov's text-book, which I held in both hands, above my head.

Having nothing better to do, I opened the book where the lesson was and began to read. It was a long lesson and a difficult one. I knew nothing about it and saw that I should not have time to get any of it into my head, especially as I was in that state of nervous excitement in which one's thoughts refuse to concentrate on any subject whatever.

After the last history lesson, which always seemed to me the hardest and most tedious of all subjects, Lebedev had complained about me to St-Jérome, and given me a two[1] in the mark-book, which was considered very bad. St-Jérome told me that if I got less than three next time I should be severely punished. This next lesson was now imminent and I was, I confess, in an awful fright.

I was so absorbed in reading the lesson I did not know that the sound of goloshes being taken off in the hall startled me. I had barely time to glance round before the pock-marked and to me loathsome face and the too-familiar awkward figure of the master in his blue swallow-tailed coat with the schoolmaster's brass buttons appeared in the doorway.

The teacher slowly deposited his hat on the window-sill, our exercise-books on the table, and separating the tails of his coat with both hands (as though that was most necessary) seated himself puffing on his chair.

'Well, gentlemen,' he said, rubbing one clammy hand on the other, 'let us first go over what we talked about at our previous lesson, and then I will endeavour to acquaint you with the further events of the Middle Ages.'

This meant, 'Say over the last lesson.'

While Volodya was answering him with the ease and assurance proper to one who knows a subject well I wandered aimlessly to the stairs and as I was not allowed to go down it was very natural that I should find myself, without noticing it, on the landing. But just as I was about to take up my usual post of observation behind the door Mimi, who was always the cause of my misfortunes, stumbled upon me.

1. Out of five.

'You here?' she said, looking sternly at me, then at the door of the maids' room and then at me again.

I felt thoroughly guilty – first because I was not in the schoolroom and secondly because I was in a place where I had no business to be, so I remained silent and, hanging my head, assumed a most pathetic expression of penitence.

'Now who ever saw the like!' said Mimi. 'What are you doing here?' I did not answer. 'No, this cannot be passed over,' she went on, rapping the banisters with her knuckles. 'I shall tell the countess.'

It was five minutes to three when I returned to the schoolroom. The master, as though oblivious alike of my absence and of my presence, was explaining the following lesson to Volodya. When he had done and was putting his note-books together, while Volodya went to the other room to fetch the lesson-ticket, the comforting thought occurred to me that the whole thing was over now and they would forget about me.

But suddenly the master turned to me with a malicious half smile.

'I hope you know your lesson,' he said, rubbing his hands.

'Yes, sir,' I answered.

'Be so kind as to tell me something about the crusade of Saint Louis,' he said, rocking his chair and gazing thoughtfully at the floor by his feet. 'Start by telling me the reasons which induced the French king to take the cross,' he said, raising his eyebrows and pointing his finger at the ink-pot. 'Next explain the general characteristics of the crusade,' he added, making a movement with his wrist as if he were trying to catch something, 'and finally, the influence of this crusade on the European states in general,' he said, striking the left side of the table with the note-books, 'and on the French monarchy in particular,' he concluded, tapping the right side of the table and inclining his head to the right.

I swallowed several times, coughed, bent my head to one side and remained silent. Then, picking up a quill pen that lay on the table, I began pulling it to pieces, still without uttering a word.

'Let me have that quill, pray,' said the master, stretching out his hand. 'It may come in useful. Well, sir?'

'Ludov...King...Saint Louis was...was...was...a good and wise tsar...'

'What, sir?'

'A tsar. He conceived the idea of going to Jerusalem and *handed the reins of government* to his mother.'

'What was her name?'

'B . . . b . . . lanka.'

'What, sir? Bulanka?'[1]

I forced an awkward smile.

'Well, sir, don't you know anything else?' he said sarcastically.

I had nothing to say so I cleared my throat and began to burble whatever happened to come into my head. The master, who sat silently flicking the dust from the table with the quill he had taken from me, looked fixedly past my ear and repeated from time to time: 'Good, sir, very good.' I was conscious that I knew nothing and was expressing myself all wrong, and felt painfully concerned that the master did not stop or correct me.

'Why did he conceive the idea of going to Jerusalem?' he said, repeating my words.

'So as . . . because . . . in order, so as to . . .'

My confusion was complete – I did not say another word and felt that even if this villainous teacher were to sit and stare inquiringly in silence at me for a whole year I should still not be able to utter another sound. For about three minutes the teacher gazed at me. Then an expression of profound sorrow appeared on his face and he said in a pathetic voice to Volodya, who had just entered the room:

'Let me have the book to put down your marks.'

Volodya handed him the book and carefully placed the lesson-ticket beside it.

The master opened the book and slowly and deliberately dipping his pen in the ink entered 5 for Volodya under the heading 'Progress' and the same for 'Conduct'. Then, with the pen suspended over the column for my marks, he looked at me, shook some ink off the pen and reflected.

Suddenly his hand made a scarcely perceptible movement and in the first column opposite my name appeared an elegantly shaped 1 with a full stop after it. Another movement, and in the column for 'Conduct' stood another 1 followed by a full stop.

Carefully closing the marks-book, the master rose and went to the door as though he did not see the look of despair, entreaty and reproach that I turned upon him.

1. A name given cream-coloured horses in Russia.

'Mihail Larionych!' I said.

'No,' he said, understanding in advance what I was going to say, 'you can't do your lessons like that. I am not going to take money for nothing.'

The master put on his goloshes and a camlet overcoat, and with great care tied a scarf round his neck. To think that he could give his mind to anything after what had happened to me! To him a mere stroke of the pen but to me it meant direst misfortune!

'Is the lesson over?' asked St-Jérome, coming into the room.

'Yes.'

'Was the master satisfied with you?'

'Yes,' said Volodya.

'What marks did you get?'

'Five.'

'And Nikolai?'

I was silent.

'Four, I think,' said Volodya.

He knew it was absolutely necessary to save me, if only for that day. Let them punish me, only not that day when there were visitors.

'*Voyons, messieurs.*' (St-Jérome had a way of prefacing everything he said with '*voyons*') '*Faites votre toilette et descendons.*'[1]

12 · THE LITTLE KEY

We had hardly got downstairs and greeted all the visitors before dinner was announced. Papa was in high spirits (he had been winning of late). He had given Lyuba an expensive silver tea-service and at dinner remembered that in his apartment in the wing he had left a bonbonnière for the birthday girl.

'Why send a servant? You had better go, young Nikolai,' he said to me. 'The keys are in the shell on the big table – you know? . . . Well, take them and with the largest key unlock the second drawer on the right. There you will find a small box and some bonbons in a paper; bring them all here.'

'And shall I bring you some cigars?' I asked, knowing that he always sent for them after dinner.

1. Now then, gentlemen, make yourselves tidy, and let us go down.

140 BOYHOOD

'Yes, do, but mind you don't touch any of my things!' he called after me.

I found the keys where he said and was just about to open the drawer when it occurred to me that I should like to know what the tiniest key on the bunch opened.

On the table, leaning against the rail, among a thousand different objects lay an embroidered portfolio with a little padlock attached to it, and I felt curious to see whether the little key would fit it. My attempt met with complete success: the portfolio opened and I found a whole heap of papers inside. Curiosity prompted me so forcefully to find out what those papers were that I had no time to attend to the voice of conscience but set to work to examine the contents of the portfolio.

*

The childish feeling of unconditional respect for all my elders and especially for papa was so strong in me that my mind instinctively refused to draw any conclusion whatever from what I saw. I felt that papa must live in a totally different world – beautiful, unattainable and beyond my comprehension – and that for me to try and fathom the secrets of his life would be a kind of sacrilege.

For this reason the discoveries I made, almost accidentally, in papa's portfolio left no clear impression on me beyond a vague consciousness of having done wrong. I felt ashamed and uncomfortable.

This feeling made me eager to shut the portfolio again as quickly as possible but I was evidently fated to suffer every kind of disaster on that memorable day: inserting the key in the keyhole, I turned it the wrong way; supposing it was locked, I pulled the key out and – oh, horror! – only the top of the key was in my hand. In vain I struggled to join it to the half left in the lock and by some magic to extract it. At last I had to resign myself to the frightful thought that I had committed another crime which papa must discover that very day when he returned to his study.

Complaints from Mimi, the bad mark and the little key! Nothing worse could happen to me. Grandmamma – on account of Mimi's denunciation – St-Jérome because of the bad mark – and papa for the key . . . and all this to come upon me no later than that very evening.

'What will happen to me? Oh, oh, oh, what have I done?' I said aloud as I paced the soft carpet of the study. 'Oh well,' I said to myself

as I took out the sweets and the cigars, *'what can't be cured must be endured
. . .'* And I ran back to the house.

That fatalistic saying, overheard from Nikolai in my early childhood, has exercised a beneficial and temporarily soothing influence on
me in all the difficult moments of my life. When I entered the dining-
hall I was in a somewhat agitated and unnatural but exceedingly high-
spirited state.

13 · THE TRAITRESS

After dinner we began to play parlour games and I took the most
active part in them. In 'Cat and Mouse' I rather clumsily ran into the
Kornakova governess, who was playing with us, and accidentally trod
on her dress and tore it. Noticing that it afforded all the girls, and
especially Sonya, great satisfaction to see the governess retire upset to
the maids' room to mend her dress, I resolved to give them that pleasure
once more. In consequence of this amiable intention, as soon as the
governess returned I began to gallop round her and continued these
evolutions until I found an opportunity to catch my heel in her skirt
again and tear it. Sonya and the young princesses could hardly restrain
their laughter, which flattered my vanity most agreeably: but St-
Jérome, who must have observed my manoeuvres, came up to me and
contracting his brows (a thing I could not endure) remarked that my
liveliness boded no good and that if I did not moderate my behaviour
he would make me sorry, even though it was a holiday.

But I was in the excited state of mind of a man who, having lost at
cards more than he has in his pocket, is afraid to cast up his accounts and
continues to stake desperately – not because he hopes to recover his
losses but in order not to give himself time to stop and consider. I
smiled impudently and turned on my heel.

After 'Cat and Mouse' some one suggested a game which I think we
used to call *Lange Nase.*[1] The main point of the game was for the ladies
to sit on one row of chairs and opposite them the gentlemen on another,
and choose each other for partners.

The youngest princess chose the smallest Ivin every time, Katya
chose either Volodya or Ilinka, and Sonya's choice always fell on
Seriozha, and to my extreme amazement she was not at all embarrassed

1. Long nose.

when Seriozha went and seated himself directly opposite her. She laughed her sweet ringing laugh and nodded to show he had guessed right. But nobody chose me. To the great mortification of my vanity I realized that I was not wanted, *left out*, that every time some one must be saying of me: 'Who is left? – Oh yes, Nikolai! Well, you take him.' So when it was my turn to come forward and guess who had chosen me I always went straight either to my sister or to one of the plain princesses, and, unfortunately, I was never mistaken. As to Sonya, she seemed so absorbed in Seriozha Ivin that I did not exist for her at all. I do not know on what grounds I mentally designated her *traitress*, for she had never promised to choose me and not Seriozha; but I was firmly convinced that she had treated me very basely indeed.

When the game was over I noticed that the *traitress*, whom I despised although I could not take my eyes off her, had gone into a corner with Seriozha and Katya, and that they were mysteriously discussing something. Creeping up behind the piano to discover their secret, I saw this: Katya was holding up a cambric handkerchief by two of its ends to form a screen for Seriozha's and Sonya's heads. 'No, you've lost: pay up now!' said Seriozha. Sonya stood before him like a culprit with her arms hanging beside her, and blushing said: 'No, I haven't lost, have I, Mademoiselle Catherine?' – 'I am fond of the truth,' answered Katya. 'You have lost the wager, *ma chère*.'

Hardly were the words out of Katya's mouth before Seriozha stooped and kissed Sonya. He kissed her full upon her rosy lips! And Sonya laughed as though it were nothing, as though it were very amusing. Horrible!!! *O perfidious traitress!*

14 · ECLIPSE

I suddenly felt I despised the whole female sex, and Sonya in particular. I began to persuade myself that there was nothing amusing about such games as these, which were only suitable for *silly little girls*, and I had a strong desire to kick over the traces and play some kind of bold prank that would astonish them all. An opportunity soon presented itself.

St-Jérome had been talking with Mimi and I now saw him leave the room. I heard his steps going up the stairs, then they sounded overhead in the direction of the schoolroom. I supposed Mimi had been telling him where she had seen me during lesson-time, and that he had gone to inspect the mark-book. In those days I did not attribute to St-Jérome any other aim in life than the desire to punish me. I have read somewhere that children from twelve to fourteen years of age – that is, in the transition stage from childhood to adolescence – are singularly inclined to arson and even murder. As I look back upon my boyhood and especially when I recall the state of mind I was in on that (for me) unfortunate day, I can quite appreciate the possibility of the most frightful crime being committed without object or intent to injure but *just because* – out of curiosity, or to satisfy an unconscious craving for action. There are moments when the future looks so black that one is afraid to let one's thoughts dwell on it, refuses to let one's mind function and tries to convince oneself that the future will not be, and the past has not been. At such moments, when the will is not governed or modified by reflection and the only incentives that remain in life are our physical instincts, I can understand how a child, being particularly prone owing to lack of experience to fall into such a state, may without the least hesitation or fear, with a smile of curiosity deliberately set fire to his own house – and then fan the flames where his brothers, his father and his mother, all of whom he loves dearly, are sleeping. Under the influence of a similar absence of reflection – absence of mind almost – a peasant lad of seventeen, examining the blade of a newly-sharpened axe lying near the bench on which his old father lies face downwards asleep, suddenly swings the axe and with vacant curiosity watches the blood oozing under the bench from the severed neck. It is under the same influence – the same absence of reasoning, the same instinct of curiosity – that a man finds a certain pleasure in standing on the very brink of a precipice and thinking, 'What if I throw myself down?' Or raising a loaded pistol to his forehead says to himself: 'Suppose I pull the trigger?' Or looks at some very distinguished personage whom every one holds in servile respect and thinks: 'What if I were to go up to him, take him by the nose and say: "Now then, come along, my hearty!"'

Under the spell, then, of this inward and unthinking excitement, when St-Jérome came down and told me I had no business to be there that evening because I had behaved badly and done my lessons so ill, and that I was to go upstairs at once, I stuck out my tongue and said I would not go.

For a moment St-Jérome could not utter a word for surprise and anger.

'*C'est bien*,'[1] he said, coming up to me. 'I have promised to punish you more than once already but your grandmother has always begged you off; but now I see that nothing but the rod will teach you obedience, and today you amply deserve a whipping.'

He said this so loudly that every one heard. The blood rushed to my heart with such force that I could feel it beating hard and the colour draining from my face, and my lips quite involuntarily trembling. I must have looked dreadful at that moment for St-Jérome, avoiding my eyes, came quickly up to me and seized me by the arm; but immediately I felt his hand touch me, beside myself with rage I tore my arm from his grasp and struck him with all my childish strength.

'What is the matter with you?' said Volodya, who had witnessed my action in horror and amazement, coming up to me.

'Leave me alone!' I shrieked at him through my tears. 'You don't any of you love me or understand how miserable I am. You are all horrid and disgusting!' I added wildly, addressing the whole company.

But at this point St-Jérome with a pale set face approached me again and before I had time to resist he had gripped both my arms as in a vice and dragged me away. I was dizzy with agitation; all I remember is that I fought desperately, using my head and my knees, as long as my strength lasted. I remember that my nose several times came in contact with some one's thigh; that some one's coat got into my mouth, that I was aware of legs all round me and of a smell of dust and the *violette* scent which St-Jérome used.

Five minutes later the door of the lumber-room was closed upon me.

'Vassily,' said *he* in a revolting triumphant voice, 'bring a birch.'

*

15 · IMAGININGS

Could I possibly have believed at that moment that I should survive the misfortunes that had befallen me, and that the day would come when I could look back upon them calmly? . . .

Thinking over what I had done, I could not conceive what would become of me but I had a dim presentiment that I was lost for ever.

At first absolute silence reigned downstairs and all around me, or at least so it seemed after the violent agitation within me, but by degrees

1. Very good.

I began to distinguish various sounds. Vassily came upstairs and flinging something which might have been a broom on the window-sill lay down on the bench with a yawn. Downstairs I heard St-Jérome's loud voice (talking about me, no doubt), then children's voices, laughter, running about, and in a few minutes everything in the house began to go on as before, as though no one knew or cared about my sitting in the dark box-room.

I did not cry but something heavy as stone lay on my heart. All sorts of thoughts and fancies whirled through my troubled brain but the recollection of the disasters that had befallen me continually interrupted their fantastic sequence, and I found myself in a hopeless maze of conjectures as to the fate in store for me, of despair and of dread.

Now the thought occurred to me that there must be some unknown reason for the general dislike of me – for the hatred even. (At that time I was firmly convinced that I was detested by everybody from grandmamma down to Filip the coachman, who all rejoiced in my sufferings.) 'Perhaps I am not the son of my mother and father, and Volodya's brother, but a poor orphan, a foundling adopted out of charity,' I said to myself; and this ridiculous notion not only afforded me a certain melancholy consolation but even seemed quite plausible. I liked to think that I was unhappy not through any fault of mine but because I was fated to be so from the day of my birth, and that my destiny resembled the unfortunate Karl Ivanych's.

'But why keep it any longer a secret, now that I have discovered it myself?' I wondered. 'Tomorrow I will go to papa and say, "Papa, there is no point in hiding the secret of my birth from me: I know." He will say: "Well, my boy, sooner or later you would have found out – you are not my son but I adopted you, and if you prove worthy of my affection I will never desert you." And I shall say: "Papa, though I have no right to call you by that name – I do so now for the last time – I have always loved you and always will, and I shall never forget that you are my benefactor; but I can no longer remain in your house. Here no one loves me, and St-Jérome has sworn to destroy me. He or I must leave your house, since I cannot answer for myself: I hate that man to such a degree that I could do anything. I shall kill him." Yes, that's what I'll say: "Papa, I shall kill him." Papa will begin to entreat me but I shall wave my hand and tell him: "No, no, my friend and benefactor, we cannot live together so let me go," and I shall embrace him and say (for some reason in French): "*Oh mon père, oh mon bienfaiteur, donne moi*

pour la dernière fois ta bénédiction et que la volonté de Dieu soit faite! "[1]
And sitting on a trunk in the dark box-room I wept and sobbed at this
thought. But all at once I remember the ignominious punishment in
store for me, reality is before me in its true light, and my imaginings
take instant flight.

Next I fancy myself free and out in the world. I enlist in the Hussars
and go to war. The enemy bears down on me from all sides. I flourish
my sabre and kill one, flourish it again and kill another – and a third.
At last, faint from wounds and exhaustion, I fall to the ground with a
cry of 'Victory!' The general rides up and asks: 'Where is he – where
is our saviour?' I am pointed out to him, he flings himself on my neck
and exclaims with tears of joy: 'Victory!' I recover and walk on the
Tverskoy Boulevard with my arm in a black sling. I am a general! And
lo, I meet the *Emperor*, who inquires: 'Who is that young man who is
wounded?' they tell him it is the famous hero, Nikolai. The Emperor
comes up to me and says: 'My thanks to you. Whatever you ask of me
you shall have.' I bow respectfully and leaning on my sabre say: 'I am
happy, great Emperor, to have been able to shed my blood for my
Fatherland, and would gladly have died for it; but since you are so
gracious as to permit me to beg a favour of you, I ask one thing only –
give me leave to destroy my enemy, the foreigner St-Jérome. I long to
annihilate my enemy, St-Jérome.' I halt threateningly before St-
Jérome and say: 'You were the cause of my misfortune – *à genoux!*'[2]
But suddenly it occurs to me that the real St-Jérome may at any
moment come in with the birch, and again I see myself, not as a general saving his country, but as a most wretched piteous creature.

I begin to think of God, and defiantly ask Him what He is punishing
me for. 'I don't believe I have ever forgotten to say my prayers morning and evening so why should I be suffering like this?' I can say positively that the first step towards the religious doubts that assailed me
during my boyhood was taken by me then, not because my unhappiness led me to murmuring and unbelief but because the thought of the
injustice of Providence, which entered my head during that twenty-
four-hour period of acute mental suffering and rigorous isolation, was
like a pernicious seed which drops into soft earth soaked with rain, and
begins rapidly to germinate and send forth roots. Next I imagined that

1. Oh my father, oh my benefactor, give me your blessing for the last time,
and may God's will be done!
2. On your knees!

I was going to die there and then, and drew vivid pictures for myself of St-Jérome's surprise when he came into the lumber-room and found a lifeless corpse instead of me. I remembered Natalya Savishna's tales of how the souls of the dead do not leave their homes for forty days, and after my death I fly unseen about all the rooms in grandmamma's house, seeing Lyuba's bitter tears and hearing grandmamma's lamentations and listening to papa's conversation with St-Jérome. 'He was a fine boy,' papa would say with tears in his eyes. 'Yes,' says St-Jérome, 'but a dreadful scamp.' – 'You should respect the dead,' papa will then say. 'You were the cause of his death; you frightened him, he could not endure the humiliation you were preparing for him ... Begone, scoundrel!'

And St-Jérome will fall on his knees, weep and beg to be forgiven. At the end of the forty days my soul will fly up to heaven; there I behold something marvellously beautiful, white, transparent and tall, and I feel that it is my mother. This white something surrounds me, caresses me; but I am worried and don't seem to recognize her. 'If it really is you,' I say, 'then show yourself to me better, so that I can hug you.' And her voice answers me: 'Here we are all like this, I cannot embrace you any better. Don't you feel happy like this?' – 'Yes, I am happy, but you can't tickle me, and I can't kiss your hands ...' – 'That is not necessary, it is lovely here without that,' she says, and I feel that it really is lovely, and together we fly higher and higher. At this point I as it were wake up to find myself on the trunk in the dark box-room again, my cheeks wet with tears, mechanically repeating the words, 'and we soar higher and higher'. For a long time I try my utmost to grasp my situation; but only a single terrible black impenetrable perspective presents itself to my mental vision at this moment. I endeavour to recall the happy comforting dreams interrupted by my returning consciousness of reality, but to my astonishment so soon as I recapture the thread of my former reverie I find it impossible to go on with it and, most astonishing of all, my imaginings no longer afford me any pleasure.

16 · IT WILL ALL COME RIGHT IN THE END

I spent the night in the box-room and no one came near me; only next day, that is, on Sunday, did they move me to a little room adjoining the schoolroom, and locked me in again. I began to hope that my punishment would be limited to confinement, and after a sound invigorating sleep and under the influence of the bright sunshine playing on the frosty patterns on the window-panes, and the usual day-time noises in the streets, I began to grow more composed. Nevertheless I found my solitude very irksome: I longed to move about, to tell somebody all the things that had accumulated inside me, and there was not a living soul within reach. This state of affairs was all the more aggravating because, repulsive as it was to me, I could not help hearing St-Jérome walking about in his room and quite calmly whistling some gay tune or other. I was fully persuaded that he did not want to whistle at all but did so merely to torment me.

At two o'clock St-Jérome and Volodya went downstairs, and Nikolai brought me my dinner. When I had got into conversation with him about what I had done and what was in store for me he said:

'Eh, master, never you fret: it will all come right in the end.'

Though that saying (which in later life served more than once to keep up my spirits) comforted me somewhat, the fact that they had sent me, not bread and water, but the whole dinner, including even the pudding – cream patties – caused me to become very thoughtful indeed. If they had not sent me any pudding it would have meant that being locked up was my punishment but now it looked as though I was not punished yet but only kept away from the others as being too wicked to associate with them, and that my punishment was yet to come. While I was debating the question the key turned in the lock of my prison and St-Jérome entered with a grim official expression on his face.

'Come to your grandmamma,' he said, without looking at me.

I should have liked to brush the sleeves of my jacket which were smeared with chalk before leaving the room but St-Jérome said that was quite unnecessary, as if I were in such a deplorable moral condition that it was not worth troubling about my appearance.

Katya, Lyuba and Volodya looked at me as St-Jérome led me by the arm through the music-room in exactly the same way as we looked at the convicts who were led past our windows on Mondays. And when I went up to grandmamma's chair intending to kiss her hand she turned away from me and hid her hand under her mantilla.

'Yes, my dear,' she said after a protracted silence during which she scrutinized me from head to foot with such a look that I did not know where to turn my eyes or what to do with my hands, 'you set great store on my affection for you, and are a real comfort to me, I must say. Monsieur St-Jérome, who at my request,' she added, drawling out each word, 'undertook your education, does not wish to remain in my house any longer. Why? Because of you, my dear. I hoped you would be grateful,' she continued after a pause and in a tone which showed that her speech had been prepared beforehand, 'for his care and trouble, that you would know how to appreciate his services, and instead of that you, you baby, you silly little boy, you actually dared to raise your hand against him. Very good! Excellent! I too begin to think that you are incapable of appreciating gentle treatment, that other, more elementary methods are required for you. Beg his pardon this instant,' she added in a stern and peremptory voice, pointing to St-Jérome. 'Do you hear?'

I looked in the direction indicated by grandmamma's finger and, catching sight of St-Jérome's coat, turned away and did not stir from the spot, feeling my heart sink again.

'Well? Don't you hear what I tell you?'

I trembled all over but did not move.

'Nikky!' said grandmamma, probably noticing the inward agony I was suffering. 'Nikky,' she repeated in a voice more tender than commanding, 'can this be you?'

'Grandmamma, I won't beg his pardon for anything in the world . . .' I said, suddenly stopping short for I felt that I should not be able to restrain the tears which were choking me, if I said another word.

'I order you, I ask you. What is the matter with you?'

'I . . . I . . . won't . . . I can't,' I got out, and the sobs which had accumulated in my breast suddenly broke down the barrier that held them back and I burst into a desperate flood of tears.

'*C'est ainsi que vous obéissez à votre seconde mère, c'est ainsi que vous reconnaissez ses bontés,*'[1] said St-Jérome in dramatic tones, '*à genoux!*'[2]

'Heavens above, if she could see this!' said grandmamma, turning away from me and wiping the tears that appeared in her eyes. 'If she saw this . . . all is for the best. No, she could never have survived such sorrow – never!'

And grandmamma wept more and more. I wept too but not for a second did I think of begging pardon.

1. This is the way you obey your second mother, this is how you repay her kindness.
2. On to your knees.

'*Tranquillisez-vous au nom du ciel, Madame la comtesse,*'[1] said St-Jérome.

But grandmamma no longer heard him; she covered her face with both hands and soon her sobs became hiccoughs and hysterics. Mimi and Gasha came running into the room with frightened faces, there was a smell of ammonia, and the whole house was filled with sounds of scurrying to and fro and whispering.

'Look at what you have done,' said St-Jérome, marching me upstairs.

'O God, what have I done! How terribly wicked I am!'

As soon as St-Jérome had gone downstairs after ordering me to my room, without thinking what I was doing I rushed to the great staircase which led to the front door.

Whether I intended to run away from home altogether or to drown myself, I don't remember. I only know that I sped farther and farther down the stairs, with my hands up to my face so as to see no one.

'Where are you going?' a familiar voice asked suddenly. 'You're just the one I want, my boy!'

I tried to run past but papa caught hold of my arm and said severely:

'Come with me, my good fellow! How dared you touch the portfolio in my study?' he said, pulling me after him into the small sitting-room. 'Well, have you nothing to say for yourself, eh?' he added, taking me by the ear.

'I am sorry,' I said. 'I don't know what possessed me.'

'Ah, you don't know what possessed you, don't know, don't know, don't know, don't know,' he repeated, giving my ear a tug at each word. 'Will you poke your nose where you have no business to in future? Will you? Will you?'

Although my ear hurt very badly I did not cry but experienced an agreeable feeling of moral relief. No sooner had papa let go my ear than I seized his hand and covered it with tears and kisses.

'Hurt me again,' I said through my tears, 'do it harder, make it hurt more, I am a good-for-nothing horrid miserable wretch!'

'What is the matter with you?' he said, slightly pushing me away.

'No, I won't leave go,' I said, clutching his coat. 'Everybody hates me, I know they do, but please, *please* listen to me. Protect me or turn me out of the house. I cannot live with him, *he* is always trying to humiliate me, he makes me go on my knees before him, wants to

1. Calm yourself for heaven's sake, countess.

thrash me. I can't bear it, I am not a little boy, I won't endure it – I shall die, I shall kill myself. *He* told grandmamma that I was a good-for-nothing, and now she is ill, she will die because of me. I . . . can't . . . with . . . him . . . *Please*, you thrash me . . . why do they tor . . . tor . . . torture me?'

Tears were choking me. I sat down on the sofa and, unable to say any more, fell with my head on his knees, sobbing so that it seemed to me I should die that very minute.

'What's it all about, little one?' asked papa sympathetically as he bent over me.

'Him, that bully . . . my tormentor . . . I shall die . . . Nobody loves me!' I gasped, and fell into convulsions.

Papa took me in his arms and carried me to my bedroom. I fell asleep.

When I awoke it was very late. A solitary candle burned by my bedside and our family doctor, Mimi and Lyuba were sitting in the room. It was obvious from their faces that they were alarmed by my condition. But I felt so well and my heart felt so light after my twelve hours' sleep that I could have sprung out of bed directly, had I not disliked the idea of upsetting their conviction that I was very ill.

17 · HATRED

Yes, it was real hatred – not the hatred we only read about in novels, which I do not believe in, hatred that is supposed to find satisfaction in doing some one harm – but the hatred that fills you with overpowering aversion for a person who, however, deserves your respect, yet whose hair, his neck, the way he walks, the sound of his voice, his whole person, his every gesture are repulsive to you, and at the same time some unaccountable force draws you to him and compels you to follow his slightest acts with uneasy attention. Such was the feeling I experienced for St-Jérome.

St-Jérome had been with us for eighteen months now. Today when I consider the man in cold blood I find that he was a good Frenchman, but French to the highest degree. He was not stupid, he was tolerably well informed, and he fulfilled his duties towards us conscientiously; but he possessed the distinctive traits of his fellow countrymen which are so different from the Russian character – he was shallow and selfish, vain, domineering and full of ignorant self-conceit. All this I heartily disliked. Needless to say, grandmamma had explained to him her views on corporal punishment and he dared not beat us; but in spite of this he often threatened us, especially me, with the rod, and pronounced the word *fouetter*[1] something like *fouatter* in a detestable manner and with an intonation which suggested that it would afford him the greatest pleasure to flog me.

I was not in the least afraid of the physical pain of the punishment – I had never experienced it – but the bare idea of being struck by St-Jérome threw me into paroxysms of suppressed despair and fury.

It had happened that Karl Ivanych in a moment of irritation had personally brought us to heel with a ruler or his braces, but that I can look back upon without the slightest anger. Even at the time I am speaking of (when I was fourteen), if Karl Ivanych had happened to give me a beating I would have taken it unperturbed. I was fond of Karl Ivanych, I remembered him as long as I remembered myself and was accustomed to regard him as one of the family; but St-Jérome was an arrogant self-satisfied man for whom I felt merely the involuntary respect which all *grown-ups* inspired in me. Karl Ivanych was a comical old 'school-usher' whom I loved from the bottom of my heart but whom in my childish comprehension of social standing ranked below us.

St-Jérome, on the other hand, was an educated handsome young dandy, trying to be anyone's equal. Karl Ivanych always scolded and punished us dispassionately; one saw that he considered it a necessary but disagreeable duty. St-Jérome, on the contrary, liked to play the part of lord and master: when he punished us it was plain that he did so rather for his own pleasure than for our good. He was carried away by his own importance. His florid French phrases, which he pronounced with a strong emphasis on the last syllable of every word, with circumflex accents, I found unspeakably obnoxious. When Karl Ivanych got cross he used to say 'play-acting', 'vicket poy', 'Spanish fly' (which he always called '*Spaniard*' fly). St-Jérome called us '*mauvais sujet, vilain garnement*'[2] and so forth – names which offended my self-respect.

Karl Ivanych used to make us kneel in the corner with our faces to the wall and the punishment lay in the physical pain occasioned by such an uncomfortable position. St-Jérome stuck out his chest, made a grandiose gesture with his hand and exclaimed in a theatrical voice: '*A*

1. To flog.
2. Bad lot, knave.

genoux, mauvais sujet!' ordering us to kneel in front of him and beg his pardon. The punishment lay in the humiliation.

They did not punish me, and no one so much as mentioned what had happened to me, but I could not forget all that I had suffered during those two days – the despair, the shame, the fear and the hatred. Although after that St-Jérome apparently washed his hands of me, and hardly concerned himself with me at all, I could not get into the way of regarding him with indifference. Every time our eyes happened to meet I felt that my look only too plainly expressed my animosity, and I hastened to assume a nonchalant air; but when I fancied that he saw through my pretence I blushed and had to turn away.

In short, it was a terrible trial to me to have anything to do with him.

18 · THE MAID'S ROOM

I began to feel more and more lonely and my chief enjoyment lay in solitary reflection and contemplation. The subject of my reflections I will speak of in the next chapter, but the scene of my contemplations was primarily the maids' room, where what was for me a most absorbing and touching romance was in progress. The heroine of this romance was, of course, Masha. She was in love with Vassily, who had known her before she came into service and who had then already promised to marry her. Fate which had parted them five years before had brought them together again in grandmamma's house but had put an obstacle in the way of their mutual affection in the person of Nikolai (Masha's uncle), who would not hear of his niece's marrying Vassily, whom he called *an incongruous ungovernable fellow*.

The obstacle thus placed in their way made Vassily, who up to that time had been somewhat cool and off-hand in his attitude, suddenly fall in love with Masha – as much in love as ever a domestic serf who works as a tailor in a pink shirt and with well-pomaded hair is capable of doing.

Though the manifestations of his love were very odd and unbecoming to a degree (for instance when he met Masha he always tried to inflict upon her some bodily pain, either giving her a pinch or a slap, or else squeezing her so hard that she could hardly breathe) he really did love her, as was proved by the fact that from the day Nikolai finally refused his niece's hand the grief-stricken Vassily took to drink and began to hang about in ale-houses and create disturbances – in a word, to behave himself so badly that he more than once underwent the humiliating punishment of being locked up at the police-station. But these misdemeanours and their consequences only served to enhance his merit in Masha's sight and made her love him still more. When Vassily was in the lock-up Masha wept for days on end without drying her eyes, bemoaning her hard lot to Gasha (who took a lively interest in the unfortunate lovers) and, heedless of her uncle's scoldings and the beatings he gave her, she would steal off to the police-station to visit and console her swain.

Do not disdain, reader, the company to which I introduce you. If the chords of love and compassion have not gone slack and feeble in your soul you will hear even in the maids' room sounds which will cause them to vibrate again. Whether you care to follow me or not, I am going to the staircase landing from which I can see all that goes on in the maids' room. There is the ledge projecting from the stove on which stand a flat-iron, a dressmaker's papier-mâché dummy with a broken nose, a wash-tub and a jug; over there is the window-sill with a bit of black wax, a skein of silk, a half-eaten green cucumber and a sweetmeat box scattered about in disorder; on that side is the large red table on which lies some unfinished needlework under a chintz-covered brick, where *she* sits in the pink gingham dress I like best and the blue kerchief which particularly attracts my attention. *She* is sewing, occasionally stopping to scratch her head with her needle or to trim the candle, and I look on and think: 'Why was she not born a lady, with those bright blue eyes, thick chestnut plait and magnificent bosom? How well she would look sitting in the drawing-room with pink ribbons on her head and wearing a crimson silk gown – not like Mimi's but like one I saw on the Tverskoy Boulevard. She would have worked at an embroidery-frame and I would have watched her reflected in the looking-glass and been ready to do whatever she wanted – help her on with her cloak and myself hand the dishes to her at dinner...'

And what a tipsy face and disgusting figure that Vassily has, in his tight coat put on over the dirty pink shirt he wears outside his trousers! In every movement of his body, in every curve of his back, I fancy I see unmistakable signs of the revolting punishment which has over-taken him.

'What, again, Vasya?' said Masha on one occasion, sticking her needle into the cushion and not looking up at Vassily as he entered.

'Well what of it? As if any good thing could come from *him*!' answered Vassily. 'If only he would decide one way or the other. As it is, I'm going to the dogs, and all through *him*.'

'Would you like some tea?' asked Nadezha, another of the house-maids.

'Thank you kindly. And why does he hate me, that old thief of an uncle of yours? What for? Because I have proper clothes, because I'm a swell, or the way I walk. That's it. Oh well!' Vassily concluded, snapping his fingers.

'We must be patient,' said Masha, biting off a thread, 'but you are always so . . .'

'I can't stand it any longer, that's what it is.'

At that moment the door of grandmamma's room banged and Gasha's grumbling voice was heard as she came up the stairs.

'Give satisfaction indeed, when she doesn't know herself what she wants . . . What a cursed life, no better than a galley-slave's! If only she would make up her mind – the Lord forgive me for thinking it,' she muttered, swinging her arms.

'My respects to you, Agatha Mihailovna,' said Vassily, rising as she entered.

'Oh, get along! I've no time for your respects,' she replied, looking at him darkly. 'And why do you come here? Is the maids' room a place for men to come?'

'I wanted to see how you were,' said Vassily timidly.

'I shall soon breathe my last, that's how I am,' screamed Agatha Mihailovna still more angrily and at the top of her voice.

Vassily laughed.

'It's no laughing matter, and when I tell you to take yourself off, then quick march! Look at the heathen! Wants to marry, the scoun-drel! Now then, out of here, quick march!'

And Agatha Mihailovna stumped past to her own room and slammed the door so violently that the window-pane rattled.

She could be heard for a long time behind the partition, abusing everything and everybody, cursing her own life, flinging things about and pulling the ears of her pet cat. Finally the door opened a crack and the cat, mewing piteously, was hurled out by the tail.

'It looks as if I had better come some other day for a cup of tea,' said Vassily in a whisper. 'See you at a happier time!'

'Never mind her,' said Nadezha with a wink. 'I'll just go and see if the samovar is boiling.'

'Yes, I'll make an end of it somehow,' continued Vassily, seating himself closer to Masha as soon as Nadezha had left the room. 'Either I'll go straight to the countess and tell her, "It's like this, and it's like that," or else . . . I'll throw everything up and run off to the ends of the earth, I swear I will.'

'And I'll be left here . . .'

'It's only you I'm sorry to leave: if it wasn't for you I'd have been at large in the wide world lo-ong ago!'

'Why don't you bring me your shirts to wash, Vasya?' said Masha after a momentary silence. 'Just look how dirty this one is,' she added, taking hold of his shirt-collar.

Just then grandmamma's bell rang downstairs and Gasha came out of her room.

'Now then, you impudent fellow, what are you after with her?' she said, pushing Vassily, who had risen hurriedly when he saw her, to the door. 'See what a pretty pass you've brought the girl to, and now here you are again. I suppose you enjoy seeing her cry, you brazen face, you. Take yourself off. And don't set foot here again. And what good has he ever done you?' she went on, turning to Masha. 'Hasn't your uncle beaten you enough today on account of him? No, you will have your own way: "I won't marry any one but Vassily Gruskov." Fool that you are!'

'No, I won't have any one else. I don't love no one but him even if you kill me for it,' pronounced Masha, suddenly bursting into tears.

I looked long at Masha as she lay on a trunk wiping the tears with her kerchief, and I tried by all manner of means to alter my opinion of Vassily, hoping to discover the point of view from which he appeared so attractive to her. But though I genuinely sympathized with Masha in her distress I could not for the life of me understand how so bewitching a creature as I considered her to be could love Vassily.

'When I am grown up,' I thought to myself after I had gone back upstairs to my room, 'Petrovskoe will belong to me, and Vassily and Masha will be my serfs. I shall be sitting in my study smoking my pipe. Masha will pass with a flat-iron on her way to the kitchen. "Send Masha to me." She will come, and there will be no one else in the room . . . Suddenly Vassily will come in and seeing Masha he'll say: "It's all up with me!" and Masha will begin to cry too, and I shall say:

"Vassily, I know you love her and she loves you. Here are a thousand roubles for you. Marry her, and God grant you happiness," and I shall depart into the sitting-room.' Among the innumerable thoughts and fancies that pass through the mind and imagination without a trace there are some which do leave deep and sensitive furrows, so that often when you no longer remember the whole gist of the thought you remember that you had something good in your mind – you are conscious of the mark made by the thought and you try to repeat it. A similar profound impression has ever since remained in my heart of the idea I then had of sacrificing my own feelings for the sake of Masha's happiness, which she could find only in marriage with Vassily.

19 · BOYHOOD

My readers will scarcely believe me when I tell them what were the favourite and most constantly recurring subjects of reflection during my boyhood, so incompatible were they with my age and situation. I think, however, that the incongruity of a man's situation with his moral activity is the surest proof of his sincerity.

For the space of a year, during which I led a solitary interior life, shut in on myself, all the abstract questions concerning man's destiny, the future life, the immortality of the soul, had presented themselves to me, and my weak childish intellect with all the ardour of inexperience strove to solve these problems, the formulation of which constitutes the highest level human intelligence can reach but the solution of which is beyond it.

It seems to me that the human mind in each separate individual follows in its evolution the same lines along which it has developed during whole generations; that the ideas which serve as basis for different philosophical theories are inalienable attributes of the mind; but that each man must be more or less conscious of them before he can know of the existence of the philosophical theories.

These thoughts presented themselves to me so clearly and forcibly that I even tried to apply them to life, imagining that I was *the first* to discover such great and important truths.

At one time it occurred to me that happiness did not depend on external causes but on our attitude to those causes; that a man who could grow used to suffering need not be unhappy – and to harden myself I would hold Tatishchev's lexicon out at arm's length for five minutes at a time (despite the horrible pain) or go into the box-room and scourge my bare back with a rope so severely that the tears involuntarily appeared in my eyes.

Another time, suddenly bethinking me that death awaited me at any hour, at any moment, I came to the conclusion – wondering that people had not realized it before – that one can only be happy by enjoying the present and not thinking of the future, and acting under the influence of this idea for two or three days I cast my lesson books aside and spent my time lying on my bed indulging in a novel and eating gingerbread made with honey, bought with the last money I possessed.

Another time, standing before the blackboard and drawing various figures on it with chalk, the thought suddenly struck me: 'Why does symmetry please the eye? What is symmetry?' – 'It is an innate feeling,' I answered myself. 'What is it based on? Is there symmetry in everything in life? On the contrary, this is life' – and I drew an oval on the board. 'When life ends the soul passes into eternity – here is eternity'; and I drew a line from one side of the oval figure right to the edge of the board. 'Why is there no corresponding line on the other side? And yes, indeed, how can eternity be only on one side? We must have existed before this life, though we have lost the recollection of it.'

This argument, which seemed to me exceedingly novel and clear and whose logic I can now perceive only with difficulty, pleased me mightily, and taking a sheet of paper I thought I would put it all down in writing; but thereupon such a host of ideas surged into my head that I was obliged to get up and walk about the room. When I came to the window my attention fell upon the dray-horse that the coachman was just putting to the cart to fetch water, and my thoughts all centred on the question: what animal or man would that horse's soul enter when it died? Just then Volodya, as he passed through the room, smiled on seeing me absorbed in speculative thoughts, and that smile sufficed to make me feel that all I had been thinking about was the most awful nonsense.

I have related this occasion, which for some reason I remember, only in order to show the reader the nature of my philosophizings.

But not one of these philosophical theories held me so much as scepticism, which at one time brought me to the verge of insanity. I fancied that besides myself nobody and nothing existed in the universe, that objects were not real at all but images which appeared when I directed my attention to them, and that so soon as I stopped thinking of them these images immediately vanished. In short, I came to the same conclusion as Schelling, that objects do not exist but only my relation to them exists. There were moments when I became so deranged by this *idée fixe* that I would glance sharply round in some opposite direction, hoping to catch unawares the void (the *néant*) where I was not.

What a pitiful trivial spring of moral activity is the mind of man!

My feeble intellect could not penetrate the impenetrable, and in that back-breaking effort lost one after the other the convictions which, for my life's happiness, I ought never to have dared disturb.

All this weary mental struggle yielded me nothing save an artful elasticity of mind which weakened my will-power, and a habit of perpetually dissecting and analysing, which destroyed spontaneity of feeling and clarity of reason.

Abstract speculations are generated in consequence of man's capacity by intuition to apprehend the state of his soul at a given moment, and transfer that apprehension to his memory. My fondness for abstract reasoning developed my conscious being to such an unnatural degree that frequently, thinking about the simplest things, I would fall into the vicious circle of analysis of my thoughts, entirely losing sight of the question that had occupied my mind at the outset, and thinking, instead, about what I was thinking about. Asking myself: 'Of what am I thinking?' I would answer: 'I think of what I am thinking. And now what am I thinking of? I think that I am thinking of what I am thinking of.' And so on. I was at my wits' end.

However, the philosophical discoveries I made vastly flattered my vanity: I often imagined myself a great man discovering truths for the benefit of humanity, and gazed upon other mortals with a proud consciousness of my own worth; but strangely enough when I encountered those other mortals I felt shy of each and every one, and the higher I rated myself in my own estimation the less capable I was not only of displaying any consciousness of merit but even of schooling myself not to blush for every word and movement, however simple and unimportant.

20 · VOLODYA

Yes, the farther I proceed in the description of this period of my life the more painful and difficult it becomes for me. Too rarely among my memories of this time do I come upon moments of that genuine warmth of feeling which so brightly and constantly illumined my early years. I find myself wanting to hasten rapidly through the desert of my boyhood, the sooner to arrive at the happy time when once again truly tender, noble sentiments cast a rich lustre on the last phase of my boyhood, and laid the foundation for a new era full of charm and poetry – the period of adolescence.

I will not pursue my recollections hour by hour but throw a cursory glance only over the most important of them, from the point to which I have brought my narrative to the time when I became friends with a remarkable man who exercised a decisive and beneficial influence upon my character and ideas.

Volodya is soon to enter the University; masters come to give him private lessons, and I listen with envy and unwilling respect as he taps the blackboard boldly with the chalk and talks of functions, sines, co-ordinates and so on, which seem to me terms pertaining to inaccessible wisdom. And now, one Sunday after dinner, all the masters and two professors assemble in grandmamma's room, and in the presence of papa and several visitors have a rehearsal of the University examinations in which, to grandmamma's great delight, Volodya evinces extraordinary learning. I am asked questions too on some subjects but put up a very poor show and the professors plainly try to conceal my ignorance from grandmamma, which makes me still more ashamed of myself. However, not much attention is paid to me: I am only fifteen and so have another year before me to the examination. Volodya only comes down to dinner and spends whole days and even the evenings upstairs at his studies, not because he is made to but of his own choice. He is extremely ambitious and wants to pass the examination not just satisfactorily but with flying colours.

But now the first day of the examination has arrived. Volodya puts on a dark-blue swallow-tail coat with gilt buttons, a gold watch and patent-leather boots. Papa's phaeton is brought to the door; Nikolai throws back the apron and Volodya and St-Jérome drive off to the

University. The girls, especially Katya, look out of the window with beaming rapturous faces at Volodya's graceful form as he gets into the carriage. Papa says: 'Please God he does well! Please God he does well!' and grandmamma, who has also dragged herself to the window, with tears in her eyes continues to make the sign of the cross towards Volodya until the phaeton disappears round the corner of the street, and she murmurs something.

Volodya returns. Everyone impatiently inquires: 'How many marks did you get?' but it is evident at once from his happy face that all is well. Volodya got a five. Next day he is seen off with the same good wishes and the same anxiety for his success, and welcomed back with the same eagerness and delight. This is repeated for nine days. On the tenth day he has to face the last and most difficult examination of all – the one in Divinity, and we all stand at the window and watch for him with greater impatience than ever. Two o'clock, and still no Volodya.

'O Lord! Gracious goodness! Here they are, here they are!' screams Lyuba with her face glued to the window.

Sure enough, there is Volodya sitting in the phaeton with St-Jérome but no longer in his dark blue coat and grey cap but in the uniform of a University student with its blue-embroidered collar, three-cornered hat and short gilt sword at his side.

'Oh, if only *she* were alive!' cries grandmamma, seeing Volodya in his uniform, and falls into a swoon.

Volodya runs into the hall with a radiant face, hugs and kisses me, Lyuba, Mimi and Katya, who blushes to the tips of her ears. Volodya is beside himself with happiness. And how fine he looks in that uniform! How well the blue collar goes with his budding dark moustaches! What a long slender waist he has, and how gracefully he walks! On that memorable day we all dine in grandmamma's room, our faces beaming with joy, and with the pudding course the butler, looking decorously majestic and at the same time delighted, brings in a bottle of champagne wrapped in a napkin. Grandmamma for the first time since *maman*'s death takes champagne and drinks a whole glass as she congratulates Volodya, and again sheds tears of happiness as she looks at him. Volodya now drives out alone in his own carriage, receives his *own* friends in his *own* apartments, smokes tobacco, goes to balls, and once with my own eyes I saw him and his companions drink two bottles of champagne in his room, and heard them toast some mysterious personages at each glass, and quarrel as to who was to get *le fond de la bouteille*.[1] He dines regularly at home, however, and after dinner settles himself in the sitting-room as of old, and is for ever engaged in some secret discussion with Katya; but so far as I can hear – for I take no part in their conversation – they merely talk about the heroes and heroines in the novels they have read, about jealousy and love, and I can't begin to understand what interest they can find in such conversations, and why they smile so archly and argue with such heat.

In general I notice that besides the friendship natural between young people who have been brought up together there are other and strange ties between them which set them apart from us and in a mysterious way unite them to each other.

21 · KATYA AND LYUBA

Katya is sixteen; she is grown up. The angular figure, the shyness and awkwardness of movement usual in girls in the transition stage have given place to the harmonious freshness and grace of a budding flower; but she has not changed. The same light-blue eyes and smiling look, the same straight nose almost in line with her forehead, with the firm nostrils, and the little mouth with its gay smile, the same tiny dimples in the clear rosy cheeks, the same small white hands ... and I don't know why but the description 'pretty little creature' still suits her remarkably well. The only new things are her thick plait of light-brown hair which she wears in a grown-up fashion and her youthful bosom, the advent of which is plainly a source of pleasure and embarrassment to her.

Though she and Lyuba have grown up and been educated together Lyuba is in all respects a very different sort of girl.

Lyuba is not tall and as a result of rickets her toes turn in, and she has a very ugly figure. Her one beauty is her eyes, and her eyes really are beautiful – large, black and having such an indefinably lovely expression of dignity and naïveté that they attract everybody's attention. Lyuba is natural and unaffected in everything, whereas Katya always seems as though she were trying to be like some one else. Lyuba always looks people straight in the face and sometimes fixes them so long with her huge black eyes that she gets scolded for doing so and reminded that it is not polite. Katya, on the contrary, droops her lashes, screws

1. The last dregs.

up her eyes and declares that she is short-sighted, though I know very well that her sight is perfectly good. Lyuba does not like making herself conspicuous before strangers, and if any one kisses her when visitors are present she pouts and says she can't bear *sentiment*. Katya, on the other hand, is always particularly affectionate to Mimi in the presence of guests, and likes walking up and down the ball-room with her arm round some other girl's waist. Lyuba is a dreadful giggler and sometimes runs about the room in convulsions of laughter, gesticulating; but Katya will cover her mouth with her pocket-handkerchief or her hands when she begins to laugh. Lyuba always sits bolt upright and walks with her arms hanging down. Katya holds her head a little on one side and walks with folded hands. Lyuba is always terribly pleased when she manages to converse with a grown-up man and says she is absolutely determined to marry a hussar; but Katya says all men are horrid and she is never going to marry, and she looks quite different when any man speaks to her, as if she were afraid of something. Lyuba is always indignant with Mimi for lacing her up in tight stays so that she 'can't breathe', and she is fond of eating; while Katya often thrusts a finger under the point of her bodice to show us how loose it is for her, and she eats very little indeed. Lyuba likes drawing heads; Katya only draws flowers and butterflies. Lyuba plays Field's concertos very nicely and some of Beethoven's sonatas; Katya plays variations and waltzes, cannot keep time, thumps and uses the pedal incessantly – and, before beginning to play any piece, with much feeling strikes three chords in *arpeggio* . . .

But in those days Katya seemed to me more of a grown-up person, and so I liked her best.

22 · PAPA

Papa has been in particularly good spirits since Volodya entered the University, and comes oftener than usual to have dinner at grandmamma's. However, the reason for his good humour, as I have heard from Nikolai, is that lately he has won very large sums at cards. It even happens that before going to his club in the evening he comes to see us, sits down at the piano, gathers us round him and, tapping the floor with his soft boots (he hates heels and never has any on his boots) sings gipsy songs. And then you should have seen the comical rapture of

Lyuba, his pet, who in her turn worships him. Sometimes he will come into the schoolroom and listen with a grave face as I say my lessons, but from some of the terms he uses to correct me I perceive that he does not know much of what I am being taught. Sometimes he winks slyly and makes signs to us when grandmamma begins to scold and get into a rage with everybody without reason. 'Well, we *did* catch it, children!' he says afterwards. On the whole he is gradually descending in my eyes from the unapproachable pinnacle upon which my childish imagination had placed him. I kiss his large white hand with the same sincere love and respect, but now I allow myself to consider and pass judgment on his behaviour, and involuntarily thoughts occur to me in regard to him which scare me. Never shall I forget one particular incident which suggested thoughts of this kind and caused me much moral suffering.

Late one evening he came into the drawing-room in a black dress-coat and white waistcoat to take Volodya, who was in his room dressing, to a ball. Grandmamma was waiting in her bedroom for Volodya to come and show himself (she always used to call him to her before every ball, to bestow upon him her blessing and inspect him and instruct him as to conduct). Mimi and Katya were walking up and down the music-room which was lighted by a single lamp, while Lyuba sat at the piano practising Field's second concerto, *maman*'s favourite piece.

I have never seen such a family likeness as there was between my sister and my mother. The resemblance lay neither in the face nor the figure but in some intangible likeness in the hands, in the way of walking, in the tones of the voice especially, and in certain expressions. When Lyuba was vexed and said: 'They keep one waiting a whole age,' she pronounced the words 'a whole age', which *maman* had also been in the habit of using, so that one almost heard *maman*'s slow way of saying 'wh-o-le a-age'; but the likeness was most extraordinary of all when she was at the piano, when her every movement was the same: Lyuba smoothed the folds of her dress in exactly the same manner, turned the pages from the top with her left hand as *maman* had, and pounded the keys with her fist when she was vexed at not being able to master a difficult passage and cried, 'Oh dear!' and there was the same inimitable delicacy and precision in her playing of the beautiful piece of Field's so appropriately called *jeu perlé*, the charm of which not all the hocus-pocus of modern pianists can make us forget.

Papa entered the room with his short quick steps and went up to Lyuba, who stopped playing when she saw him.

'No, go on, Lyuba, go on,' he said, making her sit. 'You know how I like to hear you . . .'

Lyuba continued her playing and papa sat opposite her for a long time, leaning his head on his hand; then giving his shoulders a sudden twitch he rose and began pacing up and down the room. Every time he approached the piano he paused and gazed intently at Lyuba. By his movements and the way he walked I could see that he was in a state of agitation. After several turns about the room he stopped behind Lyuba's chair, kissed her dark head and then wheeling round resumed his pacing. When Lyuba finished the piece and went up to him to ask: 'Was it all right?' he silently took her head in his two hands and began kissing her on the forehead and eyes with such tenderness as I had never seen in him before.

'Oh my goodness, you are crying!' said Lyuba suddenly, letting go of his watch-chain and fixing her large wondering eyes on his face. 'Forgive me, dearest papa, I had quite forgotten that was *mama's* piece.'

'No, my dear, you must play it as often as possible,' he said in a voice quivering with emotion. 'If you only knew what a comfort it is for me to weep with you . . .'

He kissed her again and with an effort to master his feelings went with a jerk of his shoulder out of the door that led through the passage to Volodya's room.

'Voldemar! Will you soon be ready?' he shouted, stopping in the middle of the corridor. Just then Masha, the maid, was passing and, taken aback on seeing her master, lowered her eyes and tried to go round him. He stopped her.

'You grow prettier every day,' he said, leaning towards her.

Masha blushed and hung her head still lower.

'Let me pass,' she whispered.

'Come now, Voldemar, will you be long?' papa repeated, jerking his shoulder and coughing when Masha slipped past and he caught sight of me.

I love my father, but a man's mind exists independently of his heart and often harbours thoughts which wound the feelings and are incomprehensible and harsh. And though I do my best to keep them at bay it is thoughts such as these that come to me . . .

23 · GRANDMAMMA

Grandmamma grows weaker every day. The sound of her bell, Gasha's grumbling voice and the slamming of doors are heard more frequently in her apartment, and she no longer receives us in her sitting-room seated in her easy chair but in her bedroom on the high bed with lace-trimmed pillows. When I greet her I notice a pale yellowish shiny swelling on her hand, and there is the same oppressive odour in her room that I had smelt five years before in mamma's room. The doctor comes to see her three times a day and there has been more than one consultation. But her disposition, her haughty formal manner towards every one in the house and especially papa have not changed at all: she still drawls her words as much as ever, raises her eyebrows, and says: 'my dear'.[1]

And now we have not been allowed to see her for several days and one morning during lesson hours St-Jérome offers to let me go out for a drive with Lyuba and Katya. Although I notice as we get into the sledge that the street outside grandmother's window is strewn with straw, and that some men in dark-blue are standing about near our gates, the reason never dawns on me why we are being sent out at such an unusual hour. During the whole drive Lyuba and I, we don't know why, are in that particular state of high spirits when the least trifle, the least word or movement, starts one laughing.

A hawker clutching his tray crosses the street at a trot and we burst out laughing. A poor tattered sledge-driver, flourishing the ends of his reins, overtakes us at a gallop and we shout with laughter. Filip's whip catches in the sledge-runner; he turns round and says: 'Drat the thing!' and we die of laughing. Mimi looks displeased and remarks that it is only *silly people* who laugh for no reason, and Lyuba, crimson in the face with suppressed mirth, casts a sidelong glance at me. Our eyes meet and we break into such Homeric laughter that the tears fill our eyes and we cannot restrain our paroxysms although they nearly choke us. We have no sooner quieted down to some extent than I look at Lyuba and utter a private catchword which has been in favour among us for some time, and we are off again.

1. Not always a term of endearment, especially when used without the name of the person addressed.

As we drive up to the house on the way back I open my mouth to make a fine face at Lyuba when my eyes are startled by a black coffin-lid leaning against one panel of our front door, and my mouth remains fixed in its distorted grimace.

'*Votre grand'mère est morte!*'[1] says St-Jérome with a pale face, coming out to meet us.

All the time grandmamma's body is in the house I have an oppressive feeling of fear of death – that is, the dead body reminds me vividly and unpleasantly that I too must die some day. It is a feeling that is often somehow taken for grief. I do not regret grandmamma, indeed I doubt whether any one sincerely regrets her. Though the house is full of mourning callers nobody regrets her death except one person, whose vehement grief surprises me beyond expression. And that person is her maid, Gasha, who retires to the garret, locks herself in, weeps incessantly, curses herself, tears her hair, is deaf to all remonstrance and says that death is the only consolation left her after the loss of her beloved mistress.

I repeat once more that inconsistency in matters of feeling is the surest sign of their genuineness.

Grandmamma is no more but her memory still lives in our house and there is much discussion about her. These discussions relate chiefly to the will she made before her death and which nobody knew anything about except her executor, Prince Ivan Ivanych. I notice a certain agitation among grandmamma's serfs and often hear surmises as to whose property they will become, and I confess I cannot help being glad that we are to receive an inheritance.

Six weeks later Nikolai, who is always the one that knows the news of the house, tells me grandmamma has left everything to Lyuba, appointing Prince Ivan Ivanych and not papa her guardian until her marriage.

24 · MYSELF

Only a few months remain before I enter the University. I am studying hard. I not only await my masters without dread but even find a certain pleasure in my lessons.

I like reciting clearly and accurately the lesson I have studied. I am

1. Your grandmother is dead!

preparing for the Faculty of Mathematics, and to tell the truth the sole
reason for my choice is that I delight in the terms 'sines', 'tangent',
'differentials', 'integrals' and so on.

I am much shorter than Volodya, broad-shouldered and muscular.
I am as ugly as ever and still make myself miserable over my ugliness.
I try to appear original. One thing consoles me, and that is, that papa
once said I had a *clever phiz*, and I quite believe it.

St-Jérome is pleased with me and praises me, and I no longer hate
him: indeed, when he sometimes says that *with my abilities and my
intelligence* it would be a shame not to do this or that, it even seems to
me that I like him.

I have long ago given up watching the maids' room for I should now
be ashamed to hide behind doors, and besides, the certainty that Masha
really loves Vassily has contributed not a little, I must confess, towards
cooling my ardour. I am finally cured of my unfortunate attachment
by their marriage, papa's consent for which I obtain after Vassily
asks me to intercede for him.

When the newly-married pair come to thank papa, bringing a tray
with various bonbons on it, and Masha in a cap with blue ribbons
also thanks us all for something, kissing each of us on the shoulder, I
am only conscious of the rose pomade on her hair, but not of the least
emotion.

On the whole I am beginning to get the better of my boyish defects,
with the exception, however, of the principal one, which is fated to do
me a great deal of harm in the course of my life – my tendency to
philosophize.

25 · VOLODYA'S FRIENDS

Although in the company of Volodya's acquaintances I played a role
wounding to my vanity I liked to sit in his room when he had visitors
and silently watch all that went on. The two who came most frequently
were a military adjutant called Dubkov and a student, Prince Nekhlyudov, Dubkov was a small sinewy dark-haired man, no longer in
his first youth, with rather short legs but not bad-looking and always
high-spirited. He was one of those people with limited natures who
are particularly attractive because of their limitations – who are
incapable of seeing both sides of any question and are always allowing
themselves to be carried away. The judgments of such people are

often one-sided and mistaken, yet always sincere and captivating. Even their narrow egoism somehow seems excusable and attractive. Besides this, Dubkov had a two-fold fascination for Volodya and me – his military appearance and still more his years, which young people are apt to confuse with the *comme il faut* so highly esteemed at that age. And in fact Dubkov really was what is considered 'un homme comme il faut'. The only thing I did not like was that when Dubkov was present Volodya sometimes looked as if he were ashamed of me for my most innocent of actions, and still more for my youthfulness.

Nekhlyudov was not good-looking: his small grey eyes, low straight forehead and disproportionately long arms and legs could not be called handsome. His only good points were his remarkable height, his delicate complexion and his fine teeth. But such an original and energetic expression was imparted to his face by his narrow sparkling eyes and his volatile smile, at times stern, at others childishly vague, that it was impossible to pass him by unnoticed.

He was apparently very bashful, for every trifle made him blush to the tips of his ears; but his shyness did not resemble mine. The more he blushed the more determined he looked, as if he were angry with himself for his own weakness.

Though he appeared to be great friends with Dubkov and Volodya it was evident that it was only chance that had brought them together. Their tastes were entirely different: Volodya and Dubkov seemed afraid of anything resembling serious discussion or sentiment; Nekhlyudov, on the contrary, was all excitement and enthusiasm, and would often in spite of their ridicule plunge into dissertations on philosophical matters or matters of sentiment. Volodya and Dubkov were fond of talking about the objects of their affection (and they were at times suddenly in love with several ladies, and both of them with the same ladies). But Nekhlyudov was always very angry when they alluded to his love for a certain 'lady of the chestnut locks'.

Volodya and Dubkov often allowed themselves to make affectionate fun of their relations, but any disparagement of an aunt for whom he had a kind of ecstatic adoration could send Nekhlyudov quite beside himself. Volodya and Dubkov used to drive somewhere after supper without Nekhlyudov, and call him 'a fair maiden'.

Prince Nekhlyudov impressed me from the first both by his conversation and by his appearance. But though I found much in his disposition that accorded with my own – or perhaps on that very account

– the feelings he inspired in me when I first saw him were far from friendly.

I did not like his quick glance, his firm voice, his proud mien and, above all, the complete indifference with which he treated me. Often during a conversation I burned to contradict him; to punish his pride I wanted to get the better of him in an argument – to prove to him that I was clever though he did not choose to notice me. Shyness, however, restrained me.

26 · DISCUSSIONS

Volodya, lying with his feet up on the sofa and leaning his head on his arm, was reading a French novel when I paid my usual visit to his room after my evening studies. He raised his head for a second to glance at me and resumed his reading – a most simple and natural movement but one which caused me to blush. His glance seemed to inquire why I had come, and I construed the quick lowering of his head into a wish to conceal from me the meaning of his glance. This tendency to attribute a meaning to the simplest movement was characteristic of me at that period. I went to the table and picked up a book too but, before beginning to read, it occurred to me how ridiculous it was that we should not exchange a word when we had not seen each other all day.

'Will you be at home this evening?'

'I don't know. Why?'

'Oh, nothing,' I said, seeing that the conversation flagged before it started, and began to read.

Oddly enough, Volodya and I could spend hours on end without speaking if we were alone together but the presence of a third person, even a taciturn one, was enough to set us going on the most interesting and varied discussions. We felt that we knew each other too well. And to know a person either too well or too little acts as a bar to intimacy.

'Is Volodya at home?' we heard Dubkov's voice in the hall.

'Yes,' said Volodya, putting his feet down and laying his book on the table.

Dubkov and Nekhlyudov came in wearing overcoats and hats.

'What do you say, Volodya, shall we go to the theatre?'

'No, I can't spare the time,' said Volodya, turning red.

'Oh, what stuff! Do let's go.'

'Anyway, I haven't a ticket.'

'You can get as many tickets as you like at the door.'

'Wait, I'll be back in a minute,' replied Volodya evasively, and jerking his shoulder he left the room.

I knew Volodya was very keen to go to the theatre as Dubkov suggested and that he was refusing simply because he had no money; and that now he had gone to ask the butler to lend him five roubles till he received his next allowance.

'How are you, *diplomat*?' asked Dubkov, giving me his hand.

Volodya's friends called me 'diplomat' because once after dinner when they were there grandmamma had happened to say, speaking about our futures, that Volodya would go into the army but that she hoped to see me a diplomat in a black dress-coat with my hair done *à la coq*, the two essential requirements in her opinion of the diplomatic service.

'Where has Volodya gone?' Nekhlyudov asked me.

'I don't know,' I replied, blushing at the thought that they probably guessed why Volodya had left the room.

'I expect he hasn't any money. Am I right? Oh you *diplomat*,' he added, interpreting my smile as an affirmative. 'I haven't any money either. Have you, Dubkov?'

'Let's see,' said Dubkov, taking out his purse and very carefully feeling the few small coins with his squat little fingers. 'Here's five kopecks, here's a twenty, and the rest f-f-flo-wn!' he said, making a comical gesture with his hand.

At that moment Volodya entered the room.

'Well, are we going?'

'No.'

'What an odd fellow you are!' said Nekhlyudov. 'Why don't you say you have no money? Take my ticket if you like!'

'But what about you?'

'He can go to his cousin's box,' said Dubkov.

'No, I shan't go at all.'

'Why not?'

'Because as you know I don't like boxes.'

'Why don't you?'

'I don't like them. Sitting in a box makes me feel awkward.'

'The same old thing again! I don't understand why you should feel awkward where every one is glad to see you. It's ridiculous, *mon cher*.'

'What's to be done, *si je suis timide!*[1] I am sure you never blushed in your life but I do all the time, at the merest trifle,' he said, blushing as he spoke.

'*Savez-vous d'où vient votre timidité . . . D'un excès d'amour propre, mon cher,*'[2] said Dubkov condescendingly.

'What has *excès d'amour propre* to do with it?' retorted Nekhlyudov, stung to the quick. 'On the contrary, I am shy because I have too little *amour propre*; I always fancy that people must find it disagreeable, tiresome, to be with me . . . that's why . . .'

'Get changed now, Volodya,' said Dubkov, taking Volodya by the shoulders and pulling his coat off. 'Ignat, get your master ready!'

'Therefore it often happens with me . . .' Nekhlyudov went on.

But Dubkov was no longer listening to him. 'Trala-la-ta-ra-ra-la-la,' and he hummed a tune.

'You haven't escaped,' said Nekhlyudov, 'I'll prove to you that shyness does *not* proceed from *amour propre.*'

'You will, if you come along with us.'

'I have told you I'm not going.'

'Well stay here then and prove it to the diplomat; and when we return he shall tell us all about it.'

'So I will,' rejoined Nekhlyudov with childish obstinacy. 'Only come back soon . . .'

'What do you think? Am I vain?' he said, seating himself beside me.

Though I had made up my mind on this point I was so overcome with shyness at his unexpected appeal to me that I could not answer immediately.

'I think you are,' I said, feeling my voice tremble and the colour flooding my face at the thought that the time had come to prove to him I was *clever*. 'I think that every one is vain and that everything a man does is done out of *amour propre.*'

'What is *amour propre* according to you?' asked Nekhlyudov, smiling somewhat disdainfully as it seemed to me.

'*Amour propre,*' said I, 'is the conviction that I am better and wiser than everyone else.'

'But how can everybody be convinced of that?'

'Oh, I don't know, but whether it is correct or not no one but me

1. If I am shy.
2. Do you know where that shyness of yours comes from? From an excess of *amour propre*, my dear fellow.

will ever confess to it; I am convinced that I am cleverer than any one else in the world, and I am sure you think the same about yourself.'

'No, I must say that I for one have met people I acknowledged to be cleverer than myself,' said Nekhlyudov.

'Impossible,' I replied decidedly.

'Can you really think so?' said Nekhlyudov, looking at me intently.

'Quite seriously,' I answered.

And then an idea suddenly occurred to me which I immediately proceeded to expound.

'I'll prove it to you. Why do we love ourselves more than others? ... Because we consider ourselves better and more worthy of being loved. If we thought others better than ourselves we should love them more than ourselves, but that never happens. And even if it does, I am right all the same,' I added with an involuntary smile of self-satisfaction.

Nekhlyudov was silent for a moment.

'I never thought you were so clever,' he said with such a sweet good-natured smile that I straightway felt as pleased as Punch.

Praise acts so powerfully not only on the feelings but on the mind, too, that under its pleasant influence I felt as if I had become much wiser, and thought followed thought in my brain with inconceivable rapidity. From *amour propre* we passed without noticing it to love, a theme which was apparently inexhaustible. Though our arguments must have sounded sheer nonsense to any one listening – so obscure and one-sided were they – for us they possessed a lofty significance. Our minds were so well attuned that the lightest touch on any chord in one of us evoked response in the other. We found satisfaction in this mutual echoing of the diverse chords we touched in the course of our conversation. We felt we had neither words nor time enough to express to one another all the thoughts which clamoured for utterance.

27 · THE BEGINNING OF OUR FRIENDSHIP

From that day a rather strange but very pleasant relationship was established between Dmitri Nekhlyudov and myself. When other people were present he paid hardly any attention to me; but as soon as we happened to be alone we would ensconce ourselves in some snug corner and begin discussing things, forgetful of all else and oblivious of the passing of time.

We talked of the future life, of the arts, of government service, of marriage and bringing up children, and it never once entered our heads that everything we said was the most frightful nonsense – for the reason that the nonsense we talked was clever and pleasing nonsense, and when one is young one still values intellect and believes in it. In youth all the powers of the mind are directed towards the future, and that future assumes such a variety of vivid and enchanting forms under the influence of hope based, not on past experience but on the imagined possibility of happiness to come, that these dreams of future bliss, when understood and shared by another, are in themselves at that age sources of true happiness. In the metaphysical arguments which formed one of the chief subjects of our conversation I loved the moment when thought followed thought *accelerando*, becoming more and more abstract, and at last reached such a degree of vagueness that one saw no possibility of expressing what was in one's mind and meaning to say one thing ended by saying something quite different. I loved the moment when soaring higher and higher in the realms of thought one suddenly comprehends all its immensity and recognizes the impossibility of proceeding.

It happened that once during Shrovetide Nekhlyudov was so taken up with one festivity and another that though he came to the house several times a day he never addressed a single word to me, and this so hurt my feelings that again I found myself thinking him a haughty disagreeable fellow. I was only waiting for an opportunity to show him that I did not set any value whatsoever on his company and entertained no particular affection for him.

The first time he wanted to have a talk with me after the Carnival was over I said I had lessons to prepare and went upstairs; but a quarter of an hour later the schoolroom door opened and Nekhlyudov came up to me.

'Am I disturbing you?' he asked.

'No,' I replied, though I had intended to say that I really was busy.

'Then why did you come away from Volodya's room? You know, we haven't had a talk for a long while and I've grown so used to our discussions that I feel as if something were missing.'

My vexation vanished in a moment and Dmitri appeared the same kind and lovable being as before in my eyes.

'You probably know why I came away?' I said.

'Perhaps I do,' he answered, seating himself beside me, 'but if I do guess the reason I cannot speak of it, but you can,' he added.

'Yes, and I will: I came away because I was angry with you . . . not angry but upset. To put it simply: I am always afraid that you despise me for being so young.'

'Do you know why I hit it off so well with you?' he said, answering my confession with a good-humoured wise look. 'And the reason I care more for you than for people whom I know better and with whom I have more in common? I have just discovered why it is. You have a rare and wonderful quality – you speak your mind.'

'Yes, I always speak out about the things of which I am most ashamed,' I assented, 'but only to people I trust.'

'Yes, but in order to trust a man one must be friends *completely*, and you and I are not friends yet, Nicolas. Do you remember, when we discussed friendship we said that to be true friends each must be sure of the other?'

'Be sure that the things I tell you, you won't repeat to anyone else,' I said. 'But you see, our most important and interesting thoughts are just those that nothing would induce us to tell one another.'

'And what horrid thoughts they are sometimes! Such base thoughts that if we knew we should have to confess them they would never dare enter our heads . . . Do you know the idea that has come to me, Nicolas?' he added, rising from his chair and with a smile rubbing his hands. '*Let us do just that*, and you'll see how good it will be for both of us: let's promise to confess everything to one another. We shall know one another and not be ashamed; and so as not to be afraid of other people let us promise never to say *anything* about each other to *anyone*. Suppose we do that.'

'Let's!' I said.

And we really did *do that*. What came of it I will relate hereafter.

Karr[1] has said that there are two sides to every attachment: one loves, the other lets himself be loved; one kisses, the other offers his cheek. That is perfectly true; and in our friendship I did the kissing and Dmitri presented his cheek; though he in his turn was ready to pay me a similar salute. We loved equally because we knew and appreciated

1. Alphonse Karr, 1808–90, French novelist who in 1839 became editor of *Le Figaro*.

each other, but that did not prevent his exercising an influence over me, and my submitting to him.

It goes without saying that under Nekhlyudov's influence I involuntarily adopted his tendency, the essence of which was an enthusiastic reverence for the ideal of virtue and a firm belief that the purpose of man's life is continually to perfect himself. In those days the reformation of all mankind, the abolition of all the vices and miseries seemed possible – and it seemed such a simple easy matter to improve oneself, acquire every virtue and be happy.

Incidentally, God alone knows whether these lofty aspirations of our youth were actually ridiculous, and whose fault it was that they were not fulfilled. . . .

[1854]

YOUTH

I · WHAT I CONSIDER TO HAVE BEEN THE BEGINNING OF ADOLESCENCE

I have said that my friendship with Dmitri opened up to me a new view of life, its aims and relations. The essence of this view lay in the conviction that the purpose of man's life is to strive towards more perfection, and that such perfection is easy, possible and lasting. But as yet I had only revelled in the discovery of new ideas arising from this conviction, and in forming brilliant plans for an active and moral future, and my life had gone on in the same trivial, confused and indolent way.

The virtuous thoughts I and my adored friend Dmitri – 'my wonderful Dmitri', as I sometimes used to call him to myself in a whisper – discoursed on so far appealed to my mind only and left my feelings untouched. But the day arrived when these thoughts came into my head with such fresh power of moral revelation that I took fright when I reflected on how much time I had wasted in vain; and at once, that very second, I wanted to apply my new ideas to life, with the firm intention never to be false to them.

And it is from this period that I date the beginning of my youth.

I was then nearly sixteen. Tutors still came to give me lessons. St-Jérome supervised my work, and of necessity and reluctantly I prepared for the University. Apart from my studies my occupations for the most part included solitary and incoherent reveries and ponderings, gymnastic exercises – with a view to becoming the strongest man in the world – and aimless, thoughtless wandering through all the rooms of the house (and more especially along the corridor outside the maids' room) and much looking at myself in the glass, from which, however, I always turned away with a heavy feeling of depression and even disgust. My outward appearance, I was convinced, was unsightly, and I could not even comfort myself with the usual consolation in such cases – I could not say that my face was expressive, intelligent or distinguished. There was nothing expressive in it – only the most ordinary coarse plain features; my small grey eyes were stupid rather than intelligent, especially when I looked at myself in the glass. Still less could I find anything suggestive of masculine vigour: though I was tall and very strong for my years all the features of my face were mild, inert and unformed. Nor was there anything distinguished about them: on the contrary, I looked like a peasant and had the same large feet and hands; which at that time I felt very much ashamed of.

2 · SPRING

Easter came rather late in April the year I entered the University, so that the examinations were fixed for the week after Easter, and in Holy Week I had not only to prepare myself for the Sacrament but also get ready for my examination.

After the melting snow – which Karl Ivanych used to call 'the son coming after his father' – the weather had for some three days been mild, warm and bright. There was not a speck of snow left in the streets, the dirty slush on the roads had given place to a wet glistening surface and swift-running rivulets. The last icicles hanging from the roofs were fast melting in the sun, buds were swelling on the trees in the garden, the path leading across the courtyard to the stables, past a frozen heap of manure, was dry, and mossy grass was showing green between the stones around the porch. It was that particular time in spring when the season most affects the human soul – everything glittering in the bright sunshine which still lacks heat; rivulets and patches of water where the snow has thawed, a fragrant freshness in the air; and a delicate blue sky streaked with long transparent clouds. I do not know why, but the effect of these first rustlings of the birth of spring always seem to me more apparent and impressive in a great city: one sees less but feels the promise more. I stood near the window where the morning sun cast dusty rays through the double panes upon the floor of the schoolroom, of which I was so heartily sick, and tried to work out some long algebraical problem on the blackboard. In one hand I held a limp tattered copy of Franker's *Algebra*, in the other a small piece of chalk which had already smeared both hands, my face and the elbows of my jacket. Nikolai, with his apron on and his sleeves rolled up, was breaking off the putty with a pair of pincers and bending back the nails holding the frame of the window that looked out on to the garden.[1] His occupation and the noise he made distracted my atten-

1. Nikolai was removing the inner frame which is fitted to each window in winter to keep out the cold.

tion. Moreover I was in a very bad discontented state of mind. Nothing
would go right with me: I had made a mistake at the beginning of my
calculation so that I had to start all over again; twice I had dropped the
chalk; I was conscious that my face and hands were all white; the
sponge had vanished somewhere; and Nikolai's knocking was getting
painfully on my nerves. I felt like flying into a temper and growling. I
flung down the chalk and the *Algebra*, and began pacing the room. But
then I remembered that it was Wednesday in Holy Week and we had
to go to confession, and I must refrain from doing anything wrong;
and suddenly I relapsed into a peculiarly gentle mood and went up to
Nikolai.

'Let me help you, Nikolai,' I said, trying to speak as nicely as I possibly could. The thought that I was behaving well in repressing my
vexation and offering to help him still further increased my chastened
humour.

The putty was knocked out and the nails bent back but although
Nikolai tugged at the frame with all his might it would not budge.

'If the frame comes out at once when I pull with him,' I thought, 'it
will mean it would be sinful to study any more today.' The frame
gave way on one side and came out.

'Where shall I take it?' I said.

'Let me see to it, if you don't mind,' replied Nikolai, plainly surprised and apparently not over-pleased at my zeal. 'They must not get
mixed up, and I have them all numbered in the box-room.'

'I will mark this one,' I said, lifting the frame.

I believe that if the box-room had been two miles away and the
frame twice as heavy I should have been really glad. I wanted to tire
myself out helping Nikolai. When I returned to the room the little
bricks and cones of salt[1] had already been moved on to the window-
sill and Nikolai was sweeping the sand and the sleepy flies out of the
open window with a goose-feather. The fresh fragrant air had already
entered and filled the room. From the window we could hear the
murmur of the city and the sparrows chirping in the garden.

Everything looked bright, the room was gay, a light spring breeze
stirred Nikolai's hair and the pages of my *Algebra*. I went to the
window, sat down on the sill, leaned over into the garden and mused.

A new and extraordinarily keen pleasant sensation suddenly invaded

1. Salt, sand, etc., are placed between the inner and outer window-frames to
absorb moisture.

my soul. The wet earth which was pierced here and there by bright green blades of grass with yellow stalks, the rivulets sparkling in the sun and whirling along little clods of earth and chips of wood, the reddening twigs of lilac with their swelling buds nodding just below the window, the busy twitter of birds bustling about in this bush, the dark fence wet with melting snow, but most of all the sweet-smelling moist air and joyous sunshine spoke to me clearly and unmistakably of something new and beautiful; and though I cannot describe how this was revealed to me I will try to record my perceptions at the time. Everything spoke to me of beauty, happiness and virtue; told me that one was as easily attainable and as possible as the other; that one cannot exist without the other, and even that beauty, happiness and virtue were one and the same thing. 'How was it I did not realize this? How wicked I have been till now! How good and happy I might have been, and can be in future!' I said to myself. 'Now, now – yes, this very minute – I will be a different being, and begin to live differently.' Yet for all that, I continued to sit on the window-sill for a long time dreaming and doing nothing. Have you ever lain down and fallen asleep on a dull rainy day in summer, and waking just at sunset opened your eyes to see in the broadening square at the window – the space where the linen blind is blowing up and down and beating its rod against the window-sill – the rain-soaked shadowy purple vista of the linden alley and a moist garden path lit by the brilliant slanting rays of the sun, suddenly heard the merry sounds of bird life in the garden, seen insects hovering in the open window, translucent in the sunshine, smelt the fragrance of the air after rain and thought to yourself, 'How is it I wasn't ashamed to be lying in bed sleeping through such an evening as this?' and hurriedly jumping up gone out into the garden and revelled in life? If you have, then you can imagine for yourself the overpowering sensation I experienced at that time.

3 · DAY-DREAMING

'Today I will make my confession and be cleansed from all my sins,' I thought, 'and never again will I . . .' (Here I went over in my mind the sins that troubled me most.) 'I will go to church regularly every Sunday, and afterwards read the Gospels for a whole hour; then out of the twenty-five roubles I am to get every month when I enter the

University I shall without fail give two and a half roubles (one-tenth –
a tithe) to the poor, without letting any one know, and not to beggars
– I shall find out some poor people, an orphan or an old woman whom
nobody knows about.

'I shall have a room to myself (most likely St-Jérome's) and look
after it myself and keep it marvellously clean; and I will never make a
servant do anything for me: they're human beings just the same as I.
Likewise I will *walk* every day to the University (and if they give me a
droshky I will sell it and put that money, too, aside for the poor) and I
will fulfil everything precisely and accurately' (what that 'everything'
was I could not by any means have said at the time but I well understood and felt this 'everything' to mean a wise moral irreproachable
life). 'I will take notes at my lectures and even prepare the subjects in
advance so that I shall be top in the first course and write a thesis; for
the second course I shall know everything beforehand and may even
pass straight into the third course, so that at eighteen I shall graduate as
first candidate with two gold medals; then I shall take my Master's
degree, and my doctorate, and become the leading *savant* in Russia . . .
I may even be the most learned man in Europe . . . Well, and after
that?' I was about to ask myself when I remembered that these day-
dreams indicated pride, a sin I should have to confess to the priest that
very evening, and I returned to the original point of my reflections. 'To
prepare the lectures I shall walk to the Sparrow Hills; there I will
choose a spot under a tree and read them over, sometimes I will take
something to eat with me, cheese, or pastry from Pedotti's, or something of the kind. I will rest myself and then read some good book or
other, or sketch landscapes or play some instrument (I must certainly
learn to play the flute). Then *she* too will be walking on the Sparrow
Hills, and one day she will come up and ask me who I am. I shall look
at her, oh so sadly, and say that I am the son of a priest, and that I am
happy only when I am alone here, all, all alone. She will give me her
hand and say something, and sit down beside me. And so we shall go
there every day, and be friends, and I shall kiss her . . . No, that's not
right. On the contrary, from this day forth I shall never more look at a
woman. Never, never again will I go into the maids' room, I'll try not
even to go near it; but in three years' time I shall be of age and shall
certainly marry. I will make a point of taking as much exercise as I can
and practise gymnastics every day, so that by the time I am twenty-
five I shall be stronger than Rappeau. On the first day I shall hold half

a *pood*[1] out at arm's length for five minutes, the next day a twenty-one pound weight, the third day twenty-two pounds, and so on, until in the end I can hold out four *poods* in each hand, and shall be stronger than any of the serfs; and if any one should ever take it into his head to insult me, or speak disrespectfully of *her*, I shall quite simply take him by the front of his coat, lift him about five feet off the ground with one hand and just hold him in the air to let him feel my strength, and then release him. But that wouldn't be right either; no, it won't matter, it isn't as if I shall do him any harm – I shall merely show him that I – '

Let me not be reproached if the day-dreams of my adolescence were as puerile as those of my childhood and boyhood. I am convinced that if I am destined to live to extreme old age, and my narrative continues with the years, as an old man of seventy I shall be found dreaming dreams just as impossible and childish as now. I shall be dreaming of some charming Marya who will fall in love with me, a toothless old man, as she fell in love with Mazeppa,[2] and of how my feeble-minded son suddenly becomes a minister of state, or that all of a sudden I shall find myself possessed of millions. I am convinced that there is no human being and no age devoid of this benign comforting capacity to dream. But apart from one feature general to them all – the impossible magic of reverie – the dreams of each human being and of each period of life have their own distinctive character. At that time which I regard as marking the close of my boyhood and the beginning of adolescence four feelings lay at the root of my dreams: love of *her*, the imaginary woman of whom I was always thinking in one and the same way and whom I every minute expected to meet somewhere. *She* was a little like Sonya, a little like Masha, Vassily's wife, when she stands at the wash-tub washing clothes, and a little like a woman with pearls round her white neck whom I had seen long ago in the box next to ours at the theatre. The second feeling was the love of love. I wanted everybody to know and love me. I wanted to pronounce my name, Nikolai Irtenyev, and have everybody impressed by this information and surround me, thanking me for something. The third sentiment was hope of some remarkable glorious happiness, and was so rock-firm and powerful that it verged on insanity. I was so convinced that soon, very soon, by some extraordinary circumstance I should suddenly become the wealthiest and most distinguished person in the world that I lived

---

1. 20 Russian pounds = 18 English pounds.
2. An allusion to Pushkin's poem, *Poltava*.

in constant tremulous expectation of some magic good fortune be-
falling me. I was always expecting it *was about to begin* and I on the point
of attaining all that man could desire, and I was for ever hurrying from
place to place, believing that 'it' must be 'beginning' just where I
happened not to be. The fourth and most important feeling was self-
disgust and repentance, but repentance so mingled with hope of happiness that there was nothing sorrowful about it. It seemed to me so easy
and natural to tear myself free from all the past, to reconstruct, to forget all that had been and to begin my life with all its relations completely anew that the past neither troubled nor hampered me. I even
revelled in my repugnance to the past and tried to paint it darker than
it really was. The blacker the range of my recollections of all that had
gone before the fairer and brighter did the pure radiant point of the
present and the rainbow hues of the future stand out in relief against
it. That voice of repentance and passionate desire for perfection was
my main new spiritual sensation at this period of my development, and
was the factor inspiring my new approach to myself, to other people
and to God's universe. O blessed voice of comfort, how often since
then hast thou in times of sadness when my soul has silently submitted
to life's falseness and depravity raised a sudden bold protest against
every untruth, virulently denouncing the past, and pointed to me and
compelled me to love the bright spot of the present, and promised
well-being and happiness in the future? Blessed voice of comfort – can
it be that thou wilt ever cease to sound?

4 · OUR FAMILY CIRCLE

Papa was seldom at home that spring but when it did happen he was
always exceedingly gay, strumming his favourite airs on the piano,
casting affectionate glances at us and inventing jokes about Mimi and
all of us, such as that the Crown Prince of Georgia had seen Mimi out
driving and had fallen so desperately in love with her that he had
petitioned the Synod for a divorce; or that I had been appointed
assistant to the ambassador in Vienna – and he announced these items
of news to us with a serious face. He would frighten Katya with spiders,
which she was afraid of. He was very gracious to our friends Dubkov
and Nekhlyudov, and over and over again told us and our visitors his
plans for the coming year. Though these plans changed almost from

day to day and contradicted one another they were so fascinating that we drank them in, and Lyuba would stare wide-eyed at papa's lips for fear of missing a single word. Now the idea was for us to remain in Moscow at the University while he and Lyuba went to Italy for a couple of years. Then it would be to buy an estate in the Crimea, on the south coast, and go there every summer; or for the whole family to move to Petersburg; and so forth. But beside his unusual high spirits another change had occurred in papa of late which greatly astonished me. He had fashionable clothes made for himself – an olive-green dress-coat, the new trousers with straps, and a long greatcoat which suited him very well; and he often smelled of delicious scent when he went visiting, and especially when he visited a certain lady of whom Mimi never spoke without a sigh and a face which plainly said: 'Poor orphans! What an unfortunate passion! A good thing *she* is no more!' etc. I learned from Nikolai (for papa never told us about his gambling affairs) that he had been singularly lucky at cards that winter, had won enormous sums, which he had deposited in the bank, and that he did not mean to play any more that spring. Probably this was the reason he was so anxious to go to the country as soon as possible, in case he should be unable to restrain himself. He even decided not to wait till I entered the University but to go to Petrovskoe with the girls immediately after Easter, leaving Volodya and me to follow on later.

All that winter and right into the spring Volodya and Dubkov were inseparable (the friendship with Dmitri, however, had begun to cool). Their chief pleasures, so far as I could gather from conversations I overheard, consisted in constantly drinking champagne, driving in a sledge past the windows of a young lady with whom both of them were apparently in love, and dancing *vis-à-vis*, not at children's parties any more but at real balls. This last circumstance, though Volodya and I loved one another dearly, did much to separate us. We felt that the difference between a boy still having lessons at home with tutors and a man who dances at grown-up balls was too great to allow of mutual exchange of confidences. Katya was quite grown-up now and read a lot of novels, and the thought that she might soon marry no longer seemed a joke to me; but though Volodya, too, was grown up they did not get on well together and even seemed to despise one another. In general when Katya was alone at home she took no interest in anything but novel-reading, and was bored most of the time; but as soon as ever a visitor of the opposite sex called she became very lively and charming and did such strange things with her eyes that I could not in the least make out what she was trying to say with them. It was only afterwards when I heard her remark in the course of some conversation that the only form of coquetry permissible to a girl was this coquetry of glances that I could explain to myself those strange unnatural grimaces with her eyes, which did not seem to surprise other people at all. Lyuba, too, was beginning to wear much longer dresses so that her crooked legs were hardly visible, but she was still the same cry-baby as before. Now she no longer dreamed of marrying a hussar but a singer or a musician, and to this end zealously applied herself to music. St-Jérome, knowing that he would remain with us only till I had finished my examinations, had found himself a situation in the family of some count or other, and seemed after that to look upon our household rather disdainfully. He was seldom at home, took to smoking cigarettes (then the height of dandyism) and continually whistled lively airs on the edge of a piece of card. Mimi grew more embittered every day, as though now that we were beginning to grow up she expected nothing good from any one or anything.

When I came to dinner I found only Mimi, Katya, Lyuba and St-Jérome in the dining-room; papa was not at home and Volodya was preparing for an examination with his comrades in his own room and had ordered his dinner to be brought to him there. Of late Mimi, whom none of us respected, had generally occupied the head of the table and dinner had lost much of its charm. The meal was no longer what it had been in mamma's or grandmamma's time – a sort of ceremony which at a certain hour brought the whole family together and divided the day into two halves. We now did not hesitate to arrive late, to come in for the second course, to drink wine out of tumblers (St-Jérome himself setting us that example), to loll in our chairs, to get up before the meal was over, and take other similar liberties. Dinner had ceased to be the daily joyous family festival it used to be. How different it had been at Petrovskoe when at two o'clock, all washed and dressed for dinner, we gathered in the drawing-room, talking gaily and waiting for the appointed hour. Punctually at the moment the clock in the butler's pantry began to whirr preparatory to striking the hour Foka, a table-napkin on his arm, would enter quietly, with a dignified and somewhat severe expression, to announce in a loud measured voice, 'Dinner is served!'; and with bright contented faces we would all walk into the dining-room, the elders in front and the young people behind, starched petticoats rustling, boots and shoes creaking slightly, and take our appointed places, talking together in undertones. Or in Moscow how different it was, when we used to stand before the table laid in the dining-room, chatting quietly among ourselves and waiting for grand-mamma, to whom Gavrilo had gone to announce that dinner was served. Suddenly the door would open, we would hear the faint swish of her dress and the sound of her footsteps, and grandmamma in a cap with a quaint lilac ribbon would sail in sideways from her room, smiling or looking gloomily askance (according to the state of her health). Gavrilo would rush to her arm-chair, the other chairs make a scraping sound, and with a kind of shiver down your back (the harbinger of appetite) you pick up your rather damp starched table-napkin, nibble a bit of bread and, rubbing your hands together under the table, with impatient avidity watch the plates of steaming soup which the butler dispenses in order due to rank, age and grandmamma's favour.

Now I no longer feel either happiness or excitement when I come in to dinner.

The chatter between Mimi, St-Jérome and the girls about the fright-ful boots the Russian master wears or the flounced dresses the Prin-cesses Kornakova have, and so on – the chatter that normally filled me with a frank contempt which, especially so far as Lyuba and Katya were concerned, I was at no pains to conceal did not disturb my new and virtuous frame of mind. I was gentleness itself; I spoke to them with a kind of affectionate smile, politely asked them to pass me the *kvass*, and agreed with St-Jérome when he corrected a phrase I used at dinner, remarking that it was more elegant to say *je puis*[1] than *je peux*.[1] I must own, however, that I was rather disappointed that nobody took any par-ticular notice of my meekness and virtue. After dinner Lyuba showed me a piece of paper on which she had written down all her sins. I thought this a very good idea but added that it would be still better to inscribe all one's sins in one's soul, and that 'this wasn't what mattered'.

'Why not?' asked Lyuba.

'Oh, never mind; you wouldn't understand.' And I went upstairs, telling St-Jérome that I was going to work but in reality intending to spend the hour and a half before confession time in drawing up a list of duties and occupations for my whole life, committing to paper what the aim and purpose of my life was to be and the rules by which I should now unswervingly be guided.

1. I can.

5 · MY RULES

I took a sheet of paper and wanted to start straight away on a list of my
duties and occupations for the coming year. The paper had to be ruled.
But as I could not find the ruler I used the Latin dictionary for the purpose. When I had drawn the pen along the edge of the dictionary and
removed the latter I found that instead of a line I had made an oblong
smudge of ink, besides which, the dictionary was shorter than the
paper and my line curved round its soft corner. I took another sheet
of paper and by manipulating the dictionary succeeded in ruling the
paper after a fashion. Having divided my duties into three categories –
my duty to myself, my duty towards my neighbour and my duty
towards God, I began to write down the first; but they turned out to
be so numerous and of so many kinds and subdivisions that I thought I
had better start with 'Rules of Life' and then set to work on the list. I
got six sheets of paper, sewed them together and wrote on the cover
RULES OF LIFE. But these words were so crookedly and unevenly inscribed that I debated at length whether to rewrite them, and sat for a
long time in miserable contemplation of the torn-up list and disfigured
title-page. 'Why is everything so beautiful and clear in my mind, and
turns out so repulsive on paper, and in life generally, when I try to put
something I have thought of into practice?...'

'The priest has arrived, please you are to come down to hear the
preliminary prayers,' Nikolai came into announce.

I hid my note-book in the table-drawer, looked in the glass, brushed
my hair upwards (which I imagined gave me a pensive air) and went
down to the sitting-room, where a table covered with a cloth had been
prepared with an ikon and lighted tapers on it. Papa entered by another
door at the same time. The confessor, a grey-haired monk with a stern
elderly face, gave papa his blessing. Papa kissed his small broad wizened
hand and I did the same.

'Call Voldemar,' said papa. 'Where is he? Oh yes, I forgot: of
course he will perform his devotions at the University.'

'He is busy with the prince,' said Katya, looking at Lyuba. Lyuba
suddenly blushed, made a face, pretending that she felt ill, and left the
room. I went out after her. She stopped in the drawing-room and
pencilled something else on her piece of paper.

'What! Committed another sin?' I asked.

'No, nothing particular,' she replied, colouring.

At that moment Dmitri's voice was heard in the hall, bidding good-bye to Volodya.

'There's another temptation for you,' said Katya, coming into the room and addressing Lyuba.

I could not make out what was the matter with my sister: she was so upset that the tears welled to her eyes and her agitation increased until it turned to anger with herself and Katya, who was obviously teasing her.

'Any one can see you're a *foreigner*.' (Nothing offended Katya more than to be called a foreigner, which is why Lyuba said it.) 'At such a solemn moment,' she continued in a lofty tone of voice, 'you deliberately go and upset me ... You ought to understand ... this is not a time for jokes ...'

'Do you know what she has written, Nikolai?' said Katya, greatly offended at being called a foreigner. 'She has written ...'

'I never would have believed that you could be so spiteful,' said Lyuba, breaking down completely and leaving us. 'At such a moment, and on purpose, you spend your whole time leading me into sin. I don't keep on at you about your feelings and sufferings.'

6 · CONFESSION

With these and similar disjointed reflections in my mind I returned to the sitting-room when all had assembled there and the priest, rising, was about to read the prayer before confession. But as soon as the expressive stern voice of the monk saying the prayer broke the general silence, and especially when he uttered the words: 'Confess all your transgressions without false shame, concealing none and making no attempt to justify yourselves, and your souls shall be cleansed before God; but if ye conceal aught, ye commit a great sin,' the feeling of devout trepidation which I had experienced that morning at the thought of the impending Sacrament returned to me again. I even took pleasure in recognizing this condition of mine and tried to retain it by repressing all other thoughts from entering my head and striving to increase in myself a vague sense of fear.

Papa was the first to go in to make his confession. He remained a very long time in grandmamma's room, and all that while the rest of us in the sitting-room were silent, or spoke in whispers as to who should go next. At last through the door we heard the monk's voice reciting a prayer, and papa's footsteps. The door creaked and papa emerged, coughing a little and jerking his shoulder, as was his habit, and not looking at any of us.

'You go now, Lyuba, and mind you tell everything. You are my great sinner, you know,' said papa gaily, pinching her cheek.

Lyuba turned pale, then blushed, took her notes from her apron pocket and put them back again, and bowing her head and somehow making her neck look shorter, as if expecting a blow from above, went through the door. She was soon back again but when she came out her shoulders were shaking with sobs.

At last, after pretty little Katya came back smiling, my turn arrived. I entered the dimly-lighted room with the same numb feeling of awe and dread which I deliberately set out to encourage in myself. The confessor stood at the reading-desk and slowly turned his face towards me.

I only stayed five minutes in grandmamma's room but I came out happy and (so I was convinced at the time) a completely pure, morally regenerated, new man. Though I was disagreeably impressed by finding the old surroundings unchanged – the same room, the same furniture, my own appearance just the same as it had been (I should have liked every external thing to have undergone as great a change as my inner self seemed to me to have done) – in spite of all this I remained in that blissful state of mind until I went to bed.

I was already half asleep, going over in my mind all the sins from which I had been cleansed, when I suddenly remembered one shameful sin which I had kept back at confession. The words of the prayer before confession came back to me and kept ringing in my ears. All my peace of mind vanished in a flash. 'But if ye conceal aught, ye commit a great sin . . .' I heard the words over and over again and I saw myself such a dreadful sinner that no punishment was adequate for me. For a long time I tossed from side to side as I reflected on my situation, expecting every moment the punishment of God, sudden death even – a thought which threw me into indescribable terror. But suddenly a happy idea occurred to me – at daybreak I would walk or drive to the monastery to see the priest and make a second confession. After that I grew calmer.

7 · MY EXCURSION TO THE MONASTERY

I woke several times during the night, being afraid of over-sleeping, and was up before six. Through the windows day had hardly begun to break. I put on my clothes and boots, that lay crumpled and un-brushed beside my bed as Nikolai had not yet come for them, and without saying my prayers or washing I went out into the street alone for the first time in my life.

Over the way, beyond the green roof of a tall house, the red flush of dawn gleamed through the cold mist. A fairly severe spring-morning frost which had frozen the mud and the puddles crackled under foot and nipped my face and hands. There was not a single cabman in our street as yet, though I had counted on finding one to take me quickly to the monastery and back. Only a few loaded carts dragged slowly down the Arbat and a couple of bricklayers passed along the pavement chatting together. After I had gone about half a mile I began to meet people – women on their way to market with their baskets, water-carts going to fetch water, and a pieman who appeared at the cross-roads: one baker's shop was open, and at the Arbat Gate I came across an old cabman dozing and swaying as he jolted along on his shabby, patched, bluish bone-shaker of a drozhky. Still probably half asleep, he only asked twenty kopecks to drive to the monastery and back, but then he suddenly realized, just as I was about to take my seat, and touch-ing up his horse with the ends of the reins started to drive off and leave me. 'Must feed my 'orse,' he growled, 'I can't take you, sir.'

With difficulty I persuaded him to stop, and offered him forty kopecks. He pulled up his horse, eyed me narrowly and said: 'Get in, sir.' I must acknowledge I was rather afraid that he would drive me into some back alley and rob me. Catching hold of the collar of his tattered coat, thus sadly exposing the wrinkled neck above his very bent back, I climbed up into the lumpy, rickety light-blue seat, and we went jolting along Vozdvizhenka street. On the way I noticed that the back of the vehicle was upholstered with a bit of the same greenish material from which the driver's coat was made; and this for some reason re-assured me and I no longer feared that he would carry me off to an obscure side-street and rob me.

The sun had already risen pretty high and was brightly gilding the cupolas of the churches when we reached the monastery. The ground was still frozen in the shade but all along the road muddy rills ran swiftly, and the horse went splashing through the thawing mire. On entering the monastery enclosure I asked the first person I met for the father-confessor.

'There is his cell,' said a monk who was passing, stopping for a moment and pointing to a tiny house with a little porch.

'I am very much obliged to you.'

But what impression could I have made on the monks, who all looked at me as one by one they came out of the church? I was neither an adult nor a child; my face was not washed, my hair not combed, bits of fluff were sticking to my clothes and my boots were muddy and not blacked. To what class of persons were the monks assigning me – for they stared at me hard enough? However, I went in the direction the young monk had indicated.

An old man in black garments and with thick grey eyebrows met me on the narrow path leading to the cells and asked what I was looking for.

For a moment I wanted to say, 'Nothing,' and run back to the cab and drive home, but in spite of the beetling brows the old man's face inspired confidence. I said I wished to see the confessor, and gave his name.

'Very well, my young gentleman, I will show you the way,' said he, turning back and apparently at once guessing my errand. 'The father is at matins, he will be here soon.'

He opened the door and led me through a neat passage and ante-room over a clean linen drugget into the cell.

'You can wait here,' he said to me with a kindly reassuring look, and went away.

The room in which I found myself was very small and exceedingly tidy. The whole of the furniture consisted of a little table covered with oilcloth, which stood between two casement windows with a pair of geraniums in pots on the window-sills, a shelf for the ikons with a lamp hanging before them, one arm-chair and a couple of ordinary chairs. In the corner hung a wall-clock with a floral design painted on its dial and two brass weights on the chains; on the partition-wall, which was joined to the ceiling by small white-washed wooden posts (and behind which no doubt was the bed), two cassocks hung on a nail.

The windows looked out on to a white wall some five feet distant.

Between them and the wall grew a small lilac bush. No sound from outside reached the room, so that the measured friendly ticking of the clock's pendulum sounded quite loud in the stillness. As soon as I was alone in this quiet nook all my former thoughts and recollections vanished from my head as if they had never existed, and I subsided into a kind of inexpressibly agreeable musing. That faded nankeen cassock with its threadbare lining, the worn black leather bindings and brass clasps of the books, those dull green plants, the carefully watered earth and well washed leaves, and especially the monotonous broken sound of the pendulum, spoke to me so distinctly of some new hitherto unknown life, a life of solitude, prayer and quiet calm happiness.

'Months pass, years pass,' I thought, 'and he is always alone, always at peace, always knowing that his conscience is pure in the sight of God and his prayers are heard by Him.' I sat on my chair for about half an hour, trying not to move and to breathe softly lest I should disturb the harmony of sounds which told me so much. And the pendulum continued to tick, more loudly to the right, less loudly to the left.

8 · MY SECOND CONFESSION

The steps of the confessor roused me from my musings.

'Good morning,' he said, smoothing his grey hair with his hand. 'What can I do for you?'

I asked for his blessing and kissed his small yellowish hand with peculiar pleasure.

When I had explained my request he said nothing but went up to the ikons and began to read the exhortation.

When the confession was over, and mastering my shame I had told him all that was on my mind, he laid his hands upon my head and in his quiet melodious voice pronounced: 'May the blessing of our heavenly Father be upon thee, my son, and may He ever preserve thee in faith, meekness and humility. Amen.'

I was completely happy; tears of joy choked me; I kissed a fold of his cloth cassock and raised my head. The monk's countenance expressed perfect tranquillity.

I felt that I was enjoying my emotion and fearing in any way to dispel it I hurriedly took leave of the confessor, and looking neither to right nor left lest my attention be distracted, I passed through the enclosure to seat myself again in the jolting motley drozhky. But the joltings and bumping of the vehicle, the variety of objects that glided past my eyes, soon destroyed that feeling; and before long I was thinking that by this time the confessor was probably saying to himself that never in his whole life had he met, nor would meet, a young man with so beautiful a soul as mine, and indeed that there were no others like me. I was convinced of it, and the conviction produced the kind of exhilaration that demands to be communicated to some one else.

I dreadfully wanted to talk to somebody; but there being no one at hand save the cabman I addressed him.

'Was I gone long?' I asked.

'A goodish while, and my 'orse should'a bin fed long long 'afore this, I'm a night cabman, see,' replied the old man, who appeared to have become more cheerful now that the sun was up.

'It only seemed like a minute to me,' I said. 'Do you know why I went to the monastery?' I added, moving into the hollow nearer to the old driver.

'What business be it o' mine? Our job's to take our fare where 'e tells us to go,' he answered.

'Yes, but all the same, what do you think?' I persisted.

'I daresay as 'ow some one you know of 'as to be buried an' you went to buy a plot for the grave,' he said.

'No, my friend. You know why I went?'

'Can't say, sir,' he repeated.

The cabman's voice seemed to me so kindly that for his edification I decided to tell him the reason for my expedition and even the feeling I had experienced.

'Would you like me to tell you? Well, you see . . .'

And I related it all to him, and described my beautiful feelings. I blush even now at the recollection.

'Indeed, sir,' he said doubtfully.

And for a long time after that he sat silent and still except for occasionally tucking in the skirt of his coat which kept slipping from under his striped trousers as his leg in its enormous boot jolted on the step of the vehicle. I was beginning to imagine he must be thinking the same about me as the confessor – namely, that you could search the world over and not find such a fine young man as I; but he suddenly turned to me.

'I tell you what, sir. You ought to keep your affairs to yourself.'

'What?' I inquired.

'Those affairs of yours – they are your business,' he repeated, mumbling with his toothless mouth.

'No,' I thought, 'he hasn't understood me,' and all the way home I said no more to him.

Though the tender piety itself did not last till we got back, the self-satisfaction at having experienced it did, in spite of the people who dotted the streets everywhere in the bright sunshine; but I had no sooner reached home than the feeling vanished entirely. I had not got the forty kopecks for the cabman and Gavrilo, the butler, to whom I was already in debt, would not lend me any more. The cabman, seeing me twice run backwards and forwards across the courtyard in quest of money, climbed down from the box and though I had thought him so kind he began trying to mortify my vanity by loud protests that there were swindlers about who did not pay their fares.

In the house every one was still in bed so that except for the servants there was no one from whom I could borrow the forty kopecks. At last Vassily, upon my most sacred word of honour that I would repay him, which (I could see by his face) he did not put the slightest faith in, but because he liked me and remembered the service I had rendered him, paid the cabman for me. Thus all my noble sentiments vanished like smoke. When I began to dress for church in order to go and receive the Sacrament with all the others, and found that my suit had not been mended and I could not wear it, I committed one sin on top of another. Putting on another suit, I went to communion in a strange state of mental flurry and utter distrust of my fine disposition.

9 · HOW I PREPARE FOR THE EXAMINATION

On the Thursday in Easter week papa, my sister, Mimi and Katya departed for the country, so that only Volodya, myself and St-Jérome remained in grandmamma's great house. The mood I had been in on the day of my confession and of my expedition to the monastery had quite gone, leaving behind it nothing but a vague though pleasant memory, which was gradually being dulled by the new impressions of the more independent life I now led.

The note-book with the heading RULES OF LIFE was hidden away with my rough exercise-books. Though I had liked the idea that it was possible to draw up a list of rules for all the contingencies of life and always be guided by them, and the idea of doing so appeared to me an extremely simple and at the same time a very lofty one, and though I still intended to put it into practice, I again seemed to have forgotten that this should be done at once, and kept putting it off to some other time. It was a comfort to find, however, that every thought which came into my mind fitted exactly into one or other subdivision of my rules and duties: either the rules in regard to my neighbour, or to myself, or to God. 'I shall enter this there, together with many many other thoughts which occur to me later on on that subject,' I said to myself. Today I often wonder: Was I better and more on the right lines then when I believed in the omnipotence of the human intellect, or now that I have lost the capacity for development and doubt the power and importance of the human mind? – and I cannot give myself any positive answer.

The sense of independence and that spring feeling of vague expectation which I have already mentioned so unsettled me that I positively could not control myself, and I made the sorriest job of preparing for my examination. Sometimes I would sit of a morning in the schoolroom, well aware that I had to work because next day would be the examination in a subject, two whole questions of which I had not read up at all, when suddenly a sweet breath of spring air would come in through the window, and it would seem as if there were something urgently to be remembered; my hands would automatically let the book fall; my feet would automatically have me pacing up and down the room, while – as if some one had touched a spring and set a machine in action – all sorts of merry motley dreams would rush so easily and naturally and swiftly through my head that I only had time to notice their radiance. Thus an hour, two hours, would pass unnoticed. Or I would sit over my book and after a fashion concentrate all my attention on what I was reading, when suddenly I would hear a woman's step and the rustle of her dress in the corridor – and everything would fly out of my head and it would be impossible to sit still, though I knew very well that nobody could be going along the passage except Gasha, grandmother's old maid-servant. 'Yes, but suppose it were *she*?' the thought would flash across my mind. 'What if *it* is beginning now, and I were to miss it?' and I would rush out into the passage and find that it really was Gasha; but for a long time after that I would be unable to master my thoughts. The spring had been pressed and again a terrible jumble would fill my head. Or I would be sitting alone in my room in the

evening by the light of a tallow candle, and to snuff the candle or settle
myself more comfortably I would tear myself from my book for a
moment, and notice how dark it was everywhere, by the doors and in
the corners, and hear the silence over the whole house – and again it
would be impossible not to stop and listen to that silence and gaze into
the black square of the doorway opening into a dark room; impossible
not to remain motionless a long long time, or else go downstairs and
walk through all the empty rooms. Often, too, in the evening I would
sit unobserved in the hall, listening to Gasha playing 'The Nightingale'
with two fingers on the piano, sitting alone in the ball-room lit by a
tallow candle. And when the moon was bright I positively could not
help getting out of bed to lie on the sill of the window that opened into
the little garden, and gaze at the moonlit roof of the Shaposhnikov
house, at the slender belfry of our parish church, and at the evening
shadows of the fence and a shrub where they lay black across the garden
path; and I could not help it but I stayed there so long that it was ten
o'clock next morning before I was able to rouse myself from sleep.

So that if it had not been for my tutors who continued to come, and
St-Jérome, who now and then reluctantly applied a spur to my ambition, and most of all the desire to appear an intelligent youth in the
eyes of my friend Nekhlyudov, that is, to do excellently in my examination – which in his opinion was a matter of great importance – if
it had not been for all this, the spring and my new freedom would
have made me forget everything I had ever known, and I should never
have passed my examination.

10 · THE EXAMINATION IN HISTORY

On the 16th of April, escorted by St-Jérome, I entered the great hall of
the University for the first time. We had arrived in our rather smart
phaeton. For the first time in my life I wore a frock-coat, and all my
clothing, even the linen and stockings I had on, was of the newest and
best. When the door-keeper downstairs helped me off with my overcoat and I stood before him in all my finery I even felt a little ashamed
of being so dazzling. But when I stepped into the light hall with a
parquet floor full of people, and saw hundreds of young men in high-
school uniforms and others in frock-coats, a few of whom glanced at
me with indifference, and at the far end the dignified professors stroll-

ing about between the tables or sitting in large arm-chairs I was immediately disappointed in my hopes of attracting general attention, and the expression of my face, which at home and even in the vestibule of the University had denoted regret almost that I should have to present so distinguished and important an appearance, changed to one of the most acute shyness and a certain dejection. I even fell into the other extreme and was quite delighted to see on the bench nearest to me a man wearing impossibly shabby dirty clothes who though not an old man was almost completely grey. He was sitting apart from the rest on a bench at the back and I hastened to sit beside him and began to scrutinize the candidates and form conclusions about them. Many and varied were the figures and faces there but all of them according to my ideas at that time could easily be divided into three categories.

There were youths like myself who had come to the examination hall accompanied by tutors or parents; among their number were the youngest Ivin with Herr Frost, whom I knew, and Ilinka Grap with his aged father. All these had downy chins, displayed snowy linen, and sat quietly, not opening the text-books and note-books they had brought with them, and watching the professors and the examination tables with unconcealed nervousness. The second category wore high-school uniforms and many of them had started shaving. These for the most part knew one another, talked loudly and called the professors by their Christian names, prepared answers, passed note-books to each other, climbed over the benches, brought in patties and sandwiches from outside and devoured them there and then, merely putting their heads down level with the benches. And finally, the third category of examination candidate, not that they numbered very many, were quite old, some of them attired in tail-coats but the majority in frock-coats and showing no linen. These preserved a grave demeanour, sat apart and looked very gloomy. The one who had cheered me by certainly not being dressed as well as myself belonged to this last category. Leaning on his elbows with his head between his hands and his dishevelled greyish hair thrusting out between his fingers, he was reading a book, and giving us only a momentary and not very friendly glance with his glittering eyes, he frowned morosely and stuck out a shiny elbow to prevent me moving any nearer to him. The high-school students on the contrary were too sociable, and of them I was a bit afraid. One of them, pushing a book into my hands, said, 'Hand it over to him there.' Another as he passed me said, 'Mind out of the way, old man!' A third, scrambling over a bench, held on to my shoulder as if it were a desk. All this seemed wild and disagreeable to me; I regarded myself as vastly superior to these high-school boys and considered that they ought not to treat me with such familiarity. At last names were called out; the students from the high-school stepped forward boldly and answered well on the whole, and came back looking cheerful. Our set were much more diffident and apparently did not answer so well. Some of the older men gave excellent answers, others answered very badly. When the name 'Semeonov' was called my neighbour with the grey hair and glittering eyes pushed rudely by me, stepped over my legs and went up to the table. It was plain from the professors' faces that he answered well and with assurance. On returning to his place he quietly gathered up his note-books and left without waiting to hear what mark he had received. I had already started up several times in alarm at the sound of the voice that called out the names but my turn had not come yet, according to the alphabetical list, although several names beginning with a K were already being called. 'Ikonin and Tenyev!' someone suddenly shouted from the professors' corner. A chill ran down my back and through my hair.

'Who was called? Who is Bartenyev?' people near me were saying.

'Ikonin, go on, you are called. But who "Bartenyev" or "Morden-yev" is, I don't know. Show yourself!' said a tall red-cheeked high-school student standing near me.

'It's you,' said St-Jérome.

'My name is Irtenyev,' I said to the red-cheeked high-school student. 'Did they call Irtenyev?'

'Yes, of course. Why don't you go up? . . . Lord, what a dandy!' he added, not loud but so that I heard his words as I passed between the benches.

In front of me walked Ikonin, a tall young man of about twenty-five, who belonged to the third group – the older candidates. He wore a tight olive tail-coat and a blue satin cravat over which his long fair hair was carefully brushed à la moujhik.[1] His appearance had already caught my attention when we were sitting on the benches. He was not bad looking, and talkative; but what struck me most was the strange red hair which he had allowed to grow on his throat and the yet stranger habit he had of continually unbuttoning his waistcoat and scratching his chest under his shirt.

1. Peasant style – cut square all round.

Three professors were sitting at the table which Ikonin and I approached; not one of them acknowledged our bow. A young professor was shuffling the question slips like a pack of cards; another, with a star on his coat, was looking at a high-school student who was rapidly saying something about Charlemagne, ending every sentence with the word 'finally'; and the third professor, an old man, inclining his head, looked at us over his spectacles and pointed to the question slips. I felt that his gaze was directed jointly at Ikonin and me and that there was something about us that he did not like – Ikonin's red hair perhaps, for after taking another look at the pair of us he made an impatient gesture with his head for us to hurry up and draw our question slips. I was vexed and offended, first that no one had returned our bow and secondly because they apparently lumped me in with Ikonin under the one heading 'Examination Candidates', and were already prejudiced against me on account of Ikonin's red hair. I quickly drew a ticket and was about to answer the question on it but the professor with a glance indicated Ikonin. I read the question on my ticket: it was one I knew, and quietly awaiting my turn I watched what was going on before me. Ikonin was not at all intimidated – rather the reverse, for in reaching for his ticket he leaned his body sideways half across the table; then he shook back his hair and briskly read the question written on the slip. He had already opened his mouth to answer, I supposed, when the professor with the star, having dismissed the high-school pupil with a word of commendation, suddenly looked at Ikonin. Ikonin seemed to recollect something and stopped. There was a dead silence for about two minutes.

'Well?' said the professor in spectacles.

Ikonin opened his mouth and again said nothing.

'Come, you are not the only one here, you know. Are you going to answer or are you not?' demanded the young professor, but Ikonin did not even glance at him. He stared at the ticket and uttered not a word. The professor in spectacles looked at him through his glasses, and over his glasses, and without his glasses, for he had had time to take them off, wipe them carefully and put them on again. Ikonin had not said a word. Suddenly a smile flashed across his face; he shook back his hair and, again broadside on to the table, laid down his ticket, looked at each of the professors in turn, then at me, wheeled round and swinging his arms strode jauntily back to his bench. The professors exchanged glances.

'A fine bird!' said the young professor. 'Studies at his own expense.'

I moved closer to the table but the professors continued to talk almost in whispers among themselves as if none of them was even aware of my presence. At that time I was firmly convinced that all three professors were deeply interested in whether I should pass my examination, and whether I should pass it well, but that to preserve their dignity, and for this reason only, they pretended it did not matter either way and tried to look as if they had not noticed me.

When the professor with the spectacles turned to me with an air of indifference, inviting me to answer the question I had drawn, I looked him full in the face and felt slightly ashamed for him, that he had so played the hypocrite with me, and I floundered a little at first, but it soon became easier and easier, and as the question was on Russian history, which I knew inside out, I finished brilliantly, and even went so far, in my desire to make the professors realize that I was no Ikonin and must not be put on a par with him, as to offer to draw another ticket, but the professor, nodding his head, said, 'Good,' and marked something in his register. As soon as I returned to the benches I was told by the high-school students, who, heaven knows how, found out everything, that I had got a five.

11 · THE EXAMINATION IN MATHEMATICS

At the succeeding examinations I had a number of new acquaintances, besides Grap whom I deemed unworthy of my acquaintance, and Ivin, who for some reason avoided me. Some of them already exchanged greetings with me. Ikonin even seemed glad to see me and informed me that he was to be re-examined in history, that the history professor had had a spite against him since last year's examination when, as he said, he had also made him lose his head. Semeonov, who like myself was down for the Faculty of Mathematics, avoided everybody up to the very end of the exams, sat quietly by himself, leaning on his elbow with his fingers thrust through his grey hair, and passed in excellent style, coming out second – a pupil from the First High-School was first. The latter was tall, lean, dark-haired and very pale, and had a black scarf tied round his cheek, and a forehead covered with pimples. His hands were thin and red with extraordinarily long fingers, the nails so bitten away that his finger-tips looked as if they had threads tied round them. All this seemed to me very fine and exactly as it should be in the case of a First High-School student. He spoke to every one just like anybody else, and even I made his acquaintance, yet it seemed to me there was something remarkable, *magnetic*, in his walk, in the movements of his lips and his black eyes.

I arrived earlier than usual for the mathematics examination. I knew the subject pretty well but there were two algebra questions which I had somehow dodged with my tutor and which I was completely ignorant about. These were, as I still remember, the theory of combinations and Newton's binomial theorem. I seated myself on the bench at the back, and pored over the two I did not know; but not being accustomed to work in a noisy room and anticipating that I should not have enough time, I was unable to concentrate on what I was reading.

'There he is! This way, Nekhlyudov,' I heard Volodya's familiar voice behind me.

I turned round and saw my brother and Dmitri, who with their coats unbuttoned and swinging their arms were coming towards me between the benches. It was immediately apparent that they were students in their second year, who were as much at home in the University as in their own houses. The mere look of their unbuttoned coats sufficed to express their disdain for us who were only matriculating, and inspired us who were only matriculating with envy and respect. I was vastly flattered to think all the others would see that I was acquainted with two second-year students, and quickly rose to meet them.

Volodya could not even refrain from vaunting his superiority.

'Oh, you poor wretch!' he said. 'Not been examined yet?'

'No.'

'What are you reading? Aren't you prepared?'

'All but two questions. I don't understand this.'

'What? This here?' said Volodya, and began explaining Newton's binomial theorem to me, but so rapidly and unintelligibly that, reading distrust of his knowledge in my eyes, he glanced at Dmitri and, no doubt, reading the same in his, blushed, but still continued saying something I did not understand.

'No, wait, Volodya, let us go over it with him if there's time,' said Dmitri with a glance at the professors' corner as he seated himself beside me.

I saw at once that my friend was in that gentle complacent frame of mind he always fell into when feeling satisfied with himself, a mood I particularly liked in him. As he was good at mathematics and spoke clearly he explained the theorem to me so thoroughly that I remember it to this day. But he had hardly finished before St-Jérome said in a loud whisper: '*À vous*,[1] Nicolas!' and I followed Ikonin out between the benches without having had time to go through the other question I did not know. I approached the table where two professors were sitting, with a high-school student standing at the blackboard. He was vigorously working out some formula, snapping bits of chalk off against the board and writing away though the professor had already said, 'That's enough,' and told us to draw our question slips. 'Suppose I draw the theory of combinations!' I thought, picking out my ticket with trembling fingers from the soft pile of bits of paper. With the same bold gesture and sideways lunge of his whole body as at the previous examination Ikonin took the topmost ticket, glanced at it and frowned angrily.

'I always have such devilish luck!' he muttered.

I looked at mine.

Oh horrors! It was the theory of combinations! . . .

'What have you got?' asked Ikonin.

I showed him.

'I know that one,' he said.

'Will you swap?'

'No, it would be all the same if I did, I don't feel in the vein,' Ikonin just had time to whisper before the professor called us to the board.

'Well, all's lost!' I thought. 'Instead of doing brilliantly as I meant to I shall be disgraced for ever, worse than Ikonin.' But suddenly Ikonin turned to me, right under the professor's eyes, snatched the ticket from my hand and gave me his. I looked at it, it was Newton's binomial.

The professor was a youngish man with a pleasant intelligent expression, due chiefly to the extremely protruding lower part of his forehead.

'How is it you are exchanging your tickets, gentlemen?' he said.

'No, he simply gave me his to look at, professor,' Ikonin replied readily, and again 'professor' was the last word he uttered while standing there; and again as he passed me on his way back to the benches he glanced at the professor, and at me, smiled and shrugged

1. Your turn.

his shoulders as much as to say, 'Never mind, friend!' (I heard afterwards that this was the third year Ikonin had presented himself for the
entrance examination.)

I answered my question, which I had only just previously gone
over, with distinction – the professor even said I had done better than
was required, and gave me a five.

12 · THE LATIN EXAMINATION

All went splendidly until the Latin examination. The high-school
pupil with the scarf round his cheek was first, Semeonov second and I
third. I even began to swagger a little and seriously thought that in
spite of my youth I was not to be taken lightly.

From the first day of the examinations I had heard everybody speak
in fear and trembling of the Latin professor, who was said to be a brute
who delighted in the downfall of young men, especially those who
paid their own way without any help from the University funds, and
who apparently only spoke in Latin or Greek. St-Jérome, who had
coached me in Latin, tried to encourage me, and I myself thought that
since I could translate Cicero and some of the Odes of Horace without
a dictionary and knew Zumpt's grammar by heart I was no worse prepared than the rest, but it turned out otherwise. The whole morning
all the talk was of the tribulations of those who had gone up before me;
this one a nought, another, one; a third had in addition been violently
berated and threatened with expulsion, and so on and so forth. Only
Semeonov and the scholar from the First High-School went up as
calmly as usual and returned each with a five. I already had a foreboding
of disaster when Ikonin and I were called up together to the small
table at which the terrible professor sat all by himself. The terrible
professor was a small thin sallow man with long greasy hair and a most
thoughtful countenance.

He handed Ikonin a volume of Cicero's speeches and told him to
translate.

To my great surprise Ikonin not only read off some of the Latin but
even translated a few lines with the aid of the professor who prompted
him. Conscious of my superiority over such a feeble rival, I could not
help smiling, even somewhat contemptuously, when it came to
parsing and Ikonin, as on previous occasions, subsided into hopeless

silence. I thought to please the professor by that knowing slightly sarcastic smile of mine, but it had the contrary effect.

'Evidently you can do better since you smile,' said the professor to me in bad Russian. 'We shall see. Well now, you tell me.'

I learned afterwards that the Latin professor had taken Ikonin under his wing and that Ikonin actually lodged with him. I lost no time in answering the question in syntax which had been put to Ikonin but the professor pulled a long face and turned away from me.

'All right. Your turn will come and we'll see how much you know,' he said without looking at me, and proceeded to explain to Ikonin the point on which he had questioned him.

'You may go,' he said, and I saw him enter a four for Ikonin in the mark-book. 'Why,' I thought, 'he is not at all as severe as they made out.' After Ikonin had gone, for what must have been about five minutes but seemed to me like five hours he arranged his books and tickets, blew his nose, adjusted his arm-chair, sprawled back in it, looked down the hall, all round the room, and everywhere except at me. All this pretence did not, however, satisfy him; he opened a book and pretended to be reading it as though I were not there at all. I moved a little nearer and coughed.

'Ah, yes, you here still? Well, translate something,' he said, handing me a book. 'No, better take this one.' He turned over the pages of a volume of Horace and opened it for me at a passage which it seemed to me no one could ever translate.

'I have not prepared this,' I said.

'So you only want to recite what you have learned by heart – right! No, no, you translate this.'

I began to struggle with the meaning as best I could but at every inquiring glance of mine he shook his head and sighed a curt 'No'. At last, his nerves on edge, he closed the book so abruptly that his finger got caught between the pages. Angrily he pulled it out and handed me a slip with a grammar question on it, before leaning back in his chair to listen in the most ominous silence. I began to answer but the expression on his face paralysed my tongue and I felt that whatever I said was wrong.

'No, no, that's not it at all,' he suddenly broke in with his nasty accent, shifting his position and leaning forward with both elbows on the table, and playing with a gold ring that hung loosely on one of the lean fingers of his left hand. 'It won't do, sir, to prepare like that for the

higher educational institution; all fellows like you want is to wear
the uniform with its blue collar; you get a smattering of knowledge
and think you can be University students. No, my good sirs, you must
study your subject through and through . . .' and so on, and so on.

During the whole of this speech, delivered in mangled Russian, I
gazed with stupefied attention at his drooping eyes. At first I was
wretched with disappointment at not being third, then with fear that I
should not pass at all, and finally, a sense of injustice was added, of
wounded vanity and unmerited humiliation; besides this, contempt
for the professor for not being, according to my ideas, *comme il faut* – as
I discovered when I noticed his short hard round nails – still further
inflamed me until I felt venomous. Glancing at me and perceiving my
trembling lips and eyes filled with tears, he must have interpreted my
agitation as an appeal for a better mark and, as if taking pity on me, he
said (and this in the presence of another professor who had just come
up):

'All right, I will give you a pass-mark' (that meant he would give me
a two) 'though you do not deserve it. I do so only out of regard for
your youth and in the hope that you will not be so frivolous and
irresponsible when you begin your career at the University.'

This last sentence, spoken in the hearing of another professor who
looked at me as much as to say: 'There, you hear that, young man!'
completed my discomfiture. For a moment while everything went
dark before my eyes the terrible professor with his table seemed to me
to be sitting somewhere far off, and with awful one-sided distinctness
a wild idea danced into my brain: 'What if I were to . . . ? What would
happen?' But I did not do it for some reason. On the contrary, I automatically bowed most respectfully to both professors and with a faint
smile – very likely the same smile as Ikonin's had been – I left the table.

This piece of injustice affected me so strongly at the time that had I
been free to act as I chose I would not have presented myself for further
examination. I had lost every spark of my ambition (it was useless even
to think of being third) and I got through the rest of the questioning
without taking any pains, even with indifference. My marks, however,
averaged over four, but I was no longer interested. I reasoned it out and
proved very clearly to myself that it was silly in the extreme and even
mauvais genre[1] to try to be first; all that was necessary was to do not too
badly and not too well, like Volodya. It was my intention to keep to

1. Bad form.

this for the future at the University, though it meant disagreeing for the first time with my friend.

My thoughts were now only about my uniform, my cocked hat, my own trap, my own room and, above all, my freedom.

13 · I AM GROWN UP

And these thoughts had their charm.

When I returned home on the 8th of May after the examination in Divinity – the final one – I found the tailor's assistant from Rosanov's, whom I knew as he had previously brought a uniform and frock-coat of glossy black cloth which were only tacked together with the lapels marked with chalk. He now brought the finished suit with bright gilt buttons wrapped in tissue paper.

Donning the garments and finding them splendid (although St-Jérome insisted that the back of the coat wrinkled) I went downstairs to find Volodya with a self-satisfied smile which quite involuntarily spread over my face, aware but pretending not to notice that the servants were feasting their eyes on me from the passage and the ante-room. I was overtaken in the ball-room by Gavrilo, the major-domo, and congratulated on having passed into the University, and, on papa's orders, he handed me four twenty-five rouble notes and said, likewise on papa's orders, that the coachman, Kuzma, a drozhky and the bay horse, Beauty, were to be at my exclusive disposal from that day forth. I was so overjoyed at this almost unlooked-for good fortune that I could not keep up my pretence of indifference before Gavrilo but, somewhat breathless and hardly knowing whether I stood on my head or my heels, I said the first thing that occurred to me. 'Beauty is a very fine trotter,' I think it was. Then seeing all the heads protruding from the doors of the ante-room and the passage, and unable to restrain myself any longer, I ran full tilt through the ball-room in my new coat with the shining brass buttons. As I entered Volodya's room I heard behind me the voices of Dubkov and Nekhlyudov, who had come to congratulate me and to propose that we go and dine somewhere and drink champagne in honour of my matriculation. Dmitri told me that though he did not care about champagne he would come with us this time, to drink to our friendship. Dubkov remarked that for some reason I looked like a colonel. Volodya did not congratulate me and only observed very dryly that now we should be able to leave for the country the day after tomorrow. It seemed as though – while he was glad that I had got into the University – he did not altogether like my being as grown up as himself. St-Jérome, who also joined us at this moment, said in a very pompous manner that his duties were now at an end, that he did not know whether he had fulfilled them well or ill but he had done all he could and would move on the morrow to his count's. In response to all that was said to me I felt a sweet, blissful, rather foolishly complacent smile that I could not restrain playing over my countenance and I noticed that this smile even communicated itself to all who were speaking to me.

So now I have no tutor, I have a carriage of my own, my name is printed in the list of students, I wear a sword at my belt, policemen may sometimes salute me . . . I am grown up, and, so it seems, I am happy.

We decided to dine at Yar's soon after four but as Volodya went off with Dubkov, and Dmitri also disappeared in his usual fashion, saying he had business to attend to before dinner, I had two hours to dispose of as I pleased. For some while I walked through all the rooms, inspecting myself in all the looking-glasses, now with my coat buttoned up, now with it quite unbuttoned, now with only the top button fastened, and every way seemed perfect to me. Then, though ashamed to exhibit any excess of delight, I could not forbear going to the stable and coach-house to see Beauty, Kuzma and the trap. Then I went back indoors and once more began walking about the rooms, looking into the looking-glasses and counting the money in my pocket; smiling in the same blissful manner all the while. However, before an hour had passed I began to feel a bit bored and to regret that there was nobody to see me in my splendour; and I craved movement and activity. So I gave orders to harness Beauty, and made up my mind that I had better drive to Kuznetsky Bridge to do some shopping.

I remembered that when Volodya entered the University he had bought himself some lithographs of horses by Victor Adam, some tobacco and several pipes, and I felt it essential to do the same.

With people looking at me from all sides, with the sun shining on my gilt buttons, on the cockade of my hat and on my sword I drove up to Kuznetsky Bridge and stopped at Dazziaro's picture shop. With a glance all round me I stepped inside. I did not want to buy any Victor Adam horses, so as not to be accused of copying Volodya, but hurrying to make my choice as quickly as possible (I was embarrassed at the trouble to which I was putting the obliging shopman) I took a female head painted in gouache, which was in the window, and gave twenty roubles for it. Nevertheless, having paid over my twenty roubles I still felt uncomfortable at having bothered two such handsomely-dressed shopmen over such a trifle, besides which they still seemed to regard me rather too indifferently. Desirous of letting them understand what sort of person I was, I turned my attention to a little silver object which lay in a glass case, and being told that it was a *porte-crayon*[1] costing eighteen roubles I requested them to wrap it up in paper for me, and, having paid and been informed that good pipes and tobacco were to be had at the tobacconist's next door, I bowed politely to the two shop-men and went out into the street with the picture under my arm. In the neighbouring shop, which had a negro smoking a cigar on its sign-board, I bought (again not wishing to copy any one) not Zhukov but Turkish tobacco, a Stamboul pipe and two limewood and rosewood pipe-stems. On emerging from the shop and going towards my drozhky I saw Semeonov striding along the pavement in ordinary clothes with his head bent. Vexed that he did not recognize me, I said rather loudly: 'Here, Kuzma!', got into the drozhky and overtook Semeonov.

'How do you do,' I said to him.

'My respects to you,' he replied, pursuing his way.

'How is it you aren't in uniform?' I asked.

Semeonov stopped, screwing up his eyes and showing his white teeth as if it hurt him to look at the sun but in reality to express his indifference to my drozhky and my uniform, looked at me in silence and walked on.

From Kuznetsky Bridge I drove to a confectioner's in Tverskaya street and, though I tried to look as if I were chiefly interested in read-ing the newspapers they had there, I could not refrain from eating one pastry after another. In fact, for all that I felt ashamed before a gentle-man who watched me curiously from behind his paper, with extreme rapidity I devoured eight pastries, one of each sort they had in the shop.

When I got home I felt a touch of heartburn but taking no notice of it I began to examine my purchases. I liked the picture so little that I would not put it in a frame and hang it in my room as Volodya had done with his engravings but hid it carefully away behind the chest of

1. Pencil-holder.

drawers where nobody could see it. I did not like the *porte-crayon* either now that I had got it home. I put it in the table-drawer, comforting myself with the reflection that the thing was made of silver and therefore had value and was very useful for a student. The articles for smoking, however, I decided to put into use at once, and try them out.

Opening the quarter-pound packet, I carefully filled the Stamboul pipe with the reddish-yellow fine-cut Turkish tobacco, applied a hot cinder to it, and taking the long stem between my second and third fingers (a position of the hand which pleased me particularly), I began to draw in the smoke.

The smell of the tobacco was very pleasant but my mouth tasted bitter and the smoke choked me. However I made myself keep on for a fairly long time, trying to puff out rings and to inhale. Soon the whole room was filled with clouds of bluish smoke, the pipe began to wheeze, the hot tobacco to bob up and down; I felt a bitter taste in my mouth and my head was inclined to swim. I was about to give up, after just having a look at myself in the glass with my pipe, when to my astonishment I began to stagger on my feet; the room went round, and glancing into the mirror which I had reached with difficulty I saw that my face was as white as a sheet. I hardly managed to drop on the sofa before I felt so sick and so faint that, imagining the pipe to be fatal, it seemed to me I was dying. I was seriously alarmed and thought of calling for help and sending for a doctor.

However, this panic did not last long. I soon realized what the matter was, and with a dreadful headache and feeling quite weak I lay on the sofa for a long time, gazing vacantly at the trade-mark of Bostanzhoglo on the packet of tobacco, at the pipe I had thrown down on the floor, at the odds and ends of tobacco and confectioner's pastry; dejected and disillusioned I thought to myself that I could not be quite grown-up yet if I could not smoke like other people, and that evidently it was not my fate to hold a pipe between my second and third fingers, to inhale and emit smoke through a brown moustache.

When Dmitri called for me soon after four he found me in this unpleasant condition. After drinking a glass of water however, I felt almost right again and was ready to go with him.

'What do you want to smoke for?' he said, looking at the relics of my smoking bout. 'It is sheer stupidity, and a waste of money. I have promised myself not to smoke . . . But let's be off, we have still got to go and fetch Dubkov.'

14 · WHAT VOLODYA AND DUBKOV WERE DOING

The moment Dmitri entered my room I knew by his face, the way he walked and a peculiar gesture he made when he was in a bad temper – a blinking of one eye and an awkward jerking of his head to one side as if he were adjusting his neck-tie – that he was in one of the cold stubborn moods which came over him when he was dissatisfied with himself, and which always had a chilling effect upon my feelings towards him. Of late I had begun to observe and analyse my friend's character but our friendship had suffered no change in consequence: it was still so young and strong that from whatever angle I regarded Dmitri I could not help thinking him perfect. There were two different men in him, both of whom seemed splendid to me. One, whom I loved with all my heart, was kind, affectionate, mild, gay and conscious of these amiable qualities. When he was in this frame of mind his whole appearance, the sound of his voice, all his movements seemed to say, 'I am gentle and virtuous, and enjoy being gentle and virtuous, as you can all see.' The other – whom I had only now begun to discover and before whose majesty I bowed in admiration – was cold, stern towards himself and others, proud, fanatically religious and pedantically moral. At the present moment he was that second man.

With the frankness which constituted an essential condition of our relations I told him, when we had seated ourselves in the drozhky, that I was sad and pained to see him in a mood I found so irksome and disagreeable, on a day that was such a happy one for me.

'Something must have upset you. Why won't you tell me?' I asked.

'Nicolas, old man,' he replied unhurriedly, jerking his head nervously to one side and blinking, 'since I have given you my word never to conceal anything from you, you have no reason to suspect me of doing so. One cannot always be in the same mood, and if anything has upset me I can't account for it myself.'

'What a wonderfully frank and honest nature he has!' I thought, and said no more to him.

We drove the rest of the way to Dubkov's in silence. His apartments were remarkably fine, or so it seemed to me. Everywhere were rugs, pictures, hangings, bright wallpapers, portraits, carved easy chairs and lounge chairs; on the walls hung guns, pistols, tobacco-pouches and some papier-mâché heads of wild beasts. As soon as I saw his study I realized who it was Volodya had imitated in arranging his own room. We found Dubkov and Volodya playing cards. Some one I did not know (probably nobody of much importance, to judge by his unassuming attitude) was sitting by the table, following the game with close attention. Dubkov wore a silk dressing-gown and soft shoes. Volodya, with his coat off, sat on the sofa opposite him and judging by his flushed face and the impatient cursory glance he flung at us as he tore himself for a second from the cards was greatly absorbed in the game. On catching sight of me he flushed redder still.

'Your deal,' he said to Dubkov. I realized that he was not pleased at my knowing he played cards. But he did not appear at all abashed – the expression on his face seemed to say: 'Yes, I play cards, and it surprises you only because you are still so young. There's nothing wrong about it – indeed, it's the right thing at our age.'

I immediately felt and understood that what he said was true.

Dubkov, however, did not deal the cards but rose, shook hands with us, gave us chairs and offered us pipes, which we declined.

'So here he is, our diplomat, the hero of our festivities!' said Dubkov. 'Really he is terribly like a colonel.'

'Hm!' I growled, again feeling that silly complacent smile spreading over my face.

I respected Dubkov as only a boy of sixteen can respect an adjutant of twenty-seven who is said by all the grown-ups to be an exceptionally fine young man, who dances to perfection, speaks French and while at heart despising me for my youth obviously does his best to conceal the fact.

In spite of all my regard for him, during the whole of our acquaintance I always, Heaven knows why, found it difficult and uncomfortable to look him in the eyes. But I have since noticed that there are three kinds of people into whose eyes I cannot easily look – those who are far far worse than I am, those who are much better, and those who will not speak and with whom I could not speak of some particular thing of which we were both aware. Dubkov may have been a much better person than myself or he may have been a much worse, but it was certain that he often told lies without admitting it, and that I noticed this weakness of his and of course could not bring myself to tell him of it.

'Let us play one more hand,' said Volodya, jerking his shoulder like papa and shuffling the cards.

'How persistent he is!' said Dubkov. 'We can play all we want to afterwards. Well, all right then, one more round – give me the cards.'

While they were playing I watched their hands. Volodya had large well-shaped hands: the angle of his thumb and the curve of his fingers as he held the cards were so like papa's that at first I really thought he was doing it on purpose, so as to look grown-up, but a glance at his face was enough to convince me that his thoughts were entirely on the game. Dubkov, on the contrary, had small plump hands bent inwards, extremely adroit and with soft fingers; just the kind of hands, in fact, that wear rings and belong to people who are fond of using their hands and like having *objets de vertu* around them.

Volodya must have lost, for the man who was looking at the cards he held remarked that Vladimir Petrovich had terribly bad luck, and Dubkov, getting out his pocket-book, entered something in it and showing Volodya the note he had made said 'Right?'

'Right!' agreed Volodya, looking with feigned abstraction at the pocket-book. 'Now let us go.'

Volodya drove Dubkov, and Dmitri took me in his phaeton.

'What game were they playing?' I asked Dimitri.

'Piquet – a silly game. All card-playing is silly anyway.'

'And do they play for high stakes?'

'Not very, but still it's not right.'

'And don't you play?'

'No, I have vowed not to; but Dubkov can't resist not winning from some one.'

'But that is not right of him,' I said. 'I suppose Volodya does not play as well as he does?'

'Of course it's not right but there is nothing particularly bad about it. Dubkov likes playing, and knows how to play, but he is a good fellow all the same.'

'But I didn't in the least mean . . .' I began.

'And no one ought to think any harm of him for he really is a splendid fellow. I like him very much, and always shall, in spite of his weaknesses.'

It seemed to me somehow that just because Dmitri was sticking up so warmly for Dubkov he no longer liked or respected him, but he was not going to admit it out of obstinacy and lest he should be accused of being fickle. He was one of those people who love their friends for life, not so much because the friends continue to be lovable as because, having once taken a liking to any one, even mistakenly, they consider it dishonourable to cease to care for him.

15 · I AM FÊTED AT DINNER

Dubkov and Volodya knew everybody by name at Yar's, and everybody from the hall porter to the proprietor treated them with great respect. We were immediately shown into a private room and served with a wonderful dinner, which Dubkov selected from a French menu. A bottle of iced champagne, at which I tried to look as unconcernedly as possible, was ready waiting for us. The dinner passed off very agreeably and merrily, though Dubkov as usual told the strangest stories as if they were true – among others, how his grandmother had shot three highwaymen dead with a blunderbuss who were attacking her (which made me blush, lower my eyes and turn away from him) and though Volodya quailed visibly whenever I opened my mouth to speak (which was quite unnecessary for so far as I remember I did not say anything to be particularly ashamed of). When the champagne was served every one toasted me and I crossed hands with Dubkov and Dmitri and drank 'to our close friendship' with them, and we embraced each other. As I did not know who was standing the champagne (it was a joint bottle, I was afterwards told) and I wanted to treat my friends with my own money, which I kept fingering in my pocket, I stealthily extracted a ten-rouble note, called the waiter, gave him the money and in a whisper but so that everybody heard for they were all looking at me in silence asked him to 'be so good as to bring another half-bottle of champagne'. Volodya went red and writhed, and looked at me and the others in such a startled manner that I felt I had made a mistake but the half-bottle was brought and we emptied it, with the greatest satisfaction. Everything still seemed very jolly. Dubkov made up one fairy-tale after another. Volodya, too, related such funny stories, and told them far better than I should ever have expected of him, and we laughed a great deal. Their wit – Volodya's and Dubkov's – took the form of inventing variants and exaggerations of the familiar joke-sequence: 'Have you been abroad?' asks one. 'No I haven't,' the other answers, 'but my brother plays the violin.' The pair had reached such a pitch of perfection in this species of comic inanity that they changed the original reply to 'My brother never played the violin either.' They would answer all each other's questions in this fashion, or without a question did their best to unite the most incongruous ideas, and uttered this nonsense with serious faces – and the result was very funny. I began to get the hang of it, and tried to be funny myself, but the others looked embarrassed or tried not to look at me while I was speaking, and my anecdote fell flat. Dubkov said, 'Our diplomat is talking through his hat,' but I was so elated with the champagne I had drunk and the grown-up company I was in that this remark seemed hardly even a pinprick. Dmitri alone, though he had taken just as much to drink as we had, remained in his stern serious frame of mind, which put a certain check upon the general hilarity.

'Now then, listen, gentlemen,' said Dubkov. 'After dinner we must take our diplomat in hand. Supposing we go along to *Auntie's*? We could soon put him through his paces there.'

'But Nekhlyudov won't come,' said Volodya.

'The intolerable goody-goody! What an intolerable goody-goody you are!' said Dubkov, addressing Dmitri. 'You come with us, and you'll see what an excellent lady our Auntie is.'

'I am not going, and I won't let him go either,' answered Dmitri, flushing.

'Won't let who go? The diplomat? But you want to go, don't you, diplomat? Look at him, he beamed all over his face at the very mention of Auntie.'

'It's not exactly that I won't let him go,' continued Dmitri, rising and beginning to pace the room without looking at me, 'but I advise him not to go and I don't want him to. He's not a child now and if he wishes he can go by himself, without you. But you ought to be ashamed of yourself, Dubkov: because you do wrong you want others to do the same.'

'What is there wrong in my inviting you all to a cup of tea at Auntie's?' said Dubkov, winking at Volodya. 'But if you don't like to come with us, very well: let Volodya and me go on our own. Volodya, you'll come?'

'A-hah!' said Volodya affirmatively. 'We'll drive there, and afterwards go back to my place and continue our game of piquet.'

'Well, do you want to go with them or not?' asked Dmitri, coming up to me.

'No,' I answered, moving to make room for him beside me on the sofa, where he sat down. 'I didn't want to anyway, and if you are against it, nothing would induce me to. No,' I added a moment later, 'it's not true that I don't want to go with them, but I'm glad I am not going.'

'That's capital,' he said. 'Live your own way, and don't dance to any one else's tune. That's the best thing,'

This little argument not only failed to spoil our pleasure: it heightened it. Dmitri suddenly reverted to the gentle mood I liked best. The consciousness of having acted well (as I afterwards remarked on more than one occasion) had this effect on him. He was pleased with himself now for having deterred me. His spirits soared, he ordered another bottle of champagne (which was against his principles), invited a perfect stranger into our room and made him drink, sang *Gaudeamus igitur*, requested every one to join in the chorus, and proposed a drive to Sokolniki, whereupon Dubkov remarked that that would be too sentimental.

'Let us enjoy ourselves today,' said Dmitri, smiling. 'In honour of his matriculating into the University I will get drunk for the first time; so be it.' This merriment sat rather strangely on Dmitri. He was like a tutor or a kind father who is pleased with his children and has let himself go; he wants to make them happy and at the same time show them that it is possible to enjoy oneself in an honourable and decent fashion: however, this unexpected gaiety seemed to have an infectious influence on me and on the others – the more so as each of us had now drunk nearly half a bottle of champagne.

It was in this agreeable frame of mind that I went out into the main *salon* to light a cigarette which Dubkov had given me.

In rising I noticed that my head swam a little and my arms and legs behaved normally only so long as I fixed my attention on them. Otherwise my legs were inclined to betake themselves to one side while my arms described strange gestures. I concentrated all my attention on these limbs, commanded my hands to raise themselves, button my coat and smooth my hair (in doing so my elbows shot up terribly high), while I ordered my feet to walk to the door, which they did but they stepped either very firmly or too gingerly, especially my left foot, which went on tiptoe all the time. A voice called out, 'Where are you going? They'll bring you a candle.' I guessed that the voice belonged to Volodya, and I was pleased to think that after all I had guessed right, but I merely smiled airily in reply, and continued on my way.

16 · THE QUARREL

In the main *salon* a short thickset civilian gentleman with a red moustache sat eating something at a small table. Beside him was a tall dark clean-shaven man. They were speaking French. Their glance disconcerted me but I decided to light my cigarette at the candle in front of them. Looking about me so as not to meet their eyes, I went up to their table and began lighting my cigarette. When the cigarette was alight I could not resist casting a glance at the gentleman who was dining. His grey eyes were fixed malevolently upon me. I was about to turn away when his red moustache began to move and he said in French:

'Sir, I do not like people to smoke when I am dining.'

I muttered something incomprehensible.

'No, sir, I do not like it,' continued he with the moustache severely, with a swift look at the clean-shaven man as if inviting him to admire the way in which he was going to deal with me. 'Nor do I care, my good sir, for people who are discourteous enough to come and smoke under my nose. I do not care for them either.'

I realized at once that this gentleman was giving me a dressing-down, and at first it seemed to me I was very much in the wrong.

'I did not think it would incommode you,' I said.

'Ah, you did not think you were a boor but I did!' shouted the man.

'What right have you to shout?' I said, feeling that he was insulting me and beginning to get angry myself.

'This right, that I shall never allow any one to fail in respect to me, and I shall always give such fellows as you a lesson. What is your name, sir, and where do you live?'

I was so infuriated that my lips trembled and I could not get my breath. But I still felt in the wrong, probably for having drunk too much champagne, and I did not say anything impertinent but on the contrary my lips uttered my name and address in the most submissive manner.

'My name is Kolpikov, sir, and see that you are more courteous in future. You will hear from me. (*Vous aurez de mes nouvelles*),' he concluded, the conversation having been carried on in French.

To this I merely replied, 'I shall be delighted,' trying to make my voice as firm as possible, turned round, and with the cigarette, which by this time had gone out, went back to our room.

I said nothing of what had happened either to my brother or my friends, especially as they were engaged in some hot argument of their own. I seated myself alone in a corner, deliberating on this strange incident. The words 'You are a boor, sir! (*un mal élevé, monsieur*)' kept ringing in my ears, making me feel more and more indignant. My tipsiness was quite gone now. When I pondered over the way I had acted in this affair the awful thought struck me that I had behaved like a coward. What right had he to attack me? Why didn't he simply say that I was disturbing him? So it was *he* who was in the wrong then? And why, when he called me a boor, didn't I say to him: 'A boor, sir, is one who permits himself to be rude.' Or why didn't I simply tell him to hold his tongue? That would have been capital! Why didn't I challenge him to a duel? No, I did none of those things but swallowed his insults like a wretched coward. 'You are a boor, sir!' rankled incessantly in my ears. 'No, I can't leave it like that,' I thought, and I rose with the firm intention of going back to that gentleman and saying something outrageous to him, perhaps even throwing the candlestick at his head if occasion offered. This last idea afforded me vast delight, but it was not without considerable trepidation that I again entered the large room. Fortunately Mr Kolpikov had already left; only a single waiter remained, who was clearing the table. For a moment I felt like telling the waiter what had happened and explaining that I had not been one whit to blame, but for some reason I changed my mind and went back to our room in the most dismal spirits.

'What is the matter with our diplomat?' asked Dubkov. 'No doubt he's deciding the fate of Europe.'

'Oh, leave me alone,' I said, turning morosely away. After this, wandering about the room I began to think, I don't know why, that Dubkov was not a nice man at all. 'And why this everlasting jesting and calling me "diplomat" – there's nothing kindly about that. All he cares about is winning money from Volodya and going to see some "Auntie" . . . And there's nothing agreeable about him. Everything he says is a lie or a commonplace, and he is forever trying to make fun of people. In my opinion he's nothing but a fool, and a bad man into the bargain.' I spent about five minutes in such reflections, feeling for some reason a growing hostility to Dubkov. Dubkov, however, took no notice of me and this irritated me still further. I was even angry with Volodya and Dmitri for talking to him.

'I say, you fellows, we must pour some water over the diplomat,' said Dubkov suddenly, glancing at me with what I thought to be a derisive if not treacherous smile. 'He's in a bad way! By Jove, he is!'

'You want a sluicing too, you're in a bad way yourself,' I replied, smiling viciously.

My answer must have surprised Dubkov but he turned away with an air of indifference and continued his conversation with Volodya and Dmitri.

I tried to join in their talk but felt it quite impossible to dissemble, and retreated to my corner again, where I remained until our departure.

When we had settled our bill and were putting on our coats Dubkov turned to Dmitri and said:

'Well, and where will Orestes and Pylades go? Home, I suppose, to discourse of *love*. We anyhow are calling on our dear Auntie – that's better than your sour company.'

'How dare you speak like that and laugh at us?' I broke in suddenly, going up very close to him and waving my arms. 'How dare you laugh at sentiments you don't understand? I won't allow it! Hold your tongue!' I shouted, and held my own, not knowing what more to say, and breathless with agitation. Dubkov was surprised at first, then he tried to smile and take it as a joke, but finally to my great aston-ishment he looked scared and lowered his eyes.

'I am not laughing at you at all, nor at your feelings. It's just my way of talking,' he said evasively.

'I dare say!' I shouted but the next moment I felt ashamed of myself and sorry for Dubkov, whose flushed disconcerted face expressed genuine suffering.

'What is the matter with you?' Volodya and Dmitri began both at once. 'Nobody meant to hurt your feelings.'

'Yes, he wanted to insult me.'

'What a desperate fellow your brother is!' remarked Dubkov just as he was going out at the door so that he could not hear my rejoinder.

Possibly I might have flung myself after him and made some more offensive remarks, had it not been that just at that moment the waiter who had seen my encounter with Kolpikov handed me my greatcoat and I at once calmed down, only keeping up before Dmitri sufficient pretence of being angry to prevent the abrupt collapse of my wrath from seeming strange to him. Next day when Dubkov and I met in Volodya's room we did not allude to the affair but were rather aloof, and it was more difficult than ever for us to meet one another's eyes.

The memory of my quarrel with Kolpikov, who by the by did not let me 'hear from him' either the following day or on any other, remained for many a year horribly vivid and painful to me. For perhaps a full five years after the incident I writhed and groaned every time I remembered that unavenged insult, and could only comfort myself by recalling with satisfaction what a spirited young fellow I had shown myself in the affair with Dubkov. It was only very much later that I began to see the matter in quite a different light, and to look back on my quarrel with Kolpikov with comical amusement, and regret the undeserved abuse to which I had subjected 'that good fellow Dubkov'.

When that very evening I told Dmitri of my adventure with Kolpikov and described his appearance in detail Dmitri was astounded.

'It's the very same fellow!' he said. 'Fancy, that Kolpikov is a notorious good-for-nothing and card-sharper, as well as above all things a coward who was expelled from his regiment by his brother-officers because he refused to challenge some one who slapped his face. I wonder where he got his spunk from?' he added, looking at me with a kind smile. 'So he didn't say anything worse than "boor"?'

'No,' I admitted with a blush.

'It was rude, but there's no great harm done,' said Dmitri consolingly.

It was only long afterwards, on thinking the affair over quietly, that I arrived at the probable conclusion that Kolpikov, feeling that I might be attacked with impunity, in the presence of the dark clean-shaven man had avenged on me the slap in the face he had received years before, in the same way as I had at once avenged his calling me a 'boor' on the innocent Dubkov.

17 · I GET READY TO PAY SOME CALLS

My first thought on waking next morning was my adventure with Kolpikov; again I groaned and ran up and down the room but there was nothing to be done; besides, it was my last day in Moscow and papa had told me to call on the people whose names he had himself written down for me on a bit of paper. Papa's solicitude on our account was not so much for our morals or education as for our correct social behaviour. On the piece of paper was written in his broken rapid hand-writing: (1) Prince Ivan, *without fail*. (2) The Ivins, *without fail*. (3)

Prince Mihailo. (4) Princess Nekhlyudova and Madame Valakhina, if time. And of course the curator, the rector and the professors.

Dmitri dissuaded me from these last, saying that it was not only unnecessary but even not the thing, but all the other visits had to be paid that day. It was the first two on the list – those that were marked '*without fail*' that I dreaded most. Prince Ivan Ivanych held the rank of *Général-en-chef*, he was an old man, wealthy and living alone, so that for me, a sixteen-year-old student, to go and have direct personal contact with him could not, I surmised, be very flattering so far as I was concerned. The Ivins, too, were a wealthy family and their father was some highly-placed official who had called upon us only once, when grandmamma was alive. After grandmamma's death I had noticed that the youngest Ivin fought shy of us and seemed to be giving himself airs. The eldest Ivin, so I was told, had taken his degree in jurisprudence and been given a post in Petersburg; the second, Sergei, whom I had once almost worshipped, was also in Petersburg – a big fat cadet in the *Corps des Pages*.

In my youth I not only disliked having anything to do with people who considered themselves my superiors, but such intercourse was an unbearable torture for me owing to my constant dread of being snubbed and because I would strain every faculty of my intellect to show them my independence. However, if I was not going to carry out the latter part of papa's instructions I must make amends by complying with the first. I was walking about the room, examining my clothes, my sword and my hat – all laid out on chairs – and was just thinking of setting forth when old Grap, accompanied by Ilinka, arrived with his congratulations. Grap *père* was a Russianized German, intolerably specious, smooth-tongued and all too often the worse for wine: as a rule he visited us only when he wanted something, and papa occasionally invited him into his study but never had him to dine with us. His servility and his begging propensities went so much hand in hand with a kind of superficial good nature and habit of making himself at home in our house that everybody attributed great merit to him for his ostensible attachment to us all, but somehow I did not like him and always felt ashamed for him when he spoke.

I was much put out by the arrival of these visitors and made no effort to conceal my vexation. I was so accustomed to look down on Ilinka, and he was so accustomed to consider us right in doing so, that it was rather disagreeable for me to remember that he was a student like myself. It struck me, too, that he felt slightly guilty for thus being on an equal footing with me. I greeted them coldly and did not ask them to sit down because I felt embarrassed about doing so – I thought that they could do so just as well without being invited to by me – and I ordered my drozhky. Ilinka was a good-natured, most upright and by no means stupid young man but he was a fellow of moods, for ever being overcome, without apparent reason, by some extreme emotion – either tearfulness or laughter or touchiness over every trifle; and today he seemed to be in this last state. He did not speak, looked malevolently at me and at his father, and only when addressed responded with the submissive forced smile with which he was wont to hide all his feelings, and especially the shame for his father which he could not help feeling in our presence.

'So, Nikolai Petrovich,' said the old man, following me about the room while I dressed and slowly and respectfully revolving between his plump fingers a silver snuff-box my grandmother had given him, 'as soon as I heard from my son that you had passed your examination so well – though of course everybody knows what a brain you have – I hurried here at once to congratulate you, my dear boy. Why, I used to carry you about on my shoulder, and God is my witness that I love you all like my own kin, and my Ilinka kept begging to come and see you. He, too, feels quite at home with you, so he does.'

Ilinka meanwhile was sitting silently by the window, apparently gazing at my cocked hat and angrily muttering something under his breath.

'Well, and I wanted to ask you, Nikolai Petrovich,' the old man went on, 'did this Ilinka of mine do well in the examinations? He tells me he'll be in the same Faculty as yourself, so pray don't abandon him but keep an eye on him and advise him.'

'Oh yes, he passed splendidly,' I answered, glancing at Ilinka, who blushed and ceased moving his lips when he felt my glance.

'And might he spend the day with you?' asked the old man with a timid smile as if he were very much afraid of me, and following so closely wherever I went that the smell of liquor and tobacco with which he seemed to be impregnated did not leave me for a single second. I was annoyed that he was placing me in such a false position with regard to his son, and was distracting my attention from what was to me a highly important operation – my toilet; but above all I was so upset by the smell of spirits that pursued me that I replied icily that I could not stay with Ilinka because I should be out the whole day.

'Why, father, you wanted to go to sister's,' said Ilinka smiling and not looking at me, 'and I have something I want to do too.'

I felt still more vexed and uncomfortable, and to soften my refusal a little hastened to inform them that I should not be at home because I had to call on *Prince* Ivan Ivanych, *Princess* Kornakova and the Mr Ivin who held such important office, and that I should no doubt dine with *Princess* Nekhlyudova. I thought that when they heard what distinguished people I mixed with they could hardly make any more claims on me. As they were leaving I invited Ilinka to drop in and see me another time but he only muttered something and smiled with a constrained expression. It was plain that he would never set foot in the house again.

I followed them out and started on my round of visits. Volodya, whom I had asked in the morning to come with me so that I should feel less ill at ease than if I were by myself, had declined on the pretext that it would be too foolishly sentimental for two *brothers* to go driving together in one small drozhky.

18 · THE VALAKHINAS

So I set out alone. My first visit, in point of locality, was to the Valakhinas in the Sivtsev Vrazhok. I had not seen Sonya for about three years and of course my love for her had vanished long ago, yet there still lingered in my heart a vivid and affecting memory of my bygone childish affection. I had found myself more than once in the course of those three years thinking of her with such force and clarity that I had shed tears and felt myself in love again, but this had only lasted for a few minutes and did not soon recur.

I knew that Sonya and her mother had been abroad for a couple of years, and I had heard that they had been thrown out of a diligence and Sonya's face had been all cut by broken glass, which had greatly spoiled her looks. On the way to their house I pictured Sonya as she used to be and wondered what she would be like now. Somehow I imagined her extremely tall after her two years abroad, with a beautiful figure and, though sedate and imposing, extremely attractive. My imagination refused to picture a face disfigured by scars: indeed, having read somewhere of a passionate lover who remained faithful to his love though she was scarred by the smallpox, I tried to think that I was in love with

Sonya, in order to have the merit of remaining true to her despite her scars. As a matter of fact, driving to the Valakhinas' house, I had not really lost my heart but, having once stirred up old romantic memories, I was well prepared to fall in love, and very much wanted to, the more so as for some considerable time now I had felt ashamed to be left behind by my comrades when I saw all of them in love.

The Valakhinas lived in a small neat wooden house in a courtyard. The door was opened after I had rung a bell (then quite a rarity in Moscow) by a tiny trim little boy. He either could not or would not tell me whether the family were at home; and leaving me in the dark vestibule he ran off down a still darker passage.

I remained alone for quite a while in that dark hall, which in addition to the front door and that leading into the passage had a third door which was closed. I was partly surprised at the gloomy character of the house and in part supposed that it had to be so when the family had been abroad. After about five minutes the door leading into the parlour was opened from within by the same boy, who led me to a tidy but not luxurious drawing-room into which Sonya followed me.

She was seventeen, very small and thin, with a sallow unhealthy complexion. No scars were visible on her face but the lovely prominent eyes and her bright, gaily good-humoured smile were the same I had known and loved in my childhood. I had not at all expected to find her like this and so I could not at once give vent to the sentiment which I had been preparing on my way there. She held out her hand in the English fashion, which at that time was as great a novelty as the doorbell, pressed my hand frankly and made me sit beside her on the sofa.

'Oh I am glad to see you, dear Nicolas,' she said, looking into my face with so sincere an expression of pleasure that I felt a friendly and not a patronizing tone in the words 'dear Nicolas'. To my surprise, after her travels abroad she was even sweeter, more natural and like one of the family than she had been before. I noticed two slight scars, one near her nose and one on an eyebrow, but her wonderful eyes and smile were absolutely true to my memory of them and shone as of old.

'How you have changed!' she said. 'You've quite grown up. And what about me?'

'I should never have known you,' I replied, although at that very moment I was thinking that I should have known her anywhere. I again felt myself in that carefree happy mood of five years ago, when I had danced the *Grossvater* with her at grandmamma's ball.

'Why, have I quite lost my looks?' she asked, shaking her little head.

'Oh no, decidedly not!' I hastened to answer. 'You are taller, and older. And on the contrary you are . . . still more . . .'

'Well no matter! Do you remember our dances and the games, and St-Jérome and Madame Dorat?' (I did not remember any Madame Dorat; she was evidently carried away by her delight in her childhood reminiscences and was mixing them up.) 'Oh, it was a glorious time!' she continued, and I saw the same smile – a better one even – as I had kept in my memory, and the same eyes sparkled before me. While she was talking I had time to consider the condition I was in at that moment, and decided that at that moment I was in love. The instant I had decided this my happy carefree mood vanished, a dark cloud enveloped everything before me – even her eyes and smile; I felt ashamed of something, I blushed hotly and became tongue-tied.

'How times are altered,' she continued, sighing and raising her eyebrows a little. 'Everything has got much worse, and we have changed for the worse, too. Is not that so, Nicolas?'

I could not answer, and gazed at her in silence.

'Where are the Ivins now, and the Kornakovas we used to know? Do you remember them?' she pursued, scrutinizing my flushed and nervous face with some curiosity. 'Those were fine times!'

I was still unable to answer a word.

The entrance of Madame Valakhina for the moment released me from this painful condition. I rose, bowed and recovered the use of my tongue; but in return a strange change took place in Sonya on her mother's arrival. All her gaiety and friendly naturalness abruptly disappeared, even her smile was different, and all at once, except for her stature, she became the young lady returned from abroad that I had expected to find. There seemed no reason for such a transformation since her mother smiled every whit as pleasantly and all her movements were just as gentle as of old. She sat down in a large arm-chair and pointed me to a seat near by. She said something to her daughter in English and Sonya immediately left the room, which made me feel more at my ease. Madame Valakhina inquired after my relations, my brother, my father, and then spoke of her bereavement – the loss of her husband – and finally, feeling there was nothing more to speak about, looked at me in silence, as if to say: 'If you get up now, make your bow and depart you would be doing very well, my dear!' but a strange thing happened to me. Sonya returned with some needlework and sat down in another corner of the room so that I felt her eyes upon me. While her mother was telling me about the loss of her husband I had again remembered that I was in love, and, further, I fancied that the mother had already guessed this, and once more I was overcome by such a mighty fit of shyness that I felt unable to move a single limb of my body naturally. I knew that in order to get up and go away I should have to think where I was to place my feet, what to do with my head, with my hand – in short, I felt almost as I had done the evening before, after I had drunk half a bottle of champagne. I had a presentiment that I could not get through with all this and therefore *could not* rise, and I really *could not* do so. Madame Valahkina must have wondered at my face as red as a lobster and my complete immobility; but I decided it was better to sit still in that foolish state rather than risk getting up and making a ridiculous exit. Thus I sat on for a considerable while, hoping that some unforeseen occurrence would help me out of my predicament. The occurrence presented itself in the person of an insignificant young man who entered the room with an air of being a member of the household, and bowed politely to me. Madame Valakhina rose, excusing herself on the ground that she had to speak to her *homme d'affaires*, and looked at me with a puzzled expression, as much as to say, 'If you want to sit there for ever I won't turn you out.' With a tremendous effort I got to my feet but was unable to bow, and as I went out, followed by pitying looks from mother and daughter, I stumbled against a chair that had not been at all in my way – but I knocked against it because all my attention was centred upon not tripping over the rug which was under my feet. In the fresh air, however, after giving myself a shake and groaning so loudly that even Kuzma several times inquired what he could do for me, the feeling passed off, and I began to meditate calmly enough on my love for Sonya and on her relations with her mother, which struck me as singular. When I afterwards told my father how I had noticed that Madame Valakhina and her daughter were not on good terms he said:

'Yes, she leads the poor girl an awful life with her dreadful mean-ness, and it's a funny thing,' he added, with more feeling than could have been excited by mere blood relationship. 'What a charming sweet wonderful woman she used to be! I can't make out why she has changed so. You did not see a secretary fellow about, did you? And what an idea for a Russian lady to have a secretary!' he said irately, walking away from me.

'Yes, I did,' I replied.

'Well, I hope at least he's good-looking?'

'No, far from it.'

'Incomprehensible!' said papa angrily, jerking his shoulder and coughing . . .

'So here am I in love,' I thought to myself, as I rode on in my drozhky.

19 · THE KORNAKOVS

Now came my second call, the Kornakovs. They lived on the first floor of a large house in Arbat street. The staircase was extremely grand and well-kept but not sumptuous. The drugget was held down by very brightly polished brass rods but there were no plants or looking-glasses about. The ball-room, too, with its gleaming parquet, which I traversed on my way to the drawing-room, was severely cold and orderly: everything shone and looked solid though not very new, but there were no pictures, no hangings, no ornaments to be seen anywhere. Some of the princesses were in the drawing-room. They were sitting in attitudes of such studied idleness that it was at once apparent they did not sit like that when there were no visitors.

'*Maman* will be here directly,' said the eldest, seating herself a little closer to me. For the next quarter of an hour this princess entertained me, talking with such ease and fluency that the conversation never faltered for an instant. But it was too evident that she was entertaining me and so I did not like her. Among other things she told me that their brother Stepan, whom they called 'Étienne' and who had gone to the Cadet School two years ago, had already been made an officer. When she spoke about her brother, and especially when she was telling me of his having joined the Hussars against their mother's wish, she put on a frightened look and all the younger princesses, who were sitting silent, put on frightened faces too. When she mentioned grandmamma's death she assumed a mournful air and all the younger princesses did the same; but when she recalled how I had hit St-Jérome and been taken out of the room she laughed and showed her bad teeth and all the princesses laughed and showed their bad teeth.

The princess, their mother, came in – the same small wizened woman with restless eyes and a habit of looking at other people while she was talking to you. She took my hand and raised her own to my lips for me to kiss, a thing I should otherwise never have done, not realizing that it was necessary.

'I am so glad to see you,' she exclaimed with her usual ready flow of speech, looking round at her daughters. 'Ah, how like his mamma he is. Isn't that so, Lise?'

Lise agreed that it was so, though I know for a fact I possessed not the slightest resemblance to my mother.

'So now you are quite a grown-up man! And my Étienne, you remember him, of course he's your second cousin – no, not second but . . . what is it, Lise? My mother was Varvara Dmitrievna, Dmitri Nikolayevich's daughter, and your grandmother was Natalya Nikolayevna.'

'That makes him third cousin, *maman*,' said the eldest princess.

'Oh you always get things wrong,' her mother told her irritably. 'It's not third cousin at all, but *issus de germains* – cousins once removed – that's what you and my little Étienne are. He's an officer now, did you know? Only it's not good that he has so much liberty. You young people must be kept in hand – properly in hand! You are not cross with your old aunt for telling you the truth? I was always very strict with Etienne, and I believe that it has to be so.

'Yes, that's how we are related,' she continued. 'Prince Ivan Ivanych is my uncle, and he was an uncle of your mother's. So your mother and I must have been first cousins – no second cousins, yes, that's it. Well, and tell me, my dear, have you been to call on *Prince Ivan*?'

I said I had not done so yet but was going to that day.

'Oh, but how could you!' she cried. 'Your first visit ought to have been to him. You know that Prince Ivan is like a father to you. He has no family of his own so you and my children are his sole heirs. You should honour him for his age and his position in society and everything else. I know you young people of the present generation think precious little of family ties and don't like old people; but you pay attention to what your old aunt says, because I am fond of you and I was fond of your mother and your grandmother too – I loved and esteemed her very much indeed. Yes, you certainly must go and call on him, you really must, without fail.'

I said I would be sure to go, and as I thought my visit had lasted long enough I got up to leave but she detained me.

'No, wait a moment. Lise, where is your father? Tell him to come here. He will be so glad to see you,' she added, turning to me.

A couple of minutes later Prince Mihailo entered. He was a short thick-set man, extremely slovenly in his dress, unshaven, and with such a stolid expression on his face that he looked almost stupid. He was not in the least glad to see me. But his wife, of whom he was apparently very much afraid, said to him:

'Isn't Voldemar' (she had evidently forgotten my name) 'like his mother?' and she made a sign with her eyes so that the prince, who must have guessed what she wanted, came up to me and with the most apathetic, even resentful expression on his face offered his unshaven cheek, which I was forced to kiss.

'But you are not dressed yet and you have to go out,' said the princess to him immediately afterwards, in the angry tone which she was seemingly in the habit of using to her family. 'You want to provoke people again and set everybody against you.'

'I shall be ready directly, directly, my dear,' said Prince Mihailo, and left the room. I made my bow and departed too.

It was the first time I had heard that we were Prince Ivan Ivanych's heirs and the news struck me unpleasantly.

20 · THE IVINS

I now found the thought of the unavoidable visit before me still more disagreeable. But before going to the prince I had first to call on the Ivins on my way. They lived in Tverskaya street, in a large handsome house. It was not without some nervousness that I entered the great portico where a door-keeper stood holding a staff.

I asked him whether anybody was at home.

'Who do you want to see? The general's son is at home,' said the door-keeper.

'And the general himself?' I inquired bravely.

'I will announce you. Who shall I say?' he asked, and rang a bell. The gaitered legs of a footman appeared on the staircase. Without knowing why, I so completely lost my courage that I told the footman not to announce me to the general since I would first go and see his son. As I ascended the huge staircase I felt as if I had become terribly small (not in a figurative but in the literal sense of the word). I had experienced the same sensation as my drozhky drove up to the main entrance: it had seemed to me that the drozhky, the horse and the coachman had shrunk in size. The general's son was lying asleep on the sofa with an open book before him when I entered the room. His tutor, Herr Frost, who was still with them, came in behind me with his usual jaunty step, and aroused his pupil. Ivin did not show any particular pleasure on seeing me, and I noticed that he looked at my eyebrows as he talked. Although he was very polite I felt that he was entertaining me as the eldest princess had done, and that he did not feel especially drawn to me nor in any need of my acquaintance, since he no doubt had another circle of friends of his own. All this I conjectured principally from the fact that he gazed at my eyebrows. In short his attitude towards me was, distasteful as it is to admit it, much the same as mine to Ilinka. My temper began to rise; I followed Ivin's every glance and when his eyes met Frost's I interpreted his look as a mute inquiry: 'Whatever has he come here for?'

After talking to me for a short time Ivin said that his father and mother were at home and would I not like to go down and see them with him?

'Just a minute and I'll get dressed,' he added, going into another room, though he was very well dressed in this one – he had on a new coat and white waistcoat. A few minutes later he reappeared in his University uniform, buttoned up to the chin, and we went downstairs together. The reception rooms through which we passed were very large, lofty and, I thought, luxuriously furnished: there was marble and gilding, and something wrapped in muslin, and mirrors. Just as we entered a small drawing-room Ivin's mother came in through another door. She greeted me in a very friendly manner, made me sit beside her and inquired with interest after all our family.

Having seen her barely a couple of times, I now considered her carefully and liked her very much. She was tall and thin and very pale, and seemed to have a permanently mournful weary look. Her smile was a sad one but very kind; there was a slight cast in her large tired eyes which gave her a sadder and still more attractive expression. She sat not exactly bent but with her whole body limp, and all her movements were drooping. She spoke languidly but the timbre of her voice and the way she lisped her r's and l's were very pleasing. She did not try to entertain me. My answers to her inquiries about my relations apparently afforded her a melancholy interest, as if while listening to me she sadly recalled happier times. Her son went off somewhere. She gazed at me in silence for a minute or two and suddenly burst into tears. I sat before her and could not for the life of me conceive what to do or say. She went on weeping without looking at me. At first I felt sorry for her, then I wondered whether I ought not to try and comfort her, and how to do it; and finally I became vexed that she should place me in such an awkward situation. 'Can I really present such a pathetic sight?' I reflected. 'Or is she doing this on purpose to see how I behave in such circumstances? I can't very well leave now, as though I were running away from her tears,' was my next thought. And I turned on my chair at least to remind her of my presence.

'Oh, how foolish I am!' she said, glancing at me and making an effort to smile. 'There are days when one weeps without any reason.'

She fumbled about for the handkerchief beside her on the sofa and suddenly broke out crying more violently than before.

'Oh dear, how ridiculous it is to keep on crying! I loved your mother so, we were such . . . friends . . . and . . .'

She found the handkerchief, covered her face with it and continued to cry. Once more I was in an uncomfortable situation, which lasted for some considerable while. I was annoyed but also still more sorry for her. Her tears seemed genuine and yet I kept thinking that she was not crying so much over my mother's death as because she herself was feeling unhappy and things had been much better in those days. I do not know how it would have ended if young Ivin had not reappeared and said that his father wanted her. She rose and was just going when Ivin *père* came into the room. He was a short sturdily-built man with bushy black eyebrows. His hair was quite grey and cut short and the set of his mouth firm and austere to a degree.

I rose and bowed to him but Ivin *père*, who had three decorations on his green dress-coat, not only did not return my greeting but scarcely looked at me, which suddenly made me feel I was not a human being but some negligible object like an arm-chair or window – or if I were human I was still quite indistinguishable from an arm-chair or window.

'You have not yet written to the countess, my dear,' he said to his wife in French, with an impressive but rigid expression on his face.

'Good-bye, Monsieur Irtenyev,' his wife said to me, inclining her head rather haughtily all at once and looking at my eyebrows as her son had done. I bowed once more to her and her husband, and again my bow had no more effect on old Ivin than the opening or shutting of a window might have done. But the student Ivin accompanied me to the door and told me on the way that he was being transferred to the Petersburg University as his father had received an appointment there (and he mentioned some very important post).

'Well, whatever papa may say,' I muttered to myself as I got into my drozhky, 'I will never set foot in that house again: the wife snivels and cries when she looks at me as if I were some miserable wretch, while that old pig of an Ivin does not acknowledge my bow; but I'll give it him . . .' How I was going to give it him I certainly did not know but that is what I found myself saying.

In after-days I was frequently obliged to listen to the exhortations of my father, who said that it was essential to cultivate their acquaintance and that I could not expect a man in Ivin's position to take any notice of a youngster like me; but I held to my resolution for a long time.

21 · PRINCE IVAN IVANYCH

'Well, now for the last visit – Nikitskaya street,' I said to Kuzma, and we drove to Prince Ivan Ivanych's house.

Having gone through the ordeal of a round of calls, towards the end I usually acquired a measure of self-confidence, and was now approaching the prince's house in a tolerably composed state of mind when suddenly I remembered the weeping Princess Kornakova's remark that I was one of his heirs; besides which, I saw two carriages standing at the entrance and my former nervousness returned.

I thought that the old servant who opened the door, and the footman who helped me off with my greatcoat, and the three ladies and two gentlemen whom I found in the drawing-room, and especially Prince Ivan Ivanych himself, in mufti sitting on the sofa, all regarded me as an heir of his, and consequently eyed me with ill-will. The prince was very affable and kissed me – that is, he touched my cheek for an instant with his soft dry cold lips – inquired about my studies and plans, jested with me, asked whether I still wrote verses like those I had composed for grandmamma's name-day, and said I must stay to dinner. But the more gracious he was, the more I fancied that he only lavished his kindness upon me in order to conceal how much he disliked the idea that I was his heir. He had a habit, caused by a mouthful of false

teeth, of raising his upper lip towards his nose after speaking, and emit-
ting a slight snuffling sound as if he were trying to draw the lip into
his nostrils, and on the present occasion whenever he did this it seemed
to me he was saying to himself 'That boy, that boy, I don't need him
here to remind me he's my heir, my heir,' and so on.

When we were children we used to call Prince Ivan Ivanych 'grandpapa' but now in my capacity of heir my tongue could not bring
itself to say 'grandpapa' to him, and to call him 'your excellency' – as
did one gentleman who was there – seemed humiliating, so during the
entire conversation I tried to avoid addressing him in any way. But it
was an old princess, also an heir of his and who lived in his house, who
made me feel most uncomfortable of all. I sat beside her at dinner and
all the time I fancied the reason she said nothing to me was because she
hated me for being an heir like herself, and that the prince paid no
attention to our side of the table because we, the princess and I, were
both his heirs and therefore equally distasteful to him.

'No, you would not believe how disagreeable it was,' I told Dmitri
that same evening, wanting to brag to him about my aversion to the
idea of being an heir (which seemed to me a very laudable sentiment) –
'how I loathed the entire two hours I spent at the prince's. He is an
excellent man and was very affable with me,' I continued, wishing
among other things to impress on my friend that I was not saying all
this because I had been made to feel small by the prince, 'but,' I continued, 'the thought that people might class me with the princess who
lives in his house and who licks the dust off his boots is a horrible one.
He is a marvellous old man, and exceedingly kind and considerate to
every one, but it is awful to see how he *maltreats* that princess. Money is
a detestable thing and spoils every relationship!

'You know, I think it would be far better to have it out with the
prince,' I went on, 'to tell him I esteem him as a man but think nothing
of being his heir, and ask him not to leave me anything, and say it is
only on that condition that I can visit his house in future.'

Dmitri did not burst out laughing when I said this; on the contrary,
he was silent and after pondering for a while said:

'Well, I think you are wrong. Either you ought not to go about
supposing that people might be thinking about you as they think about
that princess of yours, or if you do, you should go further: I mean, tell
yourself that you know what people may be thinking of you but that
such thoughts are so foreign to your nature that you despise them and

would never do anything on that sort of basis. Now suppose that they suppose that you suppose that . . . In a word,' he concluded, feeling that his argument was getting tangled up, 'it's much better not to suppose anything at all.'

My friend was perfectly right, though it was not till long long afterwards that experience of life taught me the evil that comes of thinking – still worse, speaking – of much that may seem very noble but which every one ought to keep hidden in his own heart, and that noble speeches seldom go with noble deeds. I am convinced that once a good intention has been put into words, for that very reason it becomes difficult, nay almost impossible of fulfilment. But how refrain from giving utterance to the lofty self-satisfied impulses of youth? Only much later in life does one remember and regret them, as one regrets a flower which one has heedlessly plucked, ere it had opened, and subsequently seen lying on the ground withered and trampled on.

The very next morning I, who had just been telling my friend, Dmitri, that money spoils all human relations, before leaving for the country borrowed the twenty-five roubles in notes which he offered to lend me for the journey when I found that I had squandered all my money on pictures and Turkish pipes. And I did not repay him for a very long time.

22 · AN INTIMATE CONVERSATION WITH MY FRIEND

This talk took place in the phaeton on the road to Kuntsevo. Dmitri had dissuaded me from calling on his mother in the morning but had come after dinner to take me to spend the whole evening and perhaps even stay overnight at the summer residence where his family were living. Only after we had left the city with its dirty motley streets and exchanged the intolerable deafening clatter of its carriage-ways for a broad view of fields and the soft crunching of our wheels along the dusty road, and the fragrant spring air and the open space surrounded me on all sides – only then did I to a certain extent recover from the many new impressions and the sensation of freedom which had so completely unsettled me during the last two days. Dmitri was sociable and in his gentle mood, and did not jerk his head to adjust his cravat, or blink nervously or screw up his eyes. I was smugly content with the noble sentiments I had expressed to him, believing now he had them in mind he could quite excuse the shameful affair with Kolpikov and would not despise me for it; and we conversed in a friendly way on many an intimate subject which friends do not on each and every occasion discuss together. Dmitri told me about his family, whose acquaintance I had not yet made, about his mother, his aunt, his sister, and *her*, whom Volodya and Dubkov regarded as his lady-love and called the 'lady of the chestnut locks'. He spoke of his mother with a kind of cold and formal commendation, as though to prevent any rejoinder on that score. His aunt he extolled enthusiastically, if with a touch of condescension; of his sister he said very little, as though embarrassed to speak to me about her; but on the 'lady of the chestnut locks', whose real name was Lyubov Sergeyevna and who was a middle-aged spinster living for family reasons with the Nekhlyudovs, he discoursed with great animation.

'Yes, she's a wonderful woman,' he said, blushing shyly but looking all the more boldly into my eyes. 'She's no longer young, in fact rather elderly, and not a bit good-looking, but then what folly, what nonsense, it is to love beauty! I never can understand that, it is so silly,' (he said this as if he had just discovered a new and remarkable truth) 'but she has such a soul, such a heart, such principles . . . I am convinced you could not find another like her in the world today.' (I don't know from whom Dmitri had acquired the habit of saying that everything that was good was rare in the world today, but he was fond of repeating the expression and it suited him somehow.)

'I am only afraid,' he continued quietly, having thus completely demolished all those who were silly enough to love beauty, 'I am afraid you will not understand or appreciate her quickly: she is modest and even reserved, and not fond of displaying her beautiful, her marvellous qualities. Now my mother, who as you will see is a splendid intelligent woman, has known Lyubov Sergeyevna for years but still cannot and will not appreciate her. Even yesterday . . . I will tell you why I was out of temper when you asked me. The day before yesterday Lyubov Sergeyevna wanted me to go with her to see Ivan Yakovlevich – you must have heard of Ivan Yakovlevich: he's supposed to be crazy but really he's a remarkable man. Lyubov Sergeyevna, I must tell you, is terribly religious and understands Ivan Yakovlevich perfectly. She often goes to see him, they talk, and she gives him money for the poor which she earns herself. She is a wonderful woman, you will see. Well, so I went with her to Ivan Yakovlevich, and very grateful I am to her for giving me the opportunity to see such a remarkable man. But mother does not choose to understand: she thinks it's all superstition. And yesterday for the first time in my life I had an argument with mother – and a rather heated one, too,' he concluded, with a convulsive movement of his neck as if recalling the feeling he had experienced during the disagreement.

'Well, and what do you think? I mean, how – when do you imagine anything will come of it? . . . or have you talked about the future with her – about how your love or friendship will end?' I asked, to divert his mind from such a disagreeable recollection.

'You mean, am I thinking of marrying her?' he said, blushing again but turning and resolutely looking me in the face.

'No, of course,' I thought, reassuring myself, 'there's no harm in my asking: we are two grown-up friends, driving in a phaeton and discussing the future. Any one would enjoy overhearing us and looking at us.'

'Why not?' he went on, after I had answered in the affirmative. 'It is my aim, as it is the aim of every sensible man, to be happy and good, so far as that is possible; and with her, if only she should be willing, as soon as I am entirely independent I should be happier and better than with the greatest beauty on earth.'

Engaged in such conversation we did not notice that we were approaching Kuntsevo, neither did we notice that the sky had become overcast and rain was threatening. The sun had sunk low to the right above the old trees of the Kuntsevo garden, and one half of its brilliant red circle was shrouded by a grey slightly translucent cloud, while broken fiery rays splintered in bursts from the other half, lighting up with brilliant blinding light the thick green crowns of the old trees shining motionless against the still clear blue sky. The glitter and light of this stretch of the heavens contrasted sharply with the heavy purple cloud which hung over the young birch copse on the horizon in front of us.

A little to the right, behind the trees and shrubs, we could already see the parti-coloured roofs of the cottages round the country house, some of which reflected the lustrous rays of the sun while others assumed the melancholy character of the other half of the heavens. To the left, lower down, a pond lay deep-blue and still, surrounded by pale-green willows which were darkly mirrored on its opaque and seemingly convex surface. Half-way up the hill beyond the pond stretched a black fallow field, and a straight line of bright green which ran across it disappeared in the distance, losing itself in the threatening leaden horizon. On either side of the soft road, which our phaeton swayed evenly along, juicy belts of rye sprouted vivid green, here and there beginning to form stalks. The air was absolutely still and fragrantly fresh; the green of the trees, of the leaves and the rye was motionless and extraordinarily pure and bright. It seemed as if each leaf, each blade of grass was living its own full, happy, individual life. Beside the road I noticed a blackish footpath winding through the dark-green rye, already more than a quarter grown, and this footpath somehow reminded me in an astonishingly acute fashion of the country at home, and by some strange sequence of thought that memory reminded me in an astonishingly acute fashion of Sonya and of the fact that I was in love with her.

In spite of all my fondness for Dmitri and the pleasure his frankness afforded me I did not want to know anything more about his feelings and intentions towards Lyubov Sergeyevna but urgently desired to tell him about my love for Sonya, which seemed to be of a much higher order. But for some reason or other I could not make up my mind to tell him straight out how splendid I thought it would be when I had married Sonya and we were living in the country, and I should have tiny children crawling about on the floor who would call me 'papa', and how delighted I should be when he came and visited me in his travelling suit with his wife Lyubov Sergeyevna ... and instead of all that I remarked, pointing to the setting sun: 'Look, Dmitri, how lovely!'

Dmitri did not say anything, evidently disappointed that in response to his confession, which had probably cost him an effort, I drew his attention to nature, to which he was more or less indifferent. Nature affected him quite otherwise than it did me: it affected him not so much by its beauty as by the attraction it held for him; he loved it with his intellect rather than his heart.

'I am very happy,' I said to him after this, paying no heed to the fact that he was apparently occupied with his own thoughts and was quite unconcerned with what I might say to him. 'You remember I told you about a young lady with whom I was in love as a child? Well I saw her today,' I went on eagerly, 'and now I am in love with her in earnest.'

And in spite of the lack of interest which his face continued to express I told him about my love and my plans for future married bliss. And strange to say, no sooner had I described in detail the force of my feelings than I instantly became conscious that they were beginning to diminish.

A shower overtook us just as we turned into the birch avenue leading to the house but we did not get wet. I only knew it was raining because a few drops fell on my nose and hand, and something began pattering on the young sticky leaves of the birch-trees which, drooping their curling motionless branches, seemed to enjoy those clear transparent drops, their delight expressing itself by the fragrance with which they filled the avenue. We got out of the phaeton to run quickly through the garden to the house. But right at the door we encountered four ladies who – two with needlework, one with a book and the other with a lapdog – were rapidly approaching from another direction. Dmitri at once introduced me to his mother, his sister, his aunt and Lyuba Sergeyevna. They halted for a second but the rain coming down faster and faster the lady whom I took for Dmitri's mother said:

'Let us go to the gallery and you shall introduce him to us again there,' and we ascended the steps with the ladies.

23 · THE NEKHLYUDOVS

At first amongst the whole company I was most struck by Lyubov Sergeyevna, who in thick knitted slippers and carrying the little spaniel in her arms ascended the steps behind the other ladies, and stopping a couple of times looked round at me very attentively and then immediately kissed her dog. She was very plain, red-haired, thin, short and slightly misshapen. What made her plain face plainer still was the peculiar way her hair was done with the parting on one side (one of those coiffures which bald women devise for themselves). Try as I would for my friend's sake, I could not discover a single handsome trait in her. Even her small hazel eyes, though they had a kindly expression, were too small and dull and decidedly not beautiful; while her hands (that most revealing feature), though not large and not badly shaped, were red and rough.

Following on their heels I reached the gallery where each of the ladies – except Varya, Dmitri's sister, who only looked intently at me with her large dark-grey eyes – addressed a few words to me

before taking up their work again while Varya began to read aloud
from a book which she held in her lap with her finger between the
pages.

Princess Marya Ivanovna was a tall graceful woman of about forty.
She might have been taken for more, to judge by the greyish curls
which were frankly displayed beneath her cap. But her fresh extremely
delicate face with hardly a wrinkle, and particularly the lively gay
sparkle of her large eyes, made her appear much younger. Her eyes
were hazel and very wide open, her lips were too thin and rather severe,
her nose was regular but slightly inclined to the left. There were no
rings on her large almost masculine hands with their fine tapering
fingers. She wore a high-necked dark-blue dress, tightly fitting her
graceful and still youthful waist, which she evidently liked to show off.
She sat remarkably straight, sewing some garment. When I entered
the gallery she took my hand, drew me to her as if wishing to scrutinize
me more closely, and said, after she had gazed at me with a somewhat
cold frank look like her son's, that she had long known me from
Dmitri's accounts, and in order to get better acquainted she invited me
to stay with them until the next day.

'Do whatever you like, don't mind about us in the least, just as we
shall stand on no ceremony with you. Go for a walk, read, listen or
sleep, if you find that more amusing,' she added.

Sophia Ivanovna, the princess's sister, was a maiden lady; she was
younger than the princess but looked older. She had that peculiar
over-full figure which is only met with in very stout old maids who are
short and wear corsets. It was as if all her robustness had mounted upwards with such force that it threatened every moment to choke her.
Her short fat arms could not meet lower than the curved peak of her
bodice, and that tightly-stretched peak of her bodice she could no
longer see.

Though Princess Marya Ivanovna had dark hair and dark eyes, while
Sophia Ivanovna was fair with large vivacious and (what is very rare)
serene blue eyes, there was a strong family likeness between the sisters:
the same expression, the same nose and the same lips; only Sophia
Ivanovna's nose and lips were a little fuller and inclined slightly to the
right when she smiled, whereas her sister's inclined towards the left.
Sophia Ivanovna, judging by her dress and the way her hair was done,
still tried to look younger than her age, and would never have displayed grey curls had she had any. At first her glance and bearing

towards me seemed very haughty and made me nervous, whereas with the princess, on the contrary, I felt quite at ease. Perhaps her stoutness and a certain resemblance to the portrait of Catherine the Great, which struck me, gave her that proud look in my eyes; at any rate I shrank into myself when, gazing fixedly at me, she said: 'The friends of our friends are our friends.' I only recovered and suddenly quite changed my opinion of her when after uttering this sentiment she was silent and opening her mouth sighed heavily. It was probably on account of her corpulence that she had a habit of sighing deeply after every few words, with her mouth open a little and slightly rolling her big blue eyes. This practice of hers was somehow expressive of such sweet kindliness that after that sigh I lost all fear of her. Indeed, I liked her very much. Her eyes were charming, her voice melodious and pleasant, and even the extreme rotundity of her figure did not seem to me, at that period of my youth, wholly devoid of beauty.

As the friend of my friend, Lyubov Sergeyevna ought at once, I considered, to have said something very friendly and intimate to me, and she did look at me for some time in silence, as if undecided whether what she intended to say would not be too familiar, but she broke the silence only to ask me what Faculty I was in. Then she again stared at me intently for quite a while, apparently hesitating whether to say those intimate friendly words or not, and I, noticing this hesitation, mutely entreated her with my eyes to speak freely, but she only remarked: 'They say nowadays not many young men study science at the University,' and then called her little dog, Suzette.

All that evening Lyubov Sergeyevna made pronouncements of a kind which generally had no connexion with the matter in hand or with each other: but I had such faith in Dmitri, and he kept looking the whole time so anxiously now at me, now at her, with an expression that asked: 'Well, what do you think of her?' that I, as so often happens, though at heart convinced there was nothing so very special about Lyubov Sergeyevna, was still very far from formulating that thought even to myself.

Finally Varya, the last member of the family, was a buxom girl of about sixteen.

The only pretty things about her were her large dark-grey eyes which with their dual expression of gaiety and quiet thoughtfulness were exceedingly like her aunt's, her very thick plaits of brown hair and her exceptionally delicate beautiful hands.

'I expect you find it dull, Monsieur Nicolas, to hear the middle of the story without knowing the beginning,' said Sophia Ivanovna to me with her good-natured sigh, turning over the pieces of a garment she was making.

The reading had stopped just then because Dmitri had gone out of the room.

'Or perhaps you have read *Rob Roy* before?'

At that time I thought it incumbent on me, if only on account of my student's uniform, always to give very *clever and original* answers to even the simplest question put to me by people I did not know very well; and I should have been deeply ashamed to offer brief plain replies like 'Yes,' 'No,' 'I don't care for it,' 'I like it,' and so on. With a glance at my fashionable new trousers and the shining buttons on my coat I said that I had not read *Rob Roy* but that it was very interesting to me to listen to it because I preferred to read books from the middle rather than from the beginning.

'It is doubly interesting,' I added with a self-satisfied smile. 'One tries to guess what has gone before and what will happen further on.'

The princess laughed – a forced laugh, it seemed to me. (I noticed later that she never laughed in any other way.)

'Well, I expect that's true,' she said. 'And will you be staying long in Moscow, Nicolas? You don't mind my not calling you *Monsieur*? When will you be leaving?'

'I don't know. Tomorrow perhaps, or we may be staying on for some while,' I answered, I can't think why for I knew perfectly well that we were to start next day.

'I wish you were staying, on your own account and for Dmitri's sake,' remarked the princess with a far-away look. 'At your age friendship is a fine thing.'

I felt that everybody was looking at me and waiting to hear what I should say, though Varya pretended to be examining her aunt's work; I felt I was being put through a sort of examination and must show myself to the best advantage.

'Yes, for me,' I said, 'Dmitri's friendship is a great help but mine cannot be of much use to him: he is a thousand times better than I.' (Dmitri could not hear me or I should have been afraid of his sensing the insincerity of my words.)

The princess again laughed the unnatural laugh that was natural to her.

'Well, just listen to him,' she said, 'why *c'est vous qui êtes un petit
monstre de perfection!*'[1]

'*Monstre de perfection* – that's capital, I must remember that,' I
thought.

'However, leaving you out of it, he is an expert in this respect,' she
continued, lowering her voice (which pleased me particularly) and
indicating Lyubov Sergeyevna with her eyes – 'he has discovered in
poor auntie,' (that was what they called Lyubov Sergeyevna among
themselves) 'whom I have known these twenty years with her
Suzette, such perfections as I have never suspected. Varya, tell them to
bring me a glass of water,' she added, again gazing into space, probably
bethinking herself that it was too soon or quite unnecessary to initiate
me into their family affairs. 'No, let *him* go. He is not doing anything;
and you go on reading. Go straight through that door, my dear, and
when you have walked about a dozen steps down the passage, stop
and call out loudly: "Piotr, bring Marya Ivanovna a glass of water
with some ice in it,"' she said to me, and again laughed lightly with her
unnatural laugh.

'I expect she wants to talk about me,' I thought as I left the room.
'No doubt she wants to say she has observed that I am a very very
intelligent young man.' I had not gone the dozen paces before the
stout Sophia Ivanovna, puffing but walking with light swift steps,
overtook me.

'*Merci, mon cher*,' said she. 'I am going, so I'll tell them myself.'

24 · LOVE

Sophia Ivanovna, as I afterwards came to know her, was one of those
rare middle-aged women who, born for family life but denied that
happiness by fate, suddenly decide to pour out on a few chosen individuals all the reserve of love intended for husband and children so
long stored up and grown and strengthened in their hearts. And in old
maids of this kind their store of love is sometimes so inexhaustible
that though there may be many chosen ones there still remains an
abundant surplus of affection which they lavish on all around them –
on all, good or bad, whom they happen to meet in their lives.

There are three kinds of love:

1. It's you who are a little monster of perfection!

(1) Poetical love.
(2) Self-denying love.
(3) Practical love.

I am not speaking of the love of a young man for a young woman, and vice versa: I am afraid of such billing and cooing, and I have been unfortunate enough in my life never to have seen a single spark of truth in that kind of love but only a lying pretence in which sensuality, marital relations, money, the wish to bind or unbind one's hands have so confused the feeling itself that there is no making head or tail of it. I am speaking about love for humanity, which according to the greater or lesser power of the heart concentrates itself upon one individual or upon several, or pours itself out upon many – the love for our mother, father, brother, children, our comrade, our friend, our compatriot – love for our fellow-creatures.

Poetical love is love of the beauty of the sentiment itself and its expression. For people who love thus the beloved object is dear only in so far as it arouses that agreeable feeling, the consciousness and expression of which they enjoy. People who love with poetic love are very little concerned with reciprocity, an item which does not affect the beauty and charm of their feeling. They frequently change the object of their love, since their principal aim is that the pleasant feeling of loving should be continually excited. In order to maintain this pleasant sensation in themselves they never stop talking in the choicest terms of their love, both to the subject of it and to everybody else; even to those who have nothing at all to do with it. In our country people of a certain class who love *poetically* not only tell everybody of their love but are sure to tell of it in French. It may seem a strange and ridiculous thing to say, but I am convinced that there have been, and still are, many people, belonging to a certain class of society, women especially, whose love for their friends, husbands and children would expire tomorrow if they were debarred from dilating upon it in French.

The second kind of love – *self-denying* love – is love of the process of sacrificing oneself for the beloved, regardless of whether such sacrifice does good or harm to the loved one. 'There is no unpleasantness I would not undergo to prove my devotion to *him* or *her* in the eyes of the whole world,' is the formula for this kind of love. People who love in this way do not believe in love being returned (for there is still greater merit in sacrificing myself for someone who does not understand me), they are always sickly, which again enhances the merit of their sacrifice; they are usually constant, for it would be hard for them to lose the credit of the sacrifices they have made for their beloved; they are always ready to die to convince *him* or *her* of their devotion but they neglect small everyday demonstrations of love which do not require any particular burst of self-sacrifice. It is all the same to them whether you eat well or sleep well, whether you are enjoying yourself and feel well, and they do nothing to bring you these blessings supposing it lies within their power to do so; but they would face a bullet, go through fire and water, and waste away for love – for all this they are always ready, if only the opportunity presented itself. Moreover, people who go in for self-sacrificing love are always proud of their love, and exacting, jealous and distrustful, and, oddly enough, desire dangers for their adored one, that they may rescue him, unhappiness that they may comfort him – and even welcome vice that they may reform him.

You live alone in the country with your wife, who loves you with self-sacrificing love. You enjoy good health and peace of mind, you have work which you like; your loving wife is so delicate that she cannot attend to the housekeeping, which is left to the servants, nor to the children, who are in the hands of nurses, nor even to any kind of hobby, which she might have cared for, for she cares for nothing but you. She is *patently* ill, yet she will not mention it to you for fear of distressing you; she is *patently* bored but for your sake is prepared to endure boredom her whole life long; she is *patently* depressed because you stick so persistently to your occupations (whatever they may be: sport, books, farming or official work); she sees that these pursuits will be your undoing – but keeps silent and suffers. But then you fall ill – and your loving wife forgets her own ill-health and, though you entreat her not to worry herself needlessly, never leaves your bedside; and every second you feel her suffering eyes on you, saying: 'Didn't I tell you so, but for all that I shall not leave you.' In the morning you feel a little better and go into another room. The fire has not been lit and no one has tidied the room; the soup, the only food you can take, has not been ordered in the kitchen, nor has your medicine been sent for; but your loving wife, worn out by her night's vigil, still keeps gazing at you with the same look of commiseration, walks on tiptoe, and gives confused and uncustomary orders in a whisper. You want to read – your loving wife tells you with a sigh that she knows you will not listen to her – you will be vexed with her but she is used to that – but that it would be better for you not to read; you want to walk about the room – it would be better for you not to do that either; you want to talk to a friend who has called to see you – you had better not talk. In the night you are feverish again and want to doze off but your loving wife, thin, wan, sighing from time to time, sits in an arm-chair beside you in the dim glimmer of the night-light, and the slightest sound or movement on her part rouses you to feelings of irritation and impatience. You have a servant who has been with you for twenty years, to whom you are accustomed, who would tend you gladly and efficiently because he has had his sleep during the day and gets paid for his service; but she will not let him look after you. She does everything herself with her weak unskilled fingers, and you cannot help watching with suppressed animosity as those pale fingers do their best to uncork a medicine bottle or snuff the candle, as they spill the medicine or touch you squeamishly. If you happen to be an impatient irascible man and ask her to go away your irritated overwrought ears hear her submissively sighing and crying outside the door and whispering some nonsense to your man. Finally, if you do not die, your loving wife – who has not slept the whole three weeks of your illness (as she continually reminds you) – falls ill, droops, suffers and becomes still less capable of doing anything, and when you are in a normal state of health expresses her self-sacrificing affection only by a gentle *ennui* which involuntarily communicates itself to you and to every one in the vicinity.

The third kind – *practical love* – consists in a longing to satisfy all the needs, wishes, caprices and even the vices of the beloved one. People who love thus love for life, because the more they love the more they get to know the loved one and the easier it becomes to love – that is, to satisfy all his or her desires. Their love rarely expresses itself in words and if it does so it is not in a self-satisfied poetical way but timidly and awkwardly, for they are always afraid that they do not love enough. Such people even love the faults of their beloved because those faults furnish them with opportunities for satisfying fresh desires. They long for reciprocity, believe in it, even readily deceiving themselves, and are happy if they find it; but they go on loving just the same even if their feelings are not reciprocated, and not only desire the loved one's happiness but by all moral and material means in their power, great and small, try to promote it.

It was this kind of practical love for her nephew, her niece, her sister, Lyubov Sergeyevna and even for me because Dmitri cared for me –

which Sophia Ivanovna radiated by her eyes, her every word and movement.

Only long afterwards did I learn to appreciate Sophia Ivanovna at her true worth; but even at this time it occurred to me to wonder why Dmitri, who tried to conceive of love in a fashion totally different from the general run of young people, and who had dear loving Sophia Ivanovna always before his eyes, suddenly fell passionately in love with that incomprehensible Lyubov Sergeyevna, at most admitting that his aunt did also possess many good qualities. 'A prophet is not without honour, save in his own country,' is obviously a true saying. It must be for one of two reasons: either there really is more bad than good in every man, or because we are more susceptible to the bad than to the good. Dmitri had known Lyubov Sergeyevna only a short time, but the love his aunt bore for him he had known all his life.

25 · I GET ACQUAINTED

When I returned to the gallery they were not talking about me at all, as I had expected; but Varya had left off reading and having laid her book aside was hotly arguing something with Dmitri, who was pacing up and down the room, adjusting his cravat with his neck and blinking his eyes. The ostensible subject of their discussion was Ivan Yakovlevich and superstition but the wrangling was too heated for its underlying meaning not to be something which touched the whole family more nearly. The princess and Lyubov Sergeyevna sat silently listening to every word, evidently tempted at times to take part in the dispute but refraining and leaving it to the pair to speak for them – Varya for the one and Dmitri for the other. When I entered Varya gave me a glance of such indifference that it was plain she was wholly absorbed in the quarrel and did not care whether I heard what she said or not. The princess's face wore the same expression: she was evidently on Varya's side. But Dmitri began to argue even more passionately now that I was there, while Lyubov Sergeyevna seemed startled by my coming and remarked, addressing no one in particular: 'Old people are quite right when they say – *si jeunesse savait, si vieillesse pouvait.*'[1]

This dictum, however, did not check the dispute but only made me think that Lyubov Sergeyevna and my friend were in the wrong.

1. If youth but knew, if old age could.

Although I felt rather awkward at being present at a petty family disagreement it was pleasant to observe the real relations of this household among themselves, which came out in the discussion, and to feel that they were not hindered by my presence from speaking their minds.

How often it happens that you see a family under one and the same deceitful cloak of propriety for years, and the true relations between its members remain hidden from you. (I have even noticed that the more impenetrable and therefore the more decorous the cloak is, the nastier are the actual relations it hides from you.) Yet once let some unexpected, apparently insignificant point arise in that family circle – about the colour of somebody's hair, a visit, or the husband's horses – and without any apparent cause the discussion becomes more and more embittered until the cloak of decorum is stretched too tightly to allow for any settlement of the argument, and suddenly, to the horror of the disputants themselves and the astonishment of those present, all the real savagery of their relations with one another comes to the fore and the cloak, now no longer hiding anything, flutters uselessly between the contending parties and serves merely to remind you how long you were deceived by it. It is often less painful to knock your head violently against the lintel of a door than to touch a sore and sensitive spot, however lightly. And almost every family has a sore and sensitive spot of this kind. In the Nekhlyudov family the sore spot was the strange love of Dmitri for Lyubov Sergeyevna, which excited in his sister and mother, if not a feeling of jealousy, at least one of wounded family pride. That is why the difference of opinion about Ivan Yakovlevich and superstition was for all of them a subject of such grave importance.

'You always try to see something extraordinarily good in what other people laugh at and despise,' Varya was saying in her musical voice, precisely articulating every syllable.

'In the first place, only the most *unthinking* person could ever speak of despising such a remarkable man as Ivan Yakovlevich,' retorted Dmitri, convulsively jerking his head away from his sister, 'and secondly, on the contrary, it is *you* who purposely set out not to see the good that stands before your eyes.'

When Sophia Ivanovna returned to us she kept glancing anxiously now at her nephew, now at her niece, and then at me, and once or twice she opened her mouth and sighed deeply, as if she had said something mentally.

'Varya, please go on reading,' she pleaded, handing her the book and affectionately patting her hand. 'I must know whether he found her again.' (I don't think there was any mention in the novel of any one finding anybody.) 'And Dmitri, you, had better wrap up your cheek, my dear, for it is getting cold and you will have toothache again,' she said to her nephew, in spite of the cross look he gave her, presumably because she had broken the logical thread of his argument. The reading was resumed.

This little dispute in no way upset the family peace and common-sensible harmony which reigned in that feminine circle.

Evidently deriving its tendency and tone from the Princess Marya Ivanovna, it was a circle which, for me, had a wholly novel character that fascinated by being somehow down to earth and at the same time artless and refined. All this I could discern in the grace, neatness and solidity of everything about me – the bell, the binding of a book, an easy chair, a table – and in the straight tightly-laced figure of the princess, the unconcealed grey hair, and the way she called me simply Nicolas and *he* (not Monsieur) the first time she saw me; in their occupations, their reading and their sewing, and in the remarkable white-ness of the ladies' hands. (Their hands all had in common a family trait, the fleshy part of the palm on the outer side being pink and sharply divided in a straight line from the pure whiteness of the back of the hand.) But the character of this feminine circle was best expressed in the excellent way all three spoke Russian and French, pronouncing every letter distinctly and finishing every word and sentence with pedantic accuracy. All this, and in particular the fact that in their com-pany I was treated as simply and seriously as a real grown-up – they telling me their opinions and listening to mine – to which I was so little accustomed that in spite of my bright buttons and blue cuffs I went in constant fear of suddenly hearing some one say to me: 'Surely you do not think people are talking *seriously* to you? Run along and get on with your lessons' – all this, I say, caused me to feel an entire absence of restraint in this society. I ventured to rise, move about and speak freely with everybody except Varya, whom I did not think it proper or for some reason permissible to speak to at this first meeting.

Listening to her pleasant melodious voice while she read, looking now at her, now at the sandy path in the flower-garden where the rain was making round dark patches, and thence to the lime-trees on whose leaves occasional drops of rain still splashed down from the pale bluish edge of the thinning thunder-cloud which hung suspended over us, then at her again, then at the last crimson rays of the setting sun which lit up the thick old birch trees, all wet with rain, and then once more at Varya – I decided that she was not at all bad-looking, as I had at first thought her to be.

'It is a pity I am already in love,' I reflected, 'and that Varya is not Sonya. How nice it would be suddenly to become a member of this family: I should gain a mother, an aunt and a wife all at once.' While I was thinking this I gazed intently at Varya as she read, and imagined I was hypnotizing her and that she would have to look up at me. Varya raised her head from her book, looked at me and, meeting my eyes, turned away.

'However, it has not stopped raining yet,' she said.

And suddenly a strange feeling came over me: I seemed to remember that all this that was happening to me now was a repetition of what had happened before – then, too, the same fine rain was falling, and the sun was setting behind the birch-trees, and I had looked at *her*, and she was reading and I had hypnotized her into looking round, and I had even recollected that this had happened before.

'Can this be *she*?' I wondered. 'Is it really *beginning*?' But I soon decided that she was not *the* she and that it was not beginning yet. 'In the first place, she is plain,' I reflected, 'and she is just a girl whose acquaintance I have made in the most ordinary manner but the *she* whom I shall meet somewhere in some *not* ordinary place will be anything but ordinary; and then the only reason why I like this family so much is because I have not seen anything yet,' I thought. 'No doubt there are families like this everywhere and I shall come across many of them in my life.'

26 · I SHOW MYSELF TO THE BEST ADVANTAGE

At tea time the reading was interrupted and the ladies began talking among themselves about people and incidents I was not acquainted with, expressly, so I imagined, for the purpose of making me feel, in spite of the friendly welcome I had received from them, the difference in age and social position which existed between them and myself. But when the conversation became general and I could take part in it, to make up for my previous silence I tried to show my exceptional intelligence and originality, which I considered myself bound to do on account of my uniform. The talk turned on country-houses and I suddenly remarked that Prince Ivan Ivanych possessed a summer villa near Moscow that people came from London and Paris to see; that it had balustrading which had cost three hundred and eighty thousand roubles, and that Prince Ivan Ivanych was a near relation of mine, and I had dined with him that day and he had specially invited me to spend the whole summer with him at that country house but that I had refused because I knew the house very well, having been there a number of times, and that all those railings and bridges did not interest me in the least for I could not bear the sumptuous, particularly in the country, but liked the country to be countrified . . . Having uttered this frightfully involved story, I grew confused, and blushed, so that everybody must have seen that I was lying. Varya, who was just handing me a cup of tea, and Sophia Ivanovna, who had been gazing at me while I spoke, both turned away from me and started another topic, with an expression which I often encountered subsequently on the faces of kind people when a very young man looks them in the eye and begins on an obvious string of lies – an expression which implies: 'Of course we know there isn't a word of truth in what he's saying but why does the poor fellow do it?' . . .

The reason I spoke about Prince Ivan Ivanych having a country villa was because I could find no better pretext for mentioning that I was related to him and the fact that I had dined with him that day; but why I had told them about balustrading costing three hundred and eighty thousand roubles and about my having often visited him at his country house when I had never been there at all – nor could have (for Prince Ivan Ivanych, as the Nekhlyudovs very well knew, never lived anywhere but in Moscow or Naples) – why I said all that I cannot possibly imagine. Neither in my childhood nor in my boyhood nor afterwards in my riper years have I ever detected in myself the vice of falsehood: on the contrary, I have always been rather too truthful and outspoken; but during this first stage of my adolescence I was often seized by a strange desire to tell the most desperate lies for no apparent reason. I say *desperate* advisedly, for I lied about matters on which I could so easily be caught out. I think that a vainglorious desire to appear quite a different person from what I was, combined with the impossible hope of lying without being detected, were the chief causes of this peculiar impulse.

After tea, the rain having stopped and the evening, when twilight fell, being still and clear, the princess suggested that we should go for a stroll to the bottom of the garden and admire her favourite spot. Acting on my principle of always being original, and holding that clever people such as myself and the princess should be above commonplace politeness, I replied that I could not bear walking about aimlessly and that if I did care to take a walk I liked to walk alone. I had no idea that this was downright rude; all I thought then was that, even as nothing could be more degrading than empty compliments, so nothing could be more pleasing and original than a little unmannerly outspokenness. However, feeling very well satisfied with my reply, I nevertheless went out with the rest of the party.

The princess's favourite spot was a little bridge spanning a narrow marsh right at the far end of the garden. The view was very restricted but very pensive and lovely. We are so accustomed to confound art with nature that very often natural phenomena which we have never encountered in pictures seem artificial to us, as if nature herself were unnatural; and vice versa: those phenomena which have been too frequently repeated in art seem to us hackneyed, while some which are too much associated with a single idea or a single sentiment, when we meet them in nature seem artificial. The view from the princess's favourite spot was of that kind. It consisted of a small pond overgrown with weeds round the edge, just behind it a steep hill covered with enormous old trees and bushes whose various foliage sometimes twisted into a tangled mass; at the foot of the hill was an ancient birch-tree which leaned over the pond, its roots clinging partly to the moist bank of the pond, its crown resting against a tall slender aspen, and i tscurling branches swinging over the smooth surface of the water, which reflected these drooping boughs and the surrounding verdure.

'How lovely!' said the princess with a nod of her head, addressing no one in particular.

'Yes, marvellous, only it seems to me awfully like stage-scenery,' I said, wishing to show that I had an opinion of my own about everything.

The princess continued to admire the view as though she had not heard me, and turning to her sister and Lyubov Sergeyevna pointed out various details to them – the twisted overhanging branch and its reflection in the water, which particularly pleased her. Sophia Ivanovna said that it was all beautiful and remarked that her sister would spend hours together at this spot, but it was evident she only said this to please the princess. I have noticed that people endowed with a loving disposition are seldom receptive to the beauties of nature. Lyubov Sergeyevna also went into raptures, asking among other things: 'How does that birch manage to support itself? Will it stand much longer?' and kept watching her Suzette who, fluffy tail wagging, fussed about the bridge on her little crooked legs as if this were the first time in her life she found herself out of doors. Dmitri began to argue very logically to his mother to prove that it was impossible to have a beautiful view if the horizon was limited. Varya did not speak. When I looked round at her she was standing with her profile to me, leaning on the railing of the bridge and gazing straight in front of her. Something must have been absorbing, even affecting her deeply, for she seemed wrapped in thought and quite oblivious of herself and of being looked at. Her large eyes showed such steady attention, such quiet concentrated thought, the way she stood was so natural and, for all her shortness, so stately even, that again I was struck by something like a memory of her and again asked myself: 'Is *it*, then, beginning?' And again I told myself that I was already in love with Sonya, and that Varya was an ordinary young lady, my friend's sister. But I felt a liking for her at that moment and in consequence a vague desire to do or say something mildly unpleasant to her.

'Do you know, Dmitri,' I said to my friend, stepping nearer to Varya so that she should hear what I was going to say, 'I think that even without mosquitoes there would still be nothing nice about this place; but as it is,' added I, slapping myself on the forehead and actually squashing a mosquito, 'it is simply awful.'

'Then you don't care for nature?' said Varya to me without turning her head.

'I consider it an idle futile pursuit,' I replied, greatly pleased to have said something a little bit disagreeable to her and at the same time original. Varya gave a faint lift of her eyebrows for an instant, with an expression of pity, and then went on gazing in front of her as serenely as before.

I was annoyed with her but for all that the grey hand-rail of the bridge on which she was leaning, with its faded paint, the reflection in the dark pond of the overhanging birch-tree's drooping bough which seemed to be reaching up to join the branches overhead, the smell of the marsh, the feeling of the crushed mosquito on my

forehead, Varya's intent look and statuesque pose – many a time afterwards quite unexpectedly recurred to my imagination.

27 · DMITRI

When we returned to the house after our stroll Varya declined to sing
as she generally did in the evening, and I was conceited enough to
suppose this was my doing, because of what I had said on the bridge.
The Nekhlyudovs never had supper and they retired early, but that
day, since Dmitri's toothache had started up as Sophia Ivanovna had
predicted, we went to his room even earlier than usual. Believing that
I had done all that my blue collar and my buttons required of me, and
that everybody was highly pleased with me, I was in an extremely
amiable contented state of mind. Dmitri, on the other hand, owing to
the dispute with his sister and his toothache, was silent and morose.
He seated himself at the table, took out his note-books – a diary and the
book in which he used every evening to enter tasks performed or
awaiting him – and perpetually frowning and touching his cheek with
his hand wrote for a considerable time.

'Oh, do leave me in peace,' he shouted to the maid sent by Sophia
Ivanovna to ask how his toothache was and whether he would not like
a hot poultice. After that, saying that a bed would be made up for me
directly and he would be back in a moment, he went to Lyubov
Sergeyevna.

'What a pity Varya is not pretty – that she is not Sonya, in fact,' I
reflected, finding myself alone in the room. 'How nice it would be after
I have left the University to come here and propose to her. I would say:
"Princess, I am no longer young: I cannot love passionately but I will
always cherish you like a dear sister." – "And you," I would continue
to her mother, "I already greatly respect. And you, Sophia Ivanovna,
believe me, I esteem very highly." – "So tell me simply and frankly:
will you be my wife?" – "Yes." And she will give me her hand, I shall
press it and say, "I love not in words but in deeds." . . . But then,' I
suddenly thought, 'what if Dmitri should fall in love with Lyuba –
after all, Lyuba is in love with him – and want to marry her? Then one
or other of us would not be allowed to marry.[1] That would be fine
too. This is what I would do. I should realize it at once but not say any-

1. It was illegal in Russia for a brother-in-law to marry a sister-in-law.

thing. Then I would go to Dmitri and say: "It would be no use, my
dear friend, for us to try to conceal anything from one another. You
know that my love for your sister will cease only with my death; but I
know all – you have deprived me of my highest hope, you have rendered me an unhappy man; but do you know how Nikolai Irtenyev
avenges the misery entailed upon him for his whole life? – Here, take
my sister!" – and I should put Lyuba's hand in his. He would say, "No,
not for all the world! . . ." And I should say, "Prince Nekhlyudov! It
is useless for you to try to outdo Nikolai Irtenyev in magnanimity. The
world does not contain a man more magnanimous than he." Then I
would bow and retire. Dmitri and Lyuba would run out after me in
tears and entreat me to accept their sacrifice. And I might consent and
be very happy, if only I were in love with Varya . . .' These imaginings
were so enjoyable that I wanted very much to communicate them to
my friend but in spite of our vow to be outspoken with each other I
somehow felt it physically impossible to do so.

Dmitri returned from Lyubov Sergeyevna, who had applied some
drops to his teeth, in even more pain and consequently more morose
than ever. No bed had yet been made up for me, and a little boy who
acted as Dmitri's valet came to ask him where I was to sleep.

'Go to the devil!' exclaimed Dmitri, stamping his foot. 'Vaska!
Vaska! Vaska!' he shouted the instant the boy had left, raising his
voice at each repetition. 'Vaska, make up my bed on the floor.'

'No, better let me sleep on the floor,' said I.

'Well, it doesn't matter, make it anywhere you like,' Dmitri went
on in the same angry tone. 'Vaska, why aren't you making the bed?'

But Vaska evidently did not understand what was required of him,
and did not move.

'Well, what's wrong with you? Make the bed, make the bed!
Vaska! Vaska!' shouted Dmitri, suddenly flying into a kind of frenzy.

But Vaska, still not comprehending, and becoming frightened, stood
motionless.

'So you are determined to be the death of . . . to drive me mad, are
you?'

And springing from his chair Dmitri rushed at the boy and several
times punched him on the head for all he was worth, and Vaska ran
helter-skelter from the room. At the door Dmitri stopped and looked
round at me, and the expression of rage and cruelty which his face had
borne for a moment changed to such a gentle, shamed and loving,

childlike look that I felt sorry for him, and much as I wanted to I could not bring myself to turn away. He did not say anything but for a long time paced the room in silence, now and then glancing at me with the same look which seemed to plead for forgiveness. Then he got his note-book out of the table-drawer, wrote something in it, took off his coat and folded it carefully, went to the corner where an ikon hung, clasped his large white hands on his breast and began to say his prayers. He prayed so long that Vaska had time to bring in a mattress and spread it on the floor, as I whispered to him to do. I undressed and lay down on the bed on the floor but Dmitri still went on with his prayers. Looking at Dmitri's slightly rounded shoulders and the soles of his feet, which seemed to expose themselves to me in a sort of submissive way every time he bowed his forehead to the ground, I loved him more than ever before and kept wondering whether or not to tell him what I had been day-dreaming about our sisters. When he had finished his prayers Dmitri lay down on the mattress beside me, and propped on his elbow looked at me for a long time in silence, with an expression that was affectionate and shamefaced. This was evidently painful to him but apparently he was punishing himself. I smiled as I looked at him. He smiled too.

'Why don't you tell me that I behaved abominably?' he asked. 'You were thinking so just now, weren't you?'

'Yes,' I answered, although my mind had been on something else, but it seemed to me that that *was* what I had been thinking. 'Yes, it was very wrong and I did not expect it of you,' said I, particularly pleased to be talking intimately with him. 'Well, how is the toothache?' I added.

'Gone. Ah, Nicolas, my friend!' Dmitri began, so fondly that I thought there must be tears in his eyes, 'I know, I feel, how wicked I am, and God is witness how I long to be better and pray for help; but what am I to do with my unfortunate horrible nature? What am I to do? I try to check myself, to reform, but you know it can't be done all of a sudden and it can't be done all alone. I need some one to support, to help me. Now Lyubov Sergeyevna understands me and has helped me a lot. I can tell by my *Journal* that I have improved a good deal during the past year. Oh my dear Nikolai,' he continued with a peculiar and un-wonted tenderness and a tone that was calmer now after this confession, 'how much the influence of a woman like her means! Think how good it could be to have a friend like her when I am independent! With her I am quite a different being.'

Whereupon Dmitri began to unfold to me his plans for marriage, life in the country, and constant efforts at self-improvement.

'I shall live in the country, you will come and stay, and perhaps you will be married to Sonya by then,' he said. 'Our children will play together. Of course all this sounds funny and silly but it may happen.'

'I should think so, and very easily!' I said, smiling and at the same time thinking it would be better still if I were to marry his sister.

'Do you know what?' he said after a brief silence. 'You only imagine you are in love with Sonya but it's fiddlesticks, I can see that, and you don't know yet what the real feeling is like.'

I did not protest because I almost agreed with him. We were silent for a while.

'You must have noticed that I was in a bad temper again today and had a horrid argument with Varya. I felt dreadful about it afterwards, especially since you were there. Although she has a lot of wrong ideas she's a splendid girl and very good, as you'll find out when you know her better.'

His change of topic from my not being in love to praise of his sister delighted me beyond measure and made me blush, but I still did not say anything to him about his sister and we went on talking of other things.

Thus we chatted till the cocks crew a second time, and the pale dawn of day had peeped in at the window before Dmitri went to his own bed and put out the light.

'Well, now for sleep,' he said.

'Yes,' I answered, 'but just one thing.'

'What?'

'Is it good to be alive?' said I.

'It is good to be alive,' he replied in a voice which made me fancy that in spite of the dark I could see his merry affectionate eyes and childlike smile.

28 · IN THE COUNTRY

The next day Volodya and I set out with post-horses for the country. Turning over various Moscow recollections in my mind as we drove along, I thought of Sonya Valakhina – but that was only in the evening after we had already covered five stages of the road. 'It is strange that I should be in love and forget all about it: I must think about her,' I said to myself. And I did begin to think of her, as one thinks when travelling – disconnectedly but vividly – and thought to such effect that for two days after my arrival in the country I somehow considered it incumbent upon me to appear sad and pensive before all the household, and especially before Katya whom I regarded as a great expert in such matters and to whom I hinted at the state of my heart. Yet for all my efforts to deceive other people and myself, and my assiduous adoption of all the symptoms I had observed in other *inamorati*, I only succeeded for two days – and that not continuously but mostly in the evenings – in reminding myself that I was in love, and in the end, as soon as I had settled into the new routine of country life and pursuits, I quite forgot about my love for Sonya.

We arrived at Petrovskoe at night and I was sleeping so soundly that I saw neither the house, the birch avenue nor any of the family, who had all gone to bed and for long been fast asleep. Hunchbacked old Foka, barefooted and with his wife's wadded jacket over his shoulders, came with a candle in his hand to unbolt the door. On seeing us he trembled all over with joy, kissed both of us on the shoulder, hurriedly put away the felt rug on which he usually slept, and started to dress himself. I passed through the hall and up the stairs not yet fully awake, but in the ante-room the lock of the door, the latch, a warped floor-board, the chest, the old candlestick splashed with tallow as it always had been, the shadows cast by the crooked wick of the tallow candle, which was cold, having only just been lighted, the ever-dusty double panes of the window that was never taken out, behind which, as I recollected, there grew a mountain-ash – were all so familiar, so full of memories, so harmonious, united as it were by a common idea, that I suddenly felt that the dear old home was tenderly welcoming me back. Involuntarily I asked myself: 'How was it we, the house and I, were able to live so long apart?' And I ran about in haste to see if all the other rooms were still the same. Yes, everything was unchanged but smaller and the ceilings were not so high, while I seemed to have grown taller, heavier and coarser. Still, even so, the house received me joyously into its embrace, and every floor-board, every window, each step of the staircase and every sound stirred up in me a host of shadowy forms, physical sensations and memories of events belonging to the irrecoverable happy past. We reached the night nursery of our childhood – all my childish terrors lurked again in the dark corners and

behind the doors; we passed through the drawing-room – the same
gentle tender mother-love breathed over everything in the room; we
crossed the ball-room – boisterous carefree childish mirth seemed to
reside there still, only waiting to be revived. In the sitting-room, where
Foka took us and where he had made up our beds, everything – the
looking-glass, the screens, the old wooden ikon, every unevenness of
the white-papered wall – spoke of suffering, of death and of what would
never be again.

We got into bed and Foka left us after wishing us good night.

'Mama died in this room, surely?' said Volodya.

I made no reply and pretended to be asleep. If I had said a word I
should have burst out crying. Next morning when I woke, papa in his
dressing-gown, wearing soft boots and with a cigar between his teeth,
was sitting on Volodya's bed, talking and laughing with him. With a
merry jerk of his shoulder he jumped up and came across to me, slapped
me on the back with his large hand, put his cheek to my lips and pressed
it against them.

'Well done, thank you, diplomat,' he said in his own half-bantering,
half-affectionate way, gazing at me with his little sparkling eyes.
'Volodya tells me you got through your examinations like a trump –
that's splendid! When you make up your mind not to play the fool
you're my fine fellow too. Thank you, my boy. Now we'll have a
grand time of it here, and in the winter perhaps move to Petersburg;
only it's a pity the hunting season is over, otherwise I should have
given you a treat. Can you shoot, Voldemar? There's no end of game,
I shouldn't mind going out with you myself one day. And when the
winter comes, God willing we'll transfer ourselves to Petersburg and
you'll meet people and make useful acquaintances; I've got a couple of
grown-up lads now and, as I was just saying to Voldemar, you are
standing on life's highway now, and my task is over. You can go on by
yourselves; but if ever you want to ask my advice, do so. I am no longer
your dry-nurse but your friend: at any rate I want to be your friend
and comrade and adviser, so far as I can, and nothing more. How does
that fit in with your own ideas, Nicky, eh? Well or ill, eh?'

Of course I said it was splendid, and I really thought so. That day
papa had a particularly winning gay and happy expression on his face,
and the new relations between him and myself, as if we were equals
and comrades, made me fonder of him than ever.

'Well now, tell me, did you call on all the relations? The Ivins? Did

you see the old man? What did he say to you?' he went on asking me.
'Did you go to see Prince Ivan Ivanych?'

And we talked so long before dressing that the sun had already
begun to move away from the window, and Yakov, as old as ever and
twiddling his thumbs behind his back and saying, 'And furthermore
. . .' just as he used to, came into our room to tell papa that the small
carriage was ready.

'Where are you going?' I asked papa.

'Oh, I almost forgot,' said papa with a jerk of vexation and a slight
cough, 'I promised to go and see the Epifanovs today. You remember
Mademoiselle Epifanova – *la belle Flamande*? She used to visit your
mamma. They are very nice people.' And with a self-conscious (or so
it seemed to me) shrug of his shoulder papa left the room.

Lyuba had several times come to the door while we were chatting,
and asked: 'May I come in?' but papa each time shouted to her through
the door: 'Utterly impossible, we're not dressed.'

'What does that matter? I've often seen you in your dressing-gown,
haven't I?'

'You cannot see your brothers without their *inexpressibles*,' he called
to her, 'but they will both of them rap on the door to you. Will that
do? Rap now, you two. It's not proper even for them to speak to you
in such dishabille.'

'Oh, how unbearable you are! Well at least hurry up and come to
the drawing-room. Mimi is longing to see you,' shouted Lyuba outside the door.

As soon as papa had gone I put on my student's uniform as fast as I
could and went to the drawing-room. But Volodya, on the contrary,
did not hurry himself and stayed upstairs for a long time talking to
Yakov and asking him where snipe and double-snipe were to be found.
As I have already said, there was nothing in the world he hated so much
as sentimentality with his 'little brother', 'dearest papa' or 'baby sister',
as he expressed it, and in avoiding every show of feeling he went to the
opposite extreme and affected a coldness which often hurt people who
did not understand its cause. In the ante-room I collided with papa, who
was on his way to the carriage with short brisk steps. He had on his
fashionable new coat from Moscow and smelled of scent. On seeing
me he gave a cheerful nod, as much as to say, 'I look all right, don't I?'
and again I was struck by the happy expression of his eyes I had noticed
that morning.

The drawing-room was still the same bright lofty room with the yellow birchwood English grand piano in it, and large open windows looking on to the green trees and gravel paths of the garden. After kissing Mimi and Lyuba I was approaching Katya when it suddenly occurred to me it would no longer be proper for me to kiss her, and I stopped short, tongue-tied and blushing. Katya, not in the least embarrassed, held out her little white hand and congratulated me on getting into the University. When Volodya came into the drawing-room and met Katya the same thing happened to him. It was indeed difficult to decide how, having grown up together and seen each other every day all that time, we were to behave now on meeting again after our first time of separation. Katya blushed redder than all the rest of us. Volodya suffered no embarrassment and, bowing lightly to her, went over to Lyuba and having talked for a little, but not seriously, departed somewhere for a solitary walk.

29 · OUR RELATIONS WITH THE GIRLS

Volodya had such strange ideas about the girls that although he could interest himself in whether they had had enough to eat, had slept well, were properly dressed and would not make mistakes in French that would shame him before strangers, he would never admit that they could think or feel like human beings, still less that it was possible to converse with them sensibly about anything. If they happened to appeal to him on some serious matter (a thing, by the way, which they had learned to avoid) – if they asked his opinion about some novel or inquired about his work at the University – he would pull a face at them and walk away without speaking, or else answer in mangled French such as 'Com ce tri jauli'[1] or, putting on a grave purposely stupid expression, say something absolutely meaningless and bearing no relation whatever to the question they had asked him, or else, suddenly making his eyes look vacant, utter words like *bun*, *gone driving*, *cabbage*, or the like. When I chanced to repeat to him something Lyuba or Katya had told me he always said:

'H'm, so you still talk to them, do you? Yes, I can see you are still in a bad way.'

---

1. *Comme c'est très joli* – How very pretty that is.

And one had to see and hear him at the time to appreciate the profound immutable contempt which echoed in this remark. Volodya
had been grown up for a couple of years now and was always falling in
love with every pretty woman he met; but though he saw Katya every
day and she had been wearing long dresses for two years and growing
prettier and prettier the possibility of falling in love with her never
entered his head. Whether this was because the prosaic recollections of
childhood – the ruler in the schoolroom, the bath-sheet, childish
tempers – were still too fresh in his memory; or was due to the aversion
very young people feel for everything to be found at hand, or to the
general human tendency to pass over the good and beautiful they first
meet, telling themselves that they will come across many such in the
course of their lives, at all events up to this time Volodya had not
looked upon Katya as a woman.

Volodya evidently felt time hang heavily on his hands all that summer; his boredom proceeded from his scorn for us which, as I have
said, he made no effort to conceal. He went about with an expression
which said: 'What a bore it all is, and there's no one to talk to!' Perhaps he would go out by himself with his gun in the morning, or sit
reading in his room and not dress till dinner-time. If papa was not at
home he would even bring his book to the table and went on reading
without exchanging a syllable with any of us, so that we all felt somehow in the wrong in his presence. In the evenings, too, he would lie
with his feet up on the sofa in the drawing-room and sleep, leaning on
his arm, or with a very solemn face talk dreadful, sometimes rather
improper nonsense, which made Mimi furious and caused her to turn
red in patches, while we nearly choked with laughter; but except with
papa, and very occasionally with me, he never deigned to speak seriously to any member of the household. Quite unconsciously I copied
my brother in his views about the girls, though I was not so much
afraid of sentiment as he was and my contempt for them was far from
being so deep and firmly rooted. I even made more than one effort that
summer to get closer to Lyuba and Katya and chat with them in order
to beguile the tedium of the day; but each time I found such an absence
of all ability to think logically, and such ignorance of the most simple,
everyday matters (as, for instance, the nature of money, the subjects
studied at universities, the nature of war, etc.) and such indifference to
my explanations of all these things, that my attempts only confirmed
my unfavourable opinion of the pair.

I remember one evening Lyuba for the hundredth time repeating some intolerably tiresome passage on the piano while Volodya lay dozing on the drawing-room sofa, now and then muttering to no one in particular with a sort of malevolent irony: 'Hark at her pounding away!... A musician she is, a *Bithoven*!' (He pronounced the name with particular sarcasm.) 'Tremendous... now once again... that's it!' and so on. Katya and I were still at the tea-table and, I don't remember how, Katya brought the conversation round to her favourite topic – love. I was in a mood to philosophize and began in a lofty way defining love as the desire to acquire in another that which one lacks oneself, etc. But Katya replied that, on the contrary, it is not love at all if a girl contemplates marrying a rich man, and in her opinion wealth was of no importance, and only the affection which can stand the test of separation is true love (I understood this as an allusion to her love for Dubkov). Volodya, who must have heard us, suddenly raised himself on his elbow and cried out on a note of interrogation: 'Katya – *thè Russians?*'

'Oh, your eternal nonsense!' said Katya.

'*Old pepper-pot?*' Volodya went on, stressing each vowel. And I could not help thinking he was quite right.

Apart from the general faculties, which are more or less developed according to the individual, of intellect, sensibility and artistic feeling, there exists a special capacity that is more or less developed in different circles of society and especially in families, which I call mutual *understanding*. The essence of this capacity lies in an agreed sense of proportion and an accepted and identical outlook on things. Two members of the same set or the same family possessing this faculty can always allow an expression of feeling up to a certain point beyond which they both see only empty phrases. Simultaneously both perceive where commendation ends and irony begins, where enthusiasm ceases and pretence takes its place – all of which may appear quite otherwise to people possessed of a different order of apprehension. People of the same understanding see everything they come across in an identically ludicrous, beautiful or repellent light. To facilitate this common understanding the members of a circle or a family often invent a language of their own with expressions peculiar to them, or even words which indicate shades of meaning non-existent for others. In our family this sort of mutual understanding was developed in the highest degree between papa and us boys. Dubkov, too, fitted into our circle pretty well and *understood* but Dmitri, though far more intelligent, was obtuse in this respect. With no one, however, had I brought this faculty to such a pitch as with Volodya, who had grown up with me in identical circumstances. Papa had lagged behind us long ago and much that was as clear to us as twice two are four was incomprehensible to him. For instance, Volodya and I had adopted – heaven knows how and why – certain words to which we attached some peculiar meaning: *raisins* signified an ostentatious desire to show that one had money, *shell* (with fingers joined and special stress on the *sh*) meant something fresh, sound and comely but not showy; a noun used in the plural indicated an undue partiality for that respective thing; and so on and so forth. However, the meaning depended more on the expression of the face and the general context, so that no matter what new word or phrase one of us might invent to express a new shade of meaning the other at the first hint would interpret it in exactly the same way. The girls did not have this *understanding* of ours, and this was the principal cause of our mental separation and of the contempt we felt for them.

It may be they had their own private *understanding* which coincided so little with ours that where we were ready to descry empty phrases they saw feeling, and what to us was irony to them was truth, and so on. But at the time I did not realize this was not their fault and that a lack of understanding between us did not prevent their being nice clever girls, and I despised them. Besides, having once lit upon the idea of frankness and carrying the application of this idea to extremes in my own case, I accused the placid trustful Lyuba of being secretive and insincere because she did not find it necessary to dig up and examine all her thoughts and impulses. For instance, the fact that Lyuba made the sign of the cross over papa every night, that she and Katya wept in the chapel where we went to attend memorial services for mamma, or that Katya sighed and rolled her eyes when she played the piano – all this seemed to me sheer make-believe and I asked myself when they could have learned to sham like grown-up people, and how it was they were not ashamed to do it.

30 · MY OCCUPATIONS

For all that, I became closer friends with our young ladies this summer than in other years by reason of a sudden passion for music which sprang up in me. In the spring a neighbour came to call on us in the country – a young man who as soon as he entered the drawing-room fixed his eyes on the piano and kept edging his chair towards it as he talked to Mimi and Katya. Having discussed the weather and the pleasures of country life, he adroitly led the conversation to a piano-tuner, to music, to the piano, and ended by saying that he could play, and very soon he had given us three waltzes, with Lyuba, Mimi and Katya standing round the piano watching him. The young man never came again but I was much taken by his playing, his pose at the piano, the way he shook back his hair and especially his method of taking octaves with his left hand, rapidly stretching his little finger and thumb over an octave span, then slowly bringing them together and quickly stretching them again. This graceful movement, his easy posture, the way he tossed his hair and the attention our ladies paid to his talent inspired me with the idea of playing the piano. Having persuaded myself, because of this, that I was gifted and had a passion for music, I set myself to learn. In this respect I behaved like millions of the male, and still more of the female sex who try to learn without a good teacher, without real vocation and without the slightest understanding of what art can give and of how to approach it so that it may yield them something. For me music, or rather piano-playing, was a means to capture young ladies through their sensibilities. With the help of Katya, who taught me my notes, and having to a certain degree broken in my thick fingers – in which effort, by the way, I consumed two months of such assiduity that I even exercised my refractory fourth finger on my knee at dinner and on my pillow in bed – I immediately began to play *pieces*, and of course played them with feeling (*avec âme*),[1] as even Katya admitted, but not keeping time at all.

My choice of pieces was the familiar one – waltzes, galops, romances, arrangements for the piano, etc. – all by those charming composers a little pile of whose works any one with a modicum of healthy taste will pick out for you from the stacks of beautiful things in a music-shop, and say: 'These are what ought *not* to be played, because nothing more tasteless was ever written;' and which, no doubt for that very reason, you will find on the pianoforte of every Russian young lady. True we also had the *Sonate pathétique* and Beethoven's C Sharp Minor Sonata, which are for ever being murdered by young ladies and Lyuba played in memory of mamma, and other good music, which her music-teacher

1. With soul.

in Moscow had set her, but there were likewise compositions by that same master, absurd marches and galops, which Lyuba also played. Katya and I, on the other hand, did not like serious stuff: we preferred above all *Le Fou* and *Nightingale*, which Katya played so fast one could not follow her fingers and I already began to play pretty loudly and fluently. I adopted the gestures of the young man and often regretted that there was no stranger present to see me play. But Liszt and Kalbrenner soon proved beyond my powers and I realized I should never catch up with Katya. Accordingly, fancying that classical music was easier, and partly for the sake of being original, I suddenly decided I loved German music, went into raptures when Lyuba played the *Sonate pathétique* though, if the truth be told, I had long been heartily sick of it, and began to play Beethoven myself and to pronounce the name as Germans do. But at the back of all this chopping and changing and pretence, as I now see it, there must have been something in the nature of talent in me, for music often affected me so deeply that my eyes filled with tears and the things I liked I could somehow pick out on the piano by ear; so that had any one at that time taught me to consider music as an end in itself, as an enjoyment on its own and not as a means of charming girls by the swiftness and soulfulness of my playing, I might possibly have really become a decent musician.

Reading French novels, of which Volodya had brought a large store with him, was another of my occupations that summer. At that time *Monte Cristo* and the various *Mystères* were only just beginning to appear, and I devoured volume after volume of Sue, Dumas and Paul de Kock. All the most unnatural characters and adventures were as much alive to me as reality. I not only never dared suspect the author of lying but the author himself did not exist for me, and real live people and real events appeared before me out of the printed book. If I had never come across people like those I read about, I never doubted for a moment that I should one day.

I discovered in myself all the passions described in every novel, as well as a likeness to all the characters – both heroes and villains – in the same way as a nervous man who reads a medical work detects in himself symptoms of every possible disease. I enjoyed alike the cunning thoughts, the fiery sentiments, the magical events and the characters who were all black or all white in these romances: the good was out and out good, the bad out and out bad, just as I imagined people to be in my early youth. It also pleased me very much that all this was in

French, and that I could lay to heart the noble words which the noble heroes spoke, so as to make use of them when an opportunity of performing some noble deed presented itself. How many French phrases I concocted with the aid of those novels for Kolpikov, should I ever encounter him again, and for *her* when I should at last meet her and reveal my love to her: I prepared such speeches to say to them that they would be quite overcome when they heard me. I even formed, on the basis of these novels, new ideals of the moral qualities I desired to acquire. Firstly in all my actions and conduct I wanted to be *noble* in the French sense, for the word has a different connotation in French, as the Germans understood when they adopted the word which they write *nobel* and did not confuse it with *ehrlich*;[1] then to be *passionate*, and finally to be what I already had an inclination to be, as *comme il faut* as possible. I even tried in my looks and bearing to resemble the heroes who possessed any of these qualities. I remember that in one of the hundreds of novels I read that summer there was an extremely passionate hero with bushy eyebrows, and I so much wanted to be like him in appearance (in character I felt I was exactly like him) that one day looking at my eyebrows in the glass I conceived the idea of clipping them a little to make them grow thicker, but when I began to cut them I accidentally sheared off too much in one place–they had to be trimmed down evenly, with the result that, to my horror, I beheld myself in the glass without any eyebrows at all and consequently very ugly. However, I comforted myself with the hope that my eyebrows would soon sprout again as bushy as my passionate hero's, and was only uneasy as to what to say to all the household when they saw me without eyebrows. I got some of Volodya's gunpowder, rubbed it on my eyebrows and put a light to it. Though the powder did not explode I looked sufficiently as if I had scorched my face, so that no one found out, and indeed, by the time I had forgotten about the passionate man my eyebrows had grown much thicker than they had been before.

31 · COMME IL FAUT

In the course of this narrative I have repeatedly referred to the idea behind the French words at the head of this chapter, and now I feel it

---

1. *nobel* means noble, generous; *ehrlich* signifies honourable, faithful, and so forth.

necessary to devote a whole chapter to this notion – which in my own life has been one of the most pernicious and fallacious ideas inculcated into me by my upbringing and social *milieu*.

The human race may be divided into innumerable categories – into rich and poor, good and bad, soldiers and civilians, wise men and fools, and so forth; but everyone inevitably has a pet classification of his own which he unconsciously applies to every new person he comes across. At the time of which I am writing my own favourite and principal system of division in this respect was into people *comme il faut* and *comme il ne faut pas*. The latter I subdivided into those inherently not *comme il faut* and the lower orders. The *comme il faut* people I respected and looked upon as worthy to consort with me as my equals; the *comme il ne faut pas* I pretended to despise but in reality detested, nourishing a sort of injured personal feeling where they were concerned; the lower classes did not exist for me – I despised them utterly. *My comme il faut* consisted first and foremost in having an excellent knowledge of the French tongue, especially pronunciation. Any one who spoke French with a bad accent at once aroused my dislike. 'Why do you try to talk like us when you don't know how?' I mentally inquired with biting irony. The second condition of being *comme il faut* was to have long well-kept clean finger-nails. The third was to know how to bow, dance and converse. The fourth, and a very important one was indifference to everything and a constant air of refined supercilious ennui. Further, I had certain general signs by which, without speaking to him, I could determine what category a person belonged to. Chief among these indications (the others being the arrangement of his room, his signet-ring, his handwriting and his carriage) were his feet. The relation of boots to trousers in my way of thinking immediately determined a man's social status. Heelless boots with square toes wedded to trousers narrow at the bottom and having no foot-straps – this was *common*; boots with round narrow toes and with heels accompanied either by narrow trousers strapped under the instep or by wide trousers similarly strapped but projecting in a peak over the toe proved a man to be *mauvais genre*,[1] and so on.

It was a curious thing that I who lacked positively all ability for the *comme il faut* should have become so obsessed by the idea. But perhaps the very reason it took such deep root in me was because it cost me such enormous labour to acquire this *comme il faut*. It is awful to think how

1. Bad form.

much of the best and most priceless period of life – the time when I was sixteen – I wasted on acquiring this quality. To all those whom I used to imitate – Volodya, Dubkov and most of my friends – it seemed to come easily. I gazed at them with envy, and laboured secretly at my French, at the art of bowing without looking at the person I was bowing to, at making conversation, at dancing, at cultivating indifference and ennui, at my finger-nails – trimming the skin around them with scissors – and yet I felt that there was still a great deal to be done if I was ever to attain my object. As to my room, my writing-table, my carriage, I did not in the least know how to give them an air of *comme il faut*, although I tried hard in spite of my disinclination for practical work of any kind. With others everything seemed to go perfectly without any trouble, as if it could not be otherwise. I remember once, after much useless exertion over my nails, I asked Dubkov, who had wonderfully good nails, how long they had been like that and what he did to make them so. 'As far back as I can remember,' Dubkov replied; 'and I have never done anything about them, and I don't understand how a gentleman's finger-nails could be any different.' This answer considerably upset me. I did not then know that one of the chief conditions of being *comme il faut* is secrecy as to the efforts by which that *comme il faut* is attained. I considered *comme il faut* not merely an important plus, an admirable quality, a perfection I was anxious to achieve, but an indispensable condition of life without which there could be no happiness, no glory, nor anything good in the world. I should have had no esteem for an eminent artist, a savant or a benefactor of the human race unless he were *comme il faut*. A man *comme il faut* stood incomparably higher than they: he left it to them to paint pictures, compose music, write books and do good – he even commended them for it (why not commend the good in whomever it be found?) but he could never put them on a level with himself; he was *comme il faut* and they were not, and that was enough. In fact, I believe, that if I had had a brother, a mother or a father who was not *comme il faut* I should have said it was a misfortune but that such being the case there could be nothing in common between them and me. But it was not the loss of the golden hours wasted in a constant striving to observe all the, for me, difficult conditions of the *comme il faut* which prevented any serious pursuit, nor the detestation and scorn which I felt for nine-tenths of the human race, nor my disregard of all the beauty that lay outside the narrow circle of the *comme il faut*, that did me most harm. The greatest

The gtest

evil this idea wrought in me lay in my conviction that the *comme il faut* was a self-sufficient status in society, that a man need not exert himself to become an official, a carriage-maker, a soldier, a scholar, so long as he were *comme il faut*; that, having attained this state, he was already fulfilling his destiny and was even superior to the majority of mankind.

Usually at a given period in youth, after many blunders and excesses, every man recognizes the necessity of taking an active part in social life. He chooses some kind of work and devotes himself to it; but this seldom happens to one who is *comme il faut*. I have known, and still know many, very many people – old, proud, self-confident, opinion-ated – who if they were asked in the next world: 'What manner of man are you, and what have you done down there?' would only be able to answer: '*Je fus un homme très comme il faut.*'[1]

This fate awaited me.

32 · YOUTH

Notwithstanding the jumble of ideas in my head I was young, innocent, free and therefore almost happy that summer.

Sometimes, and not infrequently, I got up early. (I slept in the open air on the terrace and the bright slanting rays of the morning sun would wake me.) I would dress quickly, take a towel under my arm and a French novel and go and bathe in the river, in the shade of a birch wood about a quarter of a mile from the house. Then I would lie in the shade on the grass and read, occasionally lifting my eyes from the book to watch the purple surface of the shaded stream beginning to ripple in the morning breeze; the field of yellowing rye on the opposite bank and the bright-red sheen of the morning sunlight as it struck lower and lower down the white trunks of the birch-trees which, hiding behind each other, receded from me into the depths of the thick forest; and I rejoiced in the consciousness of having within me the same fresh young vigour of life as Nature breathed forth all around me. When there were grey morning cloudlets in the sky and I felt chilled after my bathe I often set out on a pathless tramp across forest and meadow, enjoying getting my boots wet through in the fresh dew. At such times my head would be full of vivid dreams of the heroes of the last novel I had read, and I imagined myself now a general, now a minister,

1. I was a most respectable man.

now some marvellous Hercules, or a man passionately in love, and would constantly look about me in the tremulous hope of suddenly meeting *her* in the glade or behind a tree. When in the course of such wanderings I came across some peasants or peasant women at work, despite the fact that the *common people* did not exist for me, I never could help feeling horribly uncomfortable, and tried to avoid being seen by them. When the sun was up but our ladies had not yet come down for breakfast I often went into the kitchen-garden or orchard to eat whatever vegetables or fruit were ripe. And this was one of the occupations which afforded me the most satisfaction. Get into an apple-orchard and dive right into the heart of the thick overgrown raspberry-canes. Overhead is the hot clear blue sky, around you the pale-green prickly foliage of the raspberry-canes tangled with weeds. Dark-green nettles with their slender flowering tops stretch gracefully upwards; broad-leaved burdocks with strange pinkish-blue prickly blossoms grow up rankly, higher than the raspberry-canes and higher than your head, and here and there, in company with the nettles, reach up to the pale-green hanging branches of the old apple-trees high up on which, close to the burning sun, round green apples ripen, lustrous as bone. Below, a young raspberry bush, leafless and almost withered, twists and turns as it stretches towards the sun; green needles of grass and young dockleaves thrusting up through last year's dew-drenched leaves grow lush and green in the eternal shade, as though unconscious of the sun playing brightly on the leaves of the apple-tree.

It is always damp in this thicket; redolent of confined perpetual shade, of spiders' webs and fallen apples turning black where they lie on the rotting leaf-mould, of raspberries and sometimes of the forest-bugs which you swallow unwittingly with your berry and then hastily eat another berry to take the taste away. As you advance you startle the sparrows that live in this covert; you hear their anxious twittering and the beating of their tiny fluttering wings against the branches; in one spot you catch the droning of a bumble-bee and somewhere on the path the gardener's footsteps (it is half-daft Akim), as he hums his eternal sing-song to himself. 'No, neither he nor any one in the world can find me here!' you say to yourself, while with both hands you pluck the juicy berries right and left from their little white cones and cram them one after another into your mouth with gusto. Your legs are wet through to far above the knee; your head is full of some fright-ful nonsense (you repeat mentally a thousand times in succession:

'a-an-d by twen-ty-ty-ties and by se-e-e-vens'), your arms, and your legs through your soaking trousers, are stung with nettles; the perpendicular rays of the sun penetrating into the thicket begin to scorch your head; you feel you can eat no more but you still sit on in the wilderness, looking, listening, thinking, and mechanically picking and swallowing the best berries.

I would generally repair to the drawing-room just after ten when the ladies had finished their breakfast and settled to their various occupations. At the nearest window, with the unbleached linen sunblind drawn down, stands an embroidery-frame on whose white linen the flies promenade drowsily; the sun casts such brilliant fiery circles through the mesh of the blind on everything which falls in its way that one's eyes ache to look at them. At the embroidery-frame sits Mimi, constantly shaking her head irritably and moving from place to place to escape the sun, which suddenly breaking through somewhere or other throws a burning streak now here, now there, on her face or her hand. Through the other three windows, with the shadows of their frames, regular bright squares fall on the unstained wood of the drawing-room floor, upon one of which, from old habit, lies Milka, who, pricking her ears, watches the flies as they walk over the squares of light. Katya knits or reads, sitting on the sofa, and impatiently flicks off the flies with her small white hands that seem transparent in the bright light, or frowning tosses her head to shake off a buzzing fly entangled in her thick golden hair. Lyuba either paces up and down the room with her hands behind her, waiting until they should go into the garden, or plays some piece on the piano with every note of which I have long been familiar. I sit down somewhere and listen to the music or the reading until such time as I can take possession of the piano myself. After dinner I occasionally condescend to ride horseback with the girls (to go for a walk I considered unsuitable to my years and position in society). And these excursions of ours, during which I lead them through unaccustomed places and over ravines, are very enjoyable. Sometimes we meet with adventures in which I exhibit great gallantry and the ladies praise my riding and courage and consider me their protector. In the evening if we have no visitors, after tea, which we drink on the shady verandah, and after a stroll with papa round the estate, I lie back in my old place, the lounge chair, and read and ponder as of yore, while I listen to Katya or Lyuba at the piano. At other times, left alone in the drawing-room with Lyuba playing some bygone tune, I find myself putting down my book and gazing through the open door of the verandah at the drooping leafy branches of the tall birch-trees over which the evening shadows are already falling, and at the pure heavens where, if you look intently enough, a misty yellowish spot will suddenly appear and then vanish again; and listening to the music from the ball-room, to the creaking of the gate, the voices of peasant-women and the herds returning to the village, I suddenly and vividly recall Natalya Savishna, and mamma, and Karl Ivanych, and for a moment feel sad. But my spirit at that time is so full of life and hope that these memories only brush me with their wings and fly away again.

After supper, followed sometimes by an evening stroll in the garden with some one – I was afraid to walk down the dark avenues by myself – I would repair to my solitary sleeping-place on the verandah floor, which I enjoyed very much in spite of the millions of gnats which devoured me. When the moon was full I often spent whole nights sitting up on my mattress watching the light and the shadows, listening to the sounds and the stillness, dreaming of one matter and another but more particularly of poetic and voluptuous bliss which then seemed to me the highest happiness in life, and grieving because, so far, it had only been granted me to imagine it. On other nights, as soon as every one had retired and the lights had gone from the drawing-room to the apartments upstairs, where I could hear feminine voices and windows being opened or shut, I would go out on to the verandah and walk up and down, breathlessly listening to every sound from the house as it gradually sank to rest. So long as there is the slightest unfounded hope of realizing even a fraction of the happiness I long for I cannot calmly give myself up to dreams of imaginary happiness.

At every sound of a bare footstep, of a cough or sigh, at every touch given to a window, at the rustle of a dress, I would spring from my mattress, listen stealthily, peer about me and for no obvious reason become wildly excited. But now the lights disappear from the windows upstairs, the sounds of footsteps and conversation give place to snores, the night-watchman begins to beat his board, the garden looks both darker and lighter as soon as there are no more streaks of red light on it from the windows, the last candle flits from the pantry to the ante-room, throwing a glimmer of light upon the dewy garden, and I can see through the window the bent figure of Foka on his way to bed, clad in a jacket and with a candle in his hand. Often I would find a great and fearful pleasure in stealing through the wet grass in the dark shadow of the house to the ante-room window, to listen with bated breath to the page-boy's snoring and Foka's grunts – who thought no one could hear him – and the sound of his aged voice as for a long long while he recited his prayers. At last his candle is put out, the last one, the window slammed to, and I am quite alone, glancing timidly about me on all sides lest haply there might be a woman in white near the flower-bed or standing by my mattress. I run full speed to the verandah and then, and only then, lie down with my face towards the garden, cover myself as best I can from the mosquitoes and bats, and gaze into the garden, listening to the sounds of the night and dreaming of love and happiness.

Everything looked so different then: the ancient birch-trees with their leafy boughs glistening in the moonlight on one side and on the other casting black shadows on the bushes and carriage-drive, and the calm rich glitter of the pond, ever swelling like a sound, and the moon-light sparkle of the dewdrops on the flowers in front of the verandah, which also threw their graceful shadows across the grey flower-bed; and the cry of a quail on the far side of the pond, the voice of some one on the road, and the soft almost inaudible scraping of two old birch-trees against each other, the hum of a mosquito over my ear under the coverlet, and an apple catching on a twig as it falls on the dry leaves, the frogs which sometimes come hopping right up to the verandah steps, their greenish backs shining mysteriously in the moonlight – all has assumed a strange significance for me, the significance of beauty too great and happiness somehow incomplete. And now *she* would appear with her long dark plait of hair and her full bosom, ever pensive and lovely, with bare arms and voluptuous embraces. She loved me and for one moment of her love I would sacrifice my whole life. But the moon rose higher and higher, brighter and brighter, in the sky, the rich glitter of the pond steadily filling out like an organ-note shone clearer and clearer, the shadows became blacker and blacker, the light more and more limpid, and as I gazed upon and listened to it all something told me that even *she*, with her bare arms and passionate embraces, was very very far from being the whole of happiness, and love for her very very far from being the only bliss; and the longer I gazed at the high full moon, the loftier, purer and nearer to Him, the source of all beauty and bliss, did real beauty and happiness appear to me, and tears of unsatisfied but tumultuous joy would fill my eyes.

And still I was alone, and still it seemed to me that Nature in her mysterious grandeur drawing to herself the shining sphere of the moon, which for some reason hangs in some high uncertain spot in the pale-blue sky and yet was everywhere and seemed to fill the infinity of space, and I, an insignificant worm already defiled by all the mean paltry earthly passions but endowed also with a mighty power of imagination and love – it seemed to me at such moments as though Nature, the moon and I were all one and the same.

33 · OUR NEIGHBOURS

I was astounded the day after our arrival to hear papa speak of our neighbours, the Epifanovs, as extremely nice people, and still more astounded when I found that he visited them. We had long been engaged in litigation over a piece of land with the Epifanovs. As a child I had more than once heard papa rage about this litigation, storm at the Epifanovs and send for various people in order, so I understood, to protect himself against them. I had heard Yakov call them 'our enemies' and 'black people', and I remember mamma requesting that their names should never be mentioned in her house and in her presence.

On these facts I had constructed for myself in my childhood so firm and clear a notion that the Epifanovs were our *enemies*, prepared to knife or strangle not only papa but his son too if they got hold of him, and that they were in a literal sense *black people*, that when I beheld Avdotya Vassilyevna Epifanova, *la belle Flamande*, nursing mamma the year she died I could hardly believe she came from the family of black people, and I still retained the lowest possible opinion of them all. Though we often saw them during this summer I remained strangely prejudiced against the whole family. In point of fact their household consisted only of a widowed mother of about fifty, still a fresh and lively old lady, a beautiful daughter, Avdotya Vassilyevna, and a stammering bachelor son, a retired lieutenant of very grave disposition, Piotr Vassilyevich.

For some twenty years before his death Madame Epifanova had lived apart from her husband, occasionally in Petersburg where she had relatives but mostly in the country on her estate, Mytishchi, a couple of miles from us. Such horrible tales circulated in the neighbourhood concerning her manner of life as made Messalina seem an innocent child by comparison. This was why mamma had requested that even the name of Epifanov should not be mentioned in our house; but speaking quite without irony one couldn't believe even a tithe of the most malicious of all gossip – scandal among country neighbours. When I first met Madame Epifanova, though she had in her house a serf, a clerk called Mitusha, who was always pomaded and curled and wore a Circassian coat and stood behind her chair at dinner, while she frequently invited her guests in French in his presence to admire his handsome eyes and mouth, there was nothing in the least like what rumour continued to report. Indeed, it appeared that ten years previously, when Anna Dmitrievna had called on her dutiful son, Piotr, to leave the army and come home, she had entirely altered her manner of life. Her estate was a small one, a round hundred serfs, and the sums she had spent during her gay life had been considerable, so that ten years ago the payments on her mortaged and re-mortgaged estate were naturally overdue, and the property was inevitably put up for auction. In this extremity Anna Dmitrievna, supposing that the trusteeship, the inventory taken of her property, the arrival of the sheriffs, and other similar unpleasantnesses, arose not so much from her failure to pay the interest as from the fact that she was a woman, wrote to her son, then serving with his regiment, to come and save his mother in this strait. Though Piotr Epifanov was doing so well in the Service that he hoped soon to be able to keep himself he threw up all his prospects, resigned the Service and like a dutiful son who considered it his first obligation to comfort his mother in her old age (as he quite sincerely wrote to her in his letters) returned to the country.

Notwithstanding his plain face, uncouth demeanour and his stammer, Piotr Vassilyevich was a man of exceptionally firm principles and unusually practical mind. In one way or another, by the aid of small loans, various expedients, petitions and promises he managed to preserve the estate. Having become a landed proprietor, he donned his father's short fur jacket, which had been laid up in the store-room, dispensed with the carriages and horses, kept visitors away from Mytishchi, dug drains, increased his arable land, cut down the peasants' allotments, had his woods felled by his own serfs, sold the timber profitably and brought his affairs into order. Piotr vowed, and kept his word, that until all debts were paid he would not wear any coat except his father's short jacket or a canvas coat he made for himself, and would

not ride in anything but a peasant cart drawn by peasant horses. This
stoic life he tried to impose on the whole family in so far as his obsequi-
ous respect for his mother, which he considered his duty, allowed him.
In the drawing-room he stammered and deferred in all things to his
mother, fulfilled her every wish and scolded the servants if they did
not do as she told them; but in his study and in the office he would haul
every one sternly to account if a duck were killed for the table without
his orders, or at Anna Dmitrievna's bidding a serf left his work to go
and inquire after a neighbour's health, or serf-girls went to the woods
to gather raspberries instead of weeding in the vegetable garden.

Within four years or so the debts were all paid and Piotr went to
Moscow and returned in a tarantass with new clothes. But in spite of
the flourishing state of his affairs he still kept to the same stoical style of
living in which he seemed to take a gloomy pride before his own people
and strangers, and often said with a stammer: 'Any one who really
wants to see me will be glad to see me even in a peasant sheepskin, and
will not refuse my cabbage-soup and buckwheat porridge. After all I
eat them myself,' he would add. His every word and gesture expressed
pride founded upon consciousness of having sacrificed himself for his
mother and redeemed the estate, and scorn for others who had done
nothing of the sort.

The mother and daughter had totally different temperaments from
Piotr's, and were in many respects very unlike each other. The mother
was one of the most agreeable, uniformly good-natured and cheerful
women one could possibly meet. She really delighted in everything
that was pleasant and light-hearted. She even possessed in the highest
degree a faculty only to be found in the kindest of elderly folk – she
liked to see young people enjoying themselves. Her daughter, Avdotya
Vassilyevna, was, on the contrary, of a grave turn of mind, or rather
had that peculiarly apathetic, absent-minded, gratuitously distant
bearing which commonly distinguishes unmarried beauties. When she
tried to be gay her mirth seemed unnatural – as if she were laughing at
herself or at those she was talking to, or the world in general, which
she assuredly did not mean to do. She often surprised me, and I asked
myself what she could have meant, by such remarks as 'Yes, I am
awfully good-looking! Of course everybody is in love with me!' and
so on. Madame Epifanova was always bustling about: she had a passion for arranging the house and garden, for flowers, canaries and
pretty trifles. Her rooms and her garden were not large or luxurious

but everything was so neat and clean, and suggested the gentle gaiety of a pretty waltz or polka that the adjective 'toy' was often used by her guests in praising her house and garden and it fitted them perfectly. And Anna Dmitrievna, *petite* and slim, with a fresh complexion and pretty little hands, always bright and always becomingly dressed, looked like a toy herself. Only the rather too puffy dark-purple veins that showed on her small hands marred the general effect. But her daughter was just the opposite: she hardly ever did anything, cared nothing for flowers and knick-knacks and even neglected her appearance, so that she invariably had to run away and change when visitors arrived. But when she did come down having put on another dress she looked remarkably well, except for the cold unvarying expression of eyes and smile which all very handsome faces have in common. Her classically regular beautiful features and graceful figure forever seemed to be saying to you, 'You may admire me if you like.'

But notwithstanding the mother's vivacious character and the daughter's distant indifferent manner something told you that the former had never – either now or in the past – loved anything but pretty trifles while Avdotya Vassilyevna was one of those natures which, once they love, will sacrifice their whole life for the loved one.

34 · FATHER'S MARRIAGE

Father was forty-eight when he took Avdotya Vassilyevna Epifanova for his second wife.

I suspect that when he came to the country alone with the girls that spring papa had been in that restlessly happy and sociable state of mind gamblers usually are in who call a halt after winning heavily. He felt that he was in luck – luck which if he did not choose to expend it in card-playing might help him to success in other things in life. Moreover it was spring-time, he had far more money than he could normally have expected, he was entirely alone and had nothing to do. Discussing business affairs with Yakov and recalling the interminable lawsuit with the Epifanovs, and the beautiful Avdotya Vassilyevna whom he had not seen for a long time, I can imagine him saying: 'Do you know, Yakov Kharlapych, instead of bothering about that lawsuit why don't I simply let them have that damned bit of ground, eh? What do you think?'

I can imagine Yakov's fingers twisting disapprovingly behind his back at such a question, and hear him argue: '*And furthermore* we have the rights of that business, sir.'

But papa ordered the calash, put on his most fashionable olive-green coat, brushed what hair he had left, sprinkled scent on his pocket-handkerchief and in the gayest spirits because he felt that he was acting like a gentleman and most of all because he hoped to meet a good-looking woman, drove off to call on his neighbours.

I only know that on his first visit papa did not find Piotr Epifanov who was out in the fields, and spent an hour or two with the ladies. I imagine how he scattered compliments about, how he charmed them, tapping the floor with his soft boot, lowering his voice and looking sentimental. I imagine, too, how the merry old lady conceived a sudden tender liking for him, and how her cold beautiful daughter brightened up.

When a maid-servant ran panting to inform Piotr Epifanov that old Irtenyev himself had arrived I can fancy him answering sullenly: 'Well, what if he has?' – and how in consequence he walked home as slowly as he could, and perhaps even first stepped into his own room to put on his dirtiest coat, and sent a message to the cook that on no account – no, not even if the mistress so ordered – was there to be anything extra for dinner.

I often saw papa and Epifanov together afterwards, and so I can form a very good idea of their first meeting. I am sure that though papa offered to settle the dispute amicably Piotr Vassilyevich remained morose and resentful because he had sacrificed his career for his mother while papa had done nothing of the kind, which he found not in the least surprising; and how papa, taking no notice of his ill-humour, was sprightly and debonair, treating him as an astonishingly whimsical fellow – which Piotr Vassilyevich sometimes took amiss and sometimes could not resist. Papa, with his bent for making fun of everything, for some reason or other would call Piotr Vassilyevich 'colonel', and though I myself once heard him say, stammering worse than usual and flushing with vexation that he was not a *p-p-p-polkovnik* (colonel) but a *p-p-p-porutchik* (lieutenant) five minutes later papa again addressed him as 'colonel'.

Lyuba told me that before our arrival in the country they saw the Epifanovs every day, and had had an extremely jolly time. Papa, who had a talent for arranging everything with a touch of originality and wit, as well as simply and with good taste, devised shooting and fishing parties and fireworks, at which the Epifanovs had been present. 'And it would have been jollier still,' said Lyuba, 'if that insufferable Piotr Vassilyevich had not been there, sulking, stammering and spoiling everything.'

After our arrival the Epifanovs only visited us twice, and we drove over to them once, while after St Peter's day, when they and a whole crowd of other visitors called, for it was papa's name-day, our relations with the Epifanovs, I don't know why, entirely ceased, and only papa continued to go and see them.

During the short time that I saw papa with Avdotya – or Dunichka as her mother called her – this is what I contrived to observe: papa was always in the same buoyant frame of mind which had struck me on the day of our arrival. He was so gay, so young, so full of life and so happy that he radiated this happiness on all about him and involuntarily infected us all with the same mood. He never stirred from Avdotya's side when she was in the room, and paid her such sugary compliments that I felt ashamed for him; or he sat gazing at her in silence, twitching his shoulder in a sort of passionate and complacent way, coughed and sometimes, smiling, even whispered in her ear; but all this he did in the jesting manner characteristic of him even in the most serious matters.

The look of happiness I had noticed on my father's face seemed to have imparted itself to Avdotya Vassilyevna's as well, and shone in her large blue eyes almost continually except when she was suddenly seized with such shyness that I, who knew the feeling, was quite sorry and upset for her. At such moments she seemed to be afraid to look up or move, fancying that she was the object of every one's attention and their only concern and that they found everything about her disgraceful. She would glance in a scared way from one person to another, the colour coming and going in her cheeks, and then begin to talk loudly and defiantly, generally making some foolish observation, until presently, realizing this, and realizing everybody including papa had heard her, she would blush more painfully than ever. But on such occasions papa did not even remark the nonsense but giving his little cough went on gazing at her just as passionately, in happy ecstasy. I noticed that though these fits of shyness attacked Avdotya Vassilyevna without any cause they not infrequently followed the mention of some young and pretty woman in papa's hearing. Her frequent transitions from pensiveness to that strange awkward gaiety of hers to which I have just referred, the way she would repeat papa's favourite words and turns of speech, and continue with others a conversation begun with him – all this would have opened my eyes to the state of things between papa and Avdotya Vassilyevna had the chief actor not been my father, or had I been a little older; but at the time I suspected nothing, although I was in the room when papa received a letter from Piotr Vassilyevich which upset him very much, and he ceased his visits to the Epifanovs until the end of August.

At the end of August papa again began to visit our neighbours, and the day before we (Volodya and I) left for Moscow he announced to us that he was going to marry Avdotya Vassilyevna Epifanova.

35 · HOW WE TOOK THE NEWS

The day before this formal announcement every one in the house knew already and reacted to it in their various ways. Mimi never left her room all day and wept. Katya stayed with her and only came down for dinner, with an injured expression on her face evidently adopted from her mother; Lyuba on the other hand was in high spirits and mentioned at dinner that she knew a splendid secret but was not going to tell any one.

'There's nothing splendid about your secret,' Volodya said to her, not sharing her satisfaction. 'If you were capable of thinking seriously about anything, you would understand that, on the contrary, it's a bad business.'

Lyuba stared at him in amazement and said no more.

After dinner Volodya was on the point of taking my arm but fearing, I suppose, that this would look soft, merely touched my elbow and nodded towards the ball-room.

'You know the secret Lyuba was speaking about?' he said, when he was sure we were alone.

Volodya and I seldom had a tête-à-tête on any serious matter so that when such a thing did occur we both felt awkward and 'specks began to dance in our eyes,' as Volodya put it; but that day, in response to my embarrassed looks, he continued to gaze gravely straight into my eyes with an expression which seemed to say: 'There's nothing to be alarmed about, after all we're brothers and must consult together upon an important family matter.' I understood him and he proceeded:

'You know papa is going to marry the Epifanova girl?'

I nodded because I had already heard.

'Well, it's not at all a good thing,' continued Volodya.

'Why not?'

'Why not?' he repeated irritably. 'It will be very nice, won't it, to have that stammering "colonel" and all his family for relations? And though she seems kind enough now, who knows what she will turn out to be later? True, it makes no difference to us, but Lyuba will soon be making her début in society. With a stepmother like that it won't be very pleasant. She doesn't even speak French properly, and has no manners to teach her. She's a fishwife, that's all she is – a kindly one, perhaps, but nevertheless a fishwife,' concluded Volodya, evidently much pleased with this designation 'fishwife'.

Odd as it was to me to hear Volodya so coolly criticizing papa's choice it struck me that he was right.

'Why is it papa wants to marry?' I asked.

'Oh, it's a dubious business, heaven only knows what it means. All I can say is that Piotr Vassilyevich tried to induce him to marry her – insisted on it – that papa didn't want to, and then got some cock-eyed notion about chivalry. It is a mysterious affair altogether. I am only now beginning to understand father,' Volodya continued. (That he called him 'father' and not 'papa' stabbed me to the heart.) 'He's a fine man, kind and intelligent, but amazingly thoughtless and irresponsible! He can't look at a woman without losing his head. You know yourself that he falls in love with every woman he meets. You know it's so – even Mimi.'

'What do you mean?'

'What I say. I found out a short time ago, he was in love with Mimi when she was young, wrote poems to her, and there was something between them. Mimi is still heart-broken.' And Volodya laughed.

'Impossible!' I cried in astonishment.

'But the chief thing,' Volodya went on, becoming serious again and suddenly beginning to speak in French, 'is how pleased all our relations will be at such a marriage! And, of course, she's sure to have children.'

I was so struck by Volodya's common sense and foresight that I did not know what to say in reply.

At this point Lyuba approached us.

'So you know?' she said with a glad face.

'Yes,' said Volodya. 'Only I am surprised, Lyuba – after all, you are not a babe in arms. How can you be pleased that papa is marrying a bit of trash?'

Lyuba's face fell, and she looked grave.

'Oh, Volodya! Why ever a bit of trash? How dare you speak of Avdotya Vassilyevna like that? If papa intends to marry her, she can't be a bit of trash.'

'Well, not trash – I only put it like that, but all the same . . .'

'There's no "all the same" about it,' Lyuba interrupted him hotly. 'You have never heard me call the girl you are in love with a bit of trash: how can you speak like that about papa and a splendid woman? You may be my elder brother but don't say such things to me. You ought not to.'

'But why shouldn't we discuss . . .?'

'Because we shouldn't,' Lyuba interrupted again. 'We oughtn't to discuss a father like ours. Mimi may, but not you, our elder brother.'

'Oh, you still don't understand anything,' said Volodya scornfully. 'Listen. Is it a good thing that some Epifanova woman – some "Dunichka" – should take the place of your dead mother?'

Lyuba was silent for a moment, then the tears suddenly started to her eyes.

'I knew you were stuck-up but I didn't think you were so spiteful,' she said, and left us.

'Bosh!' said Volodya, pulling a rueful grimace but with his eyes rather dim. 'That's what comes of trying to argue with them,' he continued, as though in self-reproach for having so far forgotten himself as to condescend to converse with Lyuba.

The weather was bad on the following day and neither papa nor the ladies had come down to breakfast when I entered the drawing-room. There had been a cold autumnal rain during the night; odds and ends of cloud that had emptied themselves overnight were scudding across the sky, with the sun's luminous disc (already high in the heavens) shining faintly through them. It was a windy damp grey morning. The door was open into the garden and the puddles left by the night's rain were drying on the floor of the verandah, dark with moisture. The open door, fastened back with an iron hook, shook in the wind; the paths were damp and muddy; the old birch-trees with their bare white branches, the bushes and the grass, the nettles, the currants, the elder with the pale side of its leaves turned outwards, all fought and struggled where they stood, as if trying to tear themselves from their roots.

Round yellow leaves whirled and chased each other along the avenue of lime-trees until soaked through and through they came to rest on the wet path and on the damp dark-green aftermath of the meadow. My thoughts were taken up with my father's impending marriage, which I looked at from the same point of view as Volodya. The future seemed to bode no good for my sister, for us boys, or even for my father. I hated to think that an outsider, a stranger, and above all a *young* woman having no right to at all would suddenly take the place in many respects of – *whom*? An ordinary young lady to usurp the place of my dead mother! I felt depressed and my father seemed to me more and more in the wrong. Just then I heard his voice and Volodya's talking in the pantry. I did not want to see my father at that moment so I stepped outside but Lyuba came for me and said that papa was asking for me.

He was standing in the drawing-room, resting one hand on the piano and looking impatiently and at the same time portentously in my direction. His face no longer wore the youthful happy expression which had struck me during all this period. He looked sad. Volodya was walking about the room with a pipe in his hand. I went up to my father and wished him good morning.

'Well, my friends,' he said resolutely, raising his head and speaking in the peculiarly brisk tone people adopt when they have something obviously unwelcome to say which it is too late to reconsider, 'you know, I think, that I am going to marry Avdotya Vassilyevna.' He paused. 'I never meant to marry again after your mamma . . . but – ' he hesitated for a moment 'but . . . but fate evidently wills otherwise. Dunya is a good kind-hearted girl, and not so very young; I hope you will learn to love her, children, and she loves you whole-heartedly already, she is a nice person. And now,' he said, turning to me and Volodya and apparently making haste to speak for fear we might interrupt him, 'it is time for you two to leave here but I shall stay on till the New Year, and then follow you to Moscow with – ' he hesitated again '– my wife and Lyuba.' It was painful to me to see my father seem so nervous and guilty with us, and I moved closer to him. But Volodya, continuing to smoke, went on walking about the room with his head bent.

'So, my dears, now you know what your old father has taken it into his head to do,' papa concluded, colouring, coughing and holding out his hands to Volodya and me. There were tears in his eyes as he said this and I noticed that the hand he held out to Volodya, who was at the other end of the room at that moment, trembled a little. The sight of that trembling hand tore my heart-strings and a strange thought occurred to me which troubled me still more – the thought that papa had served in the campaign of 1812 and had been, as every one knew, a brave officer. I kept hold of his large muscular hand and kissed it. He squeezed mine hard and suddenly, gulping down his tears, took Lyuba's dark little head in both hands and kissed her again and again on the eyes. Volodya pretended to drop his pipe and, bending down, furtively wiped his eyes with his fist, and, trying not to be noticed, went out of the room.

36 · THE UNIVERSITY

The wedding was to take place in a fortnight's time; but our lectures at the University were starting and Volodya and I went back to Moscow at the beginning of September. The Nekhlyudovs also returned from the country. Dmitri (we had promised when we parted to write often to each other and of course we had not done so once) came straight to me and we arranged that the following day he should escort me to the University for my first lecture.

It was a bright sunny day.

As soon as I entered the auditorium I felt my personality disappearing in this throng of gay young people who surged noisily through all the doors and corridors, in the brilliant sunshine streaming in through the large windows. The consciousness that I was a member of this great company was very pleasant. But I knew only a very few of all these people, and my acquaintance even with them went no farther than a nod and greeting: 'How d'you do, Irtenyev?' All around me, though, they were shaking hands, jostling one another, and friendly words, smiles, expressions of goodwill and *badinage* showered from all quarters. I was aware right and left of the bond which bound all these young folk together, and felt with sorrow that this bond somehow seemed to miss me. But it was only a momentary impression. My vexation at being thus overlooked soon made me think it was even a very good thing that I did not belong to all that society, that I must have my own little circle of nice people, and I took a seat on the third bench where Count B., Baron Z., Prince R., Ivin and some other young gentlemen of the same class were sitting – of whom I knew Ivin and Count B. But these gentlemen, too, looked at me in a way that made me feel I did not belong to their set either. I turned to observe what was going on around me. Semeonov with his rumpled grey hair, white teeth and unbuttoned coat sat not far away and, leaning on his elbows, gnawed a quill pen. The high-school lad who had come out first at the examinations had established himself on the front bench, with a black neck-cloth still tied round his cheek, and was toying with a silver watch-key which hung on his satin waistcoat. Ikonin, who had got into the University after all, was sitting on a raised bench, wearing pale-blue trousers with piping down the seams which completely hid his boots, and laughing and shouting that he was on Parnassus. Ilinka, to my surprise greeting me not only coldly but even contemptuously, as if wishing to remind me that here we were all equals, was just in front with his thin legs resting carelessly on the bench opposite (for my benefit, it seemed); he was talking with a fellow-student, every now and then glancing in my direction. Beside me Ivin's set were talking French. These gentlemen I thought awfully stupid. Every word I heard of their conversation seemed not only silly but incorrect, simply not French at all ('*Ce n'est pas français,*' I said to myself), while the gestures, sayings and manners of Semeonov, Ilinka and the rest I decided were vulgar, common and not *comme il faut.*

I did not belong to any group, and feeling isolated and unable to make friends I grew resentful. A student on the bench in front of me was biting his nails, which were all hang-nails already, and this so disgusted me that I moved farther away from him. I remember I felt very down that first day.

When the professor entered and everybody first shifted about and then settled in their seats I remember extending my satirical observations to him, too, and was amazed that he should begin his lecture with an introductory sentence which, in my opinion, did not make sense. I wanted the lecture to be so clever from beginning to end that it would be impossible to omit or add a single word. Disappointed in this, I immediately proceeded to sketch, under the heading *First Lecture* inscribed in the handsomely-bound note-book I had brought with me, eighteen profiles joined together in a circle like a wreath, and only occasionally moved my hand across the page to make the professor (who I felt sure was much interested in me) think that I was taking notes. Having come to the conclusion at this same lecture that it was unnecessary and would even be foolish to take down everything each of the professors said, I stuck to this principle to the end of the course.

At subsequent lectures I did not feel so isolated; I made a number of acquaintances, shook hands and chatted, yet for some reason real intimacy between me and my comrades was still lacking, so that I often found myself depressed and shut in on myself. I could not join up with the set of Ivin and the 'aristocrats', as everybody called them, because, as I remember now, I was unsociable and rude with them, only bowing when they bowed to me, and they seemed to have very little need of my company. With the majority, however, the cause was quite a different one. As soon as I discerned a willingness to be friendly on the part of a fellow-student I at once gave him to understand that I often dined with Prince Ivan Ivanych and had my own trap. This was said only to show myself off to better advantage and to induce him to like me more; but on the contrary, in almost every instance, to my amazement, my comrade, as a result of the information that I was related to Prince Ivan Ivanych and had a trap of my own, suddenly became cold and distant.

We had among us a bursary-student named Operov, an unassuming, very able, industrious young man who always shook hands with his fingers rigid and straight and his hand as stiff as a board, so that the wags among his comrades frequently did the same to him and called it the 'deal board' way of shaking hands. I nearly always sat next to him and we often talked. I particularly liked Operov for the freedom with which he would pass judgement on the professors. Very clearly and precisely he would point out the merits and defects of their respective ways of teaching, and even occasionally make fun of them, which produced a peculiarly strange and startling effect upon me, spoken in his quiet voice and coming from his minute little mouth. Nevertheless he never failed to make full and careful notes in his small handwriting of each and every lecture. We were becoming friends and had decided to prepare our lectures together, and his small grey short-sighted eyes were beginning to turn to me and look pleased when I took my seat at his side, until one day in the course of conversation I found it necessary to tell him that my mother on her death-bed had begged my father never to send us to any institution supported by the State, and that I was beginning to think that all Crown scholars, though they might be very erudite, were not at all the thing – 'Ce ne sont pas des gens comme il faut,'[1] I said, faltering and conscious that for some reason I

---

1. They aren't *comme il faut* people.

was going red. Operov said nothing but at the next lecture he did not greet me first, did not hold out his 'deal board' to me or speak, and when I took my seat he bent his head sideways close to his note-books, as if he were intent upon them. I was surprised by this coolness on Operov's part for which I could see no grounds. But I considered it beneath the dignity of a *jeune homme de bonne maison*[1] to run after a bursary-student like Operov and I left him alone, though I confess his aloofness hurt me. Once I arrived before him and since the lecture was to be delivered by a popular professor whom students came to hear who did not always attend, and all the places were occupied, I took Operov's place, laid my note-books on the desk and went out. When I returned to the auditorium I saw that my note-books had been moved to a place at the back and Operov was in his usual seat. I remarked to him that I had put my note-books there.

'I know nothing about that,' he retorted, suddenly flushing and not looking at me.

'I tell you I put my books here,' said I, purposely working myself up and thinking to intimidate him with my defiance. 'Everybody saw me,' I added, glancing round at the other students, but though many of them looked at me with curiosity no one responded.

'Places aren't bought outright here, whoever comes first gets the seat,' said Operov, settling himself angrily where he was and flashing me an indignant glance.

'That means you're a cad,' said I.

I have an idea that he muttered something, it might even have been that I was a 'silly kid', but I decided not to hear. Besides, what would have been the use if I had heard? Were we to brawl like a couple of *manants*[2] over less than nothing? (I was very fond of that word *manant* and it served me as an answer and a solution in many an awkward juncture.) Perhaps I might have said something more but at that moment the door slammed and the professor in his blue tail-coat bowed and hastily ascended the platform.

However, before the examinations when I was in need of notes, Operov, remembering his promise, offered me his and invited me to study with him.

1. Young man of good family.
2. Louts.

37 · AFFAIRS OF THE HEART

Affaires du cœur occupied me a good deal that winter. I was in love three times. The first time I became passionately enamoured of a very buxom lady who rode in Freitag's riding-school, in consequence of which I went to the school every Tuesday and Friday – the days on which she rode – in order to gaze at her, but I was always so afraid lest she should see me that I stood so far away from her and bolted so precipitately from the place she had to pass, and turned away so negligently when she chanced to look my way, that I actually never saw her face properly and to this day do not know whether she was really pretty or not.

Dubkov, who knew the lady, catching me one day at the riding-school lurking behind the footmen and the fur wraps they were holding, and having heard from Dmitri of my infatuation, put me into such an awful fright by offering to introduce me to my amazon that I fled headlong from the place; and the mere idea that he had told her about me prevented my ever daring to set foot in the riding-school again, even as far as the place where the footmen waited, for fear of meeting her.

Whenever I fell in love with ladies whom I did not know, and especially married women, I was overwhelmed with shyness a thousand times worse than I had ever felt with Sonya. I dreaded nothing in the world so much as that the object of my love should learn of my passion or even know of my existence. It seemed to me that if she had an inkling of my feelings it would be such an insult to her that she would never be able to forgive me. And indeed if the lady at the riding-school had known in detail how, watching her from behind the footmen, I had imagined myself seizing and carrying her off to live in the country, and pictured what I would do with her there, she might perhaps with justice have felt very much outraged. I did not realize that knowing me would not suddenly make her aware of all my thoughts about her and that there could, therefore, be nothing shameful in simply being introduced.

Then I fell in love with Sonya when she came to see my sister. My second period of being in love with her was long a thing of the past but I fell in love a third time after Lyuba showed me a book full of pieces of poetry copied out by Sonya, in which several gloomily amorous passages from Lermontov's *The Demon* were underlined in red ink and marked with pressed flowers. Remembering how Volodya the year before had kissed his lady-love's purse, I essayed the same; and, in fact, alone in my room in the evening I fell into reveries, looking at one of the flowers, laid it to my lips and felt a sort of agreeably tearful emotion, and was in love again, or fancied I was, for several days.

Finally I fell in love for the third time that winter with a young lady with whom Volodya was in love and who visited at our house. So far as I remember now, there was nothing attractive about her – at least, nothing of the kind that usually appealed to me. She was the daughter of a well-known intellectual and learned lady of Moscow, small, thin, with long flaxed curls after the English fashion and a limpid profile. Everybody said she was even cleverer and more learned than her mother but I had no opportunity of judging of this as, feeling a kind of servile awe at the thought of her intellect and accomplishments, I only spoke to her once, and then with unaccountable trepidation. But the enthusiasm of Volodya, who was never deterred by the presence of others from giving vent to his rapture, communicated itself to me with such force that I became passionately enamoured of the young lady. Aware that Volodya would not be pleased to know that *two brothers were in love with the same maiden* I did not speak to him of my love. On the contrary, I took especial delight in the thought that our love was so pure that though the object of it was the same charming being we should remain friends and be prepared, if the occasion arose, to sacrifice ourselves for one another. As regards self-sacrifice, however, I suspect that Volodya did not quite share my views for he was so passionately in love that he was for giving a member of the Diplomatic Corps, who was said to be going to marry her, a slap in the face and a challenge to a duel. But for my part I gladly sacrificed my feeling, perhaps because it cost me no great effort since I had only had one – affected – conversation with the young lady, on the merits of classical music, and my passion, for all my attempts to keep it alive, expired the following week.

38 · SOCIETY

I was utterly disillusioned that winter by the social pleasures to which I had intended, on entering the University, to surrender myself in

imitation of my brother. Volodya danced a great deal and papa also
went to balls with his young wife; but I suppose I was still considered
either too young or inept for such pleasures, and no one introduced me
in the houses where balls were given. Notwithstanding my promise to
be perfectly open with Dmitri I did not tell him how I longed to go to
balls, and how wounded and vexed I felt at being overlooked and
evidently regarded as a sort of bookworm – which I consequently
pretended to be.

But that winter Princess Kornakova gave an evening party and
herself called to invite us all, including me; and I was to go to a ball for
the first time. Before starting, Volodya came to my room to see how I
was dressed – which greatly surprised me and took me aback. I had
always thought it highly shameful to care about being well dressed,
and that one must conceal the wish; while he, on the other hand, considered it so entirely natural and essential that he said outright he was
afraid I might bring disgrace upon myself. He told me to be sure to put
on patent-leather boots and was horrified that I wanted to wear suède
gloves; he arranged my watch for me in a particular manner and
carried me off to a hairdresser's on the Kuznetsky Bridge, where they
curled my hair which Volodya stepped back to inspect from a distance.

'There, that's not bad, but can't you keep those tufts down?' he
said, turning to the hairdresser.

But however much Monsieur Charles greased the tufts with some
sticky essence they still stood up the same as ever when I put my hat
on, and altogether my curled hair seemed to make me look uglier than
before. My only salvation lay in an affectation of casualness. Solely in
that way was my appearance tolerable.

Volodya seemed to think so too, for he begged me to get rid of the
curl, and when I had done so and was still not right he did not look at
me any more, and was silent and gloomy all the way to the Kornakovs.

I entered the drawing-room boldly with Volodya; but when the
princess invited me to dance and I for some reason said that I did not
dance – though my one idea in coming had been to dance as much as
possible – I lost my nerve, and left among strangers I lapsed into my
customary state of insuperable and mounting shyness. I stood dumbly
in one place the entire evening.

During a waltz one of the young princesses came up to me and with
the formal courtesy common to the whole family asked me why I was
not dancing. I remember my alarm at this question, yet how at the

same time, quite involuntarily, a self-satisfied smile spread over my face and I began to utter, in the most pompous French with many parentheses, such rubbish as I am still ashamed to recall many decades later. It must have been the effect the music had, exciting my nerves and drowning (so I supposed) the not altogether intelligible portion of my speech. I said something about high life, about the inanity of people and of women, until I got myself so tied up that I was forced to stop short in the middle of a word in some sentence it was quite impossible to complete.

Even the princess with her innate social tact was embarrassed and looked at me reproachfully. I was smiling. At the critical moment Volodya, who had noticed that I was speaking with great animation and probably wanting to find out if I was making up for not dancing by talking well, approached with Dubkov. Seeing my smiling face and the princess's startled mien, and hearing the frightful stuff with which I wound up, he reddened and turned away. The princess rose and left me. I went on smiling but suffered such agonies from the consciousness of my foolishness that I was ready to sink through the floor and felt that at all costs I must move about and say something which would somehow alter the situation. I went up to Dubkov and asked him how many times he had waltzed with *her*. Ostensibly I was being humorous and jolly but in reality I was imploring help from that very Dubkov to whom I had cried 'Hold your tongue!' at the dinner at Yar's. Dubkov pretended not to hear, and walked away. I moved towards Volodya and with a desperate effort, again trying to impart a jesting tone to my voice, said, 'Well, Volodya, tired out?' But Volodya stared at me as much as to say, 'You don't talk to me like that when we are alone,' and left me without a word, evidently afraid I should hang on to him.

'Oh heaven, even my own brother deserts me!' I thought.

Yet somehow I had not the resolution to leave. I stayed to the end, morosely standing where I was, and only when everybody was departing and crowding into the ante-room, and a footman in helping me on with my overcoat caught the brim of my hat so that it tipped up, did I laugh painfully through my tears, and not addressing any one in particular said: *'Comme c'est gracieux!'*[1]

1. How pleasing!

39 · THE CAROUSAL

Although thanks to Dmitri's influence I had never as yet indulged in
any of those traditional festivities known to students as 'wines' that
winter saw me participate in one such function, and carry away a not
altogether pleasant impression. It happened like this.

At a lecture soon after the New Year Baron Z., a tall fair-haired
young man with a very grave face and regular features, invited us all to
spend a sociable evening with him. 'All' of course meant all the first-
year students who were more or less *comme il faut*, which, it followed,
did not include Grap, Semeonov, Operov or common people of that
sort. Volodya smiled disdainfully when he heard that I was going to a
carouse of first-year men but I expected great things from this, to me,
still entirely novel pastime, and punctually at the appointed hour of
eight I was at Baron Z's.

Baron Z., with his coat unbuttoned over a white waistcoat, was
receiving his visitors in the brightly-lit ball-room and drawing-room
of a small house in which his parents lived: they had let him have the
reception rooms for the party. I caught sight of the skirts and heads of
inquisitive maids in the passage, and once had a glimpse of the dress of
a lady, whom I took to be the baroness herself, in the pantry. There
were about twenty of us invited, all students except Herr Frost, who
had come with the Ivins, and a tall ruddy-complexioned gentleman in
plain clothes, who acted as master of ceremonies and was introduced to
every one as a relation of the baron's and a former student of Dorpat
University. The excessive lighting and the usual formal arrangement
of the reception rooms at first had such a chilling effect on the youthful
company that every one involuntarily hugged the walls, except for a
few bold spirits and the ex-Dorpat student who, having already unbuttoned his waistcoat, seemed to be in every room at once, and in
every corner of every room, filling the whole place with his agreeable, resonant, never-silent tenor voice. But the fellows were mostly
silent or talked modestly about their professors, studies, examinations,
and serious and uninteresting topics in general. Every one without
exception kept watching the door of the supper-room and though they
tried to conceal it their expressions seemed to say: 'Well, isn't it time
to begin?' I, too, felt it was time to begin and awaited *the beginning* with
pleasurable impatience.

After tea, which the footman handed round among the guests, the Dorpat student asked Frost in Russian:

'Can you make punch, Frost?'

'O ja!'[1] replied Frost, wriggling his calves, but the Dorpat student again addressed him in Russian:

'Well then, you take it on,' (as ex-fellow-students at the Dorpat University they knew each other well); and Frost with giant strides of his bowed muscular legs began moving backwards and forwards from drawing-room to pantry and from pantry to drawing-room, and soon a large soup-tureen appeared on the table with a ten-pound sugar loaf poised above it on three crossed student's swords. Baron Z. meanwhile had been going round among his guests who had assembled in the drawing-room and were gazing at the soup-tureen, and saying to each one, with a face of immutable gravity, and in almost the same words: 'Let us all pass the cup round, student-fashion, and drink Bruderschaft,[2] otherwise there is no good fellowship at all in our set. But unbutton your coats or take them off altogether as he has done.' And indeed the Dorpat student had taken off his coat and tucked up the white sleeves of his shirt above his elbows, and now, planting his feet firmly apart, was already setting fire to the rum in the soup-tureen.

'Gentlemen, put out the lights!' cried the Dorpat student suddenly, as loudly and insistently as though we had all been shouting. But we were all silently watching the soup-tureen and the Dorpat student's white shirt, and felt that the solemn moment had arrived.

'Löschen Sie die Lichter aus, Frost!'[3] the Dorpat student shouted again, this time in German, because he was getting excited, I suppose. Frost and all of us set about extinguishing the lights. The room grew dark, only the white sleeves and the hands supporting the sugar-loaf on the swords were illuminated by the bluish flame. The Dorpat student's loud tenor was no longer the only voice heard, for talking and laughter came from every corner of the room. Many of the guests took off their coats (especially those who had fine and perfectly clean shirts). I did the same and was aware that *it had begun*. Though nothing jolly had happened so far I was firmly convinced all the same that things would be

---

1. Oh yes!

2. Drinking *Bruderschaft* is a German custom: the company drinks with arms linked and afterwards address each other in the second person singular as a sign of intimacy.

3. Put out the lights.

first-rate once each of us had drunk a glass of the potion now in course of preparation.

The drink was ready. The Dorpat student ladled the punch into glasses, spilling a good deal on the table, and shouted: 'Now then, gentlemen, come along!' When each of us had taken one of the brimming sticky tumblers the Dorpat student and Frost struck up a German song in which the exclamation *Juche!*[1] was frequently repeated. We all joined in discordantly, clinked glasses, shouted something, praised the punch, and with arms linked or not began drinking the strong sweet liquor. After that there was no further waiting: the 'wine' was in full swing. The first glassful consumed, a second was poured out: my temples throbbed, the flame looked blood-red, round me every one was shouting and laughing yet it not only did not seem jolly but I was even convinced that I and all the others were finding the affair rather dull, and that I and all the others for some reason considered it necessary to pretend we were thoroughly enjoying ourselves. The only one perhaps who was not pretending was the Dorpat student; he grew redder and redder in the face and more and more ubiquitous, filling up everybody's empty tumbler and spilling more and more on the table which had become all sweet and sticky. I do not remember the precise sequence of events but I can recall being awfully fond that evening of the Dorpat student and Frost, that I tried to learn a German song by heart and kissed them both on their sticky-sweet lips. I remember, too, that I took a violent dislike to the Dorpat student that evening and wanted to throw a chair at him but restrained myself. I remember also that besides the refusal on the part of all my limbs to comply with my will which I had experienced on the night of the dinner at Yar's my head so ached and swam that evening that I was terribly afraid I was going to die there and then. I remember, too, that we all sat down on the floor – I don't know why – and swung our arms to and fro as if we were rowing, and sang: 'Adown the river, adown our Mother Volga', and that I thought at the time that all this was quite unnecessary. I recollect, further, lying on the floor and wrestling, gipsy-fashion with interlocked legs, twisting some one's neck and reflecting that it would not have happened had he not been drunk; also that we had supper and drank something else; that I kept going out into the courtyard to get some fresh air, and felt very cold about the head, and that going home I noticed that it was dreadfully dark, that the step of my trap had

1. Hurrah!

become slanting and slippery, and that it was impossible to hold on to Kuzma because he had gone all weak and swung about like a rag. But above all I remember feeling throughout the whole evening that I was behaving very stupidly, pretending to be enjoying myself vastly, to be fond of drinking a great deal and not even to think of being drunk; and that I felt all the time that the others were likewise behaving very stupidly in pretending the same. It seemed to me that each of the others privately disliked the whole business as much as I did but in the belief that he was the only one to find it disagreeable considered himself bound to feign gaiety for fear of spoiling the general hilarity. Also, strange to relate, I felt it incumbent on me to keep up the pretence merely because into the soup-tureen had gone three bottles of champagne at ten roubles a bottle and ten bottles of rum at four roubles apiece – making seventy roubles in all, without reckoning the cost of the supper. I was so sure I was right in this that I was absolutely amazed at the lecture next day when those of my comrades who had been at Baron Z.'s party, far from being ashamed of remembering what they had done, talked about the evening so that the other students should hear. They said it had been a splendid 'wine', that Dorpat men were great hands at that sort of thing and that twenty of us had drunk forty bottles of rum and many been left dead-drunk under the table. I could not understand why they not only talked about it but slandered themselves into the bargain.

40 · FRIENDSHIP WITH THE NEKHLYUDOVS

That winter I saw a great deal not only of Dmitri, who often came to our house, but of all his family with whom I was beginning to stand on intimate terms.

The Nekhlyudovs – mother, aunt and daughter – spent their evenings at home, and the princess liked to have young people come and see her – young men of the kind, as she expressed it, who were capable of passing a whole evening without cards or dancing. But there must have been few such because I went nearly every evening and seldom met any one else there. I got to know the members of the family and their different characters, formed a clear idea of their mutual relations, grew used to their rooms and furniture, and when there were no visitors felt quite at home except on those occasions when I was left alone in the room with Varya. It always seemed to me that not being a very pretty girl she longed for me to fall in love with her. But I began to lose this feeling of embarrassment too. She gave such a natural appearance of it not mattering to her whether she was talking to me or her brother or Lyubov Sergeyevna that I came to look upon her simply as a fellow-creature to whom it was in no way wrong or dangerous to show that I took pleasure in her company. All the time of our acquaintance, though on some days I thought her very plain and on others not too bad-looking, I never once asked myself whether I was in love with her or not. I chanced sometimes to address myself to her directly but more often I talked to her through Lyubov Sergeyevna or Dmitri, and I particularly liked doing this. I derived great pleasure in discoursing when she was present, listening to her singing, and in general knowing that she was in the room, but it was seldom now that I thought of what my relations with Varya might be in the future, of sacrificing myself for my friend, should he fall in love with my sister. If any such ideas or fancies did enter my head, feeling content with the present, I unconsciously strove to banish thoughts of the future.

But in spite of the friendly terms on which we stood I continued to feel it my bounden duty to conceal my real feelings and tastes from the whole Nekhlyudov family and especially from Varya; and I tried to appear quite a different young man from what I was in reality, and such, indeed, as could never possibly have existed. I tried to appear to have strong emotions, I went into ecstasies, exclaimed and made impassioned gestures when I wanted it to be thought I was particularly pleased with anything; and at the same time endeavoured to seem unmoved by anything really extraordinary which I saw or was told about. I tried to appear an ill-natured cynic who held nothing sacred, and at the same time to be a shrewd observer. I tried to appear logical in all I did, precise and methodical in my life, and at the same time a person who despised all material things. I can say with truth that I was far better in reality than the strange creature I made myself out to be; but even such as I pretended to be, the Nekhlyudovs grew fond of me and to my good fortune apparently saw through my play-acting. Only Lyubov Sergeyevna, who regarded me as the worst of egoists and a godless cynic, it seems, had no love for me, quarrelled with me, flew into a rage and baffled me by her abrupt and incoherent remarks. But Dmitri was still on the same strange, something more than friendly relations with her, and said that nobody understood her and that she was doing him a world of good. His friendship with her likewise continued to distress the whole family.

Once Varya in discussing with me this strange attachment which none of us could understand explained it saying:

'Dmitri is a vain person. He is very conceited and, for all his intellect, very fond of praise and admiration, and always likes to be first; and *auntie* in the innocence of her heart perpetually looks up to him and hasn't sufficient common sense to conceal her admiration, with the result that she flatters his vanity, only she does it in all honesty and sincerity.'

This summing up stuck in my memory and on thinking it over afterwards I could not help coming to the conclusion that Varya was very clever, which conclusion made me glad to exalt her in my estimation. Yet though I was always pleased enough to give her credit on every discovery in her of good sense and other moral qualities I did so with strict moderation, and I never went into raptures – the ultimate stage in this process of exaltation. Thus when Sophia Ivanovna, who never wearied of talking about her niece, told me how four years ago in the country, when still only a child, Varya had given away all her frocks and shoes to peasant children without first asking permission, so they had to be taken back afterwards, I did not instantly feel Varya's action must needs increase my opinion of her, and I scoffed at her mentally for having such an unpractical view of things.

When the Nekhlyudovs had visitors, and sometimes Volodya and Dubkov among others, I smugly retired to the background with a quiet consciousness of my power as a friend of the family, not talking but merely listening to what others were saying. And all that they said seemed to me so incredibly silly that I wondered how a clever sensible woman like the princess and her equally sensible family could listen to such rubbish and reply to it. Had it then occurred to me to compare what the others said with what I said myself when I was there alone I should certainly not have marvelled at all. Still less should I have marvelled had I believed that the women in my own family circle – Avdotya Vassilyevna, Lyuba and Katya – were just like any other women and not at all inferior, and remembered the things Dubkov, Katya and Avdotya Vassilyevna talked and merrily laughed about for whole evenings; how Dubkov seized every possible opportunity and on nearly every occasion managed to declaim with feeling '*Au banquet de la vie, infortuné convive . . .*'[1] or extracts from *The Demon*; and

1. 'At the banquet of life, unfortunate guest . . .'

in general what nonsense they talked with so much enjoyment for hours on end.

Of course when they had visitors Varya paid less attention to me than when we were alone, and we had none of the reading aloud and music which I loved listening to. When she was conversing with any visitor she lost what was for me her chief charm – her quiet good sense and simplicity. I remember what a strange surprise her conversations with my brother Volodya about the theatre and the weather were to me. I knew that Volodya shunned and despised banality more than anything in the world, and that Varya herself always made fun of forced conversations on the weather and so forth – then why when they met did they both of them talk such intolerable commonplaces and as it were disgrace one another? Always after such conversations I raged inwardly against Varya, and next day made fun of the visitors but found it pleasanter than ever to be alone with the Nekhlyudov family.

At all events I began to take more pleasure in being with Dmitri in his mother's drawing-room than in being alone with him.

41 · FRIENDSHIP WITH DMITRI NEKHLYUDOV

Just at that time my friendship with Dmitri hung by a thread. I had been considering him critically too long not to have discovered failings in him, and in early youth we love only passionately and therefore only perfect people. But as soon as the haze of passion gradually begins to dissolve, or the clear rays of commonsense automatically begin to penetrate it, and we see the object of our adoration in his true aspect, with virtues and shortcomings, it is the shortcomings alone which strike us vividly, with the exaggerated force of the unexpected; the feeling of attraction for what is new and of hope that perfection in someone else is not an impossibility incites us not only to coldness but almost to dislike for the former object of our devotion, and we cast him off without regret and hasten away in search of some new perfection. If this did not happen to me in regard to Dmitri I owe it to his stubborn, pedantic, sensible rather than fervent attachment, which I would have been too much ashamed to be false to. Besides this, we were bound together by our strange rule of frankness. We were too much afraid if we parted of leaving in each other's power moral secrets we had confessed to one

another and were ashamed of. At the same time our pact of frankness
had long ceased to be observed, as we well knew, and was often embar-
rassing and occasioned a peculiar constraint between us.

Almost every time I went to see Dmitri that winter I found Bezobedov there, a fellow-student with whom he studied. Bezobedov was
a small thin pock-marked man, with tiny freckled hands and a great
mass of unkempt red hair; he was invariably ragged, dirty, uncouth
and not even a hard worker. Dmitri's friendship with him was as unin-
telligible to me as his relations with Lyubov Sergeyevna. The sole
reason that could have prompted Dmitri to choose him from among all
his fellow-students and strike up a friendship with him was that there
was no more ill-favoured student in the whole University than Bezobedov. But probably that was enough to make Dmitri defy everybody
and extend him his friendship. 'You see, I don't care a straw who you
are – you are all one to me – I like him and that means he's all right,' was
what his haughty attitude expressed throughout his relations with
Bezobedov.

I wondered how he could bear the continual strain he put on himself, and how the wretched Bezobedov endured his uncomfortable
situation. I did not like the friendship at all.

One evening I went round to Dmitri's hoping we could spend the
evening in his mother's drawing-room, talking and listening to Varya
sing or read; but Bezobedov was upstairs with him. Dmitri told me
curtly that he could not come down because, as I could see for myself,
he had company.

'Besides, what fun is there down there?' he added. 'Much better
stay here and chat.'

Though the idea of sitting with Bezobedov for a couple of hours did
not attract me in the slightest I could not make up my mind to go to
the drawing-room alone, and vexed at my friend's eccentricity I seated
myself in the rocking-chair and began to rock without a word. I was
very much annoyed with Dmitri and Bezobedov for depriving me of
the pleasure of being downstairs; I waited, hoping Bezobedov would
soon go, and was irritated with him and Dmitri as I listened in silence
to their conversation. 'A fine visitor, I must say! Nice company he is!'
I thought, when the footman brought in tea and Dmitri was obliged
to ask Bezobedov five times to take a glass, because the shy guest considered it incumbent on him to decline the first and second glasses of
tea and say, 'No, help yourself.' Dmitri, with an obvious effort, kept

up a conversation with his visitor into which he several times tried to inveigle me. I preserved a gloomy silence.

'There's no point in putting on a face that dares any one to suspect I am bored,' I mentally said to Dmitri, as I silently and rhythmically rocked my chair. With a certain satisfaction I fanned higher and higher the flames of enmity to my friend. 'What a fool he is!' I thought. 'He might be spending a pleasant evening with his delightful family but no, he sits here with this beastly fellow, and the time is passing, it's already too late to go to the drawing-room,' and I glanced over the edge of the rocking-chair at my friend. His hand, the way he was sitting, his neck (especially the nape of it) and his knees all seemed so repulsive and offensive to me that I could at that moment gladly have done something to him, even something extremely disagreeable.

At last Bezobedov got up but Dmitri could not instantly part from such a delectable visitor: he invited him to stay the night but fortunately Bezobedov declined, and departed.

After seeing him off Dmitri returned, smiling a faintly complacent smile and rubbing his hands together – partly because he had maintained his character for eccentricity, I suppose, and partly because he was at last rid of boredom. He began to pace the room, from time to time glancing at me. I hated him more than ever. 'How dare he walk about and smile?' thought I.

'Why are you angry?' he asked suddenly, stopping in front of me.

'I am not angry at all,' I retorted, as one always does in such circumstances. 'It only vexes me that you play-act to me, and to Bezobedov, and to yourself.'

'What rubbish! I never play-act to anyone.'

'I have in mind our rule of frankness, and I speak bluntly to you. I am certain you can't bear that Bezobedov any more than I can, because he is a fool and heaven knows what else, but you like to give yourself airs before him.'

'I do not. To begin with, Bezobedov is a very good sort . . .'

'But I tell you it is so. I will also tell you that your friendship with Lyubov Sergeyevna is also based on the fact that she considers you a god.'

'No, I tell you!'

'But I tell you it is! I know by my own experience,' I said with the heat of repressed anger and hoping to disarm him by my frankness. 'I have told you and tell you again, that I always imagine I like the people who say pleasant things to me but that when I come to examine the matter closely I find that no real attachment exists.'

'No,' Dmitri insisted, adjusting his neckerchief with an irritable movement of his neck. 'When I love neither praise nor blame can make any difference to my feeling.'

'That's not true. You know I admitted to you once that when papa called me a good-for-nothing I hated him for a while and wanted him to die, just as you . . .'

'Speak for yourself! It's a great pity if you are such a . . .'

'On the contrary,' I cried, jumping up from the chair and looking him in the eyes with the courage of desperation – 'what you say is wrong; didn't you tell me about my brother? I won't remind you of that because it wouldn't be fair – but didn't you say . . . All the same I will tell you what I think of you . . .'

And in an effort to wound him even more painfully than he had wounded me I began trying to prove to him that he did not love any-one, and to heap upon him all the reproaches I thought he deserved. I was very pleased at having spoken out, entirely forgetting that the only possible purpose in doing so – to force him to acknowledge the faults I accused him of – could not be attained at that moment while he was excited and angry. Had he, on the other hand, been in a condition to plead guilty I should never have said what I did.

The argument was verging upon a quarrel when Dmitri suddenly became silent and went into the next room. I made to follow him, still talking, but he did not answer. I knew that hot temper figured in his column of vices and that he was now fighting it down. I cursed the list he had written out for himself.

This, then, was what our rule of frankness had brought us to – the rule that we should *tell each other all that was in our hearts and never discuss one another with a third person.* Our delight in frankness had more than once carried us away into making the most disgraceful confessions, describing (to our shame) speculations and idle fancies as desires and feelings, as I had just done with him, for example; and these confidences had not only failed to tighten the bond between us – they had dissipated sympathy and further separated us. And now suddenly his self-esteem would not allow him to make the most trivial admission, and in the heat of our argument we made use of the weapons with which we had previously supplied one another, and which dealt such painful blows.

42 · OUR STEPMOTHER

Although papa had not meant to come to Moscow with his wife until after the New Year he arrived in October, in the autumn while it was still possible to have excellent riding to hounds. He said he had altered his mind because a lawsuit of his was to be heard in the Senate; but Mimi told us that Avdotya Vassilyevna had found it so dull in the country, had so often spoken about Moscow, and had made such a pretence of being ill, that papa had decided to humour her wish.

'You see, she never really loved him but only dinned it into everybody's ears that she did because she wanted to marry a rich man,' Mimi would add with a pensive sigh which said: 'It's not what *some people* would have done for him if he had been capable of appreciating them.'

Some people were unjust to Avdotya Vassilyevna. Her love for papa – passionate, devoted, self-sacrificing love – revealed itself in her every word, look and movement. At the same time this love and the wish never to leave her adored husband's side did not in the least prevent her longing for a fashionable new cap from Madame Annette's, a bonnet with a wonderful blue ostrich feather, or a blue gown of Venetian velvet which would cleverly set off her fine white bosom and arms, which had never yet been seen by anyone save her husband and her maids. Katya sided with her mother, of course, while between our stepmother and us certain queer bantering relations established themselves from the very day of her arrival. The moment she alighted from the carriage Volodya, with a grave face and expressionless eyes advanced, bowing and scraping, to kiss her hand and said as though he were introducing some one:

'I have the honour to offer my congratulations on dear mamma's arrival, and to kiss her hand.'

'Ah, my dear little son!' said Avdotya Vassilyevna with her beautiful changeless smile.

'And pray do not forget the second little son,' said I, also approaching to kiss her hand and involuntarily trying to assume Volodya's expression of face and voice.

If we and our stepmother had been sure of our feelings for each other the style of our greeting might have indicated our scorn for demonstrative displays of affection; were we already ill-disposed to each other it might have been taken for irony, or contempt for pretence, or a desire to conceal our real relations from our father, and so on; but in the present instance it meant nothing at all and only pointed to an utter absence of all relations (and consorted well with Avdotya Vassilyevna's own state of mind too). I have often observed since the same false sort of facetiousness in other families when the members suspected that their real relations among themselves might not be altogether satisfactory; and it was this attitude that established itself between us and Avdotya Vassilyevna. We hardly ever departed from it: we were always artificially polite to her, spoke French, clicked our heels when we bowed, and called her *chère maman*, to which she always responded in the same half-jesting way, with the same beautiful uniform smile. Only cry-baby Lyuba with her crooked legs and innocent chatter took a liking to our stepmother and tried most naïvely and sometimes clumsily to bring her closer in touch with our whole family. In return, the only person in the world for whom Avdotya Vassilyevna had a scrap of affection – apart from papa, whom she loved passionately – was Lyuba. She even treated Lyuba with a kind of wild admiration and shy respect which surprised me very much.

At first Avdotya Vassilyevna was very fond of calling herself a stepmother and hinting at the wrong unfair way children and members of the household always look upon a stepmother and so make her position difficult. Yet though she saw beforehand all the unpleasantness of such circumstances she did nothing to avoid them: she might have said a kind word to one, made a little present to another, and not grumbled – which would have been quite easy for her since by nature she was very amiable and unexacting. Not only did she do none of these things but on the contrary, seeing what the difficulties of her position might be, she stood on the defensive before she was attacked, and taking it for granted that the whole household were determined to use every means in their power to be nasty to her and hurt her feelings, she saw evil intention in everything and considered that her most dignified course was to suffer in silence, and, naturally, her lack of effort to win affection won her dislike. Moreover she was so totally devoid of that capacity of *understanding* which was developed to such a high degree in our family and to which I have already alluded, and her ways were so contrary to the deeply-rooted customs of our house that this by itself was

enough to prejudice us against her. In our orderly methodical household she always lived as though she had just arrived: she got up and
retired now early, now late; sometimes she appeared for dinner, sometimes she did not; one evening she would have supper, another evening
go without. Almost always when there were no visitors she walked
about half-dressed and was not ashamed of appearing before us or even
the servants in a white petticoat with a shawl thrown round her shoulders and her arms bare. At first I liked this homeliness but very soon it
lost her the last vestiges of my respect. What amazed us even more was
that there were two quite different beings in her according to whether
we had visitors or not: in the presence of visitors she was a healthy cold
young beauty, who dressed elegantly, was neither stupid nor clever,
but cheerful; the other Avdotya, when we were alone, was a miserable
worn-out woman, no longer young, slovenly and bored, though
affectionate. Often, looking at her, smiling and happy in the consciousness of her beauty, when she returned from a round of calls, her cheeks
flushed by the winter cold, and taking off her bonnet went up to inspect herself in the glass; or when, rustling her sumptuous décolletée
ball-gown, abashed and yet proud before the servants, she passed to her
carriage; or when we had a small party at home and she sat in a high-
necked silk gown with some fine lace round her delicate throat, radi-
antly smiling her beautiful expressionless smile on all around – I
wondered what those who raved over her would say if they saw her as I
did on evenings when she stayed at home and wandered like a ghost
through the dimly-lighted rooms, clad in some kind of dressing-gown
and with her hair dishevelled, waiting for her husband's return from
the club after midnight. At such times she would go to the piano and
frowning with effort play the only waltz she knew, or pick up a novel,
read a few lines from the middle, then throw it aside; or else, repairing
in person to the pantry so as not to disturb the servants, she would get
herself a cucumber and some cold veal and eat them standing by the
pantry-window and then wander listlessly from room to room again,
weary and depressed. But what estranged us from her most of all was her
want of comprehension which expressed itself chiefly by the peculiar
air of indulgent attention with which she would listen when people talked about things she did not understand. She was not to blame for having
acquired an unconscious habit of smiling slightly with her lips only and
inclining her head when told things that did not particularly interest
her (and nothing did interest her except herself and her husband); but

that oft-repeated smile and inclination of the head were past bearing. Her mirth, as if she were laughing at the world at large, was *gauche* and anything but infectious; her sympathy was too forced. But worst of all – she did not blush to talk incessantly to every one of her love for papa. Although she only spoke the truth when she said that her whole life was bound up in her husband, and though she proved this all the time, we found such unrestrained continual insistence upon her affection revolting, and we were even more ashamed of her when she spoke like that before strangers than when she made mistakes in French.

She loved her husband more than anything in the world, and her husband loved her, especially at first and when he saw that he was not the only one to admire her. The sole aim of her existence was to win her husband's love; yet as if on purpose she seemed to do everything most likely to displease him, and all to demonstrate her love and devotion.

She liked smart clothes and father liked to see her as a society beauty exciting praise and admiration; yet she sacrificed her weakness for finery, for father's sake, and got more and more into the habit of sitting at home in a grey blouse. Papa, who had always considered freedom and equality essential conditions in family relations, had hoped that his darling Lyuba and his amiable young wife would be good friends; but Avdotya Vassilyevna made a victim of herself and found it necessary to pay 'the real mistress of the house', as she called Lyuba, an amount of deference which shocked and annoyed papa. He played cards a great deal that winter and towards the end lost considerable sums, and, as always, not wanting to let his gambling intrude upon his family life, he began to preserve complete secrecy concerning his play. Avdotya Vassilyevna made a victim of herself again, and though unwell (and towards the end of the winter pregnant) considered it her duty to go waddling in her grey blouse and with unkempt hair to meet papa when he returned from the club at four or five o'clock in the morning, tired, depleted in pocket and shamefaced at having had an eighth fine to pay.[1] She would ask him in a careless way if he had been lucky, and listen with a smile of indulgent attention and little nods of her head while he told her of his doings at the club and begged her, for the hundredth time, never to sit up for him. But though papa's losing or winning – on which at the rate he played his entire fortune depended – did not

1. A fine used to be exacted in Russia for staying at the club after midnight. For every half hour after the allotted time the fine was doubled.

interest her in the least she continued to be the first to meet him every night when he returned from the club. This she was incited to do, not only by her passion for self-sacrifice but by a secret jealousy from which she suffered in the highest degree. No one on earth could have persuaded her that papa returned late from the club and not from some mistress. She tried to read his love-secrets in his face and discerning nothing would sigh with a certain luxury of woe and give herself up to the contemplation of her unhappiness.

In consequence of these and other innumerable instances of her making herself into a victim, by the last months of that winter – during which papa lost heavily and was therefore generally in bad spirits – an intermittent feeling of quiet hatred began to be noticeable in papa's relations with his wife – that suppressed aversion for the object of one's affection which betrays itself by an unconscious desire to inflict on that object every possible kind of petty annoyance.

43 · NEW COMRADES

The winter had passed imperceptibly, the thaw was already beginning again, and the list of examinations had now been pinned up in the University when I suddenly remembered that I should be examined in eighteen subjects on which I had attended lectures without listening, taking notes or preparing a single one. It is strange that it never once entered my head to ask myself the plain question: 'What about the examinations?' The fact is, I had been in such a haze all that winter, so full of delight at being grown-up and *comme il faut*, that when it did occur to me to wonder how I was to pass my examinations I compared myself with my fellow-students and thought: 'They will be sitting, too, but as the majority of them are not even *comme il faut* I have the advantage over them and am bound to come out all right.' I only went to the lectures because I had got into the habit of doing so and papa would not let me stay at home. Besides, I had a great many acquaintances now and often enjoyed myself at the University. I loved the noise, the talk, the laughter in the auditorium; I loved to sit on a bench at the back during a lecture dreaming of something or other to the even tones of the professor's voice, and to contemplate my comrades; I liked to run over to Materne's with one or other of them to take a glass of vodka and have a snack, and knowing that I might be hauled over the coals for it enter the auditorium after the professor, opening the creaking door timidly; I liked having a hand in the practical jokes when students from all the Faculties congregated laughing in the corridor. All this was great fun.

By the time, however, that every one had begun to attend the lectures more regularly, and the professor of physics had completed his course and taken leave of us till the examinations, and the students were busy collecting their note-books and arranging to do their preparation in parties, it struck me that I ought to get to work. Operov, with whom I still exchanged greetings but was on the coolest terms, as I have already mentioned not only offered me his note-books but suggested we should use them together with some other students. I expressed my thanks and accepted, hoping that the honour I thus did him would wipe out our former disagreement and only requesting that the gatherings should certainly be held at my house, as I had good rooms.

I was told that they meant to take turn and turn about, meeting sometimes at one fellow's place, sometimes at another's, preferring those that lived nearer. The first time we met at Zukhin's. He had a small room behind a partition, in a large house on the Trubnoy Boulevard. I was late the first day and arrived after they had already begun the reading. The little room was thick with tobacco smoke, and not good tobacco but the shag Zukhin smoked. There was a square bottle of vodka on the table, a wineglass, bread, salt and a mutton-bone.

Zukhin, without rising, invited me to have a glass of vodka and to take off my coat.

'I don't suppose you are used to such refreshments,' he added.

They were all wearing grubby calico shirts and false shirt-fronts. Endeavouring not to show my contempt for the company, I took off my coat and stretched myself in a comradely manner on the sofa. Zukhin was speaking, occasionally referring to his notes; the others stopped him to ask questions, which he answered concisely, intelligently and accurately. I began to listen more attentively and as there was much I did not understand because I did not know what had gone before I put a question.

'Oh, my dear fellow, it's no good your listening if you don't know that,' said Zukhin. 'I'll let you have my note-books. You look them through by tomorrow; otherwise what's the use of trying to explain to you?'

I felt ashamed of my ignorance; also I felt the truth of what he said, so I left off listening and amused myself by observing my new associates. According to my classification of humanity into persons *comme il faut* and persons not *comme il faut*, they evidently belonged to the latter category and therefore excited not only my scorn but a feeling of personal hostility, which I felt towards them because, though not *comme il faut*, they seemed to regard themselves as my equals, and more, they actually patronized me in a good-natured way. This feeling was aroused in me by their feet, their dirty hands with the nails bitten down to the skin (and one long nail on Operov's little finger), by their pink shirts and false shirt-fronts, the abuse they affectionately threw at one another, the dirty room and Zukhin's habit of constantly half-blowing his nose, pressing one nostril with his finger, and, above all, by the way they spoke, employing and drawling certain words. For instance, they used the word *blockhead* instead of fool, *literally* instead of exactly, *magnificent* instead of very beautiful, and so on, which seemed to me bookish and disgustingly ill-bred. But the way they accented some Russian and, even more, foreign words aroused my *comme il faut* antagonism still further: they said m*a*chine instead of mach*i*ne, *a*ctivity instead of act*i*vity, *on* purpose instead of on p*u*rpose, mant*el*-piece instead of m*a*ntelpiece, Shakespe*a*re instead of Sh*a*kespeare, and so on and so forth.

In spite, however, of these externals, which were insuperably repellent to me at that time, I had a mental impression of something good in these people, and envying the cheerful good-fellowship which united them I felt drawn to and wanted to become friends with them, difficult as that was for me. The gentle and upright Operov I already knew, and now the brisk and remarkably clever Zukhin, who evidently reigned over the circle, pleased me immensely. He was a short thick-set little fellow, dark-complexioned with a rather puffy, invariably shiny but extremely intelligent, lively, independent face. It was his forehead especially which though not high was prominent above his deep-set black eyes, and his short bristly hair and thick black beard, always looking as if it had not been trimmed, which gave him that look. He did not appear to think of himself (a trait I particularly liked in people) but it was obvious his mind was never idle. His was one of those expressive countenances which a few hours after you first see them suddenly completely alter in your eyes. This happened to me with Zukhin towards the end of the evening. All of a sudden new wrinkles

appeared on his face, his eyes sank deeper, his smile was different and
his whole expression changed so that I should hardly have recognized
him.

When they had finished reading, Zukhin, the other students, and
I – to show my readiness to be their comrade – drank a glass of vodka
apiece, and there was hardly any left in the bottle. Zukhin asked if any
of us had a quarter-rouble to spare so that he could send the old woman
who looked after him to buy some more vodka. I offered my money
but Zukhin made as though he had not heard me and turned to
Operov, who pulled out a bead purse and gave him the required sum.

'And mind you don't start drinking!' said Operov, who did not
drink at all himself.

'No fear,' replied Zukhin, sucking the marrow out of the mutton-
bone. (I remember thinking at the time, 'It must be because he eats so
much marrow that he is so clever.') 'No fear,' Zukhin went on with a
slight smile, and his smile was one you could not help noticing and
feeling grateful for. 'Even if I do take to drinking there's no harm done.
We'll see which of the two of us gives the better account of himself –
him or me. I have it all ready here,' and he slapped his forehead with
mock boastfulness. 'It's Semeonov who had better look out – he seems
to have been drinking hard.'

Sure enough, that same Semeonov with the grey hair who had
cheered me up at the first examination by being uglier than myself,
and who afterwards came out second in the entrance examination and
attended the lectures regularly during the first month, had taken to
going on the spree before the repetitions began, and towards the end
of the course had not shown himself at the University at all.

'Where is he?' asked someone.

'I've quite lost sight of him,' Zukhin went on. 'The last time I was
with him we smashed up the Lisbon together. That was something
like! He got into a mess after that I heard . . . What a head that fellow
has! There's fire for you! What a brain! It will be a pity if he goes to
pieces. And go to pieces he certainly will – he's not the sort of lad to
stick it in the University, not with his outbursts.'

After talking for a while longer everybody got up to go, having
agreed to meet again at Zukhin's on the following days because his
quarters were the nearest for all the others. When we had all come out
into the courtyard I felt rather uncomfortable to be the only one to
drive while everybody else was walking, and, shamefaced, I offered

Operov a lift. Zukhin came out with us, and borrowing a rouble from Operov went off to make a night of it with some friends. As we drove along Operov told me a good deal about Zukhin, the sort of person he was and the life he led, and when I reached home I could not get to sleep for a long time, thinking of these new people I had got to know. I lay awake for hours, wavering between respect for them – to which their knowledge, simplicity of manner, honesty and all the poetry of their youth and spirit inclined me on the one hand, and the distaste their unseemly exterior inspired in me on the other. In spite of all my desire to do so, it was literally impossible for me at that time to become intimate with them. Our ideas were wholly at variance. There were a thousand and one nuances constituting for me the whole charm and meaning of life that were quite incomprehensible to them, and vice versa. But the principal reason why we could not possibly associate was that my coat was made of expensive cloth, that I had a gig of my own and wore cambric shirts. This had particular weight with me: I felt that involuntarily I offended them by the indications of my prosperity. I felt guilty with them, and now humbled myself and now, rebelling against my gratuitous humiliation, swung over to self-confidence, and I was quite unable to enter into equal and unaffected relations with them. But the coarse vicious side of Zukhin's character was at that time so entirely thrown into the shade by the stirring poetry of valour that I sensed in him that it did not affect me at all disagreeably.

For about a fortnight I went to Zukhin's nearly every evening. I did not study much, for as I have already said I had fallen behind my comrades and not having sufficient energy to work by myself so as to catch up with them I only pretended to listen and understand what they read. I think the others guessed that I was pretending and I noticed they often skipped passages they knew themselves, and never questioned me.

Every day I became more and more lenient towards the ungenteel manners of this circle, feeling increasingly drawn towards its mode of life and finding much that was poetic in it. Only my promise to Dmitri never to go on the spree with them restrained my desire to share their diversions.

Once I thought I would brag about my knowledge of literature, particularly French literature, and so led the conversation round to this theme. To my surprise it turned out that though they pronounced the foreign titles with a Russian accent they had read a great deal more than I, and knew and could appraise English and even Spanish authors,

and Le Sage whom I had never heard of then. Pushkin and Zhukovsky
were literature to them (and not, as they were to me, little books in
yellow covers which one read and learned as a child). They despised
Dumas, Sue and Féval alike, and their judgment, especially Zukhin's,
was much sounder and sharper than my own, as I could not but acknowledge. Neither could I beat them in my knowledge of music. Still
more to my surprise I discovered that Operov played the violin, another of the students who worked with us played the violoncello and
the piano, and both of them played in the University orchestra, were
real musicians and could appreciate what was good. In short, except for
their pronunciation of French and German they were better posted
than I in everything I had meant to boast about, nor did they seem to
think there was anything to be proud of in that. True, I might have
plumed myself on my status as a man of the world but, unlike Volodya,
I had none. What, then, was the eminence from which I looked down
on them? My acquaintance with Prince Ivan Ivanych? My French
accent? My drozhky? My cambric shirt? My finger-nails? But surely
all this was stuff and nonsense? Such were the thoughts which began to
pass dimly through my mind under the influence of the envy I felt for
the comradeship and good-natured youthful high spirits around me.
They were all close friends. The simplicity of their manners towards
one another amounted to rudeness but beneath the rough exterior
went extreme care not to hurt each other's feelings. 'Blackguard' and
'swine' used as terms of endearment only jarred on me and gave me
cause for silent ridicule, but these words did not offend them or prevent
their being on the most sincere and friendly footing with one another.
They were as careful, as delicate, in their treatment of each other as only
very poor and very young people are. But above all I sensed something
wild, dissolute and dashing in Zukhin and his adventures at the Lisbon.
I felt that those revels must be vastly different from the make-believe
with burnt rum and champagne in which I had taken part at Baron Z.'s.

44 · ZUKHIN AND SEMEONOV

I have no idea what class of society Zukhin belonged to but I know that
he had been at the S. High School, possessed no means and was not, I
think, of the gentry. He was about eighteen at that time though he
looked much older. He was exceptionally intelligent and especially

quick in the uptake: it was easier for him to grasp the whole of a complex subject, seeing all the details and deductions at a glance, than consciously to argue from the laws which led to these same deductions. He knew he was clever and was proud of it, and in consequence of this pride he was uniformly unaffected and kind in his relations with everybody. He had probably had a great deal of experience of life. Love, friendship, business and money had already left their mark on his ardent receptive nature. There was nothing he had tried, if only on a small scale or in the lowest social strata, which he did not look upon with the disdain mingled with indifference and disregard which proceeded from the facility with which he attained everything. He seemed to take up everything new with such enthusiasm only in order to despise it as soon as he had succeeded in his purpose; and his gifted nature always enabled him to achieve his object and gave him the right to despise it. It was the same with his studies: with very little work, and without taking notes he knew his mathematics inside out, and it was no boast when he said he could baffle the professor. Much of what he heard at lectures he thought rubbish but with the unconscious practical cunning natural to him he immediately adapted himself to what the professor required, and all the professors liked him. He was outspoken in his relations with the authorities but he held their regard. He not only neither respected nor cared for learning but derided those who laboured in earnest to obtain what came to him so easily. Study, as he understood it, did not require one-tenth of his capacity; his career as a student offered nothing to which he could wholly devote himself, and his impetuous active nature demanded 'life', as he phrased it, and he threw himself into such dissipations as his means allowed with feverish zest and a desire to spend himself 'to the limits of my strength'. Now, just before the examinations, Operov's prediction was fulfilled. Zukhin disappeared for a couple of weeks so that for the last part of the time we had to meet at the house of another of the students for our reading. But he appeared at the first examination pale, haggard, hands trembling, and did brilliantly, passing into the second course.

At the beginning of term there had been about eight students in the group of habitual revellers with Zukhin as the leader. Originally Ikonin and Semeonov were among their number but the former retired because he could not stand the frantic debauch to which they gave themselves up at the start of the year, and the latter left them because he found they were not wild enough. At first all the men of our class looked on them with a kind of horror, and we would relate their exploits to one another.

The chief heroes of these exploits were Zukhin and, towards the end of term, Semeonov. In course of time we all became rather appalled by Semeonov, and when he attended a lecture, which he seldom did, there was great excitement in the auditorium.

Semeonov wound up his career of dissipation a few days before the examinations in a most energetic and original fashion, as I had occasion to see, thanks to my acquaintance with Zukhin. This is what happened. One evening we had just assembled at Zukhin's, and Operov, having placed beside him, in addition to the tallow candle in a candlestick, another stuck in a bottle, had plunged his nose into his note-books and begun to read in his thin little voice from his minutely-written notes on physics, when the landlady entered the room and informed Zukhin that some one had come with a letter for him.

Zukhin went out and returned soon after with bent head and a thoughtful expression on his face, holding in his hands some unfolded lines written on a piece of grey wrapping-paper, together with two ten-rouble notes.

'Gentlemen! An extraordinary event,' he said, raising his head and surveying us in a grave solemn sort of way.

'Money for coaching, eh?' said Operov, turning over the pages of his note-book.

'Well, let's go on,' said some one.

'No, gentlemen! I'm not going on,' Zukhin continued in the same tone. 'An incredible event, I tell you! Semeonov has sent a soldier with these twenty roubles, which he borrowed at one time, and writes that if I want to see him to come to the barracks. You know what that means?' he added, looking round at all of us. We were all silent. 'I'm going to him straightaway,' Zukhin went on. 'Let's go, any one who wants to.'

In a flash we all put on our coats and prepared to go and see Semeonov.

'Won't it be awkward,' said Operov in his thin little voice, 'if we all go and stare at him like something in the zoo?'

I entirely agreed with Operov's remark, especially in so far as I who hardly knew Semeonov was concerned, but I so much liked to feel I had a share in what the others did, and I so badly wanted to see Semeonov, that I said nothing to this observation.

'Rubbish!' said Zukhin. 'What is there awkward about us all going

to say good-bye to our comrade, wherever he is? Stuff and nonsense!
Come on, whoever wants to.'

We got cabs, took the soldier with us and set off. The n.c.o. on duty
at first did not want to let us into the barracks but Zukhin managed to
persuade him, and the soldier who had come with the note led us to a
huge almost dark room feebly lit by a few lamps down both sides of
which recruits with shaved foreheads and wearing grey greatcoats
were sitting or lying on plank-beds. Entering the barracks I was struck
particularly by the smell and the snoring of several hundred men, and
following our guide and Zukhin, who stepped firmly between the
plank-beds, I peered in trepidation at each recruit, trying to fit to each
of them what I remembered of Semeonov's worn stringy figure with
the long touselled almost grey hair, white teeth and brilliant melancholy eyes. In the very far corner of the barracks by the last little earth-
enware bowl filled with black oil in which the wick, formed into a
snuff and hanging over the side, burned smokily, Zukhin quickened
his step and abruptly halted.

'Hullo Semeonov,' he said to a recruit with a shaved forehead like
the others, wearing thick army underwear and a grey greatcoat over
his shoulders, sitting with his feet up on his plank-bed and chatting
with other recruits as he ate something. It was *he*, with his grey hair
cropped, his bluish forehead shaved and his always melancholy restless
expression. I was afraid he might be upset if I looked at him so I turned
away. Operov, too, apparently shared my opinion and stood behind us
all; but Semeonov's tone as he greeted Zukhin and the others with his
customary jerky speech completely reassured us and we hurried to go
forward and give – I, my hand and Operov his 'deal board', but
Semeonov was before us in holding out his big black hand, thereby
saving us from any uncomfortable feeling that we might be doing him
an honour. He spoke quietly and reluctantly as usual.

'Hullo, Zukhin. Thanks for coming. Well, gentlemen, sit down.
Make room, Kudryashka,' he said to the recruit he had been having
supper with and chatting to. 'We can talk afterwards. Sit down now.
Well, did I surprise you, Zukhin? Eh?'

'Nothing surprises me with you,' replied Zukhin, sitting beside him
on the plank-bed, a trifle like a doctor sitting on his patient's bed. 'Now
it *would* have surprised me if you had come to the examinations, that I
can say. Tell us, where've you been, and how did it happen?'

'Where've I been?' he answered in his rich deep voice. 'In taverns, pot-houses and such like. Come, sit down, gentlemen, there's plenty of room for all of you. Move your legs up, you,' he shouted imperatively, with a flash of his white teeth, to the recruit on his left who was lying with his head on his arm and watching us with lazy curiosity. 'Well, I've been having a fling. Played the fool some of the time, and some of the time it was all right,' he went on, the expression on his active face changing with each jerky utterance. 'You heard the business about the shopkeeper: the wretch popped off. They tried to send me out of the country. As for money – I ran through all that. But none of that would have mattered. I was up to the neck in debt – and some nasty debts too. And nothing to settle them with. So there you are.'

'But how on earth did you come to do this?' said Zukhin.

'It was like this: I was on the binge once at Yaroslavl – you know, at Stozhenko's, with some merchant or other. He was a recruiting agent. "Give me a thousand roubles," I said to him, "and I'll join." And I joined.'

'But how – you belong to the gentry,' said Zukhin.

'Stuff and nonsense. Kirill Ivanov arranged it all.'

'Who's Kirill Ivanov?'

'The one who bought me,' (and his eyes flashed in an odd amused way and he gave a faint ironic smile). 'Got permission in the Senate. I played the fool a bit longer, paid off my debts, and came and joined. That's all. Besides, they can't flog me . . . I've got five roubles . . . And perhaps there'll be war . . .'

Then he started telling Zukhin about his strange incomprehensible adventures, his restless expression constantly altering and his melancholy eyes burning.

When it was impossible to stay any longer in the barracks we began to take our leave of him. He held out his hand to each of us, shook ours firmly and without rising to accompany us said:

'Drop in again some time, gentlemen. They say they won't be moving us until next month,' and again he gave a half smile.

Zukhin, however, after a few steps went back to him again. I wanted to see their parting so I hung behind and saw Zukhin take money from his pocket and offer it but Semeonov pushed his hand away. Then I saw them embrace and heard Zukhin, going close to him once more, cry in a loudish voice:

'Good-bye, man. Of course, I don't suppose I shall graduate – you'll be an officer.'

Whereupon Semeonov, who never laughed, burst into an unwonted ringing guffaw, which made an unbearably painful impression on me. We went out.

All the way home, which we walked, Zukhin was silent and kept half-sniffing, pressing his finger first to one nostril, then the other. When we arrived back he immediately left us, and from that very day drank steadily right until the examinations.

45 · I FAIL

At length came the day of the first examination, in the differential and integral calculus; but I was still in a strange kind of maze and had no clear idea of what awaited me. In the evenings after having been with Zukhin and his set it often occurred to me that many of my convictions ought to be altered, that there was something wrong about them; but in the mornings with the sun shining I became *comme il faut* again, perfectly satisfied to be so and desirous of no change whatever.

It was in this frame of mind that I attended for the first examination. I seated myself on a bench on the side where the princes, counts and barons were sitting, and began talking to them in French, and (strange as it may seem) the thought never entered my head that I should presently have to answer questions on a subject I knew nothing about. Calmly and collectedly I watched those who went up to be examined, and even allowed myself to make fun of some of them.

'Well, Grap,' I said to Ilinka when he returned from the examiners' table, 'in a blue funk, were you?'

'We'll see what happens to you,' said Ilinka, who had flatly mutinied against my influence from the day we entered the University, did not smile when I spoke to him and was ill-disposed towards me.

I smiled disdainfully at Ilinka's retort, though the doubt he conveyed alarmed me for a moment. But the feeling was short-lived, overlaid again by the fog, and I continued to be absent-minded and indifferent; so much so that I promised Baron Z. to go and have a snack with him at Materne's as soon as my examination was over (as if being examined were the veriest trifle to me). When I was called up with Ikonin I arranged the coat-tails of my uniform and stepped up to the examiner's table with perfect *sang-froid*.

A slight shiver of apprehension ran down my back only when a young professor – the same who had examined me at the entrance examinations – looked me full in the face and I stretched out for the letter-paper on which the questions were written. Ikonin, though he had drawn his ticket with the same lunge of his whole body as he had done at the previous examination, did answer after a fashion, if very badly, but I did what he had done on the previous occasion – nay, I did even worse, for I took up a second ticket and could not answer the question on that one either. The professor looked pityingly into my face and said in a quiet but firm voice:

'You will not pass into the next class, Mr Irtenyev. You need not continue your examination. We must weed out the Faculty. Nor you either, Mr Ikonin,' he added.

Ikonin implored to be allowed to undergo the examination again, as if he were begging for alms, but the professor replied that he would not be able to do in a couple of days what he had not done in the course of a year, and that he could not possibly pass. Ikonin renewed his piteous, humble appeals but the professor again refused.

'You may go, gentlemen,' he said in the same low but firm voice.

Only then did I bring myself to leave the table, and I felt ashamed of having seemed to be, by my silent presence, a party to Ikonin's humiliating entreaties. I don't remember how I traversed the hall past the students, what reply I gave to their inquiries, how I got out into the ante-room, nor how I reached home. I was aggrieved, humiliated and thoroughly miserable.

For three days I did not leave my room, saw nobody and wept copiously, like a child finding solace in tears. I looked for pistols in order to be able to shoot myself dead should I very much want to. I thought that Ilinka Grap would spit in my face when he met me and quite right too; that Operov must be rejoicing in my misfortune and telling everybody about it; that Kolpikov had justly shamed me at Yar's; that my foolish speeches to Princess Kornakova could have had no other result, and so on and so on. All the moments of my life which had been torturing to my self-love passed through my mind one after another; I tried to blame someone else for my misfortune – thought that some one had done it on purpose, imagined a whole intrigue against myself, murmured against the professors, against my comrades, against Volodya, against Dmitri, against papa for having sent me to the University; I railed at Providence for having let me live to be thus dishonoured. At last, believing myself ruined forever in the eyes of all those who knew me, I besought papa's permission to join the Hussars or go to the Caucasus. Papa was not pleased with me but when he saw my terrible distress he endeavoured to comfort me by telling me that though it was a bad business matters might still be remedied by my transferring to another Faculty. Volodya, who also did not see anything dreadful in my trouble, said that in another Faculty I should at least not have to feel ashamed before my new class-mates. The ladies did not – they either would not or could not – understand what an examination meant and what not passing meant, and were only sorry for me because they saw how distressed I was.

Dmitri came to see me every day and was most gentle and kind all the time; but for that very reason he seemed to have cooled towards me. It always seemed hurtful and offensive to have him come up-stairs and sit by my side in silence, with a look rather like that of a doctor when he seats himself by the bedside of a dangerously sick patient. Sophia Ivanovna and Varya sent me books by him which I had once said I should like to read, and hoped I would go and see them; but in these very attentions I perceived only proud, humiliating conde-scension for one who had fallen so unforgivably low. After three or four days I grew a little calmer, but up to our departure for the country I did not set foot from the house but wandered listlessly from room to room, always brooding over my woe and trying to avoid all the members of the household.

I thought and thought, and at last late one evening as I was sitting downstairs all alone, listening to Avdotya Vassilyevna playing a waltz, I suddenly leaped to my feet, ran upstairs, got out the *Journal* on which was inscribed RULES OF LIFE, opened it and experienced my first moment of repentance and moral resolution. I burst into tears, but now they were no longer tears of despair. Pulling myself together, I decided to write down a fresh set of rules, in the assured conviction that never again would I do anything wrong, nor spend a single idle minute, nor ever go back on my resolutions.

How long this moral impulse lasted, what it consisted of and what new start it gave to my spiritual development I shall relate in my account of the subsequent and happier part of my youth.[1]

24th of September, Yasnaya Polyana
[1857]

1. Tolstoy intended to publish a continuation of *Childhood, Boyhood, Youth* but never did so.